SLOUGH HOUSE

A year after the Russian Secret service left a British citizen dead from Novichok poisoning, Diana Taverner is on the warpath. What seems a gutless response from the government has pushed the Service's First Desk into mounting her own counter-offensive.

Meanwhile, the slow horses are worried they've been pushed further into the cold. Slough House has been wiped from Service records, and fatal accidents keep happening. No wonder Jackson Lamb's crew are feeling paranoid.

With a new populist movement taking a grip on London's streets, and the old order ensuring that everything's for sale to the highest bidder, the world's an uncomfortable place for those deemed surplus to requirements. The wise move would be to find a safe place and wait for the troubles to pass.

But the slow horses aren't famed for making wise decisions.

MICK HERRON

◆

SLOUGH HOUSE

Complete and Unabridged

LARGE
PRINT

ISIS
Leicester

First published in Great Britain in 2021 by
John Murray (Publishers)
London

First Isis Edition
published 2021
by arrangement with
John Murray (Publishers)
An Hachette UK company
London

A catalogue record for this book is available
from the British Library.

ISBN 978–1–78541–994–2

Published by
Ulverscroft Limited
Anstey, Leicestershire

Printed and bound in Great Britain by
TJ Books Ltd., Padstow, Cornwall

This book is printed on acid-free paper

For Jo

The simplest way to explain the behaviour of any bureaucratic organisation is to assume that it is controlled by a cabal of its enemies.

Robert Conquest's third law of politics

1

Her morning turned out shorter than she'd planned. Wearing her fur-lined coat against a biting wind, she'd been heading for a team meeting at the new facility, a granite complex on the city's edge. If it looked like the local headquarters of an insurance company, that was fine. Some things hid best in the open.

The sky was grey but unthreatening. The streets, their usual city selves.

Driving in wasn't encouraged. There was a regular shuttle, though, twice an hour, looping through the inner suburbs, and she'd pass a pharmacy on the way to her stop. She needed bath salts. Three times a week, days were full-on physical: 15K in the morning, then gym-work, then four times across the lake — twice in a boat, twice in the water — then another 15K. You needed long baths afterwards . . . Yesterday she'd dozed off in the tub, its lapping a sense-reminder of the movement of the lake, into which, rumour had it, leeches had once been poured, to keep swimmers on their mettle. But she'd never encountered one. This was a relief. Even the thought of leeches gave her the creeps; the way they were jelly, and mostly mouth. The way, if you stepped on one, it would burst like a blood-filled balloon.

Seriously, she thought: sooner this hunter on my tail than one of those nightmares fastened to my skin.

Because she'd spotted him now. Should have done sooner, but she was no more than fifteen seconds off the beat; an allowable laxity, even by the standards of her department. Already she was remapping her route, and the first detour was here: through the indoor market, a vast amphitheatre where chickens hung from hooks and sacks of vegetables formed battlements along the aisles. These were too narrow for a follower to remain hidden, though he did his best: when she paused to examine a tray of ducks' eggs, the passage behind her remained empty save for an elderly woman on sticks. But he was somewhere back there, in a black leather jacket; a little noticeable for pavement-work, which was a neat double bluff.

And the nature of her task was clear — another test. She had to ditch her tracker before reaching the shuttle bus stop. Because you could swim a hundred laps of the lake, run more K than there were minutes in the hour, and none of it would count if you couldn't shake a shadow on a city street. And if you led the shadow home, well . . . She'd heard of a department made up of failures: losers assigned to a dead-end desk, spending the rest of forever in a mist of thwarted ambition. You only got to mess up once. This was harsh but — until it happened to you — it was fair.

But it wasn't going to happen to her.

On her last job, in a foreign city, she had been the hunter. This felt curiously similar. Exiting the market, she crossed the road in the wake of a woman wearing a grey jacket and matching skirt and followed her into a lingerie shop on the opposite pavement: female territory. They were the only customers. Outside, the leather-jacketed man loitered, pretending to study his phone. She'd bottled herself in but forced him to reveal himself, and once that dawned on him, he'd have little choice but to give up. Which ideally would happen in time for her to catch the shuttle.

So what was to stop her simply tapping on the window and waving at him?

'. . . Excuse me?'

The woman was addressing her.

'Is he following you? Outside? In the leather jacket?'

She thought: okay, let's see where this leads. There were clues for future behaviour in allowing situations to play themselves out.

'He is, yes.'

The woman had quick dark eyes. 'A stalker . . . ?'

'He's been following me since I left home.'

'Shall I call the police?'

She was already reaching for a phone.

'No, I — No. He's an ex-boyfriend. Last time I called the police, he came round later and beat me up.'

It was shaky, but didn't need to stand up in court.

The sales assistant was watching from behind the counter. 'Is there a problem, ladies?'

The woman in grey said, 'There's a troublesome man. Outside.'

The assistant expressed no surprise. This was a lingerie store.

'So we wondered, is there a back way?'

'It's not really for customers.'

'But we're not customers, are we? We're victims of a man hanging round your shop.'

It was sweetly said, but with a menacing undertone. 'Well . . . '

But it was a surrender, and a graceful one.

'Of course. Maybe now, while his back's turned.'

For the man in black was facing the street, his head cocked phonewards.

She checked her watch. She could still make the

3

shuttle. And this would be more satisfying than simply tagging him, and telling him he was busted . . . As they were ushered towards the goods entrance, the woman in grey beamed at her, as if this were an adventure. Something to share with the team: *Members of the public can be a resource.*

When the door closed behind them and they were alone in an alleyway thronged with wheelie bins, she said, 'Thanks.'

The woman in grey said, 'My pleasure,' and stepped forward to envelop her in a hug.

It might have been imagination. But that would have meant everything else was unreal too; not just the sudden stiletto-shaped pain in her heart, but the intake of breath that the whole world took. The woman in grey lowered her to the ground, then stepped away smartly, leaving her to grasp, in her final moment, that this had not been a test, or, if it were, it was one in which failure cost more than she'd expected. But that was a brief epiphany, long over by the time news of her death had been composed, encrypted and sent hurtling through the ether to arrive in a busy room half the globe away, where it was delivered by an earnest young man to an older woman who wore her authority as she might an ermine gown: it kept her warm, and people noticed it.

She took the tablet he offered, read the message on its screen, and smiled.

'*Smiert spionam,*' she said.

' . . . Ma'am?'

'Ian Fleming,' said Diana Taverner. 'Means 'Death to spies'.'

And then, because he still looked blank, said, 'Google it.'

4

Part One
Stalking Horses

2

Let's be honest. Frontal aspect, first reaction: it's not the best-looking property on the market.

But consider the potential.

Conveniently located above a Chinese restaurant and a newsagent, which enterprises occupy the ground-floorage, these upper three storeys present a rare opportunity to acquire a toehold in this up-and-coming area. (Nice little mention in the *Mail* not long ago. Not the property pages, but still.) East-facing, but sheltered from morning dazzle by an imposing view of the iconic Barbican Centre, and offered further protection by being on Aldersgate Street, in the London borough of Finsbury, renowned for its temperate climate. Traffic calmed by nearby lights; buses a regular fixture. And the Tube on the doorstep, with the popular Hammersmith & City, Circle and Metropolitan lines literally a minute away.

The front door's not in use, but never mind. We'll go round the back.

To this nicely low-maintenance yard, with ample room for wheelie bins and broken furniture. Ignore the smell, that's a temporary blockage. Through this back door, sticking a bit today — doesn't usually do that — but a bit of shoulder work and Bob's your uncle. Then up the stairs, but best not put weight on that banister. It's more ornamental than load-bearing. Original feature, mind.

And so we come to the first floor, a matching pair of offices, with a view of the aforementioned heritage

7

brickwork opposite. All unspoilt, very much on-plan. Notice the fixtures and fittings. Authentic period detail there, and the seventies is a decade that's coming back, isn't it, what with the riots, the recession, the racism — ha! Our little joke. But no, really.

Nice lick of paint, put your own stamp on it. Splash of yellow, splash of grey. Nothing like a touch of colour to bring out the natural warmth of a room.

But time's wingèd chariot, eh? Onwards and upwards, onwards and upwards.

Which means another flight of stairs, a little cardio-workout. That's not damp on the plasterwork, just the discolouration you get with age. Two more offices on this level, plus a compact kitchen: bit of surface area for your kettle and your microwave, storage space for your crockery and whatnot. Washer needs a tighten, but that's easily sorted. Your facilities through here, and — oh. Eco-conscious, the previous user. Just give it a flush.

And up we go to the final two offices. Crying out to be bedroomed, our opinion. You've got your sloping roof, adds character, but leaves ample space to maximise your lifestyle requirements, once you look past the telephone directories and the overflowing ashtrays and the mess on the carpet there. Nothing a deep-clean won't set to rights. Ideally the premises would be decluttered before a viewing, but access was an issue, apologies.

Window appears to be jammed shut too. But a quick minute with a screwdriver'll see to that.

Anyway, there you have it. It's quirky — little bit different — and benefits from a colourful history. A department of the Secret Service, though not an especially active one. Paperwork, we gather. Current occupants have been in possession for an eternity, though it probably feels longer. You'd think spies would have better things to do, but then again, maybe they were never the best sort of spy. Maybe that's why they're here in the first place.

But we can see you're not convinced — it was the toilet, wasn't it? — so maybe we should head west, where more traditional premises are available, over towards Regent's Park. No, don't worry about the door. Security's never been a major concern here, which is a bit peculiar now we come to think of it.

Not that that's our business — all that matters is getting this place off the books. But sooner or later, we'll find a taker. That's the thing about this line of work; the same in yours, we'll be bound. The same the world over. When something's for sale, eventually someone'll buy it.

Just a matter of time, really.

Just a matter of time.

★ ★ ★

Looking for donor sperm? read the ad above her head.

Definitely not, though on the Central Line at rush hour, you couldn't rule it out.

But for the moment, Louisa Guy hoped herself impregnable. She was jammed into a corner, true, but had her back to the enveloping mass, and her attention fixed on the door she was pressed against. In its reflection all became disjointed, like a 3D movie without the specs, but she could make out human features: blurred mouths lip-syncing to iPods, faces shuttered against contact. While the chances of a stranger-on-stranger encounter turning nasty were

9

rare — a million passenger journeys for every incident, said the stats — you'd hate to be the one to buck the trend. Take deep breaths. Don't think about bad outcomes. And then they were at Oxford Circus, where the crowd split apart like murmurating starlings, her half spilling onto the platform, heading for exits.

She didn't normally come into town after work. Her barhopping days were largely over, largely unregretted; shopping expeditions were for weekends; and cultural outings — theatre, museums, concerts — let's face it, didn't happen: she was a Londoner, not a bloody tourist. But she needed new trainers after a ten-mile outing in the rain last week; a stupid idea but she'd been having a bad day, thoughts of Emma Flyte refusing to leave her alone. You couldn't run away from your memories, but you could tire yourself to the point where the details blurred. So anyway, the trainers had either shrunk or changed shape so fundamentally they belonged on different feet, which meant here she was, heading into town after work; the evenings lighter now the clocks had gone forward, but the air still bearing shades of winter. On the escalator, video ads encouraged her to rethink fundamental choices: change bank, change phone, change job. In a perfect world she'd have managed all three by the time she reached street level.

Where the pavements were damp from rain. Louisa circumnavigated clumps of pedestrians, crossed Regent's Street at a trot while the LED warned 3-2-1, and dipped into a sporting goods store, its neon logo a pale imitation of itself in the watery light, its tiled floor slick with grime. A yellow bollard exhorted her to take care. If she'd taken care, Emma Flyte would still be alive. But it was pointless to think such things; the clocks had gone forward since then, and only ever went so far back. Trainers were in the basement. She took an elevator again; she was always going up or down, it seemed. Always up or down.

On the back wall, running shoes were displayed like ranks of heads in *Game of Thrones*. As always there was a sale on, high-street retail being mostly zombie since You-Know-What, but even at reduced prices, trainers were mad. The ones that looked good were, anyway. And while the main thing about trainers was they had to feel right, not look good, still: they had to look good. So she picked the pair that most impressed on the wall, which proved nothing but was a sensible starting point, and sat and tried them on.

They felt okay. She walked up and down and they pinched a bit, more than when sitting, but it was hard to tell whether that was a new-shoe thing or a fitting issue. These places should have a treadmill. She flexed her leg to see if that helped, and noticed a guy noticing this — he was down the far end, examining a Nike — so did it again, and he kept on noticing, though studiously pretended not to. She crouched, and pressed the toe end of each trainer, checking for fit. He replaced the Nike on the wall and took a step back, his face a studied neutrality. Yeah, right, thought Louisa, awarding herself a mental high five.

Still got it.

She sat again, removed the trainers. They cost more than she wanted to spend, and while that had rarely stopped her in the past, it would be an idea to try on a few more pairs first. As if agreeing with this notion, her mobile trembled in her pocket, and at precisely the same moment she heard a nearby ping —

someone else's phone registering an incoming text. It was the guy who'd been watching her, or pretending not to, and he stepped out of sight behind a rack of socks and wristbands, reaching into his jacket as he did so. Could've been a meet-cute, she thought, self-mockingly. *Hey, simultaneous texts — what are the odds?* And she reached for her own mobile while having the thought, and checked her message.

. . . *Fuck!*

Louisa leaped up, shoeless, and raced to the far wall, slipping a little, steadying herself by grabbing the rack, but he was gone already — was that him on the escalator? Taking the stairs two at a time, as if alerted to a sudden emergency — yeah, she thought. You and me both. There was no point following, not with nothing on her feet. He was out of sight now anyway; would be on the street, picking the busiest direction to disappear in.

Bastard, she thought. You sly cunning bastard.

And then thought: So what the hell's going on here then?, as she padded back to her shoes, the wet floor working through her socks with every step.

★   ★   ★

If you didn't count the text that had pinged in five minutes ago, this was the first action River Cartwright's phone had seen in days. He seriously needed to do something about his social life.

'. . . Mr Cartwright?'

'Uh-huh.'

'It's Jennifer Knox?'

River kept a mental list of the women he'd had contact with over the past few years, and it didn't take long to scroll through. B to K was a blank.

'From next door to your grandfather's?'

And that explained the senior wobble in her voice, which was a relief. Not *that* desperate, whatever anyone thought.

So 'Of course' was what he now said. Jennifer Knox. A caller-in on the O.B.: supplier of casseroles and local gossip, though the visits had tailed off as the Old Bastard's grasp on gossip and solids, and such fripperies as who this woman he'd known for years might be, had slackened to nothing. She had River's number because River was who you called when the O.B. had an emergency, though the old man was beyond such contingencies now. Which Jennifer Knox knew very well, having been at the funeral.

'Of course,' he said. 'Mrs Knox. How can I help you?'

'There's someone in the house.'

His grandfather's house, she meant, which had been unoccupied for a while. It belonged to River now, technically, as his mother kept stressing — 'technically' apparently meaning in every possible sense, including the legal, barring his mother's own feeling that the natural order had been disturbed — and was, equally technically, on the market, though at a price the agent had declared 'way too optimistic. Way', in these post-You-Know-What times. Its refusal to budge suited River, for the moment. He'd grown up in his grandparents' house, having been abandoned there by a mother whose horizons hadn't, at the time, included future property rights. He'd been seven. That was a lot of history to sell.

Jennifer Knox was still talking. 'I thought about calling the police, but then I thought, well, what if

13

they're friends of yours? Or, you know, potential buyers?'

'Thanks, Mrs Knox. I should have let you know. Yes, they're old friends passing through, in need of somewhere to spend the night. And I know the furniture's gone, but — '

'It's still a roof and four walls, isn't it?'

'Exactly, and cheaper than a hotel. They're travelling at the moment, and — '

'We all do what we can, don't we? To keep the costs down.'

'They'll be gone in the morning. Thanks, Mrs Knox. I'm grateful you took the trouble.'

His flat was a rented one-bedder, 'nicely off the tourist track' as some smug git had once put it. He might have inherited a country pile, but his actual living conditions remained urban haemorrhoid. The flat was cold most times of year, and even in daylight felt dark. The nightclub over the way hosted live bands twice a week, and a nearby manhole cover had loosened; every time a car ran over it, the resulting ka-chunk ka-chunk made River's jaw spasm. It happened now, as he tucked his phone in his pocket. Not so much a soundtrack; more an audible toothache.

River raised a middle finger in the world's general direction. Then went to see who'd broken into his dead grandfather's home.

* * *

Meanwhile, Roddy Ho was doing what Roddy Ho did best.

What Roddy Ho did best was everything.

Which did tend to make such moments busy, but

14

hey: if being Roddy Ho was easy, everyone would do it — there'd be fat-thumbed Roddy Hos, bad-haired Roddy Hos; even chick-retardant Roddy Hos. Which you had to love the comic possibilities, but Roddy Ho didn't have time to dwell on them because Roddy Ho had his skinny-thumbed, good-haired, chick-delighting hands full.

And the everything he was currently deployed on involved saving Slough House from whatever deep-impact shit was headed its way.

As usual.

That shit was incoming was a given: this was Slough House. But also and anyway, it had been the Rodster himself who'd alerted Jackson Lamb to the Weird Wiping, as he'd dubbed it. The Weird Wiping meant incoming shit, no question, and that the shit would be deep impact, well: it didn't take a genius. This was the spook trade, and when things went awry on Spook Street, they generally went the full Chris Grayling. So Roddy was checking the shit for depth and durability; trying to ascertain exactly which direction the shit was travelling in, and if, by now, he'd gone past the stage where the whole shit metaphor was proving useful, he'd at least made his point. Shit was coming, and everyone was looking to Roddy Ho to provide the double-ply bog roll.

Though actually, when you thought about it, that would involve Roddy doing the wiping.

Momentarily derailed, he reached for a slice of pizza. Roddy was in his office; it was way past sayonara time, but when the HotRod was on a mission, he didn't watch the clock. Besides, some things you don't want showing on your domestic hard drive, and tinkering around in Service records was one of them.

Because the first problem he'd identified, the direction of travel of the incoming effluent, was a no-brainer: any time Slough House was under the hammer, you could bet your chocolate buttons it was Regent's Park at the anvil. And in this particular instance, the Weird Wiping, what had been wiped was Slough House itself.

By 'wiped', Roddy meant erased from the Service database. Not just Slough House but the horses themselves, from the new guy Wicinski to Jackson Lamb; each and every one of them taken off the board. Oh, they were still around on the deep-level data sets; the ones involving salaries and bank accounts, all of which — after a nasty hack some years ago — were ascribed to employee numbers rather than names, so they were still getting paid, and still had jobs to do, but their personal files, their personnel jackets: they were gone, baby, gone. Anyone checking out Roddy Ho on the Service database would find zero, nada, zilch. Like the RodBod had ceased to exist.

Everything came to an end, he knew that. Take those huge statues of Jedi Knights the Taliban bombed to dust. But he'd figured his own legend would remain intact for a while yet.

So he'd thought about putting himself back up there — easy enough when you had the Rodinator's talent set: he could hoist a dick-pic as the Service's screensaver if he had a mind to — but best not. Over at the Park, they had to know who they were messing with, and it stood to reason they'd have extra security in place for when Roddy-O came putting their wrongs to rights. Which meant ninja skills were called for, stealth and cunning, and that was basically Roddy's user profile. He was near-invisible was the plain fact. Half the time, people didn't notice he was in the room. So for now he trod panther-like among the pixels, melding with the matrix. Gathering information was one thing; gathering the absence of information called for a whole different kind of cool. And Roddy Ho was cooler than a bowl of Frosties.

Pausing for a moment to wipe pizza topping from his keyboard, he summed up his progress so far.

What he'd mostly discovered was that whoever'd done the wiping had made an impressively thorough job of it.

In fact, it occurred to him, any newbies out there — any junior spooks just starting at the Park — would have no idea Slough House existed at all.

And the image came to his mind of an empty space on the street, an unfilled gap ignored by passers-by; and Roderick Ho found himself wondering, just for half a moment, what difference that would make to anyone.

★ ★ ★

Dance like no one's watching, thought Shirley Dander.

What cockwomble came up with that?

Because the point of dancing is everyone's watching, or they are if you're doing it right. The wallflowers chugging flavoured gin and wishing they had the moves. The wannabe rocking the bow-tie-and-specs on the balcony. That cute pair of kids in the corner, sizing each other up: seriously, she thought. Get a wiggle on. Before I toss a coin to choose which of you to take home.

Which could happen, she promised herself. Could so easily happen, she ought to have a sign around her neck: *Danger, Woman at Work*. Let these sad sacks know what they were dealing with.

But meanwhile, check these moves. There was no high like a natural high, and she was pretty sure the coke had worn off. What was flowing through her veins was pure Shirley-power.

That afternoon, she'd been in Slough House. Every afternoon, face it, she was in Slough House, and even the afternoons when she wasn't felt like she was. Slough House cast a portable shadow: you could hike halfway to Watford and still feel it on your back. Because Slough House sucked the juice from your veins, or tried to. The trick was showing you were juicier than it knew. So anyway: *blah*. That afternoon, she'd been in Slough House, working on one of Jackson Lamb's pet projects: the hooligan hinterland, he called it. His notion being, you didn't strap on a suicide vest and wander down your local high street without your antisocial tendencies having manifested in some way beforehand, like unpaid parking tickets, or using a mobile in the quiet carriage. Shirley wasn't so sure, but that wasn't the point: the point was, when you were in Slough House, you did what Jackson Lamb told you. The alternative was accepting that your career in the Secret Service was over, and like every slow horse before her, and every slow horse to come, Shirley Dander thought she'd be the exception to the rule that Regent's Park didn't take you back. She thought they were secretly waiting for her. She thought that somewhere in a stationery cupboard, they already had the banner they'd prepared for her homecoming.

18

On that day too, she'd dance.

Here and now, but doubtless also in that glorious future, a woman kept catching her eye and pretending it was accidental. Who knew, she might get lucky, but right at the moment she could simply gawp like everyone else, because this was *Strictly Come Dander*, and every other fucker better get their ass off the dance floor. At rest she might resemble, in the words of a former colleague, a concrete bollard with an attitude, but that was only half the story: Shirley was on the underwhelming side where height was concerned, and more cylindrical than traditionally associated with beauty, but the simple physics of it was, every body exerts gravitational pull, and when she was dancing Shirley's pulling power was up there with Newton's other laws. As for the former colleague, if he'd been asked to repeat his description a moment later, he'd have been too busy wondering what just happened to his lungs. Shirley could handle criticism as well as the next guy, but the next guy was a touchy bastard.

And still that woman was watching, and still pretending not to. You had to admire a trier, thought Shirley. You had to admire an admirer, and perhaps she should take pity on her, drag her from the crowd and jump-start her on the dance floor, but that might lead to awkwardness later, because a thing about Shirley's partners — and she meant her professional partners, but there was such a thing as mission-creep — a thing about Shirley Dander's partners was that they tended to die; their brains misted against an office wall, or their insides spilt on snowy Welsh hillsides . . . Shirley had never thought of herself as a jinx, but that hardly mattered, did it? What mattered was what everyone else thought, and — two partners down — it would be an uphill task dismantling gossip. Team up with Shirley and start counting the days. Not the kind of come-on you wanted to broadcast to those watching you from the sidelines, and pretending not to.

And the lights spun, and the dance floor pounded, and the weight of electric bass thrummed in her frame. All eyes were on Shirley Dander, and that was fine by her.

Just so long as nobody started dying again.

★ ★ ★

There was money now, a little, from his grandfather's will — his grandfather's care had gone through his savings like a landlord, but enough remained for River to have bought a car, his first for years. He'd done his due diligence, checked the wear-and-tear stats on second-hand vehicles, listened to Louisa's tip that yellow cars lost only twenty-two per cent of their value in the first three years as opposed to thirty, like every other colour, then bought something he saw stickered for sale in the street. Well, it was a bargain. And so far so good, he thought, as mid-evening London fragmented into carpet showrooms and bed shops, into garages and self-storage warehouses; he'd broken away from a pedestrian existence. It might even be symbolic of a new beginning. He had a hand on the doorknob, ready to step into whatever came next. But first he had to deal with what was happening in Kent.

His childhood home was outside Tonbridge. Jennifer Knox was a neighbour, but that was by rural standards. Central London, you'd fit fifteen dwellings into the space between her house and the O.B.'s, and never meet half the occupants. But strangers were more visible outside the city, and lights in houses that should be dark were noticed. So he had no reason to doubt her word: there was — had been — someone in his grandfather's house.

Which might be a simple case of opportunist intrusion. There'd been a death notice in the paper, and burglars were capable of research. But there were other possibilities. The O.B. had been a spook, a Service legend. His obituary had been tactful — his cover had placed him in the Ministry of Transport — but he'd lived a secret life, and the possibility that some of his secrets lived on could not be ruled out. His house was mostly empty now; the furniture mostly cleared. River's mother had taken care of that: *Let me take some of the burden off your hands.* He'd thought at first — Christ, what did this say about him? — that she was hoping to skim the cash, and had put his foot down where the study was concerned. 'The books,' he'd said. 'I'm keeping the books.'

His mother had adopted her default mode of assuming he'd gone mad. 'You don't read, River.'

'I read.'

'You don't read *that* much.'

Who did? The old man's study was a booklined cave, as if he'd grown part-hobbit in age. But his last year he'd not read at all, the words having slipped from the pages in front of him. One of the last coherent conversations he'd had with his grandson: *I'm losing anchor.* The look in his eyes bottomless.

So the study remained like a showroom in a vacant property — books, chairs, curtains; the shelf with its odd collection of trophies: a glass globe, a hunk of concrete, a lump of metal that had been a Luger; the desk with its sheet of blotting paper, like something

21

out of Dickens, and the letter opener which was an actual stiletto, and had once belonged to Beria — and if David Cartwright had left secrets in his wake they'd be somewhere in that room, on those shelves, hidden among a billion other words. River didn't know if he really believed that, but knew for sure that he didn't know he didn't, and if River thought that way others might too, and act upon the possibility. Spook secrets were dangerous to friends and foes alike, and the old man had made many of both down the years. He could see one of either breed breaking a lock, finessing a window; could see them working round the study, looking for clues. If that was happening, River needed to stop it. Any trail his dead grandfather had left, no one was going to follow but him.

Traffic grew lighter as the skies grew dark, and he made good time, parking up the lane from the O.B.'s house and approaching on foot. The house seemed empty from outside, its windows lightless. There was always the chance that the old lady had made a mistake. But there was equally a chance that she hadn't, and River skirted the front of the building, keeping in tree-shadow, and let himself in through the back door as quietly as he could.

★ ★ ★

Lech Wicinski was making dough, the instructions a list in his head.

First weigh out the flour, or make a reasonable guess.

Now add yeast and a pinch of salt. Stir it in.

Now add your warm water, your tablespoons of olive oil.

Now punch the bastard to within an inch of its life.

He faded out for a moment while this part was going on.

The day had been a bad one, which was to say, no different from most others. Jackson Lamb had taken to asking him when he planned to clean the office windows, as if this were a genetic trait, and while the other slow horses had, if not exactly warmed to him, at least defrosted slightly, the air around Slough House remained that of a half-hearted funeral. The task he'd been given, after months of staring at the walls, was slightly less energising than staring at the walls: Lamb had seen on TV, or read in a newspaper, or invented out of his own head, something about radicalised teenagers withdrawing from social media, and decided Lech might usefully pursue this topic.

'. . . You want a list of kids who've withdrawn from social media?'

'From Facepalm and Twatter and the rest, yeah.'

'Any clues as to how I might go about doing that?'

Lamb had pretended to ponder. 'I could do your job myself, if that's what you mean,' he'd said at last. 'But then there'd be even less fucking point to you than there is now.'

Which was about average for an encounter with Lamb.

So anyway, that was the shape of Lech's days: lost in a blizzard of hashtags, much like the face that looked back from every reflecting surface. Because this was a frightening mess. From a distance, he might have barely survived an acne attack; close up, you could see the razor marks obliterating what had lain beneath. As if he'd run a cheese grater over his cheeks. Bad enough, but it could have been worse: the word scored out was *PAEDO*, carved into Lech's face by the man

23

who'd infected his laptop with illegal pornography.

Thinking this, he punched the bastard dough some more.

That man was out of reach now — thanks to Lamb, as it happened — but so was Lech's career, so was his earlier life. No way would Regent's Park admit he'd been framed. His exoneration would mean their mistake, and the Park didn't do mistakes. So there was no way back to the bright lights, and no obvious future if he stepped away from Spook Street: leave now, he'd be doing so without a clean reference, looking like an extra from a horror flick. Employers wouldn't fall over themselves. While they couldn't get you for being old, gay, ethnic, disabled, male, female or stupid, when you looked like you'd crawled from wreckage of your own devising, they could throw you a pitying look: *Thank you, next.* So Slough House it was, for the foreseeable future.

It was enough to induce paranoia. That evening, on the bus heading home, he'd had the feeling of being watched; a feeling so unnervingly real he'd stepped off the bus early, and waited until it was down the road before walking the rest of the way. Unlikely, he knew; if there was any advantage to being a slow horse, it was that no one was interested. But you couldn't switch off your instincts.

He draped a cloth over the bowl. Once the dough rose he'd bash it down again, flatten it onto a tray, pour olive oil over it, along with a paste of garlic and shredded basil leaves, and leave it an hour before putting it in the oven. Then, lo, focaccia.

And tell me this, he thought. Tell me this: how could any life be broken if it included baking fucking focaccia?

24

It took all the willpower he possessed not to throw the bowl at the wall, but Lech managed it.

Look at me now.

* * *

Not long back, Catherine Standish had taken to buying bottles again; a self-conscious recreation of her drinking days, with this important distinction: she did not drink. It had been a deliberate flirtation with danger, acting out the alcoholic desire of oblivion, but in the end she had done what she had to do, and emptied her bottles down the sink, dismantling the Aladdin's cave she had wrought. It had felt, afterwards, the way she remembered the post-Christmas lulls of her childhood, when decorations were packed away and ordinary dullness re-established. But at the same time she knew a danger had been avoided, and that her regret at not having confronted it head-on was her addiction speaking. Addiction loves challenge because challenge provides an excuse to fail. Though in Slough House, opportunities to fail were never far from hand.

And if you were ever in danger of forgetting this, Jackson Lamb was usually there to see you right.

But Lamb had left the office on some mission of his own before Catherine, and she herself had left early. The evening was chill, the start of British Summer Time having been marked by hailstorms and grey skies, and she wore her winter coat as she waited at a bus stop: not her own, nor anywhere near her route. Several buses passed, and she hailed none, but when a wheelchair rounded the nearest corner and trundled past the stop, she fell into step behind it. The wheelchair's occupant gave no indication of having noticed, but continued as far as the next junction, where the chair's electric humming ceased for a moment at the pedestrian crossing. Catherine remained out of its occupant's range of vision, but the woman in the chair spoke anyway.

'Do I know you?'

'You tell me.'

'Give me a minute.'

This was as long as the traffic lights required. But once they'd done their job, the wheelchair was on the move again. As they crossed the road, to the impotent fury of London's traffic, its occupant spoke again.

'Catherine Standish,' she said. 'One-time PA to Charles Partner, late and unlamented. And now — what shall we call it? Amanuensis? Chatelaine? Dogsbody? — to the not-yet-late but lamentable Jackson Lamb.'

'Who sends his regards.'

'Does he?'

'Not really.'

'No, that didn't sound like him. You're not going to pretend this is a chance encounter, then?'

'I'd been waiting ten minutes.'

'Surprised you weren't scooped up. Sensitive to hangers-around, this neighbourhood.'

This being Regent's Park, the immediate catchment area of the Secret Service.

'One of the advantages of being a middle-aged woman,' Catherine said, 'is the cloak of invisibility that comes with it.'

'Speak for yourself.'

Which was a fair rejoinder. Molly Doran had many attributes, but invisibility wasn't among them.

'I normally take a cab,' she continued. 'You're lucky you caught me.' She halted abruptly. 'I was sorry to hear about your colleague.'

'Thank you.'

'Jackson hates losing joes.'

'I don't suppose the joes are that thrilled either.'

'Ah. She bites.' The wheelchair resumed its progress. 'The reason I'm not in a taxi heading home, Ms Standish, is that I have things to do in town. So you have two minutes to explain whatever it is you're after, and then we can both get about our business.'

Catherine said, 'We have concerns.'

'How borderline tragic for you.'

'And we were wondering if you could help.'

'And how are we defining 'we' in this context?'

'Just me, really.'

'I see.' Molly wore mockery-defying make-up, her face lifelessly white, her cheeks absurdly red. She might have been auditioning for a role in a different manner of circus, as a clown or perhaps an acrobat, though she was more than usually challenged if the latter. Her legs, for instance, ended at the knee.

She said, 'So Lamb has no idea you're talking to me?'

Catherine was aware that it could be an error to categorically state what Lamb was and was not aware of at any given time, including when he was asleep. But it was simplest to stick to supposition. 'No.'

'That's a pity. When Lamb wants a favour, I charge him through the nose.'

' . . . Really?'

'Information. Not money.' She smiled, not in a pleasant way. 'Spook currency. I'm something of a hoarder.'

27

'Which is the reason I wanted to see you.'

'It's the only reason anyone wants to see me. That's my USP. My *raison d'être*.' Molly Doran came to a halt again, and Catherine sensed a speech coming. 'I'm an archivist, Ms Standish. I deal in the paper world. My little kingdom's full of folders stuffed with the secrets people kept back when they sat at typewriters to make their reports. I used to be told, ooh, fifteen years ago, that digitisation would put an end to my kind of gatekeeping. That was before everyone got the heebie-jeebies about how vulnerable the online world is.' She mimed the flicking of a switch. 'One smart cookie in Beijing, and everything's on the Web for all to see. So I'm still around, and my records are very much hard copies. The future may not be in my keeping, but trust me, the past is my domain.' She paused. "Cookie' was wordplay, incidentally. It's a thing they have on computers.'

'Yes, I'd heard.'

'So tell me about these concerns of yours. Has someone been shaking your foundations? Slough House tumbling around your ears?'

Before Catherine could reply there was a howling in the near distance, from the direction of the zoo.

'Did you hear that?' she said.

'Ah,' said Molly. 'The big bad wolf. Coming to blow your house down, is he?'

'I think someone already has,' said Catherine.

★ ★ ★

The back door opened into a porch where coats were hung and wellington boots abandoned, or that's what used to happen. Now it was just a cold empty area between the outside world and the kitchen. River passed through it silently. That was the thing about familiar houses: you knew its squeaks and unoiled hinges; you knew where to put your weight. Here on the doorjamb was a single pencil mark, midriff height. Rose had marked it off for him. *There. That's how tall you are.* And then David had explained the rules of life: you didn't leave your details in the open for everyone to see; you didn't mark your height and age for the weasels to find. It had been River's first glimpse into his grandfather's secret world, and he'd never again asked Rose to measure him.

There was no noise. The study was ground floor, at the back: exit the kitchen, turn left. He could have done it with his eyes closed. Its door was open a fraction. Was that how he'd left it? He waited while his eyes adjusted to the gloom, acutely conscious of the emptiness around him. Even the grandfather clock, a fixture in the hallway since long before his birth, was gone. Its absence of ticking felt like a tap on his shoulder.

But in the study the shelves would be stocked with books; the rugs in place; the desk, the armchairs. There'd be a basket of logs by the fire and a transistor radio on the coffee table. It would barely be a surprise to find the O.B. there, brandy glass in hand. But his grandfather had passed into joe country, and besides: in the air was a smell of fried dust.

He put a hand flat on the study door, and pushed. It swung open.

The soft glow came from the ancient one-bar electric fire, usually kept tucked behind the O.B.'s armchair. In its halo, the room assumed the air of a Dutch painting: pin-sharp details in the centre, fading to shadow around the edges. And there, more or less where it shone brightest, his grandfather's chair, its familiar heft as much a presence in River's life as the man who'd once occupied it. The figure that sat there now watched as River entered, and didn't seem to move; didn't appear to be breathing. Might have been a ghost.

'Jesus,' he said softly.

He took two steps into the room.

' . . . Sid?'

'Hello, River,' she said.

★ ★ ★

At that precise moment, miles away, an ambulance in a hurry rounds Beech Street, its blue light strobing first Barbican Tube Station and then the buildings on the next block: the Chinese restaurant, the newsagent's; the door between the two which never opens, never closes. And for the time this takes to happen, Slough House is illuminated, its windows throwing back light as if fully engaged in London life; as if the building breathes the same air as everybody else, and harbours the same hopes and aspirations. It doesn't last. A moment later the ambulance is bombing down Aldersgate Street, its siren squealing round the rooftops, and in its wake Slough House's windows become the same black pools they were before, so that if you approached and peered in, always supposing you could hover that high above the pavement, nothing would look back at you — not the everyday nothing of casual absence, but the long-drop nothing that comes once everything's over.

But nobody ever approaches, and nobody ever

looks in. Slough House might as well not be there, for all the attention paid to it, and while this is unsurprising — the spook trade not being renowned for kerb flash — it carries too a suggestion of redundancy. Because in London, a building best hurried past is a building without reason to be, and such a building might find its days numbered; might find itself viewed not as bricks and mortar but as an opportunity; as an empty pillar of air, waiting for steel and glass to give it shape. The history embedded in its bones counts for nothing. To those who buy and sell and own and build, the past is simply a shortcut to what's yet to come, and what's yet to come offers magpie riches to those prepared to embrace the changes demanded. Or so the promises run.

For a city is an impermanent thing, its surface ever shifting, like the sea.

And like the sea, a city has its sharks.

3

There's a shop on Brewer Street. You can get Russian tobacco there. Polish chewing gum. Lithuanian snuff . . .

If the man who'd spoken those words weren't long dead, he'd have had no trouble finding the shop in question: it hadn't moved, hadn't redecorated, had barely changed at all. It was still the same stamp-sized floorspace, with a counter on which sat a till, still fondly referred to as 'electric'; it was still shelved floor to ceiling on all sides, and each shelf still bore the same bewildering array of vendibles: the same cigars with green and yellow bands; the same chocolate frogs in the same foil wrapping. The same calendar, still celebrating 1993, still hung above the door to the stairs, and the same biscuit-tin lid, its bright motif still a twinkly-eyed Stalin, was still propped on a head-height shelf, and still saw service as a percussive device when Conference was in swing, 'Conference' being the designation Old Miles bestowed on any upstairs gathering numbering more than three — any fewer, he was wont to grumble, and there was no call to count cadence, a rhythm he still observed by beating Joe Stalin in the face with a tiny hammer.

Old Miles wasn't his actual name, but it was generally held that old miles were what he walked, and nothing about the way he clung to established habits gave the lie to this.

But one reason for adhering to tradition is an awareness of impending change, and the little shop's apparent obduracy concealed a minor shift that required major rearrangement, in that what once had been a going concern was now simply a concern. Business rates were ever on the rise, and the customer base ever dwindling, reduced by mortality and age and decreasing mobility. The shop had once been part of a local network of grocers and tradesmen of every description, where the competent shopper could provision a family for a siege. But those days were gone, and Old Miles's tobacconist-cum-smuggler's cave was now marooned in a hipsters' playground. Which was the least of its worries. London altered by the day, and if the city had never been as kind nor as welcoming to strangers as it liked to pretend, it had at least thrived on the variety that strangers introduced. The political fog of the times had changed that, and political fog, as history has illustrated, is best dispelled by the waving of flags and banners, which usually foreshadows the use of truncheons and sticks. Variety was no longer a draw, and the gatherings of so-called Yellow Vests on the streets of central London were a testament to the shrinking of mental horizons that accompanies the raising of a drawbridge. Milosz Jerzinsky — Old Miles — hadn't spent his early years fighting communists from a distance only to be sandbagged by fascists on his doorstep in old age. Besides, the leasehold on his shop had precisely as many years to run as those by which he had surpassed retirement age, and the neat mirror image these spans presented was as good as a sign from the heavens. So he had taken, he admitted to his remaining customers, the land-grabber's shilling; he was folding his tent; he was making his departure. His shop would remain unchanged until its final day, but that arrived on the stroke of midnight, to mark time until which one last

Conference was being held in the upstairs room; a gathering of stalwarts and irregulars alike, who would count the hours down glass by glass, and simply by their presence prove the remainder of that long-dead customer's encomium on Old Miles's place: *At any given moment, half its customers used to be spooks.*

But the given moments, thought the man himself, were fast wearing out their welcome.

He had just sold the last three packs of his Russian cigarettes — a life-destroying brand that only a suicide could embrace — to a fat man in a dirty overcoat who looked like he worked in a betting shop, either behind the cashier's grille or on a stool beneath the TV, watching his pay packet break a leg in the 3:15 at Doncaster. Still, there was a grim focus in his eyes as he waited for his change, as if he were committing the little shop's interior to memory. Maybe he'd lost more than the odd pay packet in his time. Maybe there was a whole archive of failure shelved in that ugly head, which was perhaps the reason Old Miles spoke to him as he counted coins into his waiting hand. 'We're closing,' he said.

'So I heard.'

'There's no future in it.'

The man grunted. 'It looks like there's barely a present.'

'You've not been here before?'

The man didn't answer. He was staring at the coins, as if Old Miles had shortchanged him, or slipped an unacceptable currency into his palm. But at length he shovelled them into his trouser pocket and looked Old Miles in the eye. 'Heard about it. Never set foot inside.'

'You can't have bought that brand anywhere else in

34

these parts.'

'Maybe there's the reason you're having to close,' the man said. 'Maybe you're too nosey to survive.'

'There might be truth in that,' Old Miles conceded. 'Though up till now, I've considered survival one of my talents.' He nodded in the direction of the door to his left. 'Would you like to go upstairs?'

'You're not my type.'

'There's drink. A gathering of like-minded friends.' He leaned closer. 'You've been in the game, haven't you? I can usually tell.' He pulled back. 'Call it a wake.'

'I'm not the sentimental kind.'

'But you look like a drinker.'

The fat man produced a cigarette from nowhere. It looked like one of those that Old Miles had just sold him — the tobacco nearly black; the tube loose in its filter — but he couldn't have freed it with his hand in his pocket, surely. He slotted it into his mouth. 'Well,' he said. 'Maybe I'll pop my head in. See if I recognise any old faces.'

'And if any of them recognise yours,' said Old Miles, 'what name would they attach to it?'

'Christ knows,' said Jackson Lamb, and disappeared through the door the shopkeeper had indicated.

★ ★ ★

The speciality of the house was red meat.

If you didn't believe the menu, just look at the diners.

Diana Taverner ran the obvious numbers: if you subtracted the serving staff she'd be the only woman here, which was fine by her. Equality meant nothing if it didn't involve earning your place at the table; a table, in this instance, occupying the private upstairs

35

room of a pub, but one of those pubs reviewed in the Sunday supplements, with a named chef. He'd moved among them earlier, introducing himself, explaining the cuts he was intending to serve, and had come this close to asking if they wanted to meet the damn cow. Diana enjoyed her food, but the rituals involved could be tiresome.

A fork met a glass, repeatedly. The company fell silent.

'Thank you all.'

It was Peter Judd who'd rung for quiet, and Judd who spoke now. He'd put on weight: for a man who'd never minded being photographed jogging, he reliably resembled the 'before' slot in a set of before-and-after photos. But those paparazzi days were behind him, she supposed, even allowing for the fact that they might turn out to be ahead of him also: writing off the career of a politician whose greed for power was so naked it required a parental advisory sticker frequently turned out to be a little previous, as the barrow-boy slang had it. And barrow-boy slang was just one of the vernaculars Judd was fluent in. Another was corporate bonhomie, which, for this evening, he'd turned up to eleven.

'I'd just like to say how delightful it is to see you all here on what I'm sure will be the first of many — *many* — such occasions, being a celebration of this bold new enterprise of ours. You all know Diana Taverner, of course, and I'm sure that, like me, you're all enjoying the the *apt nomenclature* she rejoices in, for she is indeed our quick huntress, whose latest foray into the forests of international intrigue we're making a festive ah ah ah *bunfight* of tonight.'

There were those who'd said of Peter Judd, during

his years as a contender for the highest office in the land, that his clowning masked a laser-like focus on his own best interests, but it was a mistake to assume that the theatrical flourishes were nothing more than showmanship. The truth was, he enjoyed the ringmaster role too much to abjure it, while another, truer truth was, it had the added benefit of inducing even close associates to underestimate him. This, Diana knew, was a key component of his interpersonal skill set. Judd had long made a study of loyalty — the ties that bind, and how we answer to their bondage — without ever suffering its strictures himself.

'Some while ago, as none of you will have forgotten, a disgraceful episode interrupted the tranquillity of our fair and sovereign nation, when, for reasons yet to be fully established, a foreign intelligence service dispatched what can only be described as 'hitmen', a pair of *hitmen*, their actual gender notwithstanding, to commit murder on our shores. These assassins arrived in the guise of tourists, come to pay obeisance to one of the jewels in our national crown, but rather than guidebook and selfie stick they arrived armed with a toxic substance and evil intent. So far, so very like some popcorn spectacle of the kind we're accustomed to seeing on the widescreens of our nation's multiplexes, or should that be multiplices? And yet, and yet, if I were to invoke a cinematic precedent, it would be more Inspector Clouseau than ah ah James Bond. More Laurel and Hardy than *Fast and Furious*.

For in their blundering idiocy, these fools not only proved themselves unable to carry out their original mission, but left in their wake a woman dead and a man seriously impaired. Innocent bystanders, unfortunate citizens, casual victims of international skulduggery. And there are those among you, I know, who felt — like me — the the the *shame* of seeing this disgraceful episode go unpunished, to see the perpetrators paraded on their homeland television like returning heroes, and their president describe them as uninvolved passers-by, innocent of wrongdoing, and thus subject their victims, and by association every other citizen of this land, to a degree of contempt that in earlier times would have seen boots polished, kitbags packed and gunboats launched.'

He paused and his mouth assumed its usual pout, his eyes their usual cunning light. Give him a toga, Diana thought, and he'd be Nero absent his lyre.

His voice dropped.

'I should say, of course, that as deplorable and sordid as these events were, they could have been worse. Much much worse. Slathering a nerve agent on their ex-compatriot's doorknob, in a doomed attempt to murder him, was an evil, evil act, but discarding the unused portion of their toxic weapon — in a perfume bottle — in a local park — to be chanced upon by a couple on a community clean-up outing — that was heinous beyond the reach of vocabulary. That the woman died, the unfortunate woman, was quite tragic enough, but it takes no great leap of imagination to envision other outcomes. The murderous miscreants, in abandoning their poisonous armoury, gave no thought to the potential consequences such action might entail. Any number of victims might have suffered contamination. Children might have been involved. Small, British children.'

His audience was caught up in his rhetoric, their knives and forks at high noon across the bloody swirls on their plates. Damien Cantor was nodding to P. J.'s beat as if he'd first danced to it at his school disco. She'd been taken aback to see him among the company. But he, and the rest of them, had paid for this; had made it happen. So she supposed they were entitled to enjoy the moment, even if that meant — in a typically male way — that they would feel themselves its engineers.

'And in the aftermath, as I say, shame. The shame of seeing our government do nothing, of seeing sabres apparently unsheathed, but hearing only the plastic rattle of inadequacy. We pulled our aprons over our heads and hid our faces from the world. There we were, taunted and mocked by the global bully, and the best response we could muster was a cowardly wail. Is it any wonder that the common people felt affronted? Is it really a source of surprise that they began to question their leaders? Who among us wouldn't, when our leaders proved themselves so unequal to the tasks facing them? Tasks, you would have thought, that those occupying the great offices of state would be more than prepared to gird themselves for. Indeed, it's not too presumptuous to suggest that they should have arrived at said offices with loins already clenched.'

He paused, his gaze sweeping the table.

'So it is with awe and admiration that I offer our communal thanks to the fair Diana, for the efficiency and aplomb with which she turned her sights on the prize. That prize being, I don't need to tell you, an evening of the score. Two hitmen, I said, two hitmen were dispatched to our sovereign shores, though of course, as we all know, one of those hitmen was, in actual fact, in actual fact, a hit*woman*. And she, the female of the species — which we don't need our national poet to remind us is far deadlier than the male — has now been returned to the soil from which she sprang, or dung heap, rather, the dung heap which spewed her forth, one of our own unsung heroes — or possibly, who knows, heroines? — performing the ah, the ah, termination. On the instructions of our gallant huntress Diana, she who sought to take life has now herself been taken, and I can only imagine, as I'm sure we all can, the terror that must now be afflicting her erstwhile comrade-in-villainy. Vengeance, gentlemen — gentlemen and *lady* — vengeance is an oft-maligned impulse. We are told to turn the other cheek, to forgive the wrongs done to us. And this is well and good, well and good. But there is a time, too, for anger and chastisement, a time to take up the sword and lay waste those who have done us wrong. That this has now been done is a matter for celebration, and while I pay tribute, as we all do, to the fair Lady Diana, I also want to thank all of you for making her acts possible. You provided the steel and the lead, you provided the weapon. Diana took aim and her aim, as we all know, proved true. Once more we can hold our heads high in the world, even if our pride, for the time being, has to remain a matter of quiet satisfaction rather than triumphant bellowing. But the time for bellowing will come, rest assured of that. The time for bellowing will come. And when we bellow, the world will hear. Thank you.'

The boisterous reaction took some minutes to quieten down.

Taverner had to hand it to him. Judd knew which buttons to press.

★ ★ ★

It was more tree house than clubhouse, the room above Old Miles's shop; wooden floorboards, and no furniture to speak of. Packing cases along one wall provided a surface on which bottles had been set — red wine, vodka and whisky — their haphazard groupings punctuated by overflowing ashtrays. The remainder of the floor was occupied by similarly haphazard groupings of old men, or men nearly old; some in suits that had seen better days; others in peacock apparel. The common factor was that each held at least one glass. Through the small sash window, propped open the height of a tobacco tin, came a distant muddle of chanting.

Inside the room conversation was multilingual and overlapping. A blue cloud hung overhead, and the gently swaying lightbulb was the moon on an overcast night.

Lamb had found a bottle of malt and was in a corner smoking, looking like a bin someone had set fire to. Next to him, at shoulder height, hung a dartboard to which a picture of Vladimir Putin, topless on horseback, had been taped. One small postcard aside, of a wooden church in a snow-clad landscape, it was the room's only decoration.

'Are you smoking that or is it smoking you?'

The speaker was a shade younger than most others present, and wore a charcoal suit with a faint pinstripe. His thinning hair was sandy and his spectacle frames blue.

'It smells Soviet-era. Where do they make them, Chernobyl?'

Lamb gazed around the room. Though everyone had looked at him when he'd entered, most had made the effort not to appear to be doing so. 'There's a few

41

here might have been assets at one time,' he said, 'and more than a couple probably sold secrets when the weather was fair. But even Russian tobacco can't cover up the odour I'm getting from you. You're a suit.'

'Suit? I was nearly a desk at one time.'

'What happened? Someone lose your Allen key?'

The man laughed. 'Someone was better at their job than me. It happens. Smith, by the way. Corny, I know. Chester Smith.'

'And what desk did you nearly fill, Chester Smith?'

'US Liaison. Went to a woman who'd done her masters at Barnard. Turns out that was a good place to make future contacts. Form your networks early. There any spare in that bottle?'

Lamb held it up; it was three-quarters full. 'No.'

A small figure appeared in the doorway, and was immediately obscured by others.

Smith said, 'It's like the United Nations in here.'

'What, a dosshouse for the weird and lonely?'

'Exactly. Old Miles has never been on the books, did you know that? Been running this place as an out-of-hours spooks' club since the seventies, but it's always been under the bridge. More than a few ops planned here, you can bet your braces.'

'You still with the Park, Chester Smith?'

'No, I took the option when the desk job fell through. Handy little benefits package.' He sipped from his glass. 'I dabble in real estate now.'

'You don't say.' Lamb drained his own glass, then refilled it.

'Office space, mostly. A few luxury apartments. But I have this thing, call it a principle. I don't deal with Russian money.'

'That must make you very proud.'

The small figure appeared again briefly, in the space between taller bodies. The room had filled since Lamb arrived, and Old Miles himself squeezed in now, to general hubbub. The shop had closed its door for the last time. It was a sad moment, but sad moments were to be celebrated as much as happy ones, or half the liquor in the world would go undrunk. And there were no better friends than old comrades to share such moments with. This, or something like it, formed the basis of a short speech. Cheers were attempted, and glasses raised. Through the window came another burst of chanting, as if distant strangers were old comrades too.

'You were a joe, weren't you?' Smith said, once the clamour had subsided. 'That why you're here? You miss the old days?'

'What I like about the old days is, they're over,' said Lamb.

'And you know what? I think I've just worked out who you are. You're Lamb, aren't you? You're Jackson Lamb.'

Lamb's face was expressionless. But after a moment, he nodded.

' . . . Ha! Jackson Lamb! If I'd known I'd be meeting a legend I'd have brought my autograph book.'

'If I'd known this was a date I'd have freshened up.' Lamb farted, possibly in compensation, and took a last drag of his cigarette before the tube fell from the filter, scattering a Catherine wheel of sparks across the floor. Lamb ignored every part of this process apart from the inhalation: when he breathed out again, it was as if he were conjuring a storm cloud.

Smith stepped on the small fire, extinguishing it. 'Jackson Lamb. Didn't you once — '

43

'Whatever I did or didn't once, I don't now.' He produced another cigarette. 'Or did the whole 'secret' part of Secret Service pass you by?'

Chester Smith pressed a finger to his lips. 'Mea culpa. But imagine the awe a desk-man feels for the field agent.'

'I'm a desk-man myself these days. And you're, what do you call it, an investment opportunist? Property consultant? Or does wanker cover it all?'

'Now that's classic. 'Does wanker cover it all?' Priceless. Here, let me get that.' Producing a lighter, Smith snapped a flame into life. 'And I'm not exactly a civilian. I lunch with Oliver Nash once a month. A club off Wigmore Street. He keeps me in the loop.'

Nash was chair of the Limitations Committee, which oversaw the Service's spend, so technically kept Diana Taverner on a leash. It was no surprise he dined off the stories that came his way. He was every joe's nightmare: a career bureaucrat with an operational veto.

Lamb said, 'How very considerate of him. Does he print a newsletter, or just use a megaphone?'

The lighter went back in Smith's pocket. He said, 'You know your Service carried out an assassination last month?'

'Megaphone it is, then.'

'One of the GRU creeps involved in that Novichok business. Whacked her on home turf, somewhere in the Volga. That's what I call taking it to the enemy.' He swirled his empty glass. 'Word is, Putin's spitting teeth.'

'He's always spitting teeth. If not his own, someone else's.'

'You sure you couldn't squeeze a small one out of

that?'

'I hate freeloaders.' But Lamb poured a tiny amount into the proffered glass, once he'd made sure his own was full.

'Thank you.' Smith toasted the picture on the dartboard, and broke softly into song. "Rah-rah-rah Putin, homicidal Russian queen.' Gay porn lost a superstar when he went into despotism, right? Could have been the new Joe Dallesandro.'

Lamb grunted.

'That man he tried to have poisoned. Here in England.'

'What about him?'

'He was a swapped spy. Out of the game. He —'

'I know how it works,' said Lamb. 'I'm not the fucking janitor.'

'But welcome to the brave new order, eh? No holds barred. Don't get me wrong, three cheers for Lady Di. I mean, I'm all for peace and love and all that, but only once the body count's even. Otherwise we run the risk of being Russia's bunny.' He swallowed his drink in a single draught. It's possible that sarcasm was intended. 'I'm sure he'll have rolled a head or two back home, won't he? The Kremlin's Gay Hussar. Assigned some locals to Siberia. What you might call the Naughty Steppes.' He glanced slyly at Lamb saying this. 'But that won't be enough, will it? The Park carried the fight to him, he'll bring it on back. Couldn't look his photographer in the face otherwise.'

'Well, you carry right on not selling him flats. That'll take the wind out his sails.'

'Wouldn't be surprised if he weren't behind that lot, come to think of it. *Les gilets jaunes.*' Smith nodded towards the open window, through which distant

45

grumbling could still be heard. 'The real world equivalent to a bunch of internet trolls.'

'If you say so,' said Lamb. 'But I'd take them more seriously if they spent less time accessorising.' He slipped the bottle into his coat pocket, and thrust his free hand out. Chester Smith made to clasp it in his own. 'No, I need your lighter. Mine's empty.'

Smith handed it over, then watched as Lamb crossed the room, the press of bodies parting for him without fuss. At the door he halted without looking back, though Smith had the sense he was checking the room out anyway. But whatever it was he'd been looking for he didn't appear to have found, because a moment later he was gone, and the room seemed half as crowded for his absence.

'Jackson Lamb,' Smith murmured aloud, for no obvious reason. Then went to find someone new to talk to.

★ ★ ★

Judd sat next to Diana, satisfaction oozing from every pore, and she put a hand on his elbow. 'I'm not too proud to admit it,' she said. 'I nearly got an erection there.'

'Me too.'

'And thank you for those kind words.'

'Every syllable deserved.'

She was unused to praise from Peter Judd. Achievement, in other people, was not something he admired: it was like watching somebody walk around in shoes he'd planned to buy. On the other hand, he'd been running a PR company since leaving the political limelight. Perhaps he'd learned something, if only which lies to tell.

'And it achieved the required response,' he went on. 'Rage and fury from the Kremlin, I gather. He'll do such things, he knows not what they are, or something like that. *King Lear*, yes?'

'Quite possibly.'

'Did it for A level. You think he'll start a war?'

'If I'd thought that,' Diana said, 'I'd not have greenlit the operation.'

'Oh, come on. What's life without a little risk?'

'Longer?'

'You never disappoint me, Diana.'

She said, 'He won't start a war. Because he broke the rules. Sanctioning a hit on a swapped spy, that's not done. He should have known that.'

'And now you've carried out a hit on the hitter we're all square, or should be. But as you've already pointed out, he's not playing by the rules.'

'You're aware that it wasn't actually an agent who consigned the target to, as you put it, the dunghill?'

'Heap,' said Judd. Then: 'No, I'd rather assumed you acquired the services of a soldier of fortune of some sort.'

She nodded.

'But we're here to inspire national pride, and if that means blurring the odd detail, so be it.' He reached for his glass. 'Besides, the underlying point remains. The good chaps here, they provided the wherewithal. Whether to a salaried operative or a freelance journeyman hardly matters. Our political overlords, so-called, fell at every available hurdle, but these good men and true stepped up. National pride was at stake. They heard the call, and opened their chequebooks.'

'Now that's a stirring image.'

'Behave. You took their money. Don't look down

47

your nose.'

In other company she might have tried to look contrite, but Judd had as little time for social pieties as she did.

'And you have to admit, it's working nicely so far.'

It was. Or seemed to be.

It had been the tail end of winter when Judd had approached her with, as he'd termed it, an opportunity. These had felt few and far between at the time. An agent had died, in the snow, in Wales; one of Jackson Lamb's crew — a slow horse — but it all went down on the books. A recently departed Park operative had been killed in the same debacle. The way it spun, no blame was laid at Diana's door, but an odour had lingered; worse, this had happened shortly after her application for a root-and-branch overhaul of operational practices — effectively a plea for a major increase in spend — had been rejected. And that had been before the budgetary fallout from You-Know-What kicked in. The last full-scale retreat from Europe, by way of amateur armada, had seen defeat dressed up as victory; this latest version, a supposed triumph, might as well have been made on the *Titanic*. No wonder Peter Judd's siren song had fallen sweetly on her ears.

Suppose the Service were able to achieve, let's call it a self-sufficient status . . . What if she had the resources to operate as required, in situations of critical need, without requiring government approval?

We're not talking about privatisation. Simply an injection of necessary funds from sources with a vested interest in national security . . .

Funds well spent, though for now the dossier on the Kazan operation remained a miracle of invisible expenses. This was an easier ask than the more familiar inverse. Those holding the purse strings were happy not to wonder, for example, at how cheaply extra-territorial surveillance had been undertaken. And it turned out that the actual cost of having someone whacked remained one of those subjects too embarrassing to discuss in public, so that wasn't subjected to intense scrutiny either.

Judd became embroiled in something humorous to his right. Meanwhile, the man to Diana's left required her attention.

'What you said afterwards,' he said. 'Smiert spionam. It made me laugh.'

'How did you come to hear about that?'

'Oh, come on. You said it to spark a legend. You knew it would get around.'

She had a long-standing aversion to being told what she knew, though it had been a long while since anyone had dared. And this particular man — Damien Cantor — had probably still been in school then. He was mid-thirties now, treading that line between being a noise in the business world and still hip to the streets: three-day stubble and trainers. When they went on about sixty being the new forty, they forgot to add that that made thirty-something the new twelve.

'So anyway,' he went on. 'You must be pleased with the way things are going.'

'Must I?'

'All those years of being tethered to the rule book.' He was dismantling a bread roll as he spoke, though the meal was effectively over. 'And now you're a free agent. More or less.'

'I have no plans to tear up any rule books, Mr Cantor.'

'Please — Damien.' He reached for a napkin. 'I'm happy to have been of assistance. And we're all looking forward to the next adventure.'

'And I'm grateful for the backing. But the next adventure, as you put it, will more than likely consist of improved administrative processes. It's astonishing how expensive a firewall upgrade can be.'

'I'm sure. But I think we'd all prefer something a little more technicolour. I mean, after a start like this, it would be a shame to go lo-fi, wouldn't it?'

Diana stared, causing him no great discomfiture. He was easily the youngest of the assembled company; one of the new-breed media magicians, who'd started as a YouTube impresario and now owned a rolling news channel, mostly fed by citizen input. 'Make it, don't fake it' was Channel Go's mission statement, unless it was its mantra, or its logo. But its general thrust was to encourage choleric rage in its viewers, so, if nothing else, Cantor had tapped into the spirit of the times.

Judd had returned his attention her way.

'Mr Cantor was just providing me with consumer feedback,' she told him. 'Apparently I'm to work my way up to a series finale.'

'Damien has a well-polished sense of humour. Nobody here is steering your aim, Diana. We're all very much behind the scenes.'

'Of course,' Cantor agreed. 'Pay no attention to me.'

Plates were being cleared, and people starting to mill about. A group broke away, heading for the smoking area outside: 'Won't have to put up with this nonsense much longer,' one could be heard saying.

'In fact,' Cantor continued, 'I was hoping for very

much the opposite. That we all pay more attention to you.'

'Now now,' Judd said.

'Oh come on, Peter. It's the obvious next move.' He met Diana's gaze. 'Channel Go have a seven o'clock bulletin. It would be a tremendous coup for us if you were to appear. A quick rundown of, ah, recent developments. No need to go into operational details. Keep it as cloak-and-dagger as you like. But a general statement to the effect that our national pride has been reasserted, that the lion has roared — well. You hardly need me to write your script.'

'I'm starting to get the impression that that's exactly what you think I need,' Diana said.

'If you prefer, we could shoot you behind a screen.'

'I could probably arrange something similar for you.'

'Perhaps we should discuss this another time,' Judd cut in smoothly. 'If I might drag you away, Diana?'

As he rose, he let his hand fall on Diana's shoulder, and she saw Damien Cantor register this; the information slotting into place. Inaccurate information, as it happened — there was nothing between her and Judd; hadn't been for years — but that hardly devalued it. Fake news was as useful as the other kind.

She made sure to be smiling as she got to her feet.

★ ★ ★

There'd been a gathering most weeks lately, usually on a midweek evening; not precisely a march, more what was described as a display of solidarity, even though what it mostly illustrated was deep division. The Yellow Vests were a loose coalition of the disaffected — its

51

French origins an unwitting tribute to the free movement of ideas — and their anger, initially aimed at those who failed to listen to them, or at those who'd listened but had failed to act upon their demands, or at those who had acted upon their demands but in a way deemed unsatisfactory in some manner, had long been swallowed by a free-range hatred for anyone who swam into their crosshairs: Jewish MPs, gay journalists, student activists, traffic wardens; all routinely described as Nazis, which, if nothing else, suggested that the master race's membership criteria had grown less rigorous since its pomp. Tonight they had gathered along Wardour Street, where Reece Nesmith III passed them in a hurry, ignoring the jeers this provoked. Words he'd heard before, and besides, he was on a mission.

Though the man he was tailing had, for all his size, vanished inside the evening's folds.

This must have happened within minutes of his leaving Old Miles's. The streets, *gilets jaunes* aside, weren't fuller than usual; the street lights were working, there was no mist. What there was, unless it was Reece's imagination, was a whiff of foreign tobacco, as if the man had coloured the air he walked through. But of the man himself, no sign. Reece doubled back, running the gauntlet of jeers again, but he was wasting his time. The man was gone.

I know how it works, he'd said. *I'm not the fucking janitor.* The other one, the man in the suit, was a hanger-on, a spy buff. But this one, for all he was gross and dressed like he'd crawled from a charity bin, something about him suggested he was the real thing. Andy would have picked him out of a line-up: *Spook Street. No question.* But it wasn't like Andy was here to say so.

That was the whole point.

In the end he gave it up as a bad job and headed for home; along Oxford Street, up Edgware Road, under the flyover. The flat was above a dummy shop, its window display a mosaic of cards showing lettable properties but its door permanently locked. His own door was next along, in a recess, and as he opened it and stepped across the threshold, everything turned upside down. A glimpse of a yellow vest was his last conscious observation. Then he blacked out.

* * *

'I was not expecting to find fucking broadcasters among your guests.'

'Welcome to century twenty-one,' Judd said, ironising the words. 'You can't attract wealthy sponsors without involving media interests, you know that. But the Murdoch principle still applies. Why break a prime minister when you could have a whole string of them to play with instead?'

'That's not particularly comforting.'

'I'm simply pointing out that Cantor's on our side. And would much rather have a friendly, ongoing relationship with a power player than a brief headline everyone will call fake news. As for his interview, it's not going to happen.'

'Damn right it's not going to happen.'

'Though it wouldn't hurt to — '

'I'd think very carefully about the next words that emerge from your mouth.'

He paused. 'It's always a pleasure, I hope you're aware of that, Diana.'

She said nothing.

53

'But a little gratitude wouldn't hurt. Nobody's expecting you to appear on TV, that was out of order. But a fair bit of funding has been ushered your way, and those whose pockets it's come from are entitled to appreciation. Not to mention those of us who've done the ushering.'

'Does this place do rooms?' she asked. 'Because I could rent one. You could have them form a disorderly queue.'

'All I meant was, it never hurts to acknowledge largesse.'

'They're supposed to be angels, Peter. That was the word you used. Silent backers. Nothing more.'

'Even angels get their wings stroked, now and again.'

'Except the ones who plotted against God,' said Diana. 'They were eternally damned, I seem to recall.'

The unlikely angels, unless they were the legion of the damned, were scattered around the room, engaged in small conspiracies. It was not a mixed crowd: exclusively white, and middle-aged or upwards, Cantor being the exception. Their backgrounds, those she was aware of, could be summed up as urban money, but it troubled her that there were three or four among them who, like Cantor, she hadn't known would be here. This despite Judd's briefing.

She said, 'I'm grateful to have received support. But I'm starting to wonder if the arrangement's going to work.' His face didn't change while receiving this news: that wasn't a good sign. 'I didn't authorise the Kazan operation so your backers could dine out on it.'

'*My* backers?'

'You brought them to the table.'

'And I plan to join them under it before the evening

54

gets much older. So I hope you're not going to spoil everyone's enjoyment.' He studied her for a moment. 'Kazan has brought a smile to the trousers of every red-blooded Englishman — '

'Who gets to hear about it,' she put in.

'And that's more than you might think. There are whispers on the internet. And when the history books are written, you'll be there. The woman who avenged her nation's honour. And did so without expectation of glory, which should make wearing the laurels so much sweeter. More?'

She nodded.

He refreshed their glasses from the decanter at his side, and as he poured said, 'I gather you've been gifted a nice little mews property.'

'Not me personally.'

'Of course not. Heaven forfend. No, the Service, I should say, now has a little hideaway entirely off the books, which I'm sure will come in useful.' He set the decanter down. 'How did you explain that to the Limitations Committee, if you don't mind my asking?'

She said, 'Oliver Nash can be very understanding.'

'Can he indeed? Can he indeed? But I imagine even he finds it difficult to get a grasp on something when it's not actually put in front of him.'

She said, 'All right.'

He feigned innocence. 'I'm sorry?'

'It didn't go before Limitations. As you apparently know.'

And she'd have given a lot to discover how he'd come to do that.

He said, 'And nor was it intended to. It was an outright gift, the point of which was to allow you a little leeway. There's a reason they're called safe houses.

And what's the point of having new . . . sponsors, if they're not able to show their support? Were Limitations to become involved, or any one of the other ludicrously overpopulated oversight committees you're subjected to, you'd be back where you started, unable to muster the resources you need, unable to mount operations like the one we're all so happy to celebrate this evening.'

' . . . Thank you. You've made your point.'

'Have I? Because it seems to me you may not have fully grasped the import of what's happening. These good people you see around you, they're here for a reason, they're patriots. They want to help. And what do they want in return? Nothing outrageous, Diana. Nothing that might cause you to regret having accepted their largesse. But the fact is that, alongside the very warm feelings they get when they see their nation's security service prospering, they might also desire a little reflected glory themselves. A little oomph.' He swirled the glass in his hand. 'It's not like we're asking your joes to wear team shirts. We appreciate that that might be counterproductive.'

'You think?'

'But it would be a little . . . disheartening if the Limitations Committee, or, as I say, one of the other myriad parasites you're victim to, were to be presented with the full details of our little venture and find them not to their taste. What do you imagine the outcome would be? A slap on the wrists? Naughty Diana, don't do it again?'

'I hope that's not intended as a threat, Peter.'

'I'm simply indicating that this is not a good stage at which to start questioning our arrangement's efficacy. Lot of miles to travel yet. And who wants to turn the clock back on what's already been achieved?'

She thought about that, and about the humiliations of the previous year; the murderous assault that had taken place on her watch; the 'Who, me?' poses thrown in Moscow. Authorising reprisal on the slimmest of nods — *look into the possibilities, Diana, run the numbers, let's examine the viability* — had been risky, but not enough to deter her in the end. Because it mattered too much. It was the difference between apologising to the bully for being in his way and smacking him in the nose. That the bully was bigger was a given. But you shouldn't, couldn't, back down. Not unless you wanted it all to happen again.

And if taking Judd's privately organised shilling had been the only way to facilitate it, well: so be it. He was right about not turning the clock back. The time had been too well spent. She took a sip of brandy to fortify herself for the coming ordeal, that of admitting she more or less agreed with him, but he was gazing at nowhere in particular, a smile crawling across his pouty lips.

He came back to earth. 'Forgive me,' he said. 'Wool gathering.' He raised his glass in her direction. 'Something about that phrase 'naughty Diana' sent me off into dreamworld.'

'You never change, do you?' she said. 'Dog whistle politics and wolf whistle mindset.'

'You've been reading my reviews,' he said.

★ ★ ★

That smell was back: Russian tobacco. Reece Nesmith III opened his eyes, closed them, opened them again. He was on the floor of the sitting room of his upstairs flat, and there was a fat man occupying the armchair, a yellow vest puddled at his feet. The cigarette producing the Russian smell hung from his lower lip. His expression could have graced a totem pole: it was every bit as serious, and just as mobile.

'You hit me,' Reece said.

His voice came out at a higher pitch than usual.

The man didn't reply. Without taking his eyes off Reece, he gave the impression of having the whole room under surveillance, much the way he had at Miles's. Fewer bodies to keep track of, of course, and not much furniture. The armchair. A small table on which the TV sat. And bookshelves, and many more books than they could hold: tottering ziggurats of them, mostly with multiple bits of paper protruding from their pages, as if they were spawning miniature texts of their own. Tadpole writing on these slips: Andy's notes, and he always swore he could reconstruct his entire library from his high-speed jottings. Possibly an empty boast. Reece had never put him to the test.

He tried to get up, but the dizzy room prevented him. So he cleared his throat and spoke again instead. 'You hit me.' Same words, different key.

The man's cigarette glowed brightly. 'What's your name?' he said.

'Fuck off!'

'Russian, huh? Well, Comrade Fuckoff, you learn your English from watching the Superbowl? Because I'm hearing a distinctly Yankee twang.'

'You just assaulted me on my doorstep!'

'Kicked you a bit on the stairs, too. If you're keeping score.' He removed the cigarette from his mouth and examined the burning end, as if some technical error were occurring. Then put it back. 'You followed me from that spooks' parlour. Or tried to.'

'You followed me!'

'Like I say. Or tried to.' The cigarette evidently wasn't doing what it was supposed to, because he dropped it. 'You weren't much cop. Ready to tell me your name yet? I'm happy to kick you some more, if it'll help.'

Nothing about his expression suggested he was kidding.

Reece looked at the yellow jacket onto which the burning cigarette had fallen. It was work clothing, something you'd wear on a construction site, and probably wouldn't burn easily. It might be best, though, not to find out the hard way.

He said, 'Reece. Reece Nesmith.'

The man grunted.

'The third.'

'There's two more of you? That's nearly half the set. When's Snow White get here?'

'Very funny.'

'Glad you think so. Sometimes I have to explain my jokes. What is it, a condition? Or are you just, you know, a freak?'

Reece said, 'I'm not a freak.'

'Yeah, no offence. You should see the clowns I have to work with. Actual physical deformity would be an improvement.' From his overcoat pocket he produced a half-full bottle of whisky and unscrewed the cap. 'But let's get back to why you were following me. And what you were doing in the first place, hanging out with a bunch of Euro-spooks. Long-retired Euro-spooks.' He took a swallow. 'Long-retired Euro-spooks who were third division messenger boys at best.'

59

'You're a spy.'

'If you're one of those 007 nerds, hoping the glamour rubs off, you're in for a disappointment.' He farted, and produced another cigarette. 'Class takes practice.'

'Please don't light that.'

'Your growth's already been stunted. Where's the harm?'

'It's my home.'

'And burning it down would increase its value.' But he didn't light up, or not yet. 'Why were you following me?'

'I heard you talking with that guy. The other Brit. The one who acts like he's been in the game, but hasn't.'

The man nodded.

'You were talking about Putin. About the Novichok business. When toxic paste was smeared on a doorknob and the bottle left in a park.'

'Where someone found it,' the man said. 'And died. What are you, a reporter for *Metro*? That's ancient history.'

'There's a rumour there's been a vengeance killing. That you Brits took out one of the team responsible. You were talking about it.'

'If you're wanting to bid on the film rights, you're going the long way round. Nobody at Old Miles's would have the first clue what actually happened.' He raised the bottle to his mouth again, took another swallow. 'Least of all Chester Smith.'

'That's why it wasn't him I followed.'

The high-vis vest was smouldering now. Reece picked himself up, walked over and stamped on it, sending a whisper of black smoke spiralling upwards, like an evil ghost. There was only one chair in the room, but there was an upturned tea chest against one wall, and he crossed over, moved the incumbent table lamp to the floor, and sat. 'What's your name?' he said.

'I'll ask the questions, Dobby. So you followed me because I look like I know what I'm talking about. And that's why you were there in the first place, right? Looking for someone like me.' The unlit cigarette between his fingers seemed a deadly weapon. Reece wondered if he'd made a mistake, but it was done now. Besides, the fat bastard walked the walk. He'd tailed Reece half a mile across London, unseen. He doubted Chester Smith could have done that.

'Andy used to go there,' he said. 'Old Miles has gatherings, or did have. 'Conferences,' he called them. Once a month or so. Andy used to go. Some of the old guys there, he used them as sources.'

'For what?'

'He was writing a book.'

'About what?'

'Putin. He was a journalist, Andy was. He had a lot of material, he'd done a lot of research, especially about Putin's early days. He knew exactly the kind of man Putin is, what he's capable of. And Chester Smith was right, he'll be after payback if one of those assassins he sent here was killed. But Smith was wrong that it's something he's planning. It's already happening. It's already started.'

'What are you talking about, little man?'

'Putin had Andy murdered,' said Reece Nesmith III. 'He had him killed.' And then — he couldn't help it — he started to cry.

The taxi taking her home, which she was sharing with Peter Judd — though not as far as he probably hoped — became snarled in a Yellow Vest gathering. Men holding banners had overflowed the pavement, whether by accident or design was hard to say, though if the former, it added a layer of irony to the slogans about taking back control. When the driver sounded his horn, the backlash was immediate: fists were raised and obscenities unleashed. Someone thumped the bonnet, and the driver revved the engine, and the way was cleared, though the muttering from the front seat continued for some while. It might have become more than muttering if Judd hadn't barked 'Ladies present!'

'Preserving me from a fit of the vapours?' she asked. 'What a gent.'

'One of the many tragedies of feminism is that women can no longer suffer gallantry.'

'I'd be grateful if you'd spare me the others. I'm due in the office at seven.'

Judd nodded in appreciation, then gestured towards the back windscreen. 'Do you have people among them?'

'People?'

'People. Among our assembled brethren back there.'

'I'm not sure they're brethren of mine,' Diana said. 'Or of each other, come to that. A coalition of the furious is how I'd describe it.'

'Which sidesteps my question, which is an answer in itself, isn't it?' His brow furrowed, a familiar harbinger of weighty opinion. 'Are we sure that falls under your remit?'

'You're asking whether riotous assemblies are a threat to national security? Let me think about that. Yes.'

'Because you're falling into the common misapprehension that these folk are enemies of democracy. Whereas in fact they're champions of the new democracy, that's all. One that will ultimately see power being handed over to a wider spectrum of stakeholders.'

'You've changed your tune,' she said. 'A few years ago, you'd have described them as a rabble. But of course, that was when your own ambition ran along more traditional lines.'

'Things change,' he said smoothly. 'Conditions change. The old way of doing things no longer applies. There are new realities of power evolving in front of our eyes, and they're part of it. Yellow, you might say, is the new black.'

'A delicious irony if you happen to be black, I'm sure,' said Diana. 'Come to think of it, maybe irony is the new black. There's no shortage.' She glanced his way. 'It used to be you had the hard right on one side, the hard left on the other. Nowadays, they meet round the back. I suppose racists and anti-Semites are always going to find common ground, but I wish they wouldn't march up and down on it chanting.'

'They're disgruntled citizens.'

'Who vent their disgruntlement in the traditional way, by finding weaker citizens to bully. Please don't tell me you're planning on figureheading their movement, Peter. That would leave us seriously at odds.'

'Which would never do, would it?' The absence of light in his eyes belied the tone of voice he'd adopted. 'So let's not fight. Though there is another possibly

63

contentious topic I'm going to have to raise now.'

'Damien Cantor.'

'You never cease to amaze me. Yes, Damien Cantor.'

'Who didn't exactly endear himself to me. Or did you not notice that?'

'I think even he noticed that, and he's not over-burdened with self-awareness. No, opinion is divided as to young Damien. Some think he's a prick. Others that he's a cunt. But all agree he's a figure to be reckoned with. Because he has the ears of the public. Their eyes, too. And doubtless other parts of their anatomy, but for the time being it's his media clout we should consider. I know you don't want to look too closely at the books, and why should you — that's my job — but you should know that he's a major contributor to the cause, Diana. Major. And as such, it might be an idea to allow him a little access. A back-stage pass, as it were.'

'Is this meant to be funny?'

'We both knew there'd be a certain amount of flexibility required alongside these new arrangements. This is part of that. You don't have to like him, you just have to accept that he's part of the grander scheme of things. And I'm certainly not suggesting you appear on his news show. We can all agree that's not in our best interests.'

'I'm so glad to hear you're looking out for my best interests. Are you hearing yourself speak? I'm First Desk at Regent's Park, you seriously think I'm going to be best pals with an internet chancer just because he was front of the queue when you were passing the hat? This falls on your side of the line, Peter. I agreed to turn up tonight and shake a few hands and smile a

64

few smiles, but I am not taking part in the swimsuit round. If you want him entertained, waggle your own tail feathers. Are we clear on this?'

Apparently not.

He said, 'All I'm saying is, show him he's on the inside looking out. He's not an actual journalist, he doesn't care about breaking stories or finding scoops. He cares about being close to the levers of power. Let him think that, and he'll be first in the queue next time I'm, how did you put it, passing the hat.'

Diana stared, but he wouldn't meet her gaze; he was looking ahead, over the driver's shoulder, at the streets unfurling in front of the car, at the gauzy reflections in puddles and windows that turned after-hours London into a kaleidoscope, made fast-food outlets and minicab offices brief flashes of wonder. Innocence became him like a wimple does a stripper.

She said, 'What have you done?'

'I'm sure I don't know what you mean.'

'You could use that phrase as your ringtone, but it doesn't fool me. You're telling me to loosen up for Damien Cantor because you're covering your tracks. You've already let something out of your bag, haven't you? What is it?'

'Diana —'

'I won't ask twice.'

He said, 'In order to establish the right sort of backing for our venture, by which I mean people who believe in what we're trying to do, people of appropriate character, I have had to . . . allow a little light to shine here and there. Not on anything that might cause us embarrassment. You have nothing to worry about.'

'Was there ever a more confidence-sapping expression?'

'I've divulged nothing that could do us harm, Diana. You know me better than that. Just a little . . . shop gossip.'

'You're not in the shop, Peter. You're not even a customer. You're just hanging around in aisle three, hoping to nick a chocolate bar.'

'No metaphor left unpunished, that's one of the things I adore about you.' He turned to face her. 'As I say, Damien may not be anyone's pick for a dining companion, but he is a force to reckon with. An influencer. So yes, I may have allowed him a peep behind the curtain. An oeil amusé, if you like. Just to keep him onside, which is where we want him to be.'

'A glimpse of what?'

'I shared a detail or two about your special needs group, that's all. The slow horses. And the use you're putting them to.' His pout twitched. 'He thought it was funny. As do you. Which is why you told me in the first place, yes?'

'Not expecting you to pass it around the playground.'

'All shall be well, and all manner of thing shall be well,' he soothed. The taxi was slowing, approaching Diana's house. 'Remind me. Am I dropping you here? Or are we both, ah, getting off?'

'You're going home to your wife.'

'So I am.'

'And I'm giving serious thought as to whether I drop the curtain on our little arrangement,' she said, laying heavy stress on the final three words as the car drew to a halt and she opened the door, and climbed gracefully out.

Peter Judd waved through the window. 'It's interesting that you think you're still holding the rope,' he said, but the car was moving by then, and there was no chance she'd have heard.

★ ★ ★

After a while he'd got himself under control, though to be fair, he hadn't lost it all that much. A few tears: a grown man could be forgiven a few tears. Andy had been twenty-eight, same as himself. Losing someone at that age, being lost at that age: a few tears were the least you could expect.

The fat man hadn't moved from the armchair, but every time a car went past its headlights threw his shadow on the walls then sucked it out of existence, a passenger on a demonic carousel. It made Reece want to draw the curtains, but he was mesmerised by the moment. And if he moved the man might pounce. He looked capable of it, for all his size, the way a monitor lizard might seize a passing goat.

'Who's Andy?' the man asked at last.

'My partner.'

'And he's dead.'

'He was killed.'

'How?'

'They said it was a heart attack. But — '

'They?'

'He was in Moscow. But there was nothing wrong with his heart.'

'Your friend died of a heart attack in Moscow, and you think Vladimir Putin did it.'

'Because of the book Andy was writing.'

'Was he one of you?'

'In what way?'

'Jesus, so much for tact. What's the PC term for

67

diddyman?'

'I have achondroplasia. A genetic disorder.' Reece felt a familiar flash of anger. 'Do you want me to spell it for you?'

'Fuck no, we'll be here all night.' There was a glint as the man's bottle appeared again. He took a swallow, then said, 'So you were a matching pair.'

'His condition was rarer than mine. But the outcome was the same. He was a person of restricted growth, yes.'

'You'd think he'd have been better at keeping his head down.'

'Is this all a joke to you?'

'So far. What was he doing in Moscow? Research?'

'Yes. And . . . Well, he used to live there. His parents still do.'

'So he was Russian.'

'Yes. Andrey.'

'A Russian citizen who died in Russia. Were you there?'

' . . . No.'

'Did you see his death certificate?'

'No, but — '

'Any police investigation?'

'No.'

'His parents kick up a fuss?'

'No, they think he — '

'Where's his body now?'

'He was cremated.'

'Were you there?'

' . . . No.'

'So, to sum up. Something happened a long way away which you didn't see and nobody else is suspicious about. What do you think we should do?

68

Organise a telethon?'

'Putin had him murdered.'

'So what? We all know the man has blood on his hands. Let's face it, he has blood on his elbows. But he couldn't give a flying fuck for world opinion, and anything he gets up to inside his own borders is the state equivalent of behind closed doors. Besides.' He took another slug from his bottle. 'I realise the loss of your friend must have left a tiny little hole in your life. But dying in Russia doesn't automatically mean he was murdered by its president. And if you were an expert cardiac diagnostician, I doubt you'd be living in this shithole. Aren't you lot supposed to be house-proud?'

'You think all gay men are neat-freaks?'

'I meant dwarfs, to be honest. Or is it gnomes are the tidy ones? I get you mixed up.'

'Now you're just trying to be offensive.'

'There's effort involved, yes. And it wouldn't kill you to show some appreciation. I've had a long day.' He looked at the bottle in his hand. 'Fancy a drink?'

' . . . Thanks.'

'Well fetch me one while you're at it. This is good stuff. I'll save the rest for later.' He tucked it away in his pocket.

Reece mentally played back what he'd just heard, then did so again to be sure . . . He could itemise the contents of his fridge from here, and already knew all he had was beer: bottled Beck's. He got down off the tea chest, went into the kitchen, and came back carrying a pair.

'This the best on offer? Bloody hell.' But he unscrewed the cap anyway, and tossed it into a corner.

Reece said, 'Andy had done a lot of research. And he had a contact. In the GRU. That's — '

'Yeah, let's pretend I know what the GRU is.'

'This man, he told Andy about the special squad they have there. An assassination department.'

He sat back on the tea chest, and opened his own bottle.

The man said, 'If that was Andy's breaking news, what was his idea of a scoop? The charge of the Light Brigade?'

'They use two-person teams, posing as married couples. And one of them was killed not long ago, on Russian soil. In the city of Kazan. As revenge for the Novichok attacks.'

'That's the rumour, yes. And it's even reached Brewer Street.' He hoisted the bottle to his lips, and swallowed half its contents in a single gulp. 'So it's unlikely that it's worth murdering for.'

But Reece wasn't finished. 'He told Andrey, the contact did, that Rasnokov's declared war on the British Secret Service. On Putin's orders. That they'd identified a similar department here in the UK, some kind of assassination squad, and they plan to wipe them out one by one. On British soil. That's what Andy was writing about.'

'In his book,' the man said flatly.

'He was planning on selling this bit to a newspaper.'

'But he died of a heart attack first.'

'He didn't have a heart condition.'

'Nobody does. Until they do.' Impressively, if that's the word, the man's beer was already gone. He lobbed the empty after its cap and belched hugely. 'And he told you this how long before he died?'

'The day before. Ten days ago. We spoke on the

phone.'

The man said, 'Lots of people write books. Sell stories to newspapers. They don't all get murdered. Not half enough of them, frankly.'

'Andy stepped into something big, and then he died. You think that's a coincidence?'

'It's a matter of perspective. If Andy was your size, anything he stepped in must have looked big. Any more beer?'

'No.'

'Good. That one was a fucking insult.' He stood so suddenly Reece thought he was on the attack. His cigarette hung from his mouth. 'Look. People die. You should get used to that. And if you want to get all paranoid about it, that's your choice. Word of advice, though. Be careful dropping names like Rasnokov's, and keep your fantasies to yourself or you'll only be a nuisance. And you're small enough to squash. Something else you should be used to by now.'

'Fuck off,' said Reece.

'Now that's disappointing. I was hoping for 'Follow the yellow brick road'.'

And then he was gone.

Reece crossed to the window, and watched him heading down the street, trailing smoke. His high-vis vest lay on the floor, a camouflage accessory no longer required. Reece wondered where he'd stolen it from, in that brief interval after leaving Old Miles's; wondered if he'd left a genuine yellow vest wearer in a similar heap somewhere, then decided he didn't care. Andrey would have thought it a detail worth worrying over, but Andy had been a writer. And look where that had got him.

Though maybe the fat bastard had been right.

Maybe being dead was just the next thing that had happened to Andy in his short, all senses, life.

In a sudden spurt of anger, he kicked out at the nearest pile of books. Homespun bookmarks flew, snippets of Andrey's tadpole writing on them: useless clues — Reece couldn't decipher half, and the rest were in Russian. But it didn't matter. Nothing he did could bring Andy back, and his best attempt so far, snagging a real-life spook from Andy's favourite hang-out, had only resulted in a string of insults and a sitting room stinking of smoke. Everybody was a bastard. That included Andy and, probably, himself.

After a while he collected the books and set them in a pile again. The bookmarks would never find their way back to their rightful pages, so he just gathered them together and tucked them inside the top volume. Maybe, tonight, he'd set something in motion he'd never get to hear about. It was more likely, though, that all he'd done was afford half an hour's amusement to a fat spy.

He put the empty bottles in the recycling box and the scarred yellow vest in the bin.

Then he went to bed.

4

The kitchen at Slough House had been fitted in the late seventies, and had undergone renovation since, in as much as a calendar had been hung there in 2010. That had been taken down, but the nail used to fix it in place remained, now graced by a tea towel, which had previously dangled from the one drawer knob that didn't come away in the hand. This new assignment sometimes allowed the towel to nearly dry out, not that it was used much, but it did tend to absorb available moisture. The room's other main advantage was that it was of a size that could almost accommodate two people without argument erupting, provided neither one was Roddy Ho.

Who, sniffing suspiciously, said, 'What's that supposed to be?'

'Focaccia.'

'It's got bits on it.'

'It's supposed to. Don't tell me you've never seen one before. You eat enough pizza.'

'Pizza's round.'

'You're aware that being round is not a food group?' The bread Lech Wicinski had made the previous evening nestled in silver foil on the battle-scarred kitchen counter. 'Try some. It won't kill you.'

'I don't want to get crumbs on my shirt.'

Lech eyed the garment in question: a green, paisley-swirled specimen Ho had buttoned to the throat. 'Crumbs might improve it.'

Louisa joined them, bearing an empty mug. She

looked at Ho, then at Lech, then at the bread, then at Lech again. 'You made that?'

'Yes.'

'What, with like flour and stuff?'

'Flour, yes. And also stuff.'

She nodded, though not in a way that indicated she was up to speed yet. 'And then what? Did you drop it?'

'Christ, what is this? I made some bread, I didn't finish it all. So I brought the rest in. Where's the problem?'

'It's just, that doesn't happen much round here.'

'Which? The baking or the bringing it in?'

'All of it,' said Louisa. 'Including the part about not finishing it yourself.' She emptied the kettle into the sink and refilled it, a process Ho watched without comprehension. 'Fresh water?' she said. 'For coffee?' Then back to Lech: 'If you're planning on starting a bake-off, I'll tell you now, it'll end badly.'

'If I start a bake-off,' said Lech, 'it'll be to decide which of you lot to chuck in an oven.'

'Why bake stuff anyway?' asked Ho. 'It's available in shops. Duh.'

'I hate to say this,' said Louisa, 'but the shirt has a point.'

'So you're not a cook either.'

'Me? I can barely defrost.'

'What's wrong with my shirt?' asked Ho.

'It looks like a frog threw up on you.'

'It's Italian designed.'

'So's the bread,' said Lech. 'But it was made by a Pole in the East End.'

Catherine had appeared in the doorway. 'What are you all doing?'

74

'Are you our prefect now?' Louisa asked. 'Is this one of those age-flip things, and I've woken up back in school?'

'We should all be so lucky.'

'Anyway, the boiling kettle should be a clue,' Louisa added.

'I didn't so much mean what are you doing as why aren't you doing it upstairs? Team meeting, remember? Nine sharp.'

'I didn't think he was here yet.'

'He's not,' said Catherine. 'But when did that stop him expecting everyone else to be on time? Focaccia looks good, by the way.'

'Thanks,' said Lech.

'But you do realise you'll never hear the end of it.'

Louisa poured her coffee while Ho tried to read the label on his own collar without undoing buttons. Lech rewrapped the bread and looked like he was regretting various decisions, going at least as far back as bringing the bread in, and possibly extending to choice of career and not staying in Australia, where he'd holidayed in ninety-six.

'I didn't mean anything, by the way,' Louisa said. 'That crack about being back in school.'

He rolled his eyes, but she was out of the door, and didn't notice.

Upstairs, Shirley was already in place. There were no visitor's chairs in Lamb's office, or none he liked anyone to sit on — the one technically so designated currently nursed a pyramid of sauce-stained Wagamama hotboxes — but one particular standing space was deemed more desirable than others, it being thought to fall within Lamb's blind spot. The warier among them didn't believe Lamb had a blind spot, and suspected some slow-burning mind-fuck, but Shirley was playing the odds, and had positioned herself to the left of the door, nearest the corkboard on which brittle scraps of paper had long ago been pinned, presumably by Lamb, presumably for a reason. She didn't speak when Louisa, Lech and Roddy trooped in, and was possibly asleep, though upright. River arrived last. He didn't speak either, but in contrast to Shirley looked like sleep was a stranger, or an enemy.

Louisa tried to catch his eye, but he wasn't having it. This wasn't especially unusual, but there was an energy to him, a voltage, which was. Slough House didn't recharge batteries, it sapped power. It's as if there were negative ley lines, special coordinates where forceless fields met, sucking all spirit from whoever stood there, and Slough House was slap bang on that junction. Whatever had River twitching, it wasn't the prospect of a day at work.

A door banged; not the one from the yard, but the toilet on the floor below. So Lamb had floated in and up several flights of stairs without fluttering a cobweb on the way. It was unnerving to picture him doing this, like imagining a tapir playing hopscotch. The smell of stale cigarettes entered the room a moment before him, and the slow horses made way for it, then Lamb, by shuffling to either side. He arrived among them shaking his head in wonderment. 'What a dump.'

Louisa looked round: the moist walls, the grim threadbare carpet, the print of a foreign bridge which made you want to hurl yourself off it. 'You've only just noticed?'

'I meant back there,' said Lamb. 'That's going nowhere first flush.' He threw himself into his chair,

76

which, one happy day, was going to respond by dis-integrating into a hundred pieces. 'Sorry to keep you waiting. I was up late comforting a gay American dwarf.'

They stared.

'What? I can't have a social life?'

'It's more that you don't usually apologise,' Catherine said.

'Well, how often do I fall into error?' He tossed something at Shirley, which she unwisely caught. It was a paper tissue, unnaturally heavy, starting to split. 'Get rid of that, will you?'

'...You're nearest the bin.'

'I didn't want it in my nose, you don't think I want it in my bin, do you?' He looked round at the assembled team. 'Remind me, what the fuck are you doing here?'

Shirley slipped out, suppressing a gag reflex, while all present mentally erased the blind-spot theory.

'Updates,' said Catherine.

'Ah yes. Team updates. So glad we can share these moments. Means I don't have to rely on the obituary columns for giggles. So.' He placed his palms on his paunch and smiled benignly. 'Time to share. And this is a safe space, mind. No one's going to point out what a dickhead you are. Who's first?'

Louisa said, 'I was followed yesterday evening.'

'Congratulations. Did you shag him in his car or take him home?'

'He tagged me on the Central Line and stayed with me to Oxford Street. I busted him in a sports shop. And he legged it.'

Lamb surveyed the assembled company. 'You see, this is what happens when you leave your contact details on toilet walls.'

'He was Park.'

'Ah, keeping it in the family. And we know this because . . . ?'

'Because he got the same text we all got at 6.59 p.m. yesterday. One of those HR messages, checking their alert system's working.'

You are receiving this text to ensure your contact details are up to date. Reply ICON to acknowledge receipt.

Lamb's eyes narrowed. 'I thought we were wiped from Service records. This kind of spoils the magic.'

'Contact details are on the deep-level data sets,' Ho said.

'Yeah, I heard some jabbering there, but I won't pretend I followed it.'

'We've been over this,' Lech said. 'It's our personal records that have been wiped. Names, photos, active history, operational involvement, all that. The deep-level stuff, which is anonymised — like our employee numbers and bank details — that data's still on file. Else we wouldn't get our salaries, for a start.'

Lamb looked pained. 'You get salaries? I thought the whole point was to demoralise you.'

'We don't get much.'

'Just as well. If they paid you what you were worth, you'd owe them money.' He returned to Ho. 'That new, is it? The palsy-pattern shirt?

'Paisley,' said Roddy.

'If you say so. Makes you look a spastic either way.' He leaned back and put his feet on his desk. Somehow he'd managed to shed his shoes. 'So. Everyone got the same text message, right?'

'Including you,' said Catherine.

'Seriously?' He scrambled about in his pockets,

theatrically going through most of them before finding his mobile back in the first one he'd checked. Then they waited while he turned it on. 'Well, heartbreak make me a dancer. Seems I'm no better than the rest of you.' He dropped the phone, and went on, 'Okay then. One little slow horse went to market, and it turned out she had a trainee spook on her heels.'

'What makes him a trainee?'

'You spotted him, didn't you? What about the rest of you?' He pointed at Shirley, who'd slunk back in and was visibly trying to disassociate herself from her own hands. 'What were you up to last night? No, let me guess. You were jiving the small hours away. Anyone watching you?'

'I'm always watched in night clubs.'

'Yeah, they're worried you'll steal people's drinks.' He paused. 'No, hang on, you're the lush,' he said to Catherine. 'I get you confused. Have you thought about wearing badges?'

'To make your life easier? That's not going to happen,' said Catherine. 'And no, I wasn't followed last night.'

'You sure about that?'

'I just said so.'

'Ah, the wonders of sobriety. What it must be to have total recall of every passing second.' He looked at Louisa. 'And she could have given you lessons back in the day. Had a thing about sailors, if I remember rightly. A big thing. She'd have gone down on the *Titanic* given half a chance.'

He produced a cigarette out of nowhere, a lighter from the same place, and lit the one from the other. Then he stared at the lighter for a moment before tossing it over his shoulder and pointing at Lech

79

Wicinski. 'You planning on letting those facial pubes cover the art on your cheeks? Or is your electric razor on the fritz? No offence.'

'I'm Polish,' Lech said. 'Not German.'

'Well, it wasn't for lack of trying. Did you make the bread, by the way?'

'...Yes.'

'Needs more garlic.' Lamb belched. 'So, any nasty eyes tracking your private pleasures last night? Or were you too busy playing the old ham banjo to notice?'

'I'm not sure,' said Lech. 'There might have been someone.'

'Well, that opens a world of possibilities. Care to elaborate?'

'Heading home, on the bus.' He shrugged. 'It might have been nothing. But I got off a stop early just in case.'

'That'd put the fear of God into them. Anyone surrender?'

'Nobody followed me home from there.'

'Probably too scared. You're very quiet.'

This to River Cartwright.

River said, 'Nothing to report.'

'No pitter-patter of spooky footsteps trailing your moves last night?'

'They'd have had to be fast. I was driving.'

'Oh, of course, you have a car now. Spending the inheritance. What did you go with? Let me guess. An Aston Martini.'

'Something like that,' said River.

'And where were we tooling about?'

'Nowhere special. Just putting it through its paces.'

Lamb stared, but said no more.

The smoke from his cigarette was thicker than

80

usual, unless there was a local mattress fire. Eyes were starting to water; throats beginning to itch.

'You haven't asked me yet,' Roddy said.

Lamb sighed. 'Okay, Donkey Kong. Anyone pinned a tail on you lately?'

'No.'

'Well, that was a fruitful exchange.' His cigarette between his lips, Lamb slid both hands down his trousers to rearrange his underwear. That accomplished, he removed the cigarette and tapped the ash into the nearest mug. The entire tube fell off the filter. He looked bitterly at what was left for a moment, then dropped that into the mug too. 'So. Either the rest of you are too dozy to notice that the Park's keeping tabs, or it's only happening to the scarlet woman. Or she was making it up on account of being terrified she'll end up a spinster bag lady, with no man paying attention. That about sum it up?'

'Or, strange as it may seem, it was a coincidence,' said Catherine.

'Ah, thank you. We can always rely on you to play devil's asparagus.'

'Avocado,' she said automatically. Then: 'Advocate. Damn it, you've got me doing it.'

'He ran when he realised I'd clocked him,' said Louisa. 'It was no coincidence.'

Lamb shifted his feet to the floor, carefully enough that only a few things were knocked from his desk. 'No. Because if it was it would be two coincidences, on account of it happening at the same time as we've been rubbed out of the Service database.' He looked at Lech. 'Rubbed out in the technical sense, that is. Not your area of expertise.'

Lech's look, his posture, his reddening neck;

everything bar his actual voice invited Lamb to go fuck himself.

'Have you raised this with the Park yet?' Catherine said. 'Dare I ask?'

'Our refugee status? No, I haven't. On account of I prefer to know what Taverner's up to before I ask her about it, and I haven't worked out what that is yet. Too busy. Some of us have lives outside the workplace, you know.'

'Comforting gay American dwarfs,' said Shirley.

'Glad someone's paying attention.'

'Or is it dwarves?'

'There was only one of them,' said Lamb. 'His friend's dead.' He farted in a brisk, businesslike fashion. 'Anything else? God, look at you all, lined up like a choir at a hobo funeral. About as confidence-inspiring as a Spanish motorway.'

'Nothing like rallying the troops,' said Catherine.

'I have something,' said Ho.

Lamb glared. 'Pubic lice? That would explain the fidgeting.'

'I know when our records were removed.'

'Well, fuck me merrily on high. Actual information.' He leaned back. 'Come on then. Amaze us.'

'First week of January. The fifth.'

'How do you know?' said River. 'If the records aren't there, they can't tell you when they were deleted.'

Ho adopted the superior look cats give mortals. 'I checked for when the personnel database was updated, outside the regular back-ups. Then looked to find each time an update happened with no new material added.'

'How can you —'

'It gets smaller.'

'Which meant something was deleted,' Louisa said.

'Yeah, duh.' Ho interlaced his fingers importantly. 'Administrator activity's logged. But you have to know where to look.'

'And that's why we keep you,' said Lamb. 'I'd known there was a reason, beyond my famously charitable nature.' He beamed round at the rest of them. 'See? Being a dickless no-mates pays off in the long run. Okay, Austin Powers, as a reward, you can keep your shirt on. I'd been going to make you eat it.'

'And what use is that?' said Shirley. 'Knowing the date it happened?'

'Difficult as this will be for you to understand,' said Lamb, 'knowing things is better than not knowing things. Think of it as the difference between having a cocaine baggie in your pocket and not. I hope this helps.'

Shirley managed not to check her pockets, but it was a close-run thing.

'All righty,' said Lamb. 'I've had as much as I can stand for one lifetime. Piss off and do some work. And remember, all of us are lying in the gutter. But some of you are circling the drain.'

'Thanks.'

'But it could be worse. You could be a hotshot squad of international assassins. Then you'd really be in trouble.'

Nobody dared ask, and they all trooped out.

On the way downstairs, Shirley said, 'Have you gone off reservation lately?'

'Me?' said Louisa. 'No.'

'Then why would the Park be tailing you?'

'They don't need a reason,' said Louisa. 'We're Slough House. They can do what they want with us.'

She left it until after lunch before heading into River's room. He didn't seem surprised to see her. His computer was on, its screen reflected in the windowpane behind him: rows of columns, probably an electoral register. So much of what they did involved scrolling through the surface details of civic existence, looking for bumps that weren't there. But River's hands weren't on his keyboard or his mouse. They were holding something he dropped in a drawer as she entered.

'Hey,' he said.

'You okay?'

'Just peachy.'

She perched on the corner of his desk and raised an eyebrow. 'An Aston Martini?'

'It's actually a Renault Crisis.'

'Yeah, that sounds more you.' She leaned forward, and he pushed the drawer shut. 'Is that what I think it is?'

'It's nothing. Tell me about this guy who was following you.'

'He was a guy,' said Louisa, 'and he was following me. That's a barrette, isn't it?'

'A barrette's a kind of gun, right? I haven't got a gun, no.'

'That's a Beretta.'

'Or a bishop's hat? Haven't got one of those, either.'

'I've no idea what you're talking about now,' said Louisa, 'but we both know what you're not talking about.'

River said, 'I was clearing my drawers out, that's all.'

'Yeah, 'cause you're big on spring-cleaning. I've

noticed that in the past. That was Sid's barrette, wasn't it? Okay, *hair grip*.'

'Why would I have — '

'Because you found it on her desk after — afterwards. Come on, River, this is me. What's the matter? Why's she on your mind?'

His face was set in a familiar obstinate scowl.

'Because that call you got, the one you thought was her. It could have been anyone. A wrong number, a glitch on the line. Whoever it was didn't say anything, did they? You can't recognise a silence.'

Though she was recognising this one. River had pushed his chair back onto its rear two legs; was leaning against the wall, eyes half-closed.

Louisa glanced towards the room's other desk, currently vacant; its most recent former occupant a smudge on a distant hillside. And she thought about Emma Flyte, who hadn't been a slow horse; who had, let's face it, been better than any of them. Both more recent casualties than Sidonie Baker, but fresh wounds make old scars itch. It didn't take a genius to work out why River Cartwright was turning Sid's barrette over in his hands; the hair slide that was all the Park's removal men had left of her presence.

She said, 'I'm not a therapist, God knows, but — '

'She's alive.'

'I know you want to think that. I do too. But until she actually turns up — '

'No, seriously.' He let the chair fall back onto all four legs, and laid his hands flat on the desk. 'She has done. Turned up. Sid's alive.'

Louisa stared, but it didn't take her long. He meant every word, she could see that.

'You — Really? Jesus, River! *Really?*'

85

He glanced ceilingwards, and shook his head. 'Not here.' And then he was on his feet, heading for the door. His coat hung on a hook, and he scooped it free in passing.

She followed him a moment later, barely caring that Lamb might hear them, or that leaving Slough House without his permission was a hanging offence.

They were out in the yard a minute later; in the pub over the road shortly after that.

★ ★ ★

Her hair was different. Maybe that's what death does to you. It was still mostly red but now punkishly short, with a white stripe across her left temple where the bullet had passed, leaving in its wake a shallow channel, which gave her the appearance of having been imperfectly sculpted. Her dusting of freckles had faded and her skin seemed whiter, though that might have been the effect of dim lighting. She was skinnier too, her upper body swamped by a hoodie whose American university brand name disappeared inside its own folds. Once she'd been all clean lines and fresh air; now that same thought conjured up an image of her hung out with the washing. But she was still Sid. She had Sid's eyes and Sid's mouth, so she was still Sid; back from joe country, and in his grandfather's house. How had that happened?

And what did he say?

He said, 'Jesus. Sid.'

Two resurrections.

She watched as he entered, shutting the door. It seemed necessary to keep this encounter within a closed space; to seal off the emptiness outside. It was just the pair of them in a familiar room, in which nothing had changed, bar everything.

'Hello, River.'

Her voice was the same too, if a notch quieter. And there was something considered about the delivery; as if Sid were playing off-book for the first time, not entirely comfortable with her lines yet. 'I heard you coming in. I knew it was you.'

The chair she sat in was the O.B.'s. If River squinted, he could make out the smooth patches on its arms, the indentations of its upholstery, all of it adding up to the faded shape of his grandfather. His own chair, the one he'd spent so many evenings in, listening to the old man conjure stories out of memory, hadn't yet shaped itself to him. Favourite chairs were like your future; the form they would eventually take depended on your input, your commitment. River hadn't sat in his for a while. There'd been no need to, since his grandfather passed.

He crossed the room, crouched next to her. 'Sid? It's really you, right?'

'It's really me.'

He wanted to touch her, to make sure. Weird kind of hallucination this would be, one he'd driven miles to encounter at a neighbour's invitation, but still: he wanted to know her flesh was still flesh. So he reached a hand out and she took it. Her hand felt curiously warm.

'You're alive.'

'Of course I am.'

As if the alternative were out of the question, though the last time he'd seen her she'd been prone on a pavement, a pool of blood blotting out her horizons. His memory of what followed was mostly of a loud

87

journey through zombie-strewn streets, sirens jangling. *Head wounds bleed. Head wounds bleed bad.* He'd clung to that fact: that head wounds bleed bad. That Sid Baker was bleeding from the head didn't necessarily mean anything critical had happened. Could be a graze. So why had she looked so dead?

'And you're here . . . Why didn't you let me know?'

'I was going to. I knew you'd come, though. Sooner or later. I mean . . . ' She glanced around the room. 'This.'

The room, she meant; its intact status in an empty house. You didn't clear a building, leaving just one small corner of it furnished.

'What is it, a shrine? Your grandfather died, didn't he. And this is preserving his memory?'

'Not exactly. I mean, yes, in a way, but . . . It doesn't matter. What are you *doing* here? All this time. Why didn't you let me know?'

'I called you.'

He remembered. The phone had rung in his office, and nobody spoke when he picked up: he'd been sure it was Sid, though he didn't believe in any of that woo-woo nonsense. There must have been something in the quality of her breath. The short time they'd known each other, they'd spent most of it in that office, not talking. He'd grown used to her silent presence. Had known what it was like to hear her not speak.

'But I didn't know what to say.'

' . . . That you were alive?'

'But you must have known that. Didn't you know that?'

He said, 'They told us you were dead.'

'Oh . . . '

She'd disappeared from the hospital; vanished as if

88

she'd never been there. That, in fact, was the official truth: she had never been there. And when River had tried to find out what had happened, he'd been closed down. Sidonie Baker was dead: that was all he needed to know. Sid Baker was dead, and River Cartwright was Slough House, which meant he should fuck off back to his desk and stop asking questions.

The surface she'd slid under had been a murky one, and Diana Taverner had been responsible for much of the dirt. So naturally, it wasn't a pool she wanted anyone stirring a stick in.

The news that she'd been dead didn't appear to startle Sid. But then, her face was less lively now. In her long absence, she'd acquired a degree of stillness. There must have been a lot of waiting involved, and she'd clearly grown used to it.

'You could have . . .'

But it wasn't a thought worth finishing. She could have let him know, could have been in touch. But what did River know about being vanished? At least in Slough House he could open a window if he felt like it, and scream his frustration to the street below. Nobody would pay attention, but he could do that. Presumably Sid's situation had been different.

'I wasn't well for a long time.' She raised a hand to the white flash in her hair. 'I lost a couple of years.'

'I'm sorry.'

'It wasn't your fault.'

It had been, or that was the way River remembered it. A confused moment on a rainy street, and a single gunshot. A number of people had been involved, and the rest of them were all dead too.

'How did you find me? The house, I mean? How did you know to come here?'

'It was in your file. I read your file.'

Of course she had.

Because while Sid had been a slow horse, she'd also been something else; had been put in Slough House to keep an eye on him, River Cartwright. This would have been Taverner's work, but he never did hear the exact details, because Sid had been shot minutes after she'd confessed this to him.

She said, 'I lost a lot of things.'

Well, moving hospital to hospital, he could see that some of her stuff might have gone astray.

'But I remembered you.'

He wasn't sure he made any response to that. Or that any was required.

She said, 'Once I was better, they put me in Cumbria. Have you been there?'

He either had or hadn't, he was sure one of the two was true, and after a moment, he recalled which. 'Once. Long time ago.'

On a short holiday with Rose. He didn't know where the O.B. had been. Supposedly retired, there were still gaps in his family life. River recollected that much.

'It's beautiful. Hills and lakes and meadows. There's a farmhouse there, it's run like a holiday home . . . '

But would be a Service resource, thought River. There were still one or two. You could cut back here and cut back there, bow to the demands of an age of austerity, but you had to look after your joes when they'd been shot in the head. If only to ensure that future recruitment didn't get difficult.

'And you're better now? You're fully recovered?'

'I get headaches. But I'm mostly okay.'

But something had been subtracted, he was sure of

that. There was a vitality missing. But how could it be otherwise? She'd been dead. Even with the demonstrable evidence in front of him that this wasn't so, it was a difficult piece of knowledge to cast away. It was as if his past had just been rewritten. This might be what religion felt like; a thunderball, a stroke.

'So you knew where I lived,' he said. 'Where I used to live. But what made you come here? Why now?'

'I needed somewhere to hide.'

That was easy to believe. She looked like she might bolt somewhere at any moment, and cover herself with leaves.

He was still holding her hand. They'd never had this much contact back when they'd shared an office.

'Here's good then,' he said. 'You're safe here.' Which wasn't necessarily true, but felt like the right thing to say regardless.

'Maybe for the moment.'

'What are you hiding from?'

She said, 'Someone's trying to kill me.'

★ ★ ★

This seemed a suitably dramatic moment at which to pause the narrative.

The pub across the road from Slough House felt like a continuation of their work lives: more a chore than a break. The coffee was poured from a jug, but tasted like instant. River could have done with an actual drink, but that would have been a mistake: he'd be back on the road as soon as he could, behind the wheel, back to Tonbridge. Wouldn't have left her last night, except she insisted. *Keep everything normal. Don't draw attention.*

91

'And you haven't told Lamb?' Louisa said.

'What do you think?'

'I think he's going to find out anyway.'

'Sid's frightened. She asked me not to tell anyone, so that's what I'm doing.'

'Except for me.'

'Well, yes. Except you.'

'Thanks. I think. Who's trying to kill her?'

'She doesn't know. She just knew she was being watched.'

Louisa said, 'Lot of that about.'

'How do you mean?'

'What do you mean, how do I mean? I was tailed last night? Remember?'

'Yeah, sorry, right. No, I mean yeah, but what's the connection?'

'I didn't mean there was a connection, I just . . . oh, never mind. So she felt she was being watched. Doesn't she have a handler or something? They didn't just put her out to pasture, did they? Recovering from head trauma?'

After the farmhouse, after the residential care, Sid had been moved to a cottage on a newbuild estate not far from Kendal. She'd been there more than a year, relearning the steps required to live a life. The phrase had remained with River: he pictured her with L-plates on, buying groceries, feeding plastic into an ATM. Opening brown envelopes which explained her civic duties: council tax, voter registration, jury service.

'She had a handler, or a milkman anyway,' he said. 'Twice a week, she'd turn up and check everything was okay. That Sid was managing.'

Milkmen were what retired spooks got; and also

those gunned down in the field, it seemed.

'And this milkman, who's a she you say, making her a milkwoman, thanks — what did she make of it?'

'Don't know,' said River. He tried some coffee: dreadful.

'I haven't actually put thumbscrews to her yet. Sid. Haven't choked every last detail out of her.'

Louisa said, 'I hate to ask this. But is she, you know — okay?'

'In what sense?'

'Well, most of them.' River was looking obstinate again, but she ploughed on regardless. 'Look, she was shot in the head. I get it she's still alive, and you told me about the hair thing, the white stripe. But how's she looking otherwise? Still a Burne-Jones, or is she more Picasso now?'

'She hasn't lost her looks,' said River. 'She's more fragile looking.'

'And how about mentally?'

'Pretty spacey. Drifts off while she's talking. But look, I hadn't seen her in however long it's been. Years. Hard to tell what's awkwardness and what's . . . permanent.'

'No it isn't,' said Louisa. 'Sid was bright, Sid was witty, she was never at a loss for words that I remember. Which means the Sid you've been talking to's not fully come back from her wound.' She picked up her coffee cup, came to her senses and put it down again. 'There's a lot of space between thinking someone's watching you and thinking they want you dead. The mysterious watchers might be a symptom, for all we know. Paranoia.'

'Says the woman who was tailed into a sportswear shop last night.'

93

'Oh, that happened. His phone pinged, remember?'

'I believe her.'

'Okay.'

'Something happened to send her on the run.'

'Sure. But let's not forget she's not the only one who got hurt when she was shot. You've been feeling guilty ever since.'

Tell him about it. The memory was seared on his mind: the rain, and the blood gathering on the pavement. And then the night-ride to the hospital, and the slamming doors, and the body on the trolley being wheeled away. He'd ended up locked in a cupboard, guarded by one of the Dogs, until Lamb had come to rescue him.

'And that makes you more inclined to believe her.'

'I believe her because she's Sid.'

'Same difference. Look, you want my advice? Because I'm giving it anyway. Tell Lamb. Hate to say it, but. Either Sid's in danger, in which case she's better off him knowing, or she's not, in which case people need to know anyway. So they can set about making her better.'

'What if he knows already?'

'. . . That she's at your grandfather's house?'

'That she's still alive.'

'It's possible,' said Louisa. 'He knows all sorts of things he shouldn't. But either way, he's Lamb. And she's his joe, when you get down to it.'

'That doesn't always help, does it?' River said, and they both thought briefly of the empty desk in his office.

'We should get back,' said Louisa, rising to her feet. Then, buttoning her coat, said, 'Slough House, by the way.'

'. . . What?'

'That's the connection between Sid and me. Slough House.'

River just grunted.

★ ★ ★

At lunchtime, on her way out, Catherine Standish heard Jackson Lamb torturing a warthog in his room. Best thing would be to keep walking: down the stairs, through the door which jammed rain or shine, then through the alley and onto Aldersgate Street, whose traffic-choked mundanity felt a spring meadow after a morning in Slough House. But something made her peer into Lamb's office, to check no actual animals were being harmed, and she interrupted him mid-snore. His office, as always, seemed subtly different when he was its only occupant, as if enfolding him in a mouldy embrace, though the familiar medley of odours — stale alcohol, cigarettes, sweat — remained present and true. Lamb's eyes opened before she'd finished these thoughts. 'What?'

'I thought you were having one of your fits.'

'Fits? I don't have fits.'

'Pardon me. One of those coughing extravaganzas where it seems likely you'll heave your lungs up.'

'I'm allergic to interfering spinsters,' said Lamb. 'That's probably what it is.' He scratched the back of his head, and when his hand appeared again, it was holding a cigarette.

Catherine had long given up being amazed by such tricks. She was perturbed, though, by the industrial appearance of the cigarette in question. 'Wouldn't it be quicker to burn a tyre and breathe it in?'

'Possibly,' said Lamb. 'But you know what Health and Safety's like.' He slotted the cigarette into his mouth, but made no move to light it. This was just as well, as he had it in backwards. 'What is it you're not telling me?'

She paused. 'Now, that's a list I try to keep as long as possible.' But it was a forlorn defence: Lamb was growing rosily benign, the way witches in fairy tales do. She stepped further into the room and said, 'I spoke to Molly Doran last night.'

Lamb's expression didn't alter.

'Ambushed her on her way home.'

'There are those who might think that's taking unfair advantage of a cripple,' said Lamb.

'I only — '

'But that's Molly for you. And as she obviously didn't flay and hang you from the nearest branch, she must have been in a happy mood.'

'Her records are pre-digitised,' said Catherine. Sometimes, if you kept on track, you could drag Lamb's attention after you. 'I wanted to know if the paper versions of our records had been purged as well.'

Lamb looked at his watch.

' . . . What?'

'It's five past April,' he said. 'Congratulations. That little brainwave only took you, what? Three months?'

She suppressed a sigh. 'You'd already done that.'

'But Molly didn't let on. Like I said. Happy mood.' He removed the cigarette, then reinserted it the right way round. 'Nobody's looked at our folder in years. Gives you a nice tingly feeling, doesn't it? Being forgotten. Or is that just me?'

'But the paperwork's still in place,' said Catherine.

'So even when they're forgetting us, they're forgetting to forget us properly.'

'If you're getting philosophical, I need a drink.' He opened a drawer and thrust his hand into it like a bear exploring a hollow trunk. 'Anyway, it's all a tub of shit. Not what you just said, though that too. But our status as untouchables. We've not been forgotten. We've been *repurposed*.'

An audible sneer accompanied the word, like a sommelier offering an alcopop.

She stepped to one side and tipped the visitor's chair so its cargo of takeaway receptacles slid to the floor. Then she produced a tissue from the sleeve of her dress and wiped the seat down. Once more or less satisfied, she sat. 'You said you didn't know what Taverner was up to.'

He said, 'That's what I said, yes. But a funny thing about me, and this is what sets me apart from the rest of you clowns, my brain stays switched on. So while I didn't know before, I do now. Do you need me to say that again?'

'I just about followed. What's happening?'

'It's like I said to Guy. She spotted him, so he must have been a beginner.' Lamb had found a bottle in his drawer: Talisker. 'Light dawning yet?'

'It's a training exercise,' she said.

'Give that woman a goldfish.'

'That's why we've been wiped.'

'Yeah, so Lady Di can paint targets on our backs and let her junior agents off the leash,' Lamb said. He leaned back, and his chair complained angrily. 'I suppose she might have hoped that, somewhere in the dim recesses of whatever passes for you lot's mental processes, you might still remember some tradecraft.

Like making sure you're not being tailed when you go about your daily business. Or even just paying some fucking attention, the way normal people do. Which might have made it a slightly more taxing exercise for the early learners.' He unscrewed the cap off the bottle. 'Fancy a drink?'

She said, 'So the Park have been using us for practice. And they wiped us first so the newbies won't know we're spooks too.'

'To be fair,' said Lamb, 'thinking of you lot as spooks requires a mental leap. Like calling Farage a statesman.'

'And now Kay White is dead.'

Lamb was watching the liquid rope he'd made by pouring whisky very slowly from the bottle into the glass. So she couldn't see his expression as he said, 'Did Molly tell you that?'

'She didn't have to.'

When he looked up, there was nothing to suggest the news had come as a surprise.

Kay White had been a slow horse, some years back. Lamb had fired her when she'd betrayed them all — his view — to the Park, presumably on the understanding that she'd be reinstated over there. That didn't happen. It never did.

Catherine said, 'She kept in touch with a few former colleagues. And they keep in touch with me.'

'A fishwives' network,' said Lamb. 'How jolly.'

'She fell off a stepladder while clearing out her attic.'

'They say most accidents happen in people's homes,' said Lamb. 'That's why I never visit anyone.'

'No, it's why you're never invited anywhere.'

He tipped his glass in her direction, then drank

from it.

'That's not like you.'

'What isn't?'

'To have one of your crew die without batting an eyelid.'

Lamb put the glass down. His unlit cigarette was between his fingers now. 'One of mine? She's a distant memory. Wasn't even that until you brought her name up.'

'All right, so she wasn't current. But she used to be one of us. That ought to matter.'

'Might of, if I hadn't fired her for dumping us all in the shit. I mean, it was a long time ago, and it's not like I carry grudges.' He put the cigarette back in his mouth. 'But she deserved to die. Even Gandhi would admit that.'

'Did it never occur to you that for a supposed backwater of the Security Service, we suffer a lot of fatalities?'

'I've always assumed that was down to public demand.'

'So it doesn't worry you, this . . . accidental death? Now, of all times?'

'Seriously? You're seriously asking me that?' He threw his head back and barked at the ceiling. Some might call it laughter. 'Look, I trust Taverner about as far as I can fly. But she's not gunna take out a contract on Slough House just to give her learner spooks something to do. Don't get me wrong, she'd do it if she had a reason. But this isn't that.'

Catherine pursed her lips, and didn't answer.

'Christ, Standish, they've never needed to kill us. I mean, fucking look at us. What would be the point?'

'The timing worries me.'

99

'It's spring. When else do you clear out your attic?'

She stood. 'What did that crack mean, earlier? About international assassins?'

'Nothing to get your ovaries in a twist. Assuming yours aren't already knotted.'

She waited, but he wouldn't elucidate further.

'So now you've worked out what's going on,' she said, 'are you planning on taking it up with Taverner?'

'Is Notre Dame flammable? Speaking of which.'

He sparked a flame from a lighter he was suddenly holding, and applied it to his cigarette.

Catherine shuddered. 'You really need to get a grip on some health issues.'

'What I don't know about healthy living,' said Lamb, 'you could write on the back of a fag packet.' He breathed out smoke. 'And tell Cartwright and Guy that the next time they sneak out without permission, I'll hang her by his testicles. Or vice versa.'

He reached for his glass again, and Catherine left him to it.

5

Preparing to leave, Oliver Nash said, 'I saw something rather extraordinary on the way in.'

Nash being Nash, this would probably be one of those pop-up tourist experiences London pulls from its sleeve occasionally: a wondrous mechanical elephant, or a herd of fibreglass cows.

It had been a successful meeting, from both points of view; Diana's because she had got what she wanted, and Nash's because he hadn't noticed. The venue was Diana's office, down on the hub. Previous First Desks had chosen to occupy one of the upper-storey rooms, whose expensive windows afforded leafy views, but Diana preferred to be where the action was. Most of her career had been spent here, almost all of it as Second Desk (Ops), her initial meteoric rise having been followed by a hard stop. Since then, it sometimes felt she'd done little but bide her time, paying obeisance to one First Desk after another; watching mistakes made and successes forged, and knowing that if she'd been in charge, there'd have been fewer of the former, more of the latter. And now she was where she'd long wanted to be, and much of it involved taking meetings with Oliver Nash and similar examples of Whitehall mandarin: decent human beings in themselves, but lacking the sense of urgency that the times required.

Take the business of cybersecurity.

There was little official appetite for deep-cover ops, she'd reminded him; software was replacing human agency as the cornerstone of intelligence work.

Hundreds of hours of recorded conversation; miles of emails — that was how they were measured, in actual miles — and gallons, bathtubs, reservoirs of pixellated flow: all of these, gathered at a distance, were the fruits of Spook Street. And even once they were harvested, human agency remained at a remove, the intelligence pored over instead by algorithms whose acronyms were increasingly twee, but which were at least as open to subversion as the most disenchanted joe. You didn't have to buy an algorithm a drink, or set it up with an easy lay. You just had to work out what made it dance, and once that was done — once you had its number — it was your creature, and would do whatever you wanted. And that was how vulnerable everything was these days: you were only one hack away from open government.

'We need bigger firewalls, Oliver. Bigger ones, better ones. The kind you can see from space.'

'Ha, like the Great Wall of — '

'Precisely.'

'Not unironic, in the circs.'

She let him chuckle over that, accurately gauging the moment at which mirth would deflate into a sigh.

'Diana, I am on your side in this.'

'Why does that phrase drain me of confidence?'

'But you can't be unaware of the bigger picture.'

'There is no bigger picture. We're talking about national security, about protecting our virtual borders. For God's sake, look at the self-harm we've inflicted in the name of national sovereignty. You'd have thought there'd be few lengths we'd not be willing to go in pursuit of that particular grail.'

'Leaving aside your jaundiced view of recent history, you're overstating the case. Besides, and don't imagine I'm unaware of this, the last such restructuring was completed not twenty-four months back. After a significant, not to say unprecedented, budgetary dispensation.'

'Two years is a long time in cyberspace.'

'Be that as it may, this is not a case you're going to find it easy to pursue in front of Limitations. Claude Whelan had friends Down the Corridor, remember. Forgive me if I'm treading on your *amour propre*, but you're not quite as popular, perhaps because you're not as ready to, as our American cousins would say, make nice.'

'I'm not in this business to make nice, and I don't like having to make do, either. Nor am I looking to Whitehall for friends or playmates. I just expect support from that direction when I'm looking to repel our common enemies.'

'As witness the Kazan episode.'

'Which received an ovation from the committee. In case you'd forgotten.'

'It tickled the right erogenous zones, yes, but in the cold light of day, wiser opinion holds that now is not the time to pour oil on troubled wildfires. And some who've gone to the bother of examining the minutes have pointed out that at no time were you given carte blanche to perform the, ah, procedure in question. You were simply asked to examine the viability of such an operation.'

'Well, I think I did that with exceptional clarity.'

'And besides, there are other needs than yours, many of them equally pressing. I'm not saying there isn't a case to be made for the upscaling you have in mind, but that's what you have to do — make a case. Not simply assert your demands.'

'And what if I told you that I won't be making demands? That all I'm looking for is approval to refocus existing resources?' She uncrossed her legs, then crossed them again. 'All I require can be met through internal rebudgeting.'

This gave him pause.

'I'm serious, Oliver. I've identified a saving.'

'I thought you were cut to the bone.'

'We are. But I can prioritise.'

'Enlighten me further,' said Nash. 'Please.'

'There's a project called Chimera.'

'Oh, very on-message. How come I've not heard of it?'

'Because I run a tight ship. Chimera's not appeared on any agenda within the last few years because it's been doing precisely what it ought to do, when it ought to do it, within budget.'

'Good lord. Are you sure you want to close it down? We could have it mounted and put on a plinth.' He shifted in his chair. 'All right, all right. A little levity never did any harm. Remind me, what's the precise nature of this, ah, Chimera?'

'Probably best if we don't emphasise what we're losing, and focus on the gains to be made.'

'Of course. And I'm sure you're right, and there's no need to blind the committee with technical detail, but for my own peace of mind, I really do need a glimpse of precisely what we're deciding we can live without.'

'Very well,' said Diana. 'Chimera was set up in the mid nineties and involved long-term, real-time analysis of the psychological effects of operating under deep cover in domestic pressure groups.'

'Ah. Animal Liberation Front kind of thing?'

'I can neither confirm nor deny.'

'All very . . . surreptitious. Subterfuguous?'

'I don't want to hammer home the obvious, but we are the Secret Service.'

'Is there an adjective from subterfuge?'

'I'll make a note, Oliver. Have someone look into it.'

He said, 'And this was costing enough that you can make substantial savings by closing it down?'

'We're a bureaucracy. Everything we do costs money, because it all has to be discussed by committee, every member of which is claiming expenses. So do we really need to debate first principles, or can I rely on your support when it comes to the next Limitations meeting? Redirecting funds, that's all. With the committee's approval it can be done in house, and the next you'll hear about it, it'll be in place. No fuss, no fireworks.'

'I'll give it some thought. But in principle, I see no objection.'

'I'm grateful. Now, I've a call to make. Was there any other business?'

'There was something.' Nash checked his phone, which was where he kept his notes. 'Ah yes. The minister's been getting calls. An American, resident here, claiming that his partner, in the life partner sense I think, that his partner was murdered in Moscow. On Putin's orders.'

'And was he one of ours?'

'A Brit, you mean? No, I gather he was a Russian citizen.'

'So even if he was murdered, it wouldn't be our business. Why are you bringing it to me?'

'The minister had no particular instructions,' Nash

said. 'He just wants to stop receiving these phone calls.'

'That's a police matter. Really, you can't keep urging me to keep costs down on the one hand, and —'

'*Mea culpa.*'

' — offering my services to any of your Westminster cronies who have a passing problem.'

'I'm sorry, Diana, you're right. As always. Thanks for your time.' He rose to go, putting his phone away, and said, 'I saw something rather extraordinary on the way in.'

A wondrous mechanical elephant, she thought. A parade of fibreglass cows.

'Please tell.'

'There was a tour arriving as I came through the lobby,' he said. 'One of those Civil Service groups?'

These were regular outings: covens of civil servants given whistlestop tours round Regent's Park, or at least, round those non-classified areas that were close enough to thrill by association. *This is where Bond hangs his raincoat. Some floors below us lies the hub.*

'It's not that extraordinary. They've been a feature for years.'

'Ah, yes, no, I meant who was in the group. Damien Cantor? The boss of Channel Go, you know who I mean? Richest man in the country under thirty-five, I'm led to believe.'

Diana discovered something on her desk that required attention, and it was a moment before she replied. 'And he was being shown around the building?'

'Maybe he plans to make an offer for it,' said Nash. 'Diana? That was a joke.'

'Good meeting, Oliver. Thank you.'

There was something forlorn about a house stripped of its furniture, or there was if you were its departing spirit. A stranger might find potential in this wide hallway, but for River — reaching it via the kitchen; he'd used the back door again, as had been his childhood habit — it was like entering a ransacked priory: the wooden chest which had sat under that row of coat hooks was gone, as was the engraving, a Howard Phipps, which had hung on the opposite wall. But these were secondary emotions: he was here for Sid, who was in the study, and to all appearances had not moved since the early hours. *Sid was bright, Sid was sharp.* Sid now seemed mostly weary, and greeted him the way a long-term patient might a regular visitor, reaching a hand out but remaining seated, her legs tucked under her. The white stripe in her hair looked an affectation: she was a punkish waif in a modernised Dickens.

'Thank you for coming.'

He wasn't sure how the alternative would have worked. He could have gone home, he supposed, and spent the evening thinking how strange it was, that Sid was in his grandfather's study in Kent.

They ate in picnic fashion: provisions he'd bought on the way.

'You weren't followed, were you?'

River shook his head. He'd looped a roundabout twice, and doubled back on himself a couple of miles to make sure.

'Tell me again,' he said. 'About the people who came looking.'

'You're wondering if my story's going to change.'

'I'm wondering what we can do to find them.'

'I don't want to find them,' she said. 'I want them not to find me.'

'I'll keep you safe. Describe them.'

'They were a couple. A man and a woman. Dressed like missionaries.'

Black-suited, River learned. White-shirted. The man was dark, clean-shaven; the woman blonde, had her hair tied back, and wore round, plastic-framed spectacles. They'd been going door-to-door round the estate where Sid had been housed.

'And you're sure they weren't . . . well. Missionaries?'

She gave him a look he remembered well: this was Sid, he'd once shared an office with.

When they'd reached her door, she had watched from a bedroom window. They had hung on the doorstep longer than natural, and she'd had to step back sharply when the woman looked up.

'What time of day?'

'Morning.'

'Where did they go once they'd left?'

'Next door.'

And had carried on up the winding street, then down the other side. Like missionaries would have done.

Sid said, 'Maybe it wasn't just to look less suspicious. Maybe they didn't know exactly which house I was in.'

'What did you do?'

'I called it in.'

Which was standard. If you had a handler, if you had a milkman, you always called it in.

River said, 'It was supposed to be a safe house. How

could they know where to find you?'

'They could have known about the farm. Where I spent time in recovery.' A hunk of bread balanced uneaten on her chair's armrest. 'It's been used for years.'

And a link between the farm and the estate, a few miles down the road, wouldn't have been hard to establish. They might not have followed Sid's milkman to Sid's exact address — the estate was a warren of culs-de-sac and one-way streets; a tail would have burned bright as a beacon — but they could have established her general whereabouts, and then gone door to door.

'And what makes you sure they wanted to kill you?'

She picked up the bread and stared at it, puzzled. Then put it carefully down. 'What else would they have planned?'

It pulled at his heart to have her sitting here, both because it was her and because it was here. Sid, whom he'd thought dead. And here, of all places, where that same heart had put down its first roots. He'd been carted place to place by his mother, like a suitcase. Only once she'd abandoned him to his grandparents' care had he learned what home meant. And thinking that thought, he realised he had no idea what family Sidonie Baker had; what friends she might have left behind. Besides himself, he thought, then caught that: had he been her friend? They'd fought through most of their short relationship. Which was a familiar story when it came to River and women, though in his defence, by no means all of them ended up shot in the head.

And it was impossible not to think about head wounds, their long-term implications. Being shot in the head might leave you fearing being shot in the head again. Most professions this didn't happen once, let alone twice, but River could see how it might be: once shot, twice shy. Sid was a softer presence now; her colours muted. Maybe her reception in general was fuzzier, and prone to static. Strangers weren't always dangerous, but those that were were best avoided. Why wouldn't she imagine them bringing harm to her door?

Some of this might have been written on his face, because she said, 'You think I'm paranoid.'

'No.'

'Yes you do.'

'Sid, you had a bad time of it, and I'm sorry. It was my fault.'

Truth was, he could barely remember if that were so. He had been the reason Sid was there that night, on that London street in the rain, but he hadn't asked her to come.

'You didn't pull the trigger,' she said.

'No.'

'Well then.'

'Why did you come here?'

'I couldn't think of anywhere else. And you're safe.' She raised a hand to the white stripe in her hair. 'You're a slow horse. Whatever's going on, whatever's happening, you're not involved. Slow horses never are.'

Which was partly true, he thought. Slow horses spent a lot of time not being involved. And by the time things turned out otherwise, it was frequently too late.

'Why do you think they're after you?'

'Maybe I know something.'

110

'Like what?'

'I don't know . . . Maybe I used to know something, and I've forgotten what it was. But that doesn't mean I don't still know it. Back there.'

She made a vague gesture: the back of her mind, she meant. A part blocked off since the shooting. He imagined the bullet throwing up furrows as it creased her head: creating little earthworks in the brain, behind which memories piled, irretrievable clumps of information.

And that would be just like a slow horse too, he thought. To be in possession of crucial information, and still be the last to know.

'What do you think I should do?'

'You can stay here for a while.'

'That's not a solution. Just a hiding place.'

'Best I can do right now.' He wanted to move closer to her, offer reassurance, but wasn't sure that was the way to do so. Instead, he rose and turned on the lamp in the corner, dispelling the gathering gloom. 'I can try to find out more about those missionaries.'

'They weren't missionaries.'

'Whoever they were. I can get Ho to check them out, probably.'

Provided he didn't mind eating some serious shit.

'Roderick Ho . . . Is he still with you?'

'Uh-huh.'

'How is he?'

'Much the same,' said River. 'Unfortunately.'

Again, that evening, he didn't want to leave but couldn't comfortably stay. He fetched from the boot some odds and ends he'd thought to pack — his kettle, a duvet, a towel — and asked how she was doing for clothes. It was like vaulting over several levels of relationship. When he left he was clutching the list she'd scribbled — underwear, a sweatshirt, shampoo — and trying to remember if her handwriting had been so disorganised when he'd first known her. Meanwhile Sid had bedded down in a nest of cushions, and that was how he thought of her all through the night: like someone who'd lost their way in a wood, and covered themselves with leaves, hoping this would keep them safe.

★　★　★

Before the light had left the day, Diana was occupying a bench with her back to the Globe, looking out on the Thames. The bench was an old favourite, smack in the middle of a twelve-yard stretch unmonitored by CCTV, and she'd recently had its USP refreshed, this being a foul splash of birdshit covering most of its length; a plastic transfer, but realistic enough to ensure no one ever sat here. It was also somewhere she would smoke, a habit she rarely indulged in with others present. It was hard to say which of the two, fag or faeces, passing tourists found more offensive.

Sometimes, at moments like this — feeling the day's first charge of nicotine; watching the endless river heading home — she could allow her mind to empty, and simply feel alive. Today, though, that wasn't going to happen. She'd been fizzing for hours.

'Ah. A beautiful woman indulging in vice. Is there any more arousing sight?'

If Peter Judd appreciated the specifics of a clandestine meeting, he went out of his way to challenge them.

Diana peeled the transfer away, allowing him space

to sit, and as he lowered his carefully tailored bulk onto the bench, he said, 'A summons. An urgent summons, no less. Who's been putting sand in your Vaseline, Diana?'

'Why did Damien Cantor join a visitor group at the Park this morning?'

'Flattering as it is to have you think I'm pulling strings all day, I'm usually as much in the dark as you.'

'I'm not generally in the dark.'

'No. I seem to recall you prefer it with the lights on. May I have one of those?'

She took packet and lighter from her bag and handed them to him. He shuddered at his first inhalation, a parody of pleasure. 'Thank you. Look, Cantor's an investor. He wants to kick the skirting boards, check for damp. And he probably thinks he was being subtle, or even funny, joining a tour group, but you can put that down to his age. And being mega-rich. The mega-rich always think they're the dog's bollocks.'

'My understanding of dogs' bollocks,' said Diana, 'is that you can lop them off and chuck them away, and the dog will still operate.'

She finished her cigarette and ground it underfoot. A nearby gull watched with hungry interest.

'It's a little soon,' said Judd, 'to contemplate altering the composition of, what shall we call it, our caucus? Besides which, as I think I mentioned, Cantor is a major contributor. Sidelining him now would be like dropping Beckham before the semi-final.'

'I see you're letting your sporting references lapse. Now you no longer depend on the goodwill of the electorate.'

'Fuck the electorate.'

'Cantor might be a big noise in his world, but this

113

is mine,' she said. 'And his role in my world is to offer his backing and accept my gratitude, or remove himself entirely.'

'I do love it when you draw lines,' Judd said smoothly. 'It brings out the feminist in me. I'll have a word with our Damien, all right? And all shall be well, and all manner of thing and so on. Now. Crisis over, moving on. Your meeting with Nash went well, I trust?'

'. . . Passably.'

'Don't tell me. You invented a project that's no longer fit for purpose, and claimed you could make a saving by closing it down and redirecting the funds to your preferred use. And all you need the committee to do is rubber-stamp the process.'

'It's in hand.'

'And you're confident Nash won't, ah, put two and two together?'

'Two and two? He'd have trouble adding one and one.'

Which was unfair, and both knew it, but politics was the art of cutting absent parties down to size.

'Excellent. I'm glad your qualms of yesterday have settled. This work we're doing, this path we're on — it's of enormous benefit to the nation. I feel stirrings of heroism.' He glanced at his crotch. 'There is one other small thing. I've been talking with our, ah, *angels*, and there's general agreement that we'd like you to ease off on your infiltration of the Yellow Vest movement.'

The river still flowed, the breeze still blew. The evening light was still leaking away from the sky.

She eased another cigarette from the packet. The lighter wouldn't spark first time.

'I probably didn't hear you correctly. For a moment,

I thought you were daring to dictate Service policy.'

'Hardly policy. I don't wish to engage in semantic quibbles, but we're talking about one minor line of surveillance. Nothing more.'

She didn't need to look his way to know the pout was in place, the rhetoric forthcoming.

'Look, I understand your concern about the unwashed getting jiggy on the streets, but it's a minor blip. The disturbances will die down — they always do — and on the smoke-blown landscape left behind, we'll see one or two figures emerge who it's wise to pay attention to. Look at You-Know-What. A minor figure, a local joke, never even managed to get elected, somehow positions himself as head of a party everyone wrote off as a bunch of small-minded xeno-phobes, and ten years later he's changed history. This, these Yellow Jackets, who knows? Maybe they're the start of something similar. Just another stage in our political evolution. Democracy is all very well, Diana, but nobody's ever suggested it's the be-all and end-all. Especially not the end-all. Harks back to ancient Greece, thank you, but where's Greece now? Knock-ing on the back door, asking for scraps. That's where its big idea got it.'

'Thanks for the history lesson,' Diana said. 'But the big picture isn't the only thing worrying me. No, what I find concerning is you telling me that this deci-sion has apparently been made, and I'm here to take instruction. And that's not how this works.'

'You've been over-bureaucratised for too long. All those subcommittees and oversight boards, all that middle-fucking-management whose only purpose is to assert its own importance, because if anyone took a good hard look they'd see it doesn't have any. Like it or not, that's the world you're coming from. Where the only decisions you're allowed to make are either so piddlesome nobody else can be bothered with the paperwork, or so incendiary nobody wants to be caught near the fire. Sound familiar?'

'Peter —'

'No one's trying to strong-arm you, Diana. It's simply a matter of encouraging you to see things from a wider perspective, now you're heading up a team with more diversified interests.' He shook his head solemnly. 'If I thought anyone was trying to hold you over a barrel, I'd be the first to stand in their way.'

This was a familiar trope. Theoretically, Judd was always ready to lie down in front of bulldozers for a principle, even if, in practice, he tended to be out of the room when the short straw was pulled.

'Well you can let our angels know that their desires will not be considered. Not when I'm making operational decisions, or any other kind. And if any of them want to withdraw their support in light of that, they're free to do so. Are we clear?'

'As crystal. But bear in mind that if they do decide to withdraw their support, you'll be back where you started from, rattling your cup in front of a panel of thwarted pygmies.' He touched the knot of his tie with an index finger. 'Always supposing you weather any bad publicity arising.'

'Say that again?'

'I'm simply pointing out that when you disappoint rich and powerful men, they let their displeasure be known. But I'm sure it won't come to that. One small favour, Diana. Allow the Yellow Vest campaign to reach its natural end without attempting to discredit those spearheading it. Where could be the harm?'

'Have a good evening, Peter.'

She was halfway across the Millennium Bridge before she remembered she'd failed to reaffix the bird-shit transfer. But then, that was the thing about shit, real or fake: once you'd begun spreading it about, it never ended up precisely where you wanted it.

★ ★ ★

Most great ideas, or a lot of them anyway, were thought at the time to be rubbish, and you were reckoned an idiot for having them.

This was true of stupid ideas too.

Telling them apart was the tricky bit.

So a couple of years ago, when Struan Loy had his brainwave, there'd been no shortage of naysayers telling him he was dipshit crazy. But he'd had the strength of character to rise above that, to recognise the brilliance of his own invention, and to refuse to kowtow to the carping of mediocrities, so here he was, living in a shipping container, cooking past-their-sell-by sausages on a camping stove, and wondering whether that scrabbling he could hear was another rat or a Madagascan spider. These containers had been all over the world, so exotic spiders couldn't be ruled out.

At the time, though, it had been a great idea.

Back then, things had been looking handy. Momentarily between employments, he'd been a sleeping partner at a fitness centre. Well, sleeping partner — he'd been sleeping with one of the partners. This was a divorcée named Shelley, who, to piss off her ex — the other half of the operation — had given Struan a deal on hiring the hall for evening classes:

117

self-defence. Struan, as he sometimes let drop, had been in the security services in an earlier life; not to go into detail but there'd been training, there'd been combat. Put it like this: do not sneak up behind him. Which added frisson to his 'Do it to Them First' session, a fairly lively class that, with hindsight, wasn't ideal for the over fifties. Anyway, once the paramedics were off the premises, Shelley had said something about this being the last straw, which came as a surprise to Struan, who hadn't been counting straws. But it seemed they built up without you knowing.

Give Shelley her due, she'd been generous while it lasted, and the winter before they'd gone on a South African jaunt, safari included. All top job, but it was during a two-day stopover in Johannesburg that he'd had his eureka moment, and that moment was this: shipping containers. There were whole apartment blocks made out of them in Jo'burg: brightly coloured huge great building blocks stacked on top of each other like kids' toys, only with people living in them. It was like, on one hand you had a housing crisis, which everyone knew about, and on the other was this solution, which some smart guys in Johannesburg had stumbled upon, but it was up to Struan Loy to carry the message home. Shipping containers. A lot cheaper than actual buildings. This, definitely, was worth putting every penny he had into, along with a lot of pennies he didn't have but was able to borrow at rates which would seem cheap in the long run, so, post Shelley, he bought a dozen containers from a shipping company gone liquid, these particular assets being stacked behind an industrial park on the outskirts of Leicester. Struan Loy, entrepreneur. All he needed now was to recruit some of the architectural nous, *design* nous, which the bright lads back in S.A. had on tap, and his future was up and running.

Long story short: two years later he had no job, no money, and was shaving expenses where he could, which had meant moving into one of the containers, even though they hadn't exactly been customised yet. It was almost like being homeless, which was in fact exactly what it was.

It made the days when he'd been a slow horse seem a career high.

Slow horses was what they'd been called, those edged out of their roles at Regent's Park because of the envy, spite and small-minded malice of others, but also, in his case, because of an unwise group email suggesting that the then First Desk was an al-Qaeda plant. It was a lesson in how bureaucracies worked: i.e. no sense of humour. Then there'd been a thing that happened with a kid being kidnapped, and Struan's crew — the slow horses — had ended up in the middle of it, and he'd made the perfectly rational decision to save his own skin by shopping them all to Diana Taverner at the Park, in the hope that this would salvage his career. Memo to self: didn't happen. It could get you down, the obstacles a good man found in his way, but seriously, what was that scrabbling in the corner?

Except not in the corner, he realised. It was coming from outside: footsteps on the cracked concrete surface of the wasteground.

He moved to the door as silently as he could; peeped out into the near-dark, and the air that held a hint of coming rain. A few yards away, outside the next container along, stood a man and a woman, both of whom turned his way, despite his attempt at quiet. They were, he couldn't help noticing, carrying a bottle of vodka apiece.

They approached, the woman unleashing a smile. 'Struan Loy, yes? *Mr* Struan Loy?'

The honorific stressed, as if in despite of circumstance.

Loy said, 'Who are you?'

'We heard about your business scheme.'

'The shipping containers?' This was the man, and his accompanying glance took in Loy's home and its immediate neighbours. 'The *residential* shipping containers?'

Raincoats, black suits, white shirts. The woman attractive, but with her hair tied back severely enough that she might want you not to notice, or not yet; the man clean-shaven, and with a quiet, polite look to him.

'I'm him, yes. Or he's me.' Loy was conscious of how he was dressed, suddenly: an old pair of jeans and a sweater too long in the sleeves. Not exactly primed for business discussion. But his visitors didn't seem to care: they stood on what he supposed you could call his threshold, but might be more accurate not to, holding their bottles expectantly, as if awaiting an invitation.

If it weren't for the vodka, thought Struan Loy, he might have taken them for missionaries.

* * *

Diana Taverner had eaten an Italian meal, had drunk two glasses of Chilean wine, but was feeling irredeemably British as she arrived at her Notting Hill home: tired, irritable, full of dread. 'Home', anyway — when asked she'd say 'home' was the Cotswolds, careful never to name the actual village; London was her workplace, her business address. But on the few occasions when she suffered through a weekend in Temple Guiting, she found herself glued to her phone, counting the hours. The cottage had woodburning stoves and exposed beams, stone-flagged floors and a curious window-seat halfway up its narrow staircase, all of which, back in the city, she'd recount as rustic charm, and most of which was a fucking nuisance. She could see stars there, true, but indoors she had to keep her head low. Exposed beams were dangerous. Home, in fact, was Regent's Park. But the Notting Hill house was elegant and subtle and carpeted to a hush; it had spot lighting and spotless walls. It had a fridge full of wine. She shucked her shoes off, gathered the mail, padded into the kitchen and poured herself another glass. Through the sliding door, she could see the intruder light was on, which meant a fox had been doing the rounds. It would go off in a minute. She put the mail on the table, and carried the wine upstairs.

Removed her make-up. Took deep breaths. She hadn't waded out so far she couldn't make it back safely. She was First Fucking Desk. She'd taken apart bigger threats than Damien Cantor, than Peter Bloody Judd. And troublesome angels weren't an unprecedented hazard. Some had tried it on with God, and look where that got them.

Her wine finished, she left the mirror to its own reflections, and took her glass downstairs to refill it.

The intruder light was still on.

The garden was a thin strip of land, most of it paved; large plants in huge pots were kept alive by a weekly gardener. There was furniture too, in case Diana ever made any friends, and ever invited them

121

round, and they ever decided to enjoy each other's company in the garden. It was wooden, sturdy, and when the intruder light was on looked like props on a stage. She unlocked the door, opened it and stepped down onto the path. The smoke from Jackson Lamb's cigarette reached her even before she registered his bulk, squatting in one of the chairs.

He said, 'What are you doing in my garden?'

She shook her head.

'Now you say, 'No, it's *my* garden,' and we'll improvise from there.'

'Fuck off. You know how long it'll take the Dogs to get here? And it will *not* be a comfortable collection, I can promise you.'

'Might as well sit while we're waiting, then.'

Diana stared at him, then shook her head again and went back into her kitchen and filled her wineglass. Really filled it. Had to be careful carrying it outside again, in case it slopped over the rim.

She set it on the table, pulled another of the heavy wooden chairs out, and sat.

Looking at the glass, Lamb said, 'No, don't worry. I'm fine.'

'I know. There's a bottle poking out of your pocket.'

'Oh. That.' He brought it out, removed its cap. 'Cheers.'

She raised her glass in what she hoped was an aggressively sardonic manner.

'So,' he said. 'I suppose you're wondering why I invited you out here for a chat.'

'Cut the comedy and get to the point.'

'You've been using my crew for training purposes. Like they were dummies in a shooting gallery.'

'Oh, I'm sorry. Is there a reason I shouldn't be

doing that?'

'Only the obvious. That they're my fucking dummies.'

'And they do you so much credit.' She glanced at his feet, where a pile of cigarette stubs had mushroomed. 'How long have you been here?'

'Longer than I expected. Since when have you had a social life?'

'Sorry to inconvenience you.'

'Yeah, I may have had to piss in one of your plant pots.'

Diana doubted he was kidding. She motioned towards his cigarette. 'Can I have one of those?'

He sighed. 'Some people just make themselves free and easy with other people's property.' But he handed her one.

'Did you make this yourself?'

'Just hold it at an angle.'

He shoved a plastic lighter across. The first inhalation reminded her of her first one ever. 'God in heaven. Where did this come from?'

'Old Miles's.'

'Ah, Christ. It's closed down, right?' She shook her head. 'The old guard used to gather there. Back in Partner's day.'

'Just the suits,' he said. 'And the hangers-on.'

'Suits and hangers,' she said. Then: 'It's all changing though, isn't it? I thought everything had changed enough already. But it keeps on happening.'

'If I wanted to listen to a stroppy woman getting maudlin, I'd have picked a City bar.' He took a swallow from his bottle, which had a label Diana didn't recognise, then said, 'So that's why you had us all wiped. So your newbies wouldn't know they were tail-

123

ing professionals.'

She breathed out smoke that looked blacker than natural. 'It took you long enough.'

'Once I'd established I was still getting paid, it didn't seem that urgent. Besides. You didn't put anyone on me.'

'No,' said Diana. 'I didn't want any of them broken.'

Lamb nodded, as if that went without saying. Then said, 'I heard about Kazan. I'm guessing the Whitehall crowd creamed themselves then backed away.'

'Nothing I'm not used to.'

'What about Number Ten?'

'Doesn't officially know. That way, his spad doesn't have to decide what the PM thinks.'

They were silent. Way overhead, in the dark starless sky, nothing happened.

Then Lamb said, 'I've stood on bridges in my time. You watch one of your own come back to your side, watch one of theirs walk the opposite way. And that's the end of the story. They're off the board. Untouchable. This shit doesn't get written down, but that doesn't mean it's not a rule. Otherwise it's just joe country. Welcome to the badlands.' He tipped his bottle in her direction. 'Putin pissed all over that rule. You did the right thing.'

'Thanks.'

'He's probably declared war, though. You realise that.'

'No, I think he'll get the message.'

'Because I heard a rumour.'

'And you pay attention to that sort of thing?'

'Of course I fucking do. I'm a spy.' He added his cigarette end to the pile by his feet. 'Apparently we

124

have a crack assassination squad.'

'That was the rumour?'

'No, the rumour is they've been targeted. Tit for tat. You took out one of their featured artists, now they're coming for yours. Should make for an interesting summer.'

Diana said, 'We used freelance talent for Kazan.'

'I figured.'

'Because it's not as straightforward as it used to be. Not with half the agencies in Europe thinking it's funny to put our people on their watch lists. No more courtesy access, no more blind eyes turned to low-key incursions. No more shortcuts through friendly states. Cooperation strictly according to the book, which suddenly has a lot more small print than we'd thought.' She contemplated her wineglass, manoeuvring which was less complicated now it held half as much. 'The many blessings of You-Know-What.'

'Don't look at me,' said Lamb. 'I voted Lib Dem.'

'Very funny. But my point was, we have tactical teams, sure, and we have operatives who could take even you down bare-handed, though I'm sure they'd prefer rubber gloves. But we don't, as such, have an actual department. Where'd this rumour come from?'

'A little man at Old Miles's.'

'And he, what, saw it on Twitter?'

'His partner was a journo, writing a book on Putin.'

'Uh-huh.'

'And died.'

'Killed?'

Lamb shrugged.

'Where?'

'Moscow.'

'This little man,' Diana said. 'American?'

'Full-blooded Munchkin.'

'And his partner was a Russian citizen.' She made to inhale again, and thought better of it. 'He's been writing to the minister. Local reports called it natural causes.'

'And annoying Putin doesn't count?'

Diana said, 'Well, he wouldn't be the first Russian journalist to walk into a bear trap.' She drank some wine. 'If bodies start turning up, I'll know we've got a problem. To add to my ever-growing list. In the meantime, I'm tired. Would you mind pissing off back wherever you call home?'

Lamb heaved himself up. When he stretched, she thought about bear traps again. He found another cigarette somewhere, and said, 'Pretty impressive, though. Bankrolling a hit on a Moscow heavy without sanction from upstairs.'

'Maybe I've got a fairy godfather.'

'Let's hope he doesn't make an offer you can't refuse.'

Foreboding washed over her, and the words were out before she could stop them. 'I may have made a mistake, Jackson.'

He waited.

But she shook her head. 'Ah, screw it. It is what it is. Isn't that the current wisdom?'

'London rules, Taverner. If you're big enough to admit you've made an error, you're stupid enough to make another one.'

'Thanks.'

'And don't fuck with my joes.'

'They're not joes.'

'That wasn't the important bit. The important bit was, do not fuck.' He nodded towards the door. 'Can

126

I come through the house?'

'No. You can leave the way you came.'

'I came through the house.'

'No you didn't.'

She locked the sliding door behind her, and went up to the toilet. When she came back down the intruder light was off, and the garden empty.

★　★　★

'May we come in and look around?'

If it had been just her, no question.

The man said, 'Jim and Jane. By the way.'

'He's Jim,' the woman added. 'I'm Jane.'

'We're what you might call interested parties.'

'Interested in the concept, that is.'

'Shipping containers,' said Jim. 'Residential. Brilliant.'

'Just brilliant.'

'And we're very keen on exploring the potential further.'

'Possibly as a franchised opportunity,' said Jane.

'By which we mean, we would shoulder the design burden. And production costs, of course.'

'While you would retain the vision and the trademark rights.'

'We'd not ask you to sell your dream.'

'Who in their right mind would offer their dream for sale?'

'But we hope you'll be interested in leasing it,' said Jim.

It was like being washed by gentle hands, thought Struan Loy. Like being oiled and towelled and given a happy ending. 'Jim and Jane,' he said. Then he said,

'Okay, Jim and Jane. Come in. Bring your bottles.'

He couldn't help slipping into salesman mode as he stepped aside to let them enter. 'Nice and spacious, as you can see. Plenty of . . . potential.'

There was only the one light, a battery-powered lantern, but it illuminated the amenities: the armchair, and the wooden crate seeing use as both table and kitchen. The camping stove sat on top of it, along with the pan in which he'd fried his sausages; probably still hot, but here was the beauty of his current lifestyle: who cared about scorch marks?

'Bit of a campsite, to be honest. Not actually ready for moving in, but I wanted to . . . test the ambience.'

Jim was looking round with interest.

Jane said, 'What design did you have in mind? For the finished model, I mean?'

'Well,' said Loy. 'Three rooms, really. A living–sleeping space, that would be most of it. And a shower, obviously, with the necessaries. And a separate kitchen.'

'With a good big window across the living space wall,' Jane said. 'I like it. What are you using at the moment? For the — ah — necessaries?'

'Just going round back,' said Loy.

Jim was making admiring-type noises and, more importantly, unscrewing the top of the vodka bottle. It made that appealing *snap* as the seal broke. 'You have glasses? Or plastics, even. We're all friends here.'

Loy had two polystyrene beakers and a chipped mug.

'Perfect.'

Jim poured each of them a generous measure of vodka, and they toasted Struan Loy's enterprise.

Jane kept up the chatter while Jim refreshed their

128

drinks. They'd heard about the scheme while exploring investment opportunities, and their ears had pricked up. Well, housing. It was important to put something back, didn't Struan think? Struan thought. Anyway, she could see why he'd had trouble with uptake, because people were so unimaginative these days, but anyone with an ounce of vigour — hell, she wasn't afraid of the word: anyone with *spunk* — could see that what Struan had come up with, his genius brainwave, was exactly what society had been waiting for. Man with a welding torch and the right attitude could have this space sorted in no time.

And Struan was so right not to overcomplicate. Three rooms: bedroom, kitchen, bathroom. Or even — and she didn't want to tread on toes here — but even, you could make it just the two. Plenty of properties, studio flats, incorporated kitchen into living space, yes? Cut down on conversion expenses. But anyway, here was the other thing, they were stackable, shipping containers. Famous for it. What you had here, basically, was a whole apartment block waiting to be assembled. Little bit of clever with the outside staircases, and you were away. Had he thought about furnished or unfurnished? She bet the former. She could see he had an eye. Have some more vodka.

He had some more vodka.

It felt good going down. And Jane's pep talk hit the spot too, reminding Struan what it was he'd seen in Johannesburg. Not just an opportunity, but a journey; somewhere he could point himself, and keep moving. Away from the bad luck that had dogged him so long. The only trouble, far as he could see — the only wasp in the sun cream — was that things like this didn't happen. Not to Struan Loy.

Because when things were turning to shit, they kept turning to shit faster. Second law of motion. Emphasis on motion. His recent trajectory had taken a shitward direction, and no way was that going to terminate in a couple of strangers turning up with a wellyful of dosh. No, something was going on. And if they thought Struan hadn't copped on to that yet, they should have stuck to being the missionaries they resembled.

'So who was it pointed you in my direction?'

He slurred on *direction*, he thought, but then decided he hadn't, or at least, that you were supposed to slur on it, it had an *ecksh* sound. But probably the whole mental debate was itself an indication that he'd been drinking neat vodka.

Jane and Jim exchanged a look. 'His name was Peter?'

'. . . Pete Fairfax?' said Loy.

'Fairfax, yeah. I think that was it.'

It was good to have these questions answered, especially when the answer was: these people are full of crap. Loy didn't know a Peter Fairfax.

Might be good to have them not in his living space any more.

'So yeah, well, anyway,' he said. 'Good. Good. Definitely a lot to think about.'

'Definitely,' Jim agreed.

'*So* much,' Jane offered.

'But right now, and thanks for the drink and everything, but right now I'd really better get some shut-eye.' He mimed sleeping, very briefly, unsure why he was doing so. Everyone knew what sleeping looked like. 'Gotta be fresh in the morning.'

'Really? Why so?'

This was Jane again.

'Oh, you know.' A vague gesture. 'Things to do.'

Jim was unscrewing the top on the second vodka bottle. There didn't seem to be a *snap* this time, as if the seal had already been broken.

'No, really. I think I've had enough,' Loy said.

'Yeah, probably,' Jim agreed. He looked at Jane. 'We about done?'

'To a crisp,' she agreed. And then, to Loy, she said some words he didn't follow: a pattering of tongue on palate in a language from far away.

'...What?'

'Oh, just an observation.'

Jim was holding the bottle upside down now, pouring its contents onto Struan's sleeping bag.

'Hey! What the hell you doing?'

'What? Oh, this.' He stopped pouring. 'Well. You can't drink it. That's for sure.'

'That's for damn sure,' added Jane, and they both laughed.

Jim started prowling the living space, shaking the bottle on the move: liquid spattered everywhere, onto Loy's possessions, onto the metal walls.

'Will you stop that?' He moved forward, intent on delivering a physical rebuke, but he was on the floor suddenly, his legs a tangle beneath him. Jane stepped away, a small smile on her face. And then Jim was shaking the bottle in his direction, so it was spattering down the front of his sweater, his holey old sweater too long in the sleeves.

'Right. That's it. Fuck off out of here, both of you!'

'I think he's right,' said Jane.

'Bottle's empty anyway,' said Jim.

'Shall we tuck him in?'

'Not sure he's in the mood.'

'Fuck off,' Loy said. He was sober again, he was sure of it. 'Right off. Now.'

Who they were, what they wanted, other questions: they'd still be there in the morning. But one thing he knew: these people, this Jim and this Jane, were remnants of his old life, when he'd been in the Service. This was a call to action. Tomorrow he'd be back at the Park, banging on the door. Home was where, when you went there, they had to let you in. This, they'd want to know about. And he felt a spark light up inside, familiar from years ago: the feeling of belonging, and of being useful, and having something to bring to the fight. He didn't yet know what the fight was, but had a shrewd idea of who the enemy were. And there was a strange smell, too, which wasn't vodka but was more energetic, not to mention acrid, not to mention dangerous.

Not to mention this:

That Jim and Jane were leaving, the lighter Jim had just tossed towards the sleeping bag still tumbling over itself in mid-air, more slowly than gravity usually allowed, its flame somehow holding on despite the gyrations it was going through. Already Struan was getting to his feet, and had managed as far as his hands and knees before the lighter hit the bag the way shit hits the fan: with a *whump*, and an air of there being no going back. Jim and Jane were at the door, and then the door was swinging shut, and there was a ratcheting noise, something indescribable, but perfectly captured by the vision of a length of wood being inserted through a pair of metal handles. There was no way of confirming this from Struan's side of the door, but its refusal to open told a story.

He hammered on the frame, sounding like a German rock group. '*Please!*' There were flames behind him, the sleeping bag going up, and fire spreading everywhere, greedily swallowing the liquid Jim had sprayed around, and then scarfing up everything else in its path: clothes, some books, the fat in that dirty pan, the sweater he was wearing. '*Open the door! Please!*' You spent half your life pleading let me in, but when it came down to it, what you really wanted was to be set free.

But no matter how hard he banged, how loud he screamed, nothing happened next except the rest of everything, or Struan Loy's everything, which involved heat and flame and flesh and smoke and far too much noise, and then silence.

6

Damien Cantor was watching a video submission, citizen footage of police officers hassling Yellow Vests, when his office door opened and two men entered, black-jeaned, polo-necked and plugged into their mothership, judging by their earpieces. Without word they proceeded to give his office a once-over as he muted his laptop, stared in amazement, and finally said, 'Excuse me? Ex*cuse* me? What the hell?'

Neither paid attention.

He picked up his phone then replaced the receiver: if Sally wasn't in the room apologising already, she was either being forcibly restrained or had committed seppuku in reception.

So he slipped into a smile, leaned back and said, 'Okay, guys. Knock yourselves out.'

They did and they didn't. There was no self-harm involved, but they quietly, methodically, finished their tasks: the point wasn't securing the room, but letting Cantor know he was their bitch. Which made this office politics, and you didn't get to his position — the fifty-second floor of the Needle, snugly inside the Square Mile's nest of bankers, lawyers and other corporate scam artists — without knowing how to take a dagger in the back. So when they reached his desk he simply raised his arms so they could lift his laptop and check its underside. 'Want to pat me down?' he said. 'Shall I assume the position?' Not a flicker of response. 'Give me a call now,' he said as they exited. 'Don't be shy.' They left the door open, but it was closed by invisible hands once Diana Taverner was in the room.

'That was exciting,' he told her. 'I felt like a movie extra.'

'Oh, I'm sure you felt more important than that.' She sat on the opposite side of his desk, and despite the view on offer looked nowhere but at him. He supposed, once you'd had professionals do the business for you, you didn't need to pay extra attention.

'Coffee? Tea? I used to have a PA somewhere.'

'I won't be long. You were at the Park yesterday.'

'I was.'

'Can I ask why?'

'There's a visitors' tour. Fascinating stuff. Fascinating.'

'And you thought it would be cute to tag along, oohing and aahing with the common herd.'

Cantor was wearing a blue suit today, with matching tie and three-day stubble. For his common-herd outing, he'd worn windcheater and nerd-specs: plastic frames with vanilla lenses. He wasn't surprised he'd been recognised.

Taverner said, 'Do I have to explain to you why it's not a good idea that our connection be flagged?'

'And yet here you are. Openly and in broad daylight.' He smiled. 'I don't mean to teach you your trade. But doesn't the full court press compromise the, ah, *clandestine* nature of our relationship?'

'Well, now. Imagine how complicated it would be to explain away a furtive encounter.'

He was nodding already; his expression that of the bright child who understands first time of hearing. 'So your coming here in the open renders our meeting official but banal. Remind me why it's happening?'

135

'I'm curious about footage you've been airing. Wanted to quiz you on its provenance.'

'Which is something First Desk would do.'

'It's something this First Desk does. As the fact of my doing so might indicate. Mr Cantor — '

'Damien.'

'Damien, I'm going to outline how our relationship works. And then, if you see any difficulties arising, we'll know we need to rethink its viability.'

'Oh, I'm liking this. Loving it.'

'This is not a partnership, Damien. This is a strictly one-way arrangement. You, along with a number of others, dispense funding. In doing so, you're providing a service to the nation, in return for which the nation is in a better position to be able to protect those things you value and hold dear. With me so far?'

'I am.'

'What you don't get is any say in the uses to which I put that funding. That can not and will not happen. Ever. I would have hoped Peter Judd had made that perfectly clear.'

'Oh, he did. He did.'

'Further to which, I'm not saying there might not be advantages to your role. Potential priority when stories are breaking, for instance. But you can forget about my appearing anywhere near a newsroom camera.'

He showed his palms. Total surrender.

'Well then. Now I've underlined the message, we have no more to discuss.'

'Of course not. But just so I'm not getting any wires crossed,' he said. 'It's like I make a donation to the Red Cross. That doesn't give me the right to tell them how to apply bandages. Yes?'

'Yes.'

'Or say I give a dosser in the street ten quid. If he wants to piss it up against a wall, that's his choice.'

'Or perhaps he'll just piss all over you, Damien. That would be his choice also.' She stood.

'Sure you won't stay for coffee?'

'I'm sure.'

'Or a tour of the company? I mean, you've shown me yours. By the way, I keep meaning to ask, do you ever get called 'M'?'

'Enjoy your day.'

He said, 'One other thing. How's Doyle working out?'

'. . . What's that?'

'My man Tommo Doyle. Joined your internal police a few months back, what do you call them? The Dogs?'

Taverner said, 'In what way is he 'your man'?'

'He worked security for me a couple of years, but he was wasted, frankly. I'm not exactly a high-risk subject. And Tommo was SAS, back in the day. Definitely a good fit for you guys.'

'I'm not personally acquainted with Mr Doyle,' she said.

'Really? I make it my business to be on first-name terms with all my staff,' said Cantor. 'Not that I'm trying to teach you how to run your Service.'

'A wise decision.'

After she'd left, he reran the footage and approved it for that lunchtime's bulletin. Ultimately this would be the editor's decision, but ultimately he paid the editor's salary. Then he stood near the window, looking down on London: its starts and stoppages, its daily chaos. He shouldn't have mentioned Doyle really, but the worst that would happen was Doyle would lose

137

his job and there was always room for him back here. Tommo was full of good stuff once you got him loosened up. A couple of drinks and he'd tell you stories would make your hair curl.

★ ★ ★

Treat those you despise with humanity, especially if the reason you despise them is that they have none. One of those lessons you pick up along the way, a little shard of wisdom — aspirational goodness — that becomes a moral anchor, if only by virtue of the fact that the words are there, in your head. So Lech Wicinski supposed that's how he ought to regard his fellow beings — with humanity — seeing as how he seemed to be suffering the contempt of all around, but mostly what he felt was, fuck them. Especially Jackson Lamb.

'You want the good news first or the bad news? And I should warn you up front, the bad news is, there's no good news.'

Which was how Lamb had greeted them once they'd answered the summons to his room, delivered via Slough House's version of jungle drums: Lamb's foot, stamping repeatedly on Lamb's office floor.

Catherine said, 'Why don't we cut the pantomime for once, and you could just let everyone know what's up?'

Lamb, who was drinking what was probably tea from a mug the size of a bucket, raised his eyebrows. 'Dissent in the ranks? Okay, I'm a reasonable man. Let's put it to the vote. Hands up those who prefer Standish's approach. Right. Now, hands up all those in charge. Oh, just me?' He lowered his hand. 'The mes have it.'

138

River Cartwright said, 'Glad we've established that. What's the bad news?'

'You know how your self-esteem couldn't get lower? Well, congratulations. We have a new depth. Tell 'em, Standish.'

'Louisa was right,' Catherine said. 'She was being followed, by a Park junior. As are the rest of you, on and off.'

A certain amount of clamour followed this. Lamb, meanwhile, sipped tea daintily from his bucket, like a well-behaved silverback.

'As a training exercise,' Catherine said, once the noise had died down. 'That's why Slough House was wiped. To turn you all — us all — into anonymous targets.'

'So we're what now,' asked Louisa. 'Tin ducks at a fairground stall?'

'Kind of,' said Lamb. 'Only without the individual personalities.'

'And this is Taverner's doing,' said River.

'You have to admit, it has a sly charm all her own.'

Shirley Dander said, 'It's a fucking liberty is what it is.'

Ho was looking from one slow horse to another, as if trying to work out when it would be his turn to speak.

Louisa said, 'Have you suggested to Taverner that she curtail this?'

'Hell no. Why would I do that?'

'To stop your team being treated with disrespect? . . . Sorry. Forget I spoke.'

'Already done.' Lamb set his mug down carefully, then belched with all the restraint of a defrocked nun. 'Anyway, I can't see the harm, to be honest. Not like you present a challenge. And if you're now serving two purposes instead of one, it's like I've just halved all your salaries.' He beamed. 'Win win.'

'What level surveillance are we under?' asked Lech.

'What level whattery are we what?'

'Surveillance. Are they simply using us for pavement practice, or should we assume our airwaves have been tagged?'

'Ah, yes, I can see why that's an issue for you. What with all the porn out there, just waiting to be googled.' He adopted a pious expression. 'If that's what one does with porn. You're asking the wrong person, really. But as far as the surveillance question's concerned, the answer is, I have no fucking clue. But thank you, Forrest Gimp. Good input.'

Catherine said, 'So the plan is, we just put up with whatever nonsense the Park wishes upon us?'

Lamb rolled his eyes. 'God, you're a drag to have around. Moan moan moan. It's like being shackled to the ghost of Bob Marley.'

'I think you mean Jacob.'

'Depends,' said Lamb. 'Which was the one surrounded by wailers?'

After that, the morning crawled past. Lech was deep into his register of social media absconders; #gonequiet, as he'd mentally dubbed it. There seemed no useful algorithm he could apply, so mostly he was making a random trawl of hot-button issues, particularly the aftermaths of terrorist events. In the midst of grief and anger, you could always discern hate. It occurred to him that, for all his pre-digital outlook, Lamb was a walking correlative of Twitter, inasmuch as his daily outpourings of bile didn't look like drying up anytime soon. An insight he'd once have enjoyed relaying to Sara, his fiancée, when he got home, except they were no longer engaged and no longer lived together. There probably weren't many relationships could survive accusations of paedophile leanings, he thought. He couldn't blame Sara for pulling the plug, though he did.

Someone called @thetruthbomb had enjoyed the New Zealand murders. *giving it some of there own innit*, he'd opined. Almost certainly 'he'. *drink your medicin boys*. He hadn't tweeted since, unless he'd been banned, or changed his name.

Shirley Dander was standing in the doorway.

Lech assumed she'd come to see Roderick Ho, who was headphoned and might as well have been blinkered too, which was as much to say, he was being Roderick Ho. But Dander walked straight to Lech's desk and stood waiting for a reaction, like a mute charity mugger.

'. . . What?'

'You doing anything?'

Lech looked at his computer, looked at Shirley, looked at the ceiling, looked back at Shirley. 'Now?'

'For lunch.'

'What do you want?'

'I was thinking, maybe fish?'

Lech said, 'And why do you want me along?'

'Bait,' said Shirley.

★ ★ ★

The keeper of overlooked history, thought Diana. The curator of the dusty box file.

Or just an old bag in a wheelchair.

Two views of Molly Doran.

141

Elsewhere in Regent's Park, the Queens of the Database managed information: stored it, catalogued it, rendered it readily obtainable for the boys and girls on the hub. They were the digital do-it-alls, and prided themselves on the meticulous nature of their record-keeping. They also fielded a formidable pub quiz team. Molly Doran, meanwhile, stalked the perimeter of her analogue estate like an old-world gamekeeper, if admittedly one on wheels; her archive, modelled on the stacks found in its real-world counterparts, was some floors below the surface, at the end of a blue-lit corridor. It occupied a long room lined with upright cabinets, set on tracks allowing them to be pushed together accordion-style when not in use, and in these cabinets languished acres of dusty information, the Park's past lives and glories, and also its failures and dismal misadventures. All of which could be housed on a thumb drive, if the money was there for digitisation; a process which would be carried out over Molly Doran's lifeless corpse, as the woman herself had asserted, in the apparent belief that this was a disincentive. When the Beast — Molly's collective name for the array of databases and info-caches the Queens oversaw — when it broke down or, as daily seemed more likely, turned out to be also available in Mandarin, her shelves would be all that remained secret and untarnished. She'd have shielded the past from the present, which, as far as Diana Taverner was concerned, was the almost exact inverse of the task in hand.

But useful or not, one thing Molly Doran most certainly was was out of the way. Her archive was her island, and she never came to shore. Though check-in data showed she spent more time in the building than anyone bar Diana herself, she might as well have been a ghost on wheels, unnoticed by any but the most sensitive, and dismissed as a story by everyone else. And yet eight weeks ago she'd registered a complaint; reported one of the in-house police team — the Dogs — for 'unwarranted intrusion, unacceptable language and all-round arseholery', the last of which wasn't a recognised infringement of a house rule, but could probably be taken as character appraisal. The complaint had been investigated; an HR lackey sent to mollify Molly, which probably ranked as the most thankless task available to that department; and a mild wigging delivered to the miscreant, in the form of an email suggesting he read up on the disability protocols outlined in the staff handbook. Thereafter, the wheels of the Park had ground on, as had, presumably, the wheels of Molly's chair.

The Dog in question: Tommo Doyle, Damien Cantor's 'man'.

This information had come her way when Diana had looked up Doyle's employment record on her return to the Park. Cantor's impertinent valediction, *How's Doyle working out?*, had been intended as a one-fingered salute, that was clear; Cantor was a show-off, a man-child, like most men, and clearly convinced of his own cunning. She'd checked the CCTV capture of his tourist outing, and he'd been wearing glasses and a windcheater. A disguise. No wonder Oliver noticed him. And all it was, she thought, was manspreading; he was pissing on a lamppost, marking territory. There was no shortage of such behaviour in this business, or any other; there were always men in the background, imagining they were centre stage. The newer variety, who were careful to keep their inner

Weinstein on a leash; older ones like Peter Judd, who wore their chauvinism like battlefield decorations; and uncategorisable miscreants like Jackson Lamb, who probably thought the glass ceiling was a feature in a Berlin brothel. She remembered, not long back, an uncharacteristically informal conversation with Josie, who worked on the hub. It's funny, Josie had remarked, how we always end up working round male insecurities. The Bechdel test gets flunked here on a daily basis. 'Our job is tackling crises and clearing up messes,' Diana had reminded her. 'That's pretty clearly going to involve discussing men.'

It was not beyond the bounds of probability, she now thought, that whatever Tommo Doyle had been up to that pissed off Molly Doran would lead back, like an unravelled clew, to Damien smugging Cantor.

There was an alcove just inside the archive room, a wheelchair-sized cubbyhole where she expected to find Molly, but it was currently vacant, and the room silent. You could not, she thought — Molly could not — navigate her way round here without a certain amount of mayhem; the aisles were surely too narrow for a wheelchair to manoeuvre freely. There would be caution, hesitation and stop/start calculation. Except there wasn't. What there was instead was a smooth cornering on near-silent wheels, and the sudden appearance of Molly Doran barrelling towards her, like Mr Toad in a fury.

She came to a halt with her front wheels a precise inch in front of Diana's toes.

'Very impressive,' Diana said drily.

'I practise a lot,' said Molly.

Diana stepped aside, and Molly executed a neat little three-point turn which left her precisely in her alcove.

'You registered a complaint,' Diana said, once Molly was stationary.

'I most certainly bloody did.'

'About Doyle.'

'I don't care what his name is. One of your security gorillas. I've told them before, and I'll tell them again, I won't have Dogs on my floor. Not even guide ones.'

Diana suppressed irritation. 'Might I ask why?'

'You might. I don't have any tea leaves to hand, so I've no idea what'll happen next.'

'If I don't get your cooperation pretty soon, I can sketch a fair idea of what your future will entail. If that helps.'

Molly thrust her jaw out. This was not an especially attractive look for her, though compiling a list of such looks would be a challenge: some time ago — Diana was guessing it was subsequent to the event that saw Molly consigned to a wheelchair — she had taken to making her face up in a manner only a little way short of being eligible for a clown's patent, if such things existed, and weren't an internet myth. Red cheeks, pale face, almost as thick as Kevlar. Her hair in tufts. A challenge to the world in general, though Diana was the wrong person to lay a challenge down in front of, unless you were prepared to see it bent in half and thrust into the nearest bin.

'They tend to be uncivil,' said Molly.

'And what form of incivility did this particular example display?'

'Trespass.'

'Any detail you want to add?'

'I found him poking around when I arrived one morning. Which meant he'd opened up and entered without my permission. Which would not, in any case, have been forthcoming.'

'The Dogs have access rights on all floors,' said Diana. 'Regardless of your personal antipathy. What was he doing?'

'Just checking things out,' Molly said. 'That was his story.'

'You didn't believe him?'

She said, 'He called me a crip.'

'He called you *what*?'

'I asked him to leave. He said he didn't take instructions from a crip.'

'And so you reported him.'

Molly nodded.

Diana looked around. They were the only people there, which would probably have been true at most times. The secrets Molly kept didn't burn with urgency; they lay like mantraps in overgrown patches of woodland. Long forgotten, most of them, but not yet rusted shut. When she looked back at Molly, the other woman's expression was a familiar one; it spoke of an extra layer of knowledge you hadn't drilled down to yet. Slappable, really, though that wouldn't be politic. Better to probe a little deeper. There weren't many options.

She said, 'You think he was blowing smoke.'

'Not at the time,' said Molly. 'At the time, I saw red. Big man, seen some action by the look of him. Could have thrown me, chair and all, from one side of the room to the other.'

'And strong men aren't bullies. Weak ones are.'

They both knew an exception to that rule, of course, but he was a study all to himself.

'But later, when I thought about it,' Molly said,

'after that moron from HR came to pacify me, it occurred to me, that's why he'd rolled the insults out. To stop me wondering what he'd really been doing.'

'You've checked for missing files?'

Molly didn't bother to laugh. 'I'll do that, when I have a decade to spare.'

'And all he'd need was a phone,' Diana finished. Ten minutes on his own in here, he could walk away with a hundred years of history in his pocket.

It was her own fault, or could be made to look like it was, which came to the same thing. Until a few months back, Head Dog had been one Emma Flyte, whose departure Diana had much enjoyed arranging once she'd come into her kingdom. Following this, there'd been a minor exodus from the ranks, three or four of Flyte's colleagues feeling the need to move on too. It wasn't a huge issue. Replacements were found.

And as the Dogs were frequently recruited from ex-forces personnel, a former SAS officer with private security experience would have been seen as a good fit.

She left Molly and took the lift back to the hub, her mind simmering. Josie was at her office door, the overnights in her hand: reports of incidents that had come in during the dark hours. 'Bullet points?'

'Nothing too troublesome. Surveillance updates on the Manchester lot, mostly.'

'I don't need to see them. I do need some coffee.'

'Ma'am.' Josie was about to head off, but remembered something. 'Oh, and a suspicious death. Horrible really. A fire in a shipping container.'

'Christ. Immigrants?'

'No. Just the one victim.'

'We're not the police force.'

'He used to be Park,' said Josie.

147

Catherine Standish refilled Lamb's bucket several times that morning: he didn't always drink tea, but when he did, it was an Olympic performance. Her first few visits he was occupied, which is to say, in one of his waking trances: unshod feet on his desk, hands clasped across his belly, open eyes directed at the ceiling. She knew better than to attempt communication. The fourth occasion, he glared at her as if reading her mind. This being so, she spoke it.

'You might have backed them up a bit.'

'Oh, shut up. I told Taverner not to fuck with my joes. She probably won't. But having them tailed by her L-plate muppets isn't full-on fuckery. More like heavy petting.' He hefted his mug. 'Besides, I told them about it, didn't I? And I don't imagine Dander will shrug it off.'

Catherine let that sink in. Then said, 'Somebody might get hurt.'

'I'm pleased you've grasped the essentials.' He took a magnificent slurp of tea. 'Besides, Taverner's heart's not in it. She's up to something, and it's not going well.'

'And this is a cause for rejoicing? We're all on the same side, remember?'

'Jesus, have you learned nothing? When they tell you to take it one day at a time, that doesn't mean do a memory wipe each morning.' He set the mug down. It couldn't possibly be empty yet. 'If we were all on the same side, we wouldn't have to watch our own backs.'

'We can't watch our own backs. We have to watch each other's.'

148

'That, sir, is arrant pedantry,' Lamb said, in a fair approximation of Winston Churchill. 'Up with which you can fuck right off.'

He was impossible in this mood, which was something it had in common with all his other moods.

Catherine said, 'What do you mean, Taverner's not going well?'

'I mean she might have made a mistake.'

'In picking on your crew?'

'Christ, no. That's a no-brainer. No, it's what she said last night, then pretended she hadn't. She's worried about something, and as she has no personal life, it's something to do with the Park.' He squinted at the ceiling. 'And off-book, or she'd not be worried. Anything in-house, she can blame on someone else.'

'You think she's running a black op?'

'Last time she tried that, heads rolled. Well, not rolled exactly. But definitely sat on a tabletop looking alarmed.'

'Thanks for the memory. What do you plan to do?'

'I plan to have a big lunch and a long nap,' said Lamb. 'But send Ho up first. Don't see why I should be the only one making an effort.'

★ ★ ★

The hotel was just off Kingsway, and was a discreet and mildly shabby concern, the kind of place where you might bring a hooker, but only if you were classy enough to pay for the whole night. Peter Judd collected his key at reception and asked if there was a kettle in the room. He gestured to the plastic bag he held, which was all the luggage he carried. 'I've brought my own biscuits,' he said, in a tone of self-congratulation

149

that implied that walking into a supermarket, grasping the general concept, and successfully walking out with a purchase was an achievement on a par with Prince Charles posting a letter by himself.

'All our rooms are provided with full amenities,' he was assured.

'I'm very glad to hear that,' he said. 'Whatever it means. Could you ring when my guest arrives?'

Which happened within the hour.

His guest was a man in early middle age, running to fat, and with sweaty jowls which weren't shaved too closely; less a style statement than lack of care. His hair hadn't been washed of late, and his shirt was too snug a fit for bystanders' comfort, so God knew what wearing it felt like. He looked round the room suspiciously before venturing inside; stood with the door hanging open behind him, like an exit strategy for dummies. Judd, who had arranged the two available armchairs in the centre of the room, was pouring boiling water into a teapot. 'Put wood in hole,' he said, in a comedy accent. 'That's what you northerners say, isn't it?'

'I'm from Hertfordshire.'

'Yes.' He carried the teapot to a small table on which he'd already placed two teacups and the now opened packet of biscuits. 'I didn't put them on a plate,' he said. 'I assumed you don't go for airs and graces.'

The man had closed the door at last, and at Judd's invitation took one of the two chairs.

'So,' said Judd, taking the other. 'Desmond Flint. Flinty. I presume your nickname comes from adding a Y, rather than from your unyielding nature?'

Flint just stared.

'Well, it cuts down on imaginative effort, I suppose,'

said Judd. 'Forgive me if I appear ill at ease.' He was as ill at ease as a cat in a basket. 'At Oxford I quite often encountered those who, ah, identified as working class. But what they meant was, they went to only a minor public school. Do you take milk? There are little tubs.'

'Why am I here?'

'To tell me what you're doing. What you think you're doing. With the, ah, you know. The Yellow Vests.'

'And why the hell should I do that?'

'Because there'll be something in it for you.'

Flint kept staring a moment longer, then shook off whatever grim spell he'd fallen under. His words, when they came, were greased by familiarity.

'It's the will of the people being frustrated over and over. These past few years, we've seen it happen time and again, election promises broken, Parliament dragging its feet before acting on what the people want. What they demand. These politicians, they're the servants of the people, right? So how come they get to decide what orders they do and don't carry out? All that has to come to an end. And that's what we're doing. Bringing it to an end.'

Judd waited until Flint was done, then clapped politely.

'You know what I like most about that? It's that you said sweet fuck all.'

'I was explaining — '

'No, you were saying words. But don't get me wrong.' He lifted the teapot and began pouring. 'That's all you need do right now. Say the words and make the noises. Nobody's really listening, they're just tapping along to the beat.'

'I'm listened to.'

151

'No. You're noticed, that's all. But that's nothing to worry about at this stage. There's a fine line between political notoriety and political respectability, and that's where you're balanced. A good starting point for a career.'

'If I was interested in political respectability, I'd have stood for election. And a fat lot of good that would have done.' Flint picked his teacup up, but put it down without drinking from it. 'We all know the system's rigged to favour Establishment voices. Of which you're one, by the way. So why should I be interested in anything you have to say?'

'Because I've been there and walked away from it,' said Judd smoothly. 'I know what it's like to occupy one of the great offices of state, and what it's like to feel   dissatisfaction — disillusionment — with   the process.' He oozed sincerity. 'I spent most of my life believing I could do good within the walls as they currently stand. But I came to recognise that there will always be those who will do everything in their power to maintain the status quo, even when that so obviously favours such a small section of society.'

'Fuck off.'

'Yes, that's a good point. Do help yourself to a biscuit.' He did so himself, and went on, 'You know, I don't get told to fuck off half often enough, given the bullshit I spout. On the other hand, I'm in PR now. If I weren't spouting bullshit, I'd not be doing my job.'

'What do you want?'

'To see how far I can push you.'

'In what way, push?'

'Up the greasy pole. To the summit. Any metaphor you care to employ. A metaphor is when you describe something as if it were something else.'

'Fuck off again.'

'See? We're getting along famously.'

Flint took a biscuit. 'There were rumours you had no choice but to go. All sorts of mischief going on behind the scenes.'

'That's primarily what scenes are for, old man. To cover up what's going on behind them. And the fact that you don't know that underlines how much you need me on your team. As for my departure from front-line politics, the truth? Yes, I was aiming for the top, and was prevented from reaching it. But that was then and this is now. And things are changing. In your own small way you're helping bring that about, though it would be happening anyway. It might be wise not to forget that.'

'There's change coming, you got that part right. Massive change. And long overdue.'

'Well now. Let's not overestimate its impact. When the Establishment crumbles, you know what'll replace it? The Establishment. There'll be new letterheads printed, that's all. And what I'm offering you is the opportunity to climb on board. You might as well. If not you, it'll be someone else.'

'Do you think you're being funny, mate? Because I don't have to just walk out, you know? I could knock your block off first.'

'I'm sure you could. You do look, if I have the terminology right, 'well hard'. But do either of those things, and at the very least you'll miss learning something you ought to know.'

Judd sipped tea again, and waited.

Flint had his hands on the arms of his chair, ready to get up. But he didn't.

Judd sipped more tea. Waited.

At last Flint said, 'Well?'

'The Secret Service have people in your organisation.'

'...We're not an organisation, as such.'

'Aren't you really? As such? But you have people doing things, don't you? You're having leaflets printed. Who's writing the copy? Who's arranging the printing? Who's sorting them into bundles — '

'Okay.'

' — and arranging their distribution? Who decides when and where you next do whatever it is you're going to do? And who decides what that is?'

'I said okay.'

Judd smiled benevolently. 'Even if you don't have a steering committee, you have decisions to make, and people helping make them. It's possible that among that number are some who are there specifically for the purpose of reporting your intentions to what I suppose we'll have to call the authorities. Or maybe they're just hangers-on, joining your gatherings. If so, you'll soon work out who they are. They'll be the ones encouraging the others to pick up a brick and throw it through a window. Or suggesting that instead of moving on nicely when Mr Policeman instructs, you have a go at him instead. *Agents provocateurs*, they're called. Like the posh knickers, and with the same outcome in mind.' He smiled. 'Someone's going to get fucked.'

'And you're saying that's me.'

'And by association, everyone who supports your movement.' Judd put his cup down. 'More? Sure? You don't mind if I do?' He poured. 'I may already have managed to curtail these covert activities. If not, I shall do so in short order. Meanwhile, let me return to my opening argument. Political respectability. It's not about being elected, it's about having a voice.'

154

'Oh, I have a voice. And it's being heard loud and clear.'

'Is it? Because as far as mainstream media goes, you're a joke. The rabble at the gates. All that muck-raking going on, digging up your CV. Non-payment of child support, some minor cases of affray. Mortgage fraud too, wasn't it?'

'That was a clerical error!'

'Oh, I'm sure. But the point is, that's what the headlines are saying every time your picture appears. But they're not painting you a yob just because you're a yob. They're doing it because they're frightened. What you need to do is make capital out of that fear.'

Flint was rubbing his stomach abstractedly. It looked very much like that was the sort of thing he did when concentrating, so was presumably already on Judd's mental list of stuff that would need sorting out. He said, 'What are you suggesting?'

'That I help,' Judd told him. 'I can put you next to the right people, who'll give you a fair hearing, and the opportunity to have your voice heard unaccompanied by editorial condemnation.'

'And?'

'And I'll make sure you're seen in the right places, and with the right company. At the moment you're on the news pages, and a punchline on panel shows. But once you start appearing in the diary columns, well. Then you're being taken seriously.' He put his cup down. 'Channel Go will do for starters. It has aspirations, and it's looking for someone to pin its colours to. If it decides to back you, that means you'll have got clout tomorrow you didn't have today. And if that happens often enough, you become an unstoppable force.'

'You make it sound easy,' said Flint. 'But what's in it for you?'

'Power.'

'That's very . . . frank.'

'I often am. Oh, I lie my teeth off like everyone else when it's in my best interests. But here and now, there's no point lying. Your movement may be going places, and I've never wanted to be on the wrong side of history. That being the losing side, of course.'

'And what if I decide I don't want your help?'

'Then I'll put the same effort into destroying you. But don't let that upset you. It's nothing personal.'

Flint was nodding, agreeing with some conclusion he'd just reached. 'I always thought you were just another posh dick. Like him in Number Ten. But you're a hard bastard, aren't you?'

'Yes,' said Judd. 'Also, my life's not a super-injunction. And the number of children I have is a matter of public record.'

'Out of interest — '

'I said public record. I didn't say I'd committed it to memory. I'll call this evening. Have an answer ready.'

And just like that he switched his attention off, as if Desmond Flint had already left the room.

★ ★ ★

'I should warn you,' said Shirley Dander. 'Last couple of times I teamed up with someone, they're both dead.'

' . . . Did you kill them?'

'Uh-uh.' She shook her head virtuously. 'I mean, I might kill Ho given the chance. But it hasn't come up.'

156

They'd bought enchiladas at Whitecross market and carried them up to the Barbican terraces; were eating perched on the concrete border of a dystopian-looking flowerbed. It struck Lech that this was the first time he'd shared a meal in months. Even half an hour ago, the notion would have sounded absurd. Shirley wasn't a friend. She was just a nearby occurrence, like a disturbing weather pattern.

He took a mouthful and scanned both directions. There was nobody watching that he could see. That, though, would be the point of the exercise.

Shirley said, 'Don't do that.'

' . . . What?'

'Let anyone know we know.'

He ran that through translation software. 'You spotted someone?'

Shirley shrugged. 'There was a guy at the market might have been following. But once you know someone's doing it, you see the bastards everywhere. Like mice.'

Lech thought of the mousetrap he'd once put in his bin, a little surprise for Roddy Ho, who'd been going through his rubbish. Good times.

He said, 'They must be tripping over each other, if we've all got a shadow. And won't they be wondering how come we all work in the same building?'

'So we're a building full of patsies. Besides, maybe they're doing us one at a time. Who knows? The fact they're doing it at all is what pisses me off.'

'Enough to 'team up' with the in-house pariah?'

Shirley scrunched her face into make-believe misery. 'Boohoo. I got caught watching kiddy porn. Poor me.'

'Fuck you, Dander. I didn't do that, never have,

157

never would.'

'Yeah.'

'Never.'

'Yeah. That's what Catherine said.'

He almost choked. ' . . . She said what?'

'That what happened with the kiddy porn was a plant. That you'd been framed. She didn't say why. Classified.' She made quote marks with her fingers to illustrate the word, and sprayed sauce onto Lech's trouser leg. 'Oh, sorry.'

He looked at the red splashes on his chinos, then at Shirley, cramming what was left of her lunch into her mouth. She rolled her eyes at him. *I said sorry.*

'You all know I was framed. Lamb too. And you all still treat me like shit.'

Shirley spoke through food. 'So you got a tough break. Doesn't mean we have to like you. You're kind of a prick most of the time.'

'For fuck's sake! I've had my whole life destroyed!'

'None of us are in our happy place.' She swallowed, then offered him her napkin. 'You could pour some water on that. Then dab at it.'

'It'll make it worse.'

'But at least you'll be doing something.' He made no move to take the napkin, so she wiped her mouth with it instead. 'Look. Shit happened. Join the club. Meanwhile, more shit is being dropped from a height by Regent's Park's pigeon squadron. You gunna lie back with your mouth open, or grab a bow and arrow?'

Lech resisted the temptation to rub at the stain on his trousers and rubbed his cheek instead. The scarring felt strange terrain still; as if he were wearing a mask, and kept forgetting about it. Or had woken to find himself taking part in a masquerade, or an armed

158

robbery. 'You're kind of a prick yourself,' he told her.

'Yeah, well,' said Shirley. 'You get used to it. Do you do coke ever?'

' . . . No. Well, sometimes. But no.'

'I wasn't offering. Just, there's a guy on one of the stalls down there, one of the Thai places? He's your man, you get the urge.'

He had the weird feeling this was Shirley's idea of a friendship offering. The pipe of peace. Three guesses what would end up in any pipe Shirley got hold of.

'Okay,' he said at last. The terrace was empty now, apart from themselves. Shreds of blue sky were showing through rips in the cloud canopy. 'What are you planning?'

Shirley said, 'Let's take one of the bastards down.'

★   ★   ★

River was in his office, having spent the day staring at his screen, or else through the window, which had planted a square of sunlight onto the vacant desk he shared the room with. It had once been where Sid Baker sat, and that remained its chief significance even during J. K. Coe's tenure, which hadn't been fair on Coe, but Slough House wasn't big on fairness. And now Sid was back. All this time, she'd been in the world, hidden away; partly erased but still breathing, waiting for the moment to appear to him, in his grandfather's study.

For months he'd been wondering what secrets might be preserved in that room, encrypted among a wealth of facts and fictions. Bringing them into the light would be a task for an archivist — a Molly Doran. He remembered sitting in the kitchen once,

159

watching his grandmother prepare a Christmas goose: this had involved removing its organs, which Rose had set about with the same unhurried calm she had approached most things, explaining as she did so the word 'haruspicate'. To divine the future from the entrails of birds or beasts. He'd planned the opposite: to unshelve those books, crack their spines, break their wings, and examine their innards for clues to the past. His grandfather's past, he'd assumed. Instead, what he'd found in that room was something broken off from his own life. Now read on.

Roderick Ho had been summoned to Lamb's presence after the meeting this morning, but was back in his own office now. You didn't have to be a spy in Slough House: the creaky staircases and unoiled doors offered clues as to who was where. When River went downstairs, he found that Ho had set his monitors up so they were angled towards him like a tanning device. PC pallor. From behind them, he squinted suspiciously at River.

'What's happening?' River asked.

'...Why?'

'Just curious.'

Ho shook his head. 'Uh-uh.'

'Lamb got you on some special mission?'

Ho's eyes narrowed, which River took as a yes. But then, Ho always thought whatever he was doing was a special mission, even downloading menus from local takeaways.

'Well, I've got one. When you're free.'

'I don't work for you.'

'None of us work for each other. We work *with* each other. As in, cooperate.' Ho looked like he was struggling with the concept, so River offered a clue.

'Like the Avengers?'

Ho rolled his eyes.

'No, really. I can just see you as Mrs Peel.'

'You called?'

This was Louisa, who'd followed River downstairs.

Ho said, 'I'm busy. Leave me alone.'

Louisa came and stood behind him, studied his screens. Ho made a half-hearted attempt to shield them with his arms, like a schoolboy in an exam, but not being an octopus, he was a few limbs short of a barricade.

She said, 'Uber records? Whose log are you hacking?'

'I'm not hacking it. I'm just looking.'

'Suppose I gave you a street name and a date,' River said. 'Told you that some people had been going door to door, saying they were missionaries.'

'What you on about?'

'I bet you couldn't tell me if they really were or not.'

Louisa said, 'Don't try to play him. He's too smart.' She pointed to one of the screens. 'D Taverner? You're running a number on Lady Di?'

Anything to do with Lady Di grabbed River's attention. 'This is for Lamb, right? What's he up to?'

'That's strictly need to know.'

'I bet you've always wanted to say that.'

Louisa was still reading the screen, though had to lean in close: a list of dates, a list of drivers, a list of journeys. 'The beginning of January.'

'That's the week we were wiped,' said River.

Ho did something, and the screens went blank.

'Ah, come on! I was reading that!'

'Get out of my room,' said Ho.

'What's all the noise about?'

161

And now Catherine had joined them.

'Miss! Miss!' said Louisa. 'Ho's using his computer to spy on people, miss!'

'I'm sure that's very funny,' said Catherine. 'But it's also noisier than Lamb likes it when he's awake. Which he will be if this goes on much longer.'

Ho said, 'Cartwright wants me to check up on some missionaries.'

Catherine raised an eyebrow in River's direction.

'Brief moment of spiritual crisis,' said River. 'I thought Roddy might be able to help. I'd forgotten he was a dick.'

'Delete your account,' Ho told him.

'You know Lamb's expecting the next batch of safe-house possibles by five?' Catherine said.

The list River was compiling, of properties which might potentially be utilised as hideaways by non-friendlies. It was intended to cover the entire country, a codicil River always spelled out word by word when reminding himself what his job consisted of.

The. Entire. Country.

'And he'll have it,' he said. 'Just taking a little down-time with my colleagues. Always a morale booster.'

'Careful,' said Catherine. 'If Lamb takes it into his head to appoint a morale officer, it'll make all our lives miserable.'

She left.

Louisa studied Ho's blank screens. 'Probably just as well,' she said. 'Not sure how you'd go about finding a pair of anonymous doorknockers.'

Ho rolled his eyes.

'I thought you said not to play him,' said River.

'You were playing him,' said Louisa. 'I'm just

signalling his limitations.'

'Yeah, right,' said Ho. His fingers danced, and the screens came back to life. 'Street name?'

River recited the postcode and date Sid had given him.

'Watch the magic happen.'

River and Louisa shared a glance.

'I'd as soon go boil the kettle,' Louisa said.

In the kitchen, River moodily opened cupboard doors and closed them again. An ancient bag of sugar, turned to stone; damp coffee filters. He collected the broken-off handle of a ceramic mug from an otherwise empty shelf and twirled it in his fingers. 'Do you ever wonder what you'd have ended up doing?' he said. 'I mean, if you'd just said fuck it when they offered you Slough House?'

'Oh, please.' Louisa was rinsing her cafetière. 'You do realise it's not about you?' she said. 'Sid being alive, I mean?'

'What's that supposed to mean?'

'It means she's not just a chapter in your life story. It would be an idea not to forget that.'

'You're supposed to be an intelligence officer. Not an agony column.'

'No one said I can't be both.' An idea struck her. River saw this happen: she paused, the wet cafetière in her hands. 'Sid thinks she's being targeted.'

'I know. I told you that.'

'Yeah, but so are we. Right? And she was a slow horse, or used to be. Did you know that Kay died?'

'Kay? Kay White?'

'Remember her?'

'She's the one never shut up,' said River. 'How did she die? She can't have been that old.'

163

'Fell off a ladder, Catherine said. Something like that, anyway. Some kind of accident. Easy to fake.'

River looked at the broken handle in his palm, then tossed it into the sink. It made a scattering noise. 'So what, you think they're not just stalking us, these Park trainees? You think they're knocking us off? That doesn't sound likely. And besides, Kay's not been one of us for years . . .'

His voice trailed away.

'Nor has Sid,' Louisa supplied.

They shared a look.

'What do you think?'

River said, 'It's out there. Way out there.'

'Yeah, but. A lot of the things that happen round here are.'

'The Park, though. Taverner? She'd not authorise anything like that.'

One of Lamb's saws came to mind, though. *All kinds of outlandish shit goes on.*

'We should take this upstairs.'

'No,' said River. 'I promised her I wouldn't.'

'Promised who?' Roderick Ho had appeared in the doorway.

'Nobody,' said River. 'What'd you find?'

Ho ignored him, and spoke to Louisa. 'Told you I could do it.'

'Actually,' said Louisa, 'you didn't. Not in words.'

'Same difference.' He slid past River and opened the fridge, where half a pizza sat, still in its box. He wormed it out, but left the box where it was. 'Seven tweeters in that postcode,' he said, closing the fridge door. 'Two mentioned people knocking on the door the morning you said.'

'It was me said it,' River put in helpfully. 'If that

matters.'

It didn't seem to. 'One said they were from the Latter Day Church of Heaven, and the other from the Latter Day Church of Christ the Redeemer. There's no such places. So the dudes weren't righteous, doesn't look like.'

'Is English your second language or your third?'

Ho scowled.

From upstairs came a familiar thump: Jackson Lamb wanting attention.

River said, 'He wants your download on Lady Di. What's that about?'

'It's below your pay grade,' said Ho, cramming his pizza into his mouth before heading up the stairs.

'Oh, happy day,' said Louisa. 'I want him to keep saying that forever.'

River said, 'So they weren't missionaries.'

'Wouldn't appear so.'

'Which means Sid was right. They were looking for her.'

'Possibly.' The kitchen had filled with the smell of fresh coffee, and for a moment Slough House was transformed. 'So it's like I said before. You need to take this upstairs.'

'The same upstairs using us as practice dummies?'

'I meant Lamb.'

River said, 'If we've been wiped, how come these guys know who to come looking for? If that's what's happening?'

She stared. 'You're not seriously suggesting Lamb has anything to do with it?'

'I don't know. I don't know anything. Except Sid's in danger.'

'And you plan to get all Jason Statham on it.'

165

'Tell Catherine I've been taken sick, would you? Must have been something I saw Ho eat.'

Before he could leave, she said, 'River?'

'What?'

'I don't want to lose anyone else.'

'When did the Stath ever get lost?'

'Well, he's made some pretty iffy career choices,' Louisa said, but River was gone.

★ ★ ★

Afternoons dragged, but this one was reaching its apex now; tipping into evening. This happened differently than up north, where Sid had spent the last few years; differently, too, from the way it happened in cities, where you could measure sunlight's decline against the buildings. Here there were trees that ought to perform the same function, but they were too variable to rely on, too prone to arbitrary movement, and seemed as if they might be capable of pushing the day on as their moods took them, ushering in the dusk with their gently waving limbs.

They were best watched from upstairs. Sid had told River she stayed in the study, but that wasn't true. Obviously, she had to use the bathroom, and while these were brief furtive visits, tarried over no longer than necessary to get the job done, there were also times, like now, when she'd climb the stairs to the master bedroom, which had a view of the lane that wound through the trees. This was surprisingly well maintained, given its negligible importance. Eventually it joined forces with a larger road, which in turn fed into a motorway, which in turn became London. All these miles distant, that was a barely

166

imaginable turbulence. Here, in rural stillness, there was a house next door, separated by a generous strip of garden and a bossy hedge; that aside, the next dwelling was a hundred yards down the lane. Before reaching it, you could cut off along a footpath, which took you to the village. She knew all this from a map she'd found in the study. There were other footpaths, dotted lines; you could tear along them, and rip the countryside to shreds. Scatter the pieces like leaves in a wind.

Tonight, anxiety had drawn her upstairs. Being alone all day skewed her emotional thermostat. The continual silence oppressed her, yet any unexpected noise — a passing lorry, passing voices — would have her crouching against a wall, waiting for it to subside. And then she'd find herself stroking the rift in her skull, wondering how much of her identity, of Sidonie Baker, had been carved away by that bullet's passage. She had never been one to cower against walls. That was something the bullet had left her with; a whole new character trait, conjured out of pain and confusion.

There wasn't much pain, to be fair. There were occasional blinding headaches that came from nowhere and vanished just as suddenly, but they were happening less often. But her dreams had altered character, and made sleep bizarre and unrewarding. The bullet itself would appear to her, taking on the shape of a white-suited Belgian with an asymmetrical moustache. It had taken an unfeasibly long while for Sid to deduce that this was Hercule Poirot. *Your little grey cells, non?* he would twinkle. *So many of them, how you say*, smeared *on the pavement. Tt Tt Tt.* This vowelless admonition would recur during her waking hours. It

167

was her fault, was what he meant. *You got in my way.*
Tt Tt Tt.

The bullet had been removed from her head in the hours that followed the shooting. But it remained there nevertheless; her deadly passenger, with her for the long haul.

The sky grew darker and the world through the window dimmed. Before coming upstairs she had cut a slice from the loaf River had brought, and wrapped it round a hunk of cheddar. Bread, cheese. She supposed River had other things to do than plan menus, but still. That could be something to tease him about when he turned up, teasing being something requiring forethought now. If she were to re-enter her old life she'd need more than a map of the neighbourhood, which was illuminated suddenly, the neighbourhood not the map, by a pair of headlights slicing crescent shapes out of the dusk, briefly rendering bright the room: its bare painted walls, its curtainless window frame. She stopped chewing. The car wasn't River's, but it slowed anyway, and came to a halt on the verge. The engine died. Something inside Sid woke and fluttered. The car would move on soon. It would start up, drive away, and before long River would arrive, and she'd tease him about the bread and cheese.

Tt Tt Tt, said Hercule Poirot in her head. *Tt Tt Tt.*

But the car didn't move. Instead its doors opened and two people got out, a man and a woman she recognised. They had knocked on her door in Cumbria, dressed as missionaries, and here they were, come to kill her again.

All down the lane the trees shifted as a gust of wind rifled through them. If she were out there she'd hear them sigh as they moved, but from inside the house,

168

it was a silent blessing they bestowed. Their jobs were done, and night had fallen, and it seemed to Sid they were waving goodbye.

Part Two
Chasing Tails

7

They called it Silicon Roundabout, because of the tech firms clustered in its orbit, and from this end of Old Street, at the top of the sloped passage dropping into Subway 3, the landscape it commanded was a familiar London medley of the weathered and the new; the social housing estate and the eye hospital balancing the swollen glass bulb of what Lech thought was a hotel, and the complicated facade of an office block straight from an SF comic. Over the roundabout itself, part-shrouded in builders' canopy, hung a four-sided video screen, scrolling through an endless cycle of ads for the Pixel 3a, but looking as if it wanted to be broadcasting something more in keeping with the times: cage-fighting, or Rollerball, or a party leadership hustings.

They'd waited out the worst of the evening crush in a nearby pub; one blessed with a good location, relieving it of the necessity of making an effort. Lech's small red wine lasted forty minutes, during which Shirley had drained two pints of lager and explained, for reasons that escaped him, the various kinds of body-modelling on offer within a two-hundred-yard radius: tongue-splitting, ear-pointing and tunnelling, this last involving opening holes in earlobes large enough to ease a pencil through. Lech wasn't sure he hadn't preferred being ignored. Through windows partly obscured by promises aimed at passers-by — *Good Food! Happy Hour 5–7!* — he watched office workers heading for bus stop or underground.

There'd been a touch of rain in the air, a dampness on the pavements, and he wondered whether his raincoat was still on a hook in the flat he'd shared with Sara, and whether falling in with Shirley's mischief was a wise idea, and whether doubling the length of an hour made it twice as happy, or only half.

'So anyway,' Shirley said, 'I was thinking of getting my ears sharpened. What do you reckon?'

He reckoned Lamb would love that, possibly to the point where it triggered one of his seismic coughing fits. 'Sounds cool. Go for it.'

She looked pleased. 'Maybe I will.' Then checked her watch: 'Okay. Time to go.'

Lech decided to give the last mouthful of wine a miss. He stood and, when she didn't follow suit, gave her a questioning look.

'Don't worry,' she said. 'I'll be there.'

But she wasn't, or not that Lech could see. Collar upturned, he strode down the passage towards Subway 3 and turned into the underground complex that always felt to him like a colosseum, though whether that made its commuters gladiators or lion fodder was open to question. Down here, a few timid retail premises huddled; the kind that looked like they'd not survive ten minutes in the open air. On the other hand, stranger weeds flourished in London's cracks and crevices. He walked past bookshop, card shop, coffee shop, key cutters; skirted a post-box-sized screen reeling through the same ads as its monster parent overhead, and noted without pausing a sign announcing Subway 2's refurbishment. What had been its entryway was boarded over, and he could hear drilling. There were still people around, mostly heading into the Tube station, but he carried on by, veering right towards Subway 1 — the Hox-ton/Shoreditch exit — past sandwich shop and flower shop, whose brief fragrance was a shower of light in the dark. At the far end he took the stairs up to ground level, where he doubled back past the gated entrance to the housing estate then, without looking behind, made a 180-degree turn onto the slope heading back to the subway. Overground, underground. Nobody paid attention that he could tell, but he was careful not to check. He didn't see Shirley anywhere, either.

And what were the odds, he wondered, back in the underground colosseum, that this was some bastard prank; that the others had already joined her in the pub, where they were busting a gut over his gullible goose chase?

. . . Fuck them, he thought.

But not quite yet. Fuck them in ten minutes; maybe fuck them in twenty. Because he didn't have anything else to occupy him, and he'd always been a walker after dark, Lech Wicinski; a long-time stroller of the empty streets.

And if these streets weren't exactly empty, or entirely streets, they'd do for now.

★ ★ ★

I suppose you're wondering why you're gathered in the library.

That was Hercule Poirot speaking: the memory of her bullet, deep inside her brain.

And she was indeed gathered in the library, if that was what hiding in the study amounted to. But other suspects were nowhere. It was just Sid alone, and whoever was outside.

175

She'd come downstairs while they were on the garden path, and now sat with her back against the closed study door, the doorbell dying away. Nothing sounds louder than a bell in an empty house. Her heart was fluttering, her insides clammy. The study was in darkness. *Nobody here.* The bell rang again, then once more. And then the flap on the letterbox jangled, and she imagined the pair taking it in turns to drop to one knee and peer into the hallway.

Life went quiet again, the only disturbance the faint rattling of a doorknob.

In a perfect world, they'd have gone away. But in a perfect world, Sid wouldn't have been shot in the head.

There was a shelf in the study devoted to objects rather than books. This had struck Sid as strange. She hadn't known the O.B. — which was what River had called him, so it was hard for her not to — she hadn't known the O.B., but had known who he was, and it was difficult to imagine the Service legend, the man who'd steered the ship during the captaincy of various First Desks, as collecting knick-knacks. A glass globe; a hunk of concrete; a lump of mis-shaped metal. But that was how lives worked, as a slow accretion of private detail, and what mattered more was whether these objects would make useful weapons. She supposed they might, if the wielder was in decent shape. Which she wasn't, but this didn't stop her taking one in her hand, a pleasingly heavy glass globe, with just the thinnest slice removed to allow it to stand. It contained nothing. She might have expected a butterfly wing, or a whispered fragment of autumn — a leaf, a pebble — but it was only glass and weight. Crouched against the door, she cradled it in both hands, allowing herself to believe that it anchored her to the world.

Which worked up to a point, but that point was reached when she heard the tapping on the back door.

★ ★ ★

There'd been a tourist, a year or two back, who'd been separated from his party in the underground, and it was three and a half days before they found him. It was so nearly a classical myth, it wasn't even funny. Lech was starting to recognise the feeling. He turned into Subway 4 — St Luke's/Clerkenwell — passed the public toilets and turned left, up the slope, beneath its pedestrian bridge, and arrived for the fifth time at the plaza, with its trees and benches and flowerbeds, its ranks of e-bikes. The rain was holding off still, and there were fewer people. It was that lull between the end of the working day and the start of a weeknight's drinking; less frantic than the weekend version, but not without its panicky framework. Sometimes you clung onto the edges of a day because what went on in the middle ate away at your soul. Sometimes it was the other way round. Lech shook his head, dispelling the notion that his days held no safe places, and kept walking: past the appalling mural, stags and druids, and back down the stairs into the half-light.

And there he was again.

First time Lech noticed him he'd been wearing a grey mac. He was now wearing a black one, but its lapels were open enough that Lech could see the grey lining: a reversible, a swift and handy costume change. He'd been wearing specs earlier too, and wasn't now. Didn't matter. Lech had his number. Kept it to himself, though; didn't let it show in change of pace or curl of lip as he reached the central area and looped back towards Subway 3: Moorgate and Old Street West (South Side). He was starting to feel as if he could draw the colosseum freehand, and people the result with sasquatch figures, lumpen and drooling.

He climbed the stairs, waited a full two minutes, then headed for the slope and walked back down. Give his tail time to start wondering if he'd got lost in the surrounding streets.

The crowd was thinner. Still no sign of Shirley, and he was now about eighty per cent sure she'd been playing him, and would spend the rest of the week, or maybe her life, laughing herself sick whenever she passed him on the stairs: *sucker spent an evening circling Silicon Roundabout.* He supposed that meant he'd have to retaliate, which would no doubt lead to massive escalation. Well, everybody had to die sometime. When he passed the central pillar he spotted his tail again, his mac black side out, and without pausing to study him, Lech registered relief in his body language. Good good. He thought he'd messed up, and allowed Lech to get away. For now — for the next minute or so — he'd overcompensate by keeping him in sight, or that was the theory.

Lech remembered that feeling, those moments during training when you knew you'd screwed up, and wondered if this was the one that would tip the balance; lead to the brief interview where you were thanked for your time, and assured that there were plenty of avenues that someone with your talents might usefully explore. Landscape gardening or life insurance. Maybe something in IT. But Regent's Park wasn't in your future, or a subject you'd ever talk about again. *Sign here, please.*

To this kid here, that probably felt like the worst of

all possible outcomes. But trust me, thought Lech, as he walked back along Subway 4 — trust me — that's not the worst that can happen.

Instead of reaching the end and heading street-wards, he turned into the public toilet.

* * *

The tapping paused, as if a reply were expected. When none came, it started again.

And perhaps, if she stayed very still, this would stop happening. But that was frightened-animal thinking; the instinct that freezes a rabbit in a road. This rarely causes cars to disappear.

The study curtains were open. She'd tried the windows the day before, hoping to let the room breathe, but they were locked, and she hadn't found a key. An image of throwing herself through them came and went, a scene from a film, which in real life would leave her in bloody rags on the lawn.

And she couldn't call River. Her phone was in the cottage in Cumbria, or that was where she'd last seen it. When you went dark, your phone was the first thing you ditched.

Can't call for help; can't dash for safety.

This was what got rabbits killed.

She'd been padding about in socks, but her trainers were under the O.B.'s chair. Relinquishing the globe she crawled across to reach them, pulling them on and lacing them up in a supine position. Wearing them gave her a small measure of comfort; an extra protective layer. *Tt Tt Tt* said the bullet. As well as being the voice of Poirot it was the voice of reason, it seemed. Eager to remind her that any notion of safety was balls.

The tapping paused.

Sid risked a look at the window from behind the bulk of the chair. She saw nobody; just the waving shadow of a tree: *goodbye*. It might have been her heart playing tricks.

But it happened again.

Only it wasn't a tapping now; more a squeaking, like someone rubbing a finger against glass. The back door had a glass pane, she remembered. A glass pane in a wooden frame. And she had locked the door after River's departure last night because that was what you did when you were hiding; you locked doors. Even doors with glass inserts, which you didn't have to be an expert to find your way through; merely someone with a disregard for damage.

The squeaking stopped, and was replaced by a circular, scratching sound.

The glass globe might be a weapon. Or the lump of reshaped metal. Once a Luger, River had explained. Wartime details were involved in what followed. Now it was redesigned by Dalí, and all she had to load it with was the memory of a bullet. *Tt Tt Tt*. From the back of the house came a brief splintering, as glass dropped to the tiled floor. The ex-gun felt complicated in her hand; she could make out what might once have been the barrel, now curled in upon itself like a sleeping lizard, but its trigger had been swallowed up inside the metal mass. There was a clicking noise which she interpreted as the unfixing of the back door's latch, a hand reaching through a broken pane to release the sneck. 'Sneck': a word she'd acquired up north. A faint brushing sound as the door opened, sweeping shards of glass aside. If she could solve the gun, remind it what it used to be, she would not be defenceless. The air in the house shifted, a rearrangement she could feel even in the study. She listened for footsteps, two pairs. But they'd creep, she thought. She wouldn't hear them now they were in the house. Missionaries creep.

If she could remind herself what she used to be, she would not be defenceless.

The silence grew closer, as if the effort someone was making to be quiet were inching through the house.

It stopped outside the study door.

★ ★ ★

As long as he was there, Lech shut himself in a cubicle and had a piss.

This is my working life, he thought. Used to be an intelligence analyst — one of the hub's best and brightest — and now I'm in a stinking public lavatory, hoping one of my own side makes a pass. Such was the view from Slough House.

He finished, flushed, but instead of stepping out to wash his hands leaned against the door and pressed his ear to it. The noises from the subway were muffled, abstract, aquarium-like. How many men had stood where he was now, hoping for strange encounters? He closed his eyes and thought about focaccia. Imagined thumping dough: punching it over and over, only to watch it rise.

Someone entered the toilet.

'We want their ID,' Shirley had said, back in the pub. 'Their Service card, their wallet, their phone. Hell, their pocket change and their door keys too. Fuck 'em.'

'These are agents in training,' Lech had said. 'They'll be sharp. In good nick.'

'I'm in good nick.'

You're fucking high, he'd nearly said. The way she was jiggling in her seat, he'd have to scrape her off the ceiling soon. Two pints of lager had done nothing to bring her down.

The state she'd been in, he was better off on his own.

Whoever had come into the toilet was using the urinal. Lech rested his forehead against the back of his hand. The man finished, crossed the floor, ran a tap. Lech heard a paper towel pulled from the dispenser; the rustling of hands being dried. Then nothing. No footsteps; no breathing. Just a man in a public toilet, possibly holding a damp paper towel. A man in a black mac, he thought. Reversible to grey.

He opened the door, suddenly and loud, and stepped out of the cubicle.

The man was right up in front of the mirror, pulling at the corner of an eye, as if he had something in it. Maybe he did, maybe he didn't — it was a pretty obvious dawdling tactic — but what was certain was, he wasn't the man in the mac, unless he'd changed his coat in the last five minutes, and also his head. When Lech appeared he left his eye alone, and watched as Lech, after a brief hesitation, came forward and rinsed his hands.

'It's polite to flush,' he said.

'Already did.'

' . . . Right.' The man rubbed his eye again. He was staring into his own reflection when he said, 'Looking for company?'

'Go away.'

'Because this isn't the place.'

'I said go away.'

'There are websites, you know. Apps.'

'Fuck off,' said Lech.

The man dropped his paper towel in the bin. 'I'm only saying. Get with the century, right? Unless you're into this scene.'

Footsteps were approaching.

'Gotta go.'

He left as the man with the black mac stepped through the door into the gents.

★ ★ ★

She was called Jane. He was called Jim.

Surnames were not offered.

'But you're Sidonie Baker, yes? Sid to her friends.'

'Which we hope to be.'

'Oh, very much so.'

It had had an air of inevitability about it, the way the study door had opened and the couple had come in. They might have been prospective buyers, and the house a property on their list: good, airy rooms; a little question mark over the water table. So what did that make Sid, whose name they so handily knew? Their estate agent?

'River will be here soon,' she told them. 'River Cartwright.'

'That's good. But we'll be gone by then. We move quickly.'

'Do you have a coat, Sid? Or a jacket? It's not too warm out.'

'Still a little early in the year.'

Jane was blonde and Jim dark, though viewed from

183

this distance, rather than from — say — an upstairs window, neither convincingly so. Sid suspected artifice, an hour in a hotel bathroom with a packet from the nearest Superdrug. They were dressed the same as the first time she'd seen them, white shirts under dark jackets and coats, and their voices were bright and well-practised. They might not be working to a script, but they were improvising the dialogue for a planned scenario, and if the effect was a little laboured, well, what could you expect from bad actors?

'I'm not going anywhere,' she said.

'You need to reconsider that,' said Jane.

'You're not well,' Jim explained. 'Don't you remember? You were being taken care of, in a very nice place, but you left early. You're still getting those headaches, am I right?'

'And they're going to get worse without treatment,' said Jane.

'So what we'll do is, we'll leave a note for your Mr Cartwright, tell him where we're taking you so he can come visit.'

'But the sooner we get you there, the better.'

'Traffic can be murder.'

'How did you know I was here?' she said.

'Well, we popped next door, had a word with the nice lady.'

'That's the thing about the country, isn't it? People taking notice of what's going on around them. This was a city, you could be living here months, nobody would even know your name.'

'Years, even.'

'Like Jane says. Years.'

'Is this yours?'

Jane had found Sid's jacket, draped over a chair.

'You might want to put that down. It looks like a heavy nuisance.'

Sid looked at the aimless gun in her hand. Stupid choice of weaponry; like going into battle wielding a holiday souvenir.

Tt Tt Tt.

The noise it made hitting the carpet was a faint echo of assault.

'Good girl,' said Jim.

'Now here's what we do,' Jane said. 'We all get into the nice warm car out there, and we head back to where you can be taken care of. Somewhere you should never have left in the first place.'

Sid found her voice. 'You're not from there. From the farm.'

'No, dear. But we're who they call when they need someone brought back.'

'Runaways.'

'Like yourself.'

She could make it as far as the door, she thought. Or maybe not all the way to the door. She could make it most of the way to the door, and then Jim would have her. Unless Jane had her first.

Use your little grey cells, ma chère.

The ones she still had left, her bullet meant.

'Or you could keep running,' Jane told her. She stooped to pick up the metal lump, and caressed it for a moment while looking at Sid. 'You could run next door, even. Tell the nice lady we're taking you somewhere horrid.'

She replaced it on the shelf.

'But she won't believe you,' said Jim. 'On account of, we've already had a chat with her.'

'And she knows you're unstable,' said Jane. 'Apt to

185

injure yourself.'

'Save anyone else the trouble.'

'So best not make a fuss. Here, put your jacket on.'

It makes, how you say, the good sense, her bullet said.

Because she wouldn't get as far as the door.

Jim was holding her jacket for her to slip her arms into. *Be Villanelle, be Lara Croft.* But she remained Sidonie Baker, and he remained unaware of any other possibility. Allowing herself to step backwards into his nearly embrace, she felt the jacket swallow her up.

'All ready?' Jane asked.

You are, how you say, fucked, said the bullet.

Jim opened the door with a butler's flourish, and ushered Sid through it. Let's take the back door, he suggested, in such a smooth undertone it barely required speech marks. Jane, leaving last, extinguished the lights. There was a circular hole in the back door's pane, an expertly removed slice of glass through which one or other had reached to unlock the door and gain entrance. Exit was more easily achieved. As they led her to the car, Sid stared at the neighbour's house, what was visible of it behind its screen of hedge. There were lights on, but no signs of movement. She hoped they had done nothing to harm her, the neighbour lady. There was no reason why they should, of course. But recent history spoke of collateral damage; of disregarded shrapnel ripping holes through innocent lives. If there were such a thing any more, thought Sid, as an innocent life — but that thought felt way too heavy; felt like a thought for a final journey. She sat in the back, Jim next to her. The seat belt was too tight, but she made no attempt to adjust it. Some things, you learned to live with.

186

And now would be a good time to punch this man in the head.

This was principally because he was having a piss: one of the top three moments of attention being elsewhere. Except he was being remarkably quiet, so was either pretending or was one of those types — which included Lech — who couldn't urinate with a stranger nearby. So maybe he was ready for an incoming blow, and would twist aside the moment Lech launched his attack, leaving Lech with one of those cartoon wounds you get from punching a concrete wall: a throbbing boxing glove of a hand, pulsing in time to a muted trombone.

Also, Lech was more a strategy man, or had been back at the Park: gathering data, making observations; occasionally getting very particular about finicky details. Putting the anal into analyst. When someone needed punching, there were numbers he could call. It wasn't about being a wuss; it was about playing to your strengths. And besides, if he'd got it wrong, and this guy was a civilian, punching him in the head wouldn't go down well. A thing about Slough House, it wasn't so much a last-chance saloon as an out-of-options off-licence. Any mistake you made would be your last inside the Service, and punching a shy stranger in the head in a public toilet probably counted.

So instead of getting physical, Lech said, 'Busted.'

The man didn't turn round. '. . . You what?'

'I said, you're busted.'

'No idea what you're talking about, mate. Do you mind? I'm trying to have a piss.'

'You're Park. You're supposed to tail me without being spotted. But guess what? You've been spotted.'

187

The man in the mac either finished pissing or finished pretending he'd been pissing or gave up trying to piss altogether. He zipped up and turned, looking Lech in the eye. 'Don't know what your game is, but find someone else to play it with, yeah? Because keep bothering me, and you'll end up head first down one of those, get me?' He gestured towards the urinal behind him. 'Head first,' he repeated, and made hard shoulder contact as he headed for the door.

Reasonably convincing, Lech thought, and time was he'd have stepped aside and assumed he'd made a mistake, or at least allowed for the possibility. But that was back when his face was still the one he'd grown up with; before it resembled a five-year-old's drawing of a railway junction.

ID, Service card, wallet and phone.

Pocket change and door keys too.

Fuck 'em.

'You haven't washed your hands,' he said.

'Piss off,' said Black Mac, and Lech threw his punch.

It was an uppercut, without a huge amount of force behind it, and his target was the side of Black Mac's head, offering the chance that his hand would come off worst. All in all, though, it wasn't a bad punch, maybe a five out of ten, and could have been a seven or eight if it had made contact. As it was, he missed by a couple of centimetres, as Black Mac jerked his head aside, giving the distinct impression that being attacked by strangers was not entirely outside his range of experience. Better trained; in better nick. Or just better. You couldn't rule it out.

Then he hit Lech twice in quick succession, both times in the stomach, and Lech staggered backwards, crashing through a cubicle door and only remaining upright by bracing himself against the walls with out-stretched hands, essentially offering a full-body target for the next blow. Which, it turned out, was a real beauty; the kind you'd find yourself thinking about on waking for the next few months, and observing its anniversary by hiding your head under a pillow and weeping quietly.

Luckily for Lech it was Shirley delivering it, and Black Mac on the receiving end.

* * *

When River arrived the house was dark, like a line from a rock and roll song. He parked on the verge, noticing fresh ruts where another vehicle had lately stopped. Might be something, might be nothing, but instead of collecting the shopping from the back seat — he'd brought bread, cheese; a few other things Sid might like — he headed straight for the house, going round the back. The door was unlocked. Also, there was a hole in the glass — neatly engineered rather than hooligan breakage.

'Sid?'

The empty house replied in its usual fashion.

'Sid!'

Pointless, now, to essay stealth, so he charged through the hall, a memory of Rose's complaint — *Don't run in the house, darling* — rising from the tiles. The study was in darkness. Sid had been here — her blanket was puddled on the floor; there was a half-full glass of water next to a spread-eagled book — but wasn't now. River ran upstairs, in and out of empty rooms. Bare walls stared from every direction.

189

Back in the study he collected himself, and tried to remember his training. There was no sign of conflict, merely of interruption, though the large glass paper-weight presented to the O.B. on his retirement had found its way to the floor. He picked it up, surprised as always by its weight; peered into it for answers before replacing it on its shelf. Wherever Sid was, she had taken her jacket; also her shoes. If people had come for her, would they have bothered about those details? But then, if people had come for her, it was a racing certainty next door's sentinel would know about it. The thought, the deed, the space between the two: he was banging on Jennifer Knox's door within seconds.

'Oh dear. Oh dear oh dear oh dear.'

'I'm sorry. I didn't mean to — '

'So *late*.'

It wasn't late, was barely eight, but darkness was threading its way through the local lanes, and the neighbourhood nestling down like a pigeon.

'Mrs Knox, I'm sorry, I wouldn't disturb you if it wasn't an emergency, but I really need to know, were there callers next door? Did a car come?'

'Is this about your friend?'

'About my friend, yes.'

'She went off in the car with the other two. Just five minutes ago.'

'Which other two?'

'The couple from' — her voice lowered a notch — 'the hospital.'

'Okay,' said River. 'When you say a couple . . . '

'A man and a woman, yes.'

'In a car.'

'It was silver, I think. Or white. It's hard to tell with the street lights.'

190

She backed away from the front door, ushering him in. He stepped inside, leaving the door open. He would need to leave in a hurry. Would need no obstacles.

But Mrs Knox was heading into her sitting room. 'Would you close that, please? Keep the warm in?'

He pushed it to, and followed her. 'Did they say where they were going?'

'They said she wasn't well. Did I do the right thing?'

'Did they say where they were going?'

'Only she's been there days, and doesn't come out at all. And I thought the house had been cleared? What's she been sleeping on?'

'Mrs Knox — '

'They looked surprised when I said she was in there. They thought the house was empty.'

He took a moment to wrap his mind around that. They'd come looking for Sid, but hadn't expected to find her? Or hadn't been looking for Sid at all?

'But they knew who I meant when I said you had a friend staying.'

'And did they say where they were going?'

She furrowed her brow.

'Mrs Knox — '

'Please, I can't bear to be badgered.'

'I'm sorry, but it's important. I really need to know where they were taking my friend.'

'They said they'd be taking her back to the hospital. And that I shouldn't worry if she seemed upset, because she'd been off her medication for a while.'

'Did you see them leave?'

'You didn't tell me she'd been on medication. It's only fair to let people know.'

'I'm sorry.' Various stories flew in and out of mind:

191

harmless conditions requiring minor dosages. But all of this was wasting time. 'Do you know which direction they went?'

'I'm not sure, which way's the hospital?'

River said, 'There are different routes. I really need to catch up with them. Which way —'

She said, 'Down the road. Not towards the village, I mean. Else their lights would have shone through my curtains.'

Which weren't pulled shut, not entirely. There was a slight gap, in front of which a small table was positioned, a note-pad and pen waiting. Seeing this, River had a view of Mrs Knox's life as clear as if it were spotlit; saw the heart of her empty days. Without asking, he crossed the room and picked the notebook up.

'What on earth are you —'

XTH???

'That's private!'

'Was this the number plate? Part of it?'

'I'm not some kind of snoop!'

'I really don't care. Was this the number plate?'

She said, 'I live here alone, you know.'

XTH???, which he could easily remember, but didn't need to. 'Sorry,' he said, though he wasn't. He ripped the page from its spiral spine.

'You can't do that!'

But he could, and had. He thanked her, or apologised, or supposed afterwards he'd done at least one of the two. He didn't close the door behind him, either, in his rush to reach his car; a memory etched into his mind as he pulled away showed Mrs Knox framed in an oblong of light on her doorstep. She might have been wringing her hands.

'So what happened to you?'

Shirley shrugged. 'What did it look like? I was waiting for you to draw him into the net.'

'I didn't see you anywhere.'

'You weren't supposed to.'

And besides, he'd have needed super-vision, since Shirley had been half a mile away, having decided to lose her own tail before tackling Lech's. Northern Line to King's Cross seemed a good bet, and had almost certainly been successful, in that Shirley had grown confused changing platforms, resulting in a brief, unexpected excursion to Mornington Crescent. She hadn't noticed anyone else making the same tortuous journey, so assumed her follower was currently heading wherever the Northern Line went. Unless nobody had been following her in the first place. That was the trouble with this bullshit training game the Park was playing: nobody told you when it started, and when or if it stopped.

Once back at Old Street, she'd hovered by the station barriers, then walked a circuit — underground, overground — without spotting Lech, let alone his tail. So she decided she needed a little sharpener, just to keep her edges shiny, and headed into the toilets to do a line, which was when she'd heard Lech's voice coming from the gents.

But all he needed to know was that she'd been there when the chips were down.

She made a sideways gesture with a flattened hand. 'Moves like Wonder Woman.'

They were in a pub again, a different one, having left the colosseum by separate routes and regrouped on a

193

side street off Shoreditch High. Black Mac — whom Shirley had rendered comatose with a small leather sap — was last seen propped on a toilet, outstretched legs keeping the cubicle door closed.

He won't die, had been Shirley's considered opinion. And okay, she wasn't a medic, but she had considerable pharmaceutical expertise.

Lech was twitchy, his eyes flicking doorwards every time it opened. You'd think he'd never beaten up a stranger in a toilet before. And when she'd showed him the sap, he'd actually groaned.

'Put that away. It's a deadly weapon.'

'I'll just say it's a sex aid.'

'Still probably arrestable.'

She'd been interrupted in her earlier mission, so headed for the loo before she'd finished her first pint, and returned brighter-eyed, bushier-tailed, then dumped the contents of Black Mac's pockets on the table.

'For fuck's sake,' Lech hissed, scooping keys and phone up and transferring them to his pocket. 'Why don't you just hoist a banner? 'Muggers R Us'?'

'Nobody's watching.'

'You hope.' He thumbed through the wallet while Shirley took a few life-enhancing draughts of lager. She'd been in this pub before. Shoreditch was her stamping ground, though she might have to expand that definition. Stamping and bopping-on-the-head. She examined her fingers, which were a little tingly. Nothing gets the sap moving like swinging a sap . . . She thought about sharing this with Wicinski, but it was maybe too soon. He'd gone green when Black Mac hit the deck.

And now he said, 'You know what I'm not finding?'

'What?'

'A Service card.'

'Yeah, check again.'

'I already did.'

'Well, maybe he had it in his trouser pocket. I might have missed it.'

'Or he didn't have one.'

'Or he left it at home.'

'You ever do that?'

She didn't. Her card was as good as sewn onto her body: there was always the chance she'd need to flash it at a copper making a drugs bust, or use it to impress someone. Which she hardly ever did, by the way. Maybe twice.

Lech said, 'What if he wasn't the tail?'

'He probably was.'

'But what if he wasn't?'

'What's his ID say?'

There were credit cards in the wallet, their user name D Walker. Nothing with a photo on it. And no Service card.

Lech said, 'He was wearing a reversible mac. He changed it while I was doing a loop. So I wouldn't notice he was hanging around.'

'There you go. Definitely a tail.'

'Unless I got that wrong. Maybe he had it black side out all along.'

'So what was he up to?'

'Waiting for someone?'

'So why'd he follow you into the toilet?'

'Because he needed a piss,' Lech said. Then: 'Jesus, what have we done?'

'Worst case scenario,' Shirley said, 'we've decked a civilian.'

'And stolen his wallet and phone.'

'Yeah, that too.'

'This is serious!'

Which it was, but you had to see the funny side was Shirley's take. And you could trace the culpability right back to Regent's Park, if you wanted to get technical.

On the other hand, if you wanted to get evidential, you could trace it back to Shirley's leather sap.

Lech said, 'I'm not exactly unrecognisable.'

'Neither am I,' offered Shirley.

'Yes, but he didn't see you.'

Shirley thought about that. 'You might be in some shit.'

'Thanks.'

She looked at the booty on the table. 'Probably we should get rid of this.'

'We can post it back to him,' Lech said.

'Or he could pay for the next round,' she said.

It didn't seem much to ask. Not after Black Mac had wasted their time. But Lech was having none of it, and Shirley watched grumpily as the wallet joined the rest of the treasure trove in his pocket.

'Another drink?' she suggested.

'I'm going home,' said Lech.

'Might be best to avoid Old Street.'

He didn't appear any more grateful for that than he had for Shirley saving his neck in the toilet. But she was used to going unappreciated, and stayed for another drink anyway.

8

At the meetings she attended less often than she should — *My name is Catherine, and I'm an alcoholic* — they suggested that you let go; not fret over things you couldn't control. This was for the avoidance of guilt. One of the side effects of addiction, or recovering therefrom, was that you felt you had let the world down, as if you'd nodded off at a critical moment and allowed things to slide. And given the parlous state of that world, and the moral bankrupts governing it, it would be hard not to let the guilt become overwhelming. She knew all this. It was a series of small steps heading in the wrong direction: best to stick to the twelve recommended at those meetings. Make amends to those we have harmed, for instance.

Kay White was on her mind.

It was a peculiarity of Slough House that its occupants tended to know where everyone was. If some organisations had Chinese walls, to prevent confidential information spreading, Slough House's walls were Swiss, in as much as they were full of holes; both literally — occupants had been known to punch the plaster — and in the sense that there was always leakage. The anguish of the floorboards and the creaking of the stairs told you who was where: it was an aural panopticon, wired for sound. And yet, it was easy to forget about each other. The separate miseries that slow horses came wrapped in, and the ongoing drudgery that was their daily grind, meant that much of the time they were on their own. Some more so than

197

others. Kay White, for example. Nobody had liked her. She never shut up, for a start. So it felt no huge surprise when she'd betrayed them, and no huge loss when she'd been sacked. And what it felt like now she was dead, thought Catherine, was just more of the same: the woman had left no mark here, nothing to grieve over, and where there was no grief there was often guilt.

To assuage which, Catherine Standish was making mental amends. The working day was done but she remained at her desk, hands clasped on her lap, eyes closed. It might have looked like prayer, but was simply the summoning of memory: she was trying to find a moment she'd shared with Kay White, something that stood out against the background noise. But there was nothing of substance. Most moments spent with Kay had been an attempt to block her out. When she'd departed, along with — the name escaped her — it had been a relief. And that wasn't a matter of blame, Catherine told herself. It was just life, which was full of passing strangers, even if some of them hung around for years.

. . . Struan Loy. That was the name. Loy had been here at the same time as Kay, and Lamb had kicked the pair of them out together.

And Struan Loy too had joined that chorus invisible; those who'd drifted from the margins of memory. In Catherine's life, most such had been fellow drunks, who'd done their best to blur her recollection by being little more than blurs themselves, smeary with alcohol. But there were slow horses among them, which was why that prick of guilt was needling her. That prick of shame. She should go home, really. But before that — before running the gauntlet of London's bars

198

and pubs, its off-licences and supermarkets, its corner shops with their furtive shelves of booze, all calling her name as she passed — before any of that, she'd have a quick trawl through the usual search engines, and see if she could find out what Struan Loy was up to these days.

Maybe that would soothe her conscience, for a while.

★ ★ ★

Peter Judd said, 'We live in new times, with new conditions, and new alignments are coming into being. This is a natural, and indeed ah ah ah a necessary, progression. For progression it is. And those who fail to appreciate that will suffer the usual fate of those unable to adapt to new circumstances.'

'You mean political defeat.'

'I mean political extinction.'

'Give me a break,' said Diana.

It would have been a nice moment if Channel Go had indeed gone to a break then, but it chundered on regardless.

'And you believe,' the interviewer went on, 'that Desmond Flint is one of those ushering in these new conditions we're disc — '

Diana killed transmission.

Judd's TV appearances hadn't diminished in number since he'd left office, a career turn some commenters had described as his fall from grace. But grace wasn't something he'd ever aspired to, and its absence hadn't hindered him. Besides, the notion that he was a spent force only held weight if you heeded the current wisdom, and wisdom was no longer an asset when making political predictions. The paths to power of current world leaders — paths including conspiracy to assault, knee-jerk racism, indeterminate fecundity and cheating at golf — were so askew from the traditional routes that only an idiot would have dared forecast future developments. It wasn't unfitting, then, that Judd's popularity as a political pundit continued. Judd might not have been an idiot himself, but his core supporters were a different story.

She was in her office, its glass wall frosted for privacy. On the hub, the night crew was settling into business, prepared to respond to the routine emergencies of national security. One of these, she considered, was even now unfolding: Judd had gone ahead with what he'd hinted at, and was throwing his weight behind the Yellow Vest movement. There were those who'd regard this as tantamount to pitching in with the Nazi party. But then, Nazis had a lot of support these days. That old thing about learning from the past didn't always mean studying monstrous historical movements to ensure they never happened again. It could indicate an intention to perfect their trajectories, in the hope that they'd triumph next time.

Along with Judd's hint had come veiled threats.

When you disappoint rich and powerful men, they let their displeasure be known.

And when you'd painted yourself into a corner, it was best to let the paint dry before leaving the room.

Earlier that afternoon, she'd had a meeting with the Ops team, one of whose ongoing low-level engagements was infiltration of the Yellow Vest movement: nothing too significant; a couple of youngsters distributing leaflets, stacking chairs and generally making themselves useful. An eyes-on approach, with the potential to upgrade to dicks-out if the situation demanded. But Diana had announced that she was pulling the plug.

Others around the table had exchanged puzzled looks.

'Is that wise? All signs suggest that the movement's gaining ground, not withering away.'

'And we have a tightrope to walk,' Diana said. 'Our remit is security, and that doesn't include an overzealous policing of dissenting voices.'

'But —'

'I wasn't inviting discussion. I was stating strategy.'

'If you say so.'

'I'm pretty certain I do. I'm pretty certain this is me, doing just that.'

The mood had brightened when she'd gone on to outline the new funding, but the instruction had left her feeling treacherous, and she'd been glad when the meeting was over. A necessary move, though. It would give her a little breathing space while she decided what to do about Judd, about Cantor too. That a decision would be reached, a solution found, was a given. She'd wandered into the briar patch, true, but she hadn't lasted this long at the Park without learning to trust her abilities. Even unelected, Judd remained a big beast in the political jungle. But Diana had done her growing up on Spook Street, where big beasts numbered among the daily kill.

He moved fast, though, she'd give him that. She hadn't expected him to be putting down a public marker so swiftly. On the other hand, if it turned out he'd made a catastrophic error of judgement in backing Desmond Flint, he'd deal with it in his usual fashion: by pretending it hadn't happened. It was astonishing how obediently the public trotted along after him when he did this.

Josie had interrupted her contemplation just before the shift change.

'You were asking about Thomas Doyle. Recent hire with the Dogs.'

'Yes.'

'He's left us already.'

'That was quick.'

'He came to the end of his probationary period. There were question marks, like that episode with Molly Doran, but he'd probably have passed if he'd made the right noises. But he evidently didn't want to. Handed his notice in.'

'I see.'

'Do you want me to follow up?'

Diana said, 'Send me his file. Such as it is.'

'Of course. And there's an update on that death by fire outside Leicester. The former Park agent. I'll send that too.'

'Please do.'

When Josie left, she'd switched the news on, surfing her way to Channel Go from the more serious bulletins. And now she'd switched it off, having caught Judd's contribution.

Emails from Josie were in her box: Tommo Doyle's file, and a news report on the death of one Struan Loy.

She remembered Loy. Something of a joker, and so an irritation in any office space. The space he'd come to occupy outside Leicester, though, had been a shipping container, inside which he'd burned to death. Investigation remained ongoing, but it was clearly a murder. He'd been a slow horse, yes, but this was a coincidence. People got murdered. Slow horses were people. There was a Venn diagram waiting to happen, and somewhere near Leicester, it just had.

It was unlikely that Jackson Lamb would see it that way — he had a tendency to become aroused at any sign of threat — but Diana had other things to worry about. Besides, Lamb wasn't privy to the daily updates, and the story hadn't made headlines here in the capital. Chances were, it wouldn't come to his attention.

★ ★ ★

'Fuck me sideways,' said Jackson Lamb.

Then put his head back and stared at the ceiling.

Catherine said, 'The local paper said suspicious circumstances.'

'Burning to death in a shipping container? Yeah, it doesn't take Shylock Holmes.'

She decided to let that one go.

To the amateur observer, Lamb might be preparing for a nap. His feet were on his desk, his toes mostly visible through the tatters of his socks, and one arm lay across his paunch like a jovial illustration from Dickens. But Catherine, a seasoned watcher, recognised the tension enfolding him, and knew, too, that Lamb thought the way a bear hibernates. Best not interrupt him, unless you wanted a limb torn off.

She settled herself on the visitor's chair, to one side of which lay the pile of takeaway hotboxes, and waited.

Empty noises drifted up from the lower storeys. Slough House was a medley of knocks and rattles after hours, its ghosts scratching windows and walls once its occupants had left. Or perhaps, she thought, this was normal, and it was simply a building relaxing into the dark.

She thought about Kay White, tumbling off a stepladder in the comfort of her own home.

About Struan Loy, screaming his lungs out in a tin trap.

More ghosts.

When Lamb at last raised the arm that had been dangling over the side of his chair, it held a cigarette. He slotted it into his mouth and, from somewhere on his person, produced a plastic lighter, which refused to work. After staring at it in wounded disappointment, he tossed it over his shoulder, and looked balefully at Catherine.

'Can't help you,' she said.

'Christ. Remind me of your purpose?'

'You smoke too much. Like you imagine it's a virtue.'

'I can see how an idiot might think so.'

While he began the laborious process of opening drawers and rummaging through them without actually looking, she said, 'We're being watched by the Park, on and off. And hunted by someone else. At the same time?'

Lamb's only reply was the clicking of another lighter, drawn from the depths of a drawer, and equally useless. It joined its companion somewhere in the shadows behind.

She persevered. 'They must be connected.'

'How?'

'Well, I don't know!'

'So think about it. How many points of connection could there be? Jesus, a man could die trying to get a smoke round here.' But his roving hand found a box of matches even while he spoke, and he brandished it in triumph, offering her a view of stained armpit. With a dexterity that would have impressed her in a squirrel, let alone an overweight drunk, he removed a match from the box and struck it one-handed, though lost points by dropping the open box while completing the action. Matches went everywhere, but the lit one reached his cigarette, which was all that mattered. Its job done, he tossed it away. Said, 'Loy wasn't a slow horse any more. Nor was White. Why would anyone think they were?'

Catherine said, 'Because they're operating from out-of-date information.'

'And where might that come from?'

'Oh Lord . . .'

'And that would be the sound of a penny dropping, would it? If it took me that long to join a pair of dots, I'd still be wondering why my Y-fronts shrink when I look at porn.'

He paused to draw in smoke, scrunched his face in presumable pleasure, and yawned his exhalation. She'd not have been surprised to glimpse a crocodile bird, pecking shreds of meat from his teeth. 'Takes it out of you, being a genius.'

'It must be a constant strain.'

'That and coping with the ill-tempered sarcasm of subordinates.' He heaved himself more or less upright. More matches dropped to the floor. 'I met this dwarf a couple of nights ago. I might have mentioned it.'

'It cropped up.'

'He told me his journo friend heard a whisper that Rasnokov had declared war on the Park's assassination squad.' Vassily Rasnokov was the GRU's First Desk. 'All jolly hockey sticks, I'm sure, except that the Park doesn't have an assassination squad. It gives orders as and when, or hires local talent, like it did in Kazan. So the GRU has the same problem George W had back in the day. How do you declare war on something that doesn't physically exist?' He paused to smoke. 'Answer, you go ahead and do it anyway, and hope to fuck no one notices.'

'We get called a lot of things,' she said. 'But nobody's ever accused us of being assassination specialists.'

'And nobody thinks we are. But once the label's been applied, the facts cease to matter. These guys have been given our names and told we're the targets, and they're getting on with it. They must have realised while breaking Kay White's neck that she was more Milly Molly Mandy than Modesty Blaise, but so what? They're getting paid to do a job, not worry about the details.'

'But who applied the label? Or do I hear the distant clucking of chickens coming home to roost?'

'I like to think I've made a lot of enemies,' Lamb conceded. 'But seriously, this day and age? Even I'd put me way down on a list of people worth killing. You'd have to be halfway through the Cabinet first. Not to mention whoever invented fruit-flavoured beer.'

'I'm sure the GRU have similar priorities. But either way, this list they're working from, it must have come from Molly's archive.'

'Uh-huh. Can't have come from current records, because we're not on them. And while it might be out of date, it overlaps with the present. If White and Loy were on it, then Cartwright and Guy are too. Not to mention you and me.'

'And Roddy.'

'Every cloud.' He made his own final cloud, then squashed his cigarette out on the side of his bin. It was not, Catherine noticed, one of the monstrosities he'd been smoking lately. Just an ordinary filter tip.

He saw her noticing. 'What?'

'Just wondering what we do now.'

'We gather them in,' he said. 'Before more bodies hit the streets.'

★ ★ ★

The activating order came from Catherine Standish, but he knew it originated from Lamb himself.

Blake's grave. Now.

Roderick Ho stared at the text for a full five seconds, as if waiting for it to self-destruct, then tapped out his answer:

Roger that.

Then thought a few moments, and sent another:

A-OK.

Just in case she didn't understand the first one.

After that, he was locked and loaded; ready to rock and roll. *Cylinders firing and systems go: Welcome to the Rod-eo,* he thought, then thought it again, because it was a new one. Welcome to the Rod-eo.

Saddle up.

Blake's grave meant Bunhill Fields, the cemetery not far from Slough House. Blake was some dead guy, but that wasn't important; what mattered was, it was where the team assembled when heavy shit was going down, and Slough House itself was off-limits. The emergency zone. And getting the call meant dropping everything and travelling light, because when you were called to the graveside, you needed to make sure it wasn't going to turn out to be your own.

(A brief image struck him: of Lamb cradling Roddy's body in his arms. Lamb's broken gaze was directed heavenwards. *Why?* he was wailing. *Why?* For some reason Lamb was dressed as Batman, while Roddy's own sweet corpse was in Robin costume. Very strange.)

Anyway. When word came down from Lamb that he needed his team, everyone knew what the real score was: he needed the Rodster. The rest of them could stand round making up the numbers, and that was fine, but what Lamb wanted was his best guy by his side. The others were camouflage.

And this was the part of the job Dyno-Rod loved: the part where his street skills came to the fore. Roddy Ho was the Duke of Digital; everyone knew that. He was Master of the Monitor, Lord of the Laptop, but that was only half the story. Take him away from his screens and he was also King of the Kerb, Sultan of the Streets, the something of the Pavements. He scrabbled about in his cupboard for his second-best pair of trainers — your second-best pair were your best pair, every fool knew that: they were what you wore when the going got rough — and grabbed his dark-blue hoodie from its hanger. Prez, pro, padrone, *prince*. Prince of the pavements. With smooth, practised economy Roddy readied himself for action: trainers on feet, hair tousled just right, and *bang*, he was out the door, only returning twice; once to change his blue hoodie for a black one — more ninja — and again to check he'd locked up properly. After that it was showtime, all the way.

No car. This was what it meant to go dark; you surrendered to the city, let it breathe you in gently, and carry you where you needed to go. Any watchers out there, they might hold you in their gaze for a moment, but then you'd shimmer and vanish, and they'd be left shaking their heads: *what just happened?* Then return to their original stance, waiting for your appearance, not understanding that you'd been and gone. That you'd cast no shadow; had slid through the streets like a whisper, your effortless passage a silent hymn to London's dark and energising graces.

So any Regent's Park newby assigned to pin a tail on the RodMan better bring their A-game, because the Rodinator left no trail. They'd have a happier time of it chasing smoke through a hurricane: Roddy *owned* the streets.

It was threatening rain, though, so he caught a bus.

★ ★ ★

When Lech Wicinski received the word he hadn't the faintest clue what it meant, but his carefully composed reply — *What??* — elicited no response from Catherine. So he phoned Shirley.

'I just got a strange text.'

"Blake's grave"? Me too. It means get there, now.'

'Why? Do you think Lamb knows?'

'Knows what?'

For fuck's sake.

' . . . Knows we just beat up a civilian. And stole his stuff.'

'Oh, that.' Shirley fell silent. 'But why would he want us at Blake's grave? When he could just bollock us in his office in the morning?'

A bollocking, Lech thought. He was thinking more along the lines of police, arrest, trial, imprisonment.

Shirley's more relaxed approach was likely drug-addled lack of perspective, but on the other hand might be based on experience. What happened earlier probably wasn't the first time a slow horse had walked away from someone else's wreckage. He'd heard rumours: about politicians, scaffolding, tins of paint. Mind you, that sounded a lot more accidental than thumping a civilian with a sap then stealing his money. So presumably Shirley hadn't been involved.

He said, 'So what does getting to Blake's grave usually entail?'

'You mean, what does it mean?'

' . . . Yes, okay. That.'

'Means some shit has hit a fan. And we're all about to get spattered.'

'Then why so cheerful?'

Shirley said, 'Well, it beats an early night.'

So Blake's grave, Lech interpreted, was the Slough House equivalent of the Park's Apocalypse Protocol, in which all agents got out of the building and off the map, to regroup at various locations around the city. For Slough House, of course, only one rendezvous point was required. Otherwise, the slow horses would simply be several groups of a single person each, which was pretty much what they were the rest of the time.

The protocol also demanded you went dark: no phone, no vehicle, no watchers on your back. So Lech took batteries and SIM card from his phone. If Slough House had gone tits up, he'd better not paint himself bright colours. On the other hand, if this was Lamb's idea of a wind-up, he wanted the wherewithal to Uber himself home afterwards, so instead of leaving the parts behind he put them in his pocket. Then he checked himself in the mirror, as he always did now — still a mess; those scars will never heal — and left the flat at the same time that Shirley, still in Shoreditch, ordered a vodka for the road. It would take her, like, five minutes to get to Bunhill Fields? Ten, max. And she knew it was an emergency shout, that three-word text, but really: what kind of emergency could it be? And if it was a really big one, she'd need another vodka inside her.

She was still keyed up from earlier. Playing it over in her head, they'd been lucky, her and Lech; him that she'd turned up at the right moment, when the guy in the black mac had been about to make his face a bigger mess than it already was, and him and her both that nobody had come in while they were dragging a stunned body into the cubicle. Two strokes of luck: maybe this was an end to her jinx run. Maybe this time she could partner up without having to pencil in an expiry date.

Not that her last partner had been her best friend or anything. In fact, when you got right down to it, it was possible he hadn't even noticed they were partners.

And why did it matter whether she had a partner anyway?

The thought was one she'd been pushing away for as long as it had been creeping up on her. Her relationship history was back on an upward keel — she'd recently made it to a six-day anniversary — and it wasn't like she was desperate to share an office again. It was more that, when it was her turn, she didn't want to be bleeding on a hillside on her own, in the snow. She wanted somebody with her, holding her hand or saying her name. Not that she was superstitious. Shirley had no plans to die soon. But planning had nothing to do with it, as her late colleagues would no doubt testify. Or Blake, for that matter. She doubted he'd picked out his grave in advance. One day you're wondering what to do at the weekend; the next, your weekend'll never come.

But if Lech was going to fill the current vacancy, it was probably best she didn't go into too much detail.

She finished her drink, left the glass on the bar. The pub was half full, and she didn't feel eyes on her as she went, but waited in a shop doorway for two minutes anyway, checking the pavements, one hand on the window to steady herself. That last vodka: maybe not a great shout. But legend had it that being drunk caused double vision, and she wasn't even seeing one person following her, let alone two, which made her both sober and untailed. She gave it another minute, long enough for a few deep breaths and a peculiar dance-like motion involving shaking her limbs very loosely, then stepped out onto the street. Five minutes; ten max. She'd probably get there first.

★ ★ ★

'Where is everyone?' asked Louisa.

'I was wondering that myself,' Catherine said.

That there was nobody around wasn't in itself a surprise: the cemetery locked its gates after hours. That Louisa had arrived first was stranger: she had furthest to come. On the other hand, she'd ignored protocol and driven, so maybe that shortened the odds. It was one thing going dark; quite another spending the evening farting about on public transport. She lived way out of the centre because it was more affordable. Not because she enjoyed the commute.

Catherine was asking, 'Were you followed?'

'I'm pretty sure not.'

'Pretty sure?'

Louisa said, 'I spotted the guy the other day, and I've been careful since. Or maybe paranoid's the word. I don't think I was followed. Why, what's going on?'

'Let's wait till the others arrive.'

'Why's Lamb not here?'

'He will be.'

Louisa eyed Catherine's dress. It was ankle length, as usual, with sleeves that blossomed at the cuff. On any given day, she looked like she was dressed as a Victorian puppet. Not many people could have carried it off, but Louisa had to admit Catherine was one of them. On the other hand, it was hard to picture her scaling cemetery railings.

'Lamb has a key,' Catherine told her.

'I know.'

'He opened the gate.'

'How did you even know I was wondering that? And if Lamb was here then, where is he now?'

'Here's someone.'

Which was Lech. 'You do know there are two Blake's graves,' he said.

This was true. There was a small headstone, suggesting the poet-painter William Blake's remains lay near by, and a larger memorial, flat upon the ground, which seemed more confident of those remains' location.

'They're, like, twenty yards apart?' said Louisa.

'I know.'

'So we'd probably have seen each other, whichever one we were waiting at?'

'I know. I was just saying.'

Darkness was traditionally forgiving of facial blunders: ill-advised piercings, drunken-error tattoos and New Romantic make-up stylings were diminished in shadow, and seemed less stupid. Lech's scars, though, it made worse. The first thing you thought when you saw him was that you wanted to turn a light on. Probably not entirely fair to lump him with those who'd made their faces a sideshow: it hadn't been his decision to have *PAEDO* carved into his cheeks. But it had been his choice to obliterate the word with haphazard scars, so he couldn't claim not to have had a hand in it. And right now he looked nervy, Louisa thought, as if his evening had already gone wrong in some unspecified way, and he was waiting for it to go more wrong differently. Not necessarily an unwise state of mind when Lamb had sounded a siren, but still. There was such a thing as a positive attitude.

She wondered where River was. A summons like this, she'd have expected him to be first on the scene.

And now came Shirley, weaving into the graveyard's central reservation like someone who'd been drinking with barely a pause since leaving the office. Not that Louisa was one to judge, but there was a margin there in which she could feel smug.

Catherine took one look and said, 'Oh, for goodness' sake. Here.' She produced a bottle of water from somewhere.

'Oh, cheers,' Shirley said. She took a hefty slug. 'Thirsty work.'

'What is?'

'This. Whatever this is.'

The cemetery was wedged between Bunhill Row and City Road, from which the noise of traffic was still constant. That was the direction Shirley had arrived

214

from, and Louisa couldn't help wondering not whether she'd been seen climbing in, but by how many people, and what they'd done about it. Probably nothing. It wasn't that London lacked the civic-minded; more that even the civic-minded didn't much care when short drunk strangers hauled themselves over pointy railings.

Anyway, it wasn't like they were tramping on actual graves. A few luminaries apart, the dead were fenced off from the flagstoned pathways.

Shirley was peering round, checking off a mental register. 'Where's Cartwright? And douchebag? And Lamb?'

'Not here, obviously,' said Catherine. 'And a little respect for your colleagues, would you mind?'

'Sorry. *Mr* Lamb.'

And if River wasn't here yet, it probably meant he'd headed off to the O.B.'s, to be with Sid. Louisa wondered how she felt about that, not that she had a right to feel anything. Sid was one of them, she thought, one of the originals, though there'd been slow horses before them, and would be slow horses afterwards. Unless Slough House itself was headed for extinction. Being wiped from Service records wasn't an encouraging sign.

She heard a strangled cry from Bunhill Row, followed by a tearing sound and a muffled thump. The kind of noise you'd get, she thought, if you dropped a computer nerd a short distance onto a hard surface.

Roddy Ho was on his feet when she got there, one pocket of his hoodie hanging loose but a scowl fixed firmly in place.

'Hurt yourself?'

'No. Just practising my land and roll.'

'Yeah,' said Louisa. 'In case you find yourself doing a teeny-tiny parachute jump.'

Back at Blake's grave they gathered around Catherine, Shirley still unfocused, the rest of them growing impatient. Rain was in the air, and an occasional shiver shook the trees. Somewhere on City Road, brakes squealed.

Catherine said, 'Does anyone know where River is?'

'I think he went to Kent,' Louisa said.

'His grandfather's?'

'Uh-huh.'

'. . . Why?'

'He had a good reason,' Louisa said. 'But if that's where he is, even if he's heading straight back, he'll be a while.'

Catherine pursed her lips. 'He didn't respond to the text.'

If he'd been obeying protocol, Louisa thought, he'd have dumped his phone soon as the text came through. And if any of them were likely to follow the protocol, that would be River. But before she could remind Catherine of this, Catherine was speaking again. 'Okay, Lamb said that once Roddy got here, I should start.'

Ho visibly swelled.

Lech said, 'Could you run his exact words past us?'

'I'd sooner not.'

'Because I doubt they were a compliment.'

'Shut up, scarface,' said Ho.

'That's enough. All of you.' Nobody, thought Louisa, did schoolteacher quite like Catherine. 'Now. Some of you will remember Struan Loy.'

'Yes,' said Louisa.

'No,' said Lech.

'No,' said Shirley.

'No,' said Ho.

Catherine gave him a look. 'Well, you should. He was at Slough House same time as you.'

Ho shrugged.

'What's happened to him?' Louisa asked.

She had the feeling it was nothing good. Former slow horse wins the Lottery wasn't a headline waiting to be printed.

Catherine said, 'He died. In a fire.'

Another squall of wind shook the trees, and they rustled in annoyance. *Shush. Shush.*

Lech said, 'Okay, that's sad, but he was before my time. So no offence, but if you're planning a whipround for a wreath, count me out. And why the cloak and dagger, anyway?'

'Because the fire was set deliberately. And he's the second Slough House, ah, graduate, to die in the last few weeks.'

Lech paused. 'That's not a good statistic.'

'Hence, as you say, the cloak and dagger.'

'Who was the other one?' said Shirley.

'Kay White. Also before your time.'

'But not before mine,' said Louisa. 'I thought she had an accident.'

'Yes,' said Catherine. 'But the kind that might have happened on purpose.'

'We're being hunted.'

'It's a possibility.'

'That's what Lamb thinks?'

'He thinks someone's taking revenge for the Kazan hit last month.'

'I thought that was just a rumour.'

'It is a rumour, yes. But it's also true.'

'Welcome to Spook Street,' murmured Shirley.

'By 'someone', we're presumably talking GRU?' Lech said. 'They've sent a hit team?'

'Again,' said Catherine, 'it's a possibility.'

'But why us?' said Louisa. 'We're hardly in the frame for Kazan.'

Ho said, 'But you can see why they might suspect us,' and frowned meaningfully.

'The Park,' said Shirley. 'This is them, right? Dropping us in the shit as usual.'

Lech said, 'That's a stretch. Putting targets on our backs for the new intake, that's one thing. But I can't see Taverner selling us to the Russians.'

'Yeah, we've probably seen sides of her you haven't,' said Louisa. 'And anyway. This isn't the current crew, is it? Whoever's doing this has got hold of an old team list.'

'Which would nevertheless include some of us,' said Catherine. 'So you can see why I'd be happier if River had shown up. You're sure he's just out of town?'

Louisa said, 'Yeah, about that. There's something you should know.'

A rusty metal complaint interrupted her: the Bunhill Row gate was opening. It shut a moment later, and footsteps made their way along the flagstoned avenue towards where they were gathered.

Whoever it was, there were two of them.

'Scatter,' Louisa said.

She, Lech and Shirley made for the shadows round the side of the fenced-off graves. There was tree-cover, and bushes against a high brick wall: hideouts for children, but no place of safety. If whoever had come for Struan Loy and Kay White was coming for them, they'd be easy pickings. Louisa ducked into shadow and dropped to one knee, but when she peered back, Catherine and Ho remained standing in the light, staring after them.

Oh, crap.

It was Lamb making his way towards the graveside, and he wasn't alone. Leaning into him was a young Indian woman whose right arm hung at an awkward angle, her left hand gripping the opposite shoulder as if holding everything in place. Lamb was propelling her forwards with a grace unusual to him, or not often on display. Her face was scrunched up in pain, and she was coughing softly, or whimpering.

Lamb said, 'All right. Daddy's home.'

Somewhat sheepishly, Louisa led the others out of the shadows.

Ho sneered. 'I knew who it was,' he told her.

'Catherine did,' Louisa said. 'You're just slow to react.'

Catherine, meanwhile, was studying the young woman. 'Who's this? And what have you done to her? She looks hurt.'

'She's fine,' said Lamb.

'But she looks hurt,' repeated Catherine.

'Okay, I broke her arm. But other than that she's fine.'

Catherine stared at him. 'What?'

Louisa said, 'You broke her arm? For God's sake! We need to call her an ambulance.'

'First one with a phone gets fired,' said Lamb. 'You should have gone dark when you got the text. Or do I need to remind you you're supposed to be fucking spies? Here. Hold this.'

'This' was the woman, and it was Lech he was speaking to. Who looked alarmed to find himself having to

219

wrap a restraining arm around a captive, especially an injured, unhappy one. 'Are you okay?' he asked her, as Lamb shoved her into his orbit.

'Bastard,' she said.

'Who is she?' said Shirley. 'And how come you got to break her arm?'

'Bitch.'

'Can I break her other one?'

'Nobody's breaking anything,' said Catherine.

'She's Park,' said Louisa.

'Oh, somebody's awake,' said Lamb. 'Thank you, Lara Crufts. Hope you didn't trip over any tombs back there. Yes, she's Park, and she's here courtesy of the Boy Blunder. You can always rely on Odd-Rod to make the right mistake.'

Ho tried on his meaningful-frown face again.

'He means she tailed you,' said Lech. 'Idiot.'

'And you were waiting to intercept her,' said Catherine. 'But why did you have to break her arm?'

'Because if I'd broken her leg I'd have had to carry her,' Lamb said. 'I mean, it's not rocket science.'

'We need to get her seen to,' said Catherine. 'You can't just — '

'It's a clean break,' said Lamb. 'What am I, an amateur? And Taverner'll make sure she gets what she needs, just as soon as she's delivered a message.'

'What message?'

'That whatever game Diana's playing's gone sideways, and we're the ones hanging off the edge. You got that, Southpaw? These words are for your boss's ears only. Tell her I want to talk about Kay White and Struan Loy. In one hour. She knows where I'll be.' He lobbed a key at Lech, who took it one-handed. 'Best let her walk out. Watching her climb the fence'd be funny, but we're on the clock here.'

'You're sure this is — '

'What I'm sure is, I don't want to hear the next words out of your mouth.'

For a moment the little group was still, as if enacting a tableau: the end-point of a pilgrimage, gathered by this grave. Then all except Lamb watched as Lech walked the injured woman down the path towards Bunhill Row.

'All that just to get Taverner's attention?' said Catherine, once they were gone.

'Well, I considered leaving a horse's head in her bed,' said Lamb. 'But the logistics are insane.'

'Sid's alive,' said Louisa.

A revelation that didn't seem to surprise Lamb. 'And Cartwright's with her?'

'I think so.'

'Then you mean she was alive,' said Lamb. 'Him too.'

He brushed his mouth, and a cigarette appeared. 'Whoever these fuckers are, they're not amateurs either. And like I said, we're on the clock.'

When he lit his cigarette, he was briefly burnished by a halo of flame.

Louisa, thinking of River, shivered, and the first few spots of rain began to fall.

221

9

The car moved slowly along the lane, or that was how it felt to Sid. Slowly in the way that you moved slowly towards an undesirable appointment: your legs heavy, the pavement hostile, but time pouring away at its usual speed. Darkness was falling fast, in response to strange rural gravity. There were no overhead lights, but the car's beams picked out hedgerow and gatepost, painting them in brief, minute detail, some of which fluttered away when lit. Moths, Sid thought. Moths and midges. There'd be more disturbances all around, sudden startlings and departures, if she could only see them. The creatures of the night reacting to the large bomb travelling past.

Sid was in the back seat, Jim next to her. Jane driving. Jane seemed calm and deliberate, her every move in tune with the car's progress. Jim, seat belt in place, was half turned towards Sid, his expression one of benign insincerity. It would be better all round, his face suggested, if we could get this done without wasting more breath: on words, on smiles, on life. But he'd be prepared, if necessary, to lend an ear to any plea Sid might care to make, provided Sid didn't expect him to act on it.

Sid's sojourn in the study seemed like ancient history; like a walk in an orchard on a summer's day.

And that lump of concrete, she belatedly realised, had been a fragment of the Berlin Wall. Hence its presence in the O.B.'s study. Much of his life had been dedicated to bringing that wall down, or that was how it appeared in retrospect. Perhaps it had simply been dedicated to fighting those who'd put it up, the wall itself being no more than a marker of which side he'd been on. Given a different birthplace, he might have been equally happy resisting the values of the West. Either way, at the end of the long road travelled, that chunk had come to rest on his bookshelf, symbolic of a temporary victory. Because history was cyclical, of course, and more walls would be built, and there'd always be those who hoped it would be better on one side than the other, and die attempting to find out. And in the longer run those walls would fall too, along with the despots who'd built them, crushed by the bricks they'd stacked so high. Walls couldn't last. All the same, Sid wished she'd slipped that concrete lump into her pocket while she'd had the chance. There'd be something equally cyclical about using it to smash Jim's face in.

Though its weight in her pocket would have alerted him, of course. They were assuming Sid was weak, and unlikely to defend herself, but Jim would have noticed if she'd tried to smuggle a brick out in her jacket.

'Where are you taking me?' she asked at last.

'We've told you,' said Jim. 'To the hospital.'

'No, really. Where are you taking me?'

He said, 'Trust me. It amounts to the same thing in the end.'

Jane dipped the headlights to allow an oncoming car to pass undazzled, and cranked them up again once the lane ahead was clear. Sid caught a glimpse of a lone tree in a field, its limbs a crazy tangle of malice, and then it was gone.

And the end, whatever it might be, drew nearer.

From across the water drifted the sound of an old man mumbling in song, the same words, same cadence, as if he were caught in a loop of prayer. It stirred a memory in Diana that she couldn't pin down as she walked the towpath towards Islington, where the canal disappeared into a tunnel. It had rained, only briefly, but enough to disturb hidden odours that sweetened the evening air. Houseboats lined the path, some of them floating plinths for what, in the shadows, seemed Heath Robinson contraptions designed to prepare their vessels for flight, but which would disassemble in ordinary daylight into bicycles and watering cans, recycling bins, seedling trays. From houses on the other side the occasional noises of family life filtered out: voices and snatches of music. But, a solitary runner apart, the towpath was empty. Diana was heading for the farthest bench, the one just this side of the tunnel. On it waited Jackson Lamb.

From this approach he looked like an exhausted tramp, and for a moment she wondered if he were the source of that mumbled prayer. His shoes were scuffed lumps, the hems of his trousers frayed, and his overcoat might have been stitched from the tattered sail of a pirate ship. And she had little doubt that the odour of cigarettes and Scotch would grow apparent the nearer she came, interrupting the softer smells the rain had released; little doubt, too, that for all his repose he knew damn well she was approaching, had been aware of her since she set foot on the towpath. And for half a second she had a troubling glimpse of another Lamb inside the shell of this one; one who had posed for the image in front of her, and

224

whose carefully composed decrepitude was a sculptor's trick.

Best to take the offensive. Best not to be anywhere near him, in fact, but he'd sent a damaged telegram in the form of a trainee spook, and she'd had little choice but to heed his summons.

'You fractured my agent's arm,' she said, taking a place on the bench as far from him as possible.

He opened his eyes. 'I warned you not to fuck with my joes.'

'A twenty-three-year-old woman, for God's sake!'

'Yeah, I'd have done the same to a forty-year-old man. This is what a feminist looks like.' He studied her. 'Moving on. 'I might have made a mistake.' Your words. And guess what? My death count's rising faster than the PM's dick at a convent school prize day. So. Want to explain the nature of your mistake? Or should I take a stab at it myself?'

He shifted as he spoke, and for an uncomfortable moment, she wondered if he were reaching for a blade.

But no. Not Jackson Lamb's style.

She said, 'Making mistakes is something every First Desk does, it goes with the territory. But whatever's going on with your old crew, that's landed out of nowhere. Nothing to do with current operations. So best thing all round would be if you just leave things to me, to the Park.' She felt her eyelid tremble, and hoped he didn't notice. 'I gather you've gone dark. That's sensible. Stay that way until I give the all-clear, and the rest of your team will be fine.'

'That's a relief. Do I get a kiss night night now?'

'You need to trust me on this, Jackson.'

'Funny thing. When I hear the words 'trust me', I get the feeling someone's pissing in my shoe. So like

225

we were saying, you made a mistake. This have anything to do with that club on Wigmore Street? Run by Maggie Lessiter?'

Diana said, 'She tries to keep that quiet.'

'Yeah, and I tried to keep this quiet.' He farted, a three-note trumpet solo, then eased his buttock back onto the bench. 'But somehow word got round.'

'God. Don't you ever consider impersonating a human being?'

'Never met one worth pretending to be.' He put a cigarette in his mouth, but didn't light it. Possibly for fear of igniting the atmosphere. 'Public schoolboy hang-out, isn't it? Spotted dick for pudding, and matron rapping knuckles with a wooden spoon. Drawing lots to see who gets to be prime minister.'

'So I enjoy the occasional lunch off the premises,' Diana said. 'What's your point?'

'My point is, you've taken a dip in the money pit. Because nobody pulls off a hit on a foreign holiday, especially not a Russian one, without serious brass in their pocket. And everyone knows there's no spare cash for Service jollies, what with You-Know-What costing the earth. So when you greenlit that Kazan op, you did it with a suitcase full of used banknotes. And where better to find one of those than Lessiter's club?'

'This is pure fantasy.'

'Nothing pure about it. You've been there all right. Ho ran your Uber records.' He shook his head. 'I mean, seriously. You're supposed to be Head Spook. You're about as under the radar as a Goodyear blimp. But anyway, yeah, I wanted to know where you were when you starting using Slough House as a dartboard. And who you might have been hanging out with.'

Diana looked away, towards the deeper darkness of the tunnel the canal headed into, or out of. Like most things, it was a matter of perspective. She said, 'You're confusing separate issues. What happened to White and Loy had nothing to do with any of this.'

Lamb had found a lighter somewhere, and lit his cigarette at last. 'So I got Ho — and I have to tell you, he might be a twat, but he's a talented twat. I keep expecting him to start firing ping-pong balls — so anyway, I got Ho to look at who else might have been having lunch there same days as you, and guess whose credit card he found?' He exhaled smoke, making sure it blew in her direction. 'Bullingdon Fopp. Bespoke PR services to rich tossers everywhere, in the shape of one Peter Judd. Now, why was I not surprised at his name cropping up? UK politics' hardy perineum.'

Taverner winced. 'I assume you mean perennial.'

'You can assume all you like. I'm saying he's somewhere between an arsehole and a — '

'Jesus, Lamb!' She shook her head. 'He's a member of the club. Him being there means nothing.'

'Yeah, shut up. So here's what I'm thinking. Peter Judd bankrolled the Kazan operation, presumably for reasons of his own. Nothing to do with the hit itself. More to do with the power and influence that come with buying First Desk.'

'He hasn't bought me.'

'Oh believe me, Diana, he owns every last fucking inch of you.'

There was a waterborne scuffle a hundred yards down the canal: some ducks seeing to business. She let the noise distract her, as if its very irrelevance were an escape hatch; as if this reminder that the world contained a million other moments, all of them

227

happening right this second, rendered her own situation no more meaningful than anyone else's. But it was difficult to maintain that illusion with Jackson Lamb next to her. More than bones might soon be broken. And she recognised, out of nowhere, that looping prayer that had earlier leaked from a houseboat. 'Jesus' Blood Never Failed Me Yet'. It was music, that was all. Music folded so carefully into the dark that it might have been just another city noise; the misplaced optimism of a terminal case.

Lamb said, 'You invited him in and now he'll sell everything that's not nailed down, the way his kind always do. And Slough House isn't nailed down. So do you want to forget about those fucking ducks for a minute and concentrate on the big issue? You pissed off the GRU when you took out one of their agents, and they're looking to even the blood count. And thanks to Peter Judd, or someone like him, they've decided Slough House fits the bill.' He flicked his cigarette in the direction of the canal, and for a moment it was a tiny rocket, leaving stars in its wake. Then it was only a hiss. 'So this is where we are. And because I'm a people person, I'll tell you what I'll do. I'll give you one chance to decide whose side you're on. And before you do that, here's a tip. Whatever rules this wet-job crew are playing by? So am I.'

Firing that cigarette into the dark might have been a mistake; he hadn't anywhere near finished it. But another had appeared in his fist already, and he aimed it at her as if staring down its barrel.

'Start talking.'

And Diana did just that.

★ ★ ★

When his phone buzzed with Catherine's text, *Blake's grave. Now*, River switched it off and removed the battery one-handed; left the parts on the passenger seat. Gone dark. It seemed to fit.

There are states in which all moods become possible at once: fear and fury, grief and excitement, dread, bewilderment, and a sudden deep attachment to something which might already have slipped away. River had spent these last years missing Sid, though he hadn't known how much until now; the knowledge had arrived hand in hand with the awareness that she might have been taken away again. So he was driving too fast through darkness, the sky having deepened from blue to near-black, and the lane ahead, narrowed by his headlights' focus, was a constantly swirling channel hedged on both sides by a blurry green mass. He was tensed to brake, but desperate not to. They were minutes ahead of him, in a possibly white car. *XTH???* The number plate hardly mattered. The first car to swim into his vision would be the one he was chasing. There'd been nowhere to turn off, not without plunging into an unlit field.

They looked surprised when I said she was in there. They thought the house was empty.

Two of them, 'from the hospital'. They'd come looking, the same way they had come looking in Cumbria, though this time they hadn't expected to find Sid, which must mean they'd been looking for River. That bore thinking about, but not right this minute; for now, all he had to do was catch up, before they did whatever it was that missionaries did. Which River doubted involved saving souls, though it might include liberating them from the flesh.

Fear and fury, grief and excitement. Because he

could not deny there was exhilaration in this; the pleasure of hot pursuit, a live mission. River's brief tenure at the Park seemed a decade ago, and the long days at Slough House since must have seen slow poison feeding into him, because even now, with Sid's life at stake, there was part of him that was glad this was happening. He tried to banish the thought, but couldn't. He was glad this was happening, because the life he'd led since exile from the Park was not the life intended for him, not the one his grandfather had prepared him for. The O.B. had never wanted First Desk for himself, preferring to be the power behind the swivel chair, but he'd wanted it for River. That was the unspoken dream, present in the silences between the stories he'd told, but he'd never realised that it was the stories themselves River craved to be part of — that it was the danger he yearned for, not the satisfaction of moving pieces around the board. River didn't want to be the storyteller. He wanted to be living in the tale. And if he'd had flashes, these last few years, of the ice in the soul required to plot an enemy's destruction, he was just now learning the corruption that action demanded, the addictive joy in abandoning scruple and surrendering to the chase, even when someone you loved was in danger.

Which was the thought he was having when he took the corner way too fast and met the oncoming car.

★ ★ ★

The ducks concluded their meeting with some acrimony and adjourned, all parties seething. As Diana finished her account of her dealings with Peter Judd and the angels, their noise was being enfolded within the evening's other disturbances: the traffic in the near-distance, and the aimless chatter of pedestrians on the road above, muffled by trees, so their language had no more clarity than that of the ducks.

When the girl had come to her — Ashley Khan; in her sixth month of training, and no guarantee she'd reach her seventh, not after tonight's encounter — Diana had considered sending the Dogs out, to bring Lamb in under heavy manners. And then reality kicked in: if Lamb was breaking bones just to show her he was serious, then he was monumentally pissed off. Which meant he knew that his former team was being hunted down, and was looking for someone to blame. And given his talent for mayhem, and the tightrope she was currently walking, it would be safer to have him hear the facts from her than find them out for himself.

The ducks' departure had left the canal as ruffled as an unmade bed, which now quietly made itself before her eyes.

'Not just Judd, then,' said Lamb after a while. 'You've got a whole coven of the fuckers.'

'Businessmen. Entrepreneurs. Concerned about our national security.'

Even as she was saying the words, she could feel their hollowness. Lamb possibly noticed this too, as his immediate response was another fart.

'Judd's no fan of Slough House,' he said. 'Last time we locked horns, I seem to remember he ended up a butler short.'

Butler wasn't quite the word for Seb, Peter Judd's erstwhile fixer, fiend and legbreaker, but it was true that he hadn't been seen for a while.

'But what the altogether fuck's he playing at now?

231

Sponsoring a hit, okay, that puts you in his pocket, and I'm sure he's enjoying having you wiggle around there.'

'I'm not in his pocket.'

'Tell that to his stiffy. But feeding the opposition my crew, what's that about? It's as carefully planned as a Trump tweet. There's no sense playing both ends against the middle when you're the one in the middle.'

Diana said, 'It's not Judd.'

'Then who?'

She said, 'White and Loy were old news. They're off the books. And even the books have been off the books since I wiped Slough House. Which means the details this GRU team have, if that's who they are, came from Molly Doran's archive.'

'Thanks. I'd got that far.'

'And Judd hasn't had access to the archive.'

'And you're gunna tell me who has.'

'One of the angels — one of the backers — his name's Damien Cantor. Media playboy, grew up on the internet and graduated from YouTube with honours. He — '

'I don't give a shit about his CV.'

'But maybe you've noticed Channel Go? That's his baby.'

'His baby? What'd he do, screw a shopping channel?'

Diana said, 'Judd wanted Cantor on board because he's got money, a ton of it. And what floats his boat is influence. He wants to be setting the agenda, not just reporting it, because that's how it is these days. You own a news channel, it's like putting a deposit down on a government.'

'Another Murdoch Mini-Me, eh? Paint my fucking wagon.'

'He's also a narcissist and a show-off. Essentially, a PM-in-waiting. So he couldn't resist letting me know he'd put one over on me.'

Lamb gave an impressed whistle. 'Have to get up early in the afternoon to manage that.'

'Fuck you, Jackson. Give me one of those.' She meant a cigarette, but realised too late what she'd let herself in for: Lamb removed the one inserted between his lips and passed it to her. After the briefest of hesitations, she accepted.

He produced another from behind his ear and lit both.

Once that was accomplished, she said, 'He told me one of his ex-security staff had signed on with the Park. When I ran his name, I found he'd had a run-in with Molly. Lurking in her stacks. Not something she approves of.'

'Yeah. She really puts her foot down when that happens.'

'You'll like this, then. He called her a crip.'

Instead of responding, Lamb stared across the canal, at one of the houseboats moored opposite. A flickering behind its curtains suggested candlelight within, or perhaps a TV, or an iPad. Anything, really.

She said, 'Tommo Doyle's his name. And he could have photographed the Slough House file while he was in the archive. On Cantor's instructions, I mean. Because Cantor knew about Slough House. Judd told him.'

'Told him what, precisely?'

'That the department existed, that I'd wiped your records, that I was using your crew for target practice. It must have given him the idea you were a sellable commodity.'

233

'And there's nothing a rich man likes better than knowing something's for sale.'

'There were already rumours the Kremlin's furious about Kazan, and looking to take revenge. Ready to declare war on our equivalent of their murder squad. Except we don't have a murder squad, which left them punching shadows.' Diana paused. 'Cantor's not interested in ideology. But he wants to be a player, and these are the boys who stole the White House. If he offered them a viable outlet for their anger, who knows what he'll get in return?'

'Yeah, and he starts feeding tigers their breakfast, who does he think they'll eat for lunch?' said Lamb. 'The stupid fucker. And that's why my old crew are falling off ladders and burning to death. You'd think the GRU would have noticed our team list is written in faded ink on yellow paper.'

'Why would they care? They just have to be seen doing it. By us. By Rasnokov. By the Gay Hussar himself. Welcome to the fake news world, Jackson. You've been hiding in Slough House too long. Things have got nasty out here.'

'They always were,' said Lamb.

★ ★ ★

Words smeared across River's mind in the moments afterwards, each syllable flat as a fly on a windscreen, its shape still apparent amidst the mess:

Shit

No

Sid

But while it was happening there were no words, only movement. River's brain became a blank, while his

234

hands and feet did his thinking: slamming the brakes on, going into a skid so loud, so total, he had no choice but to go with it, turning the wheel so the car spun as it approached collision, like a cartoon animal trying to avoid the inevitable, pulled one way while its legs tried to go the other. The windscreen filled with light and just as suddenly emptied: there was a tooth-grinding scream of metal on metal, and directions scattered and reassembled themselves in a different order. He was no longer moving. The car he'd nearly hit was parked sideways across the narrow lane. And River was still facing it, so one of them had managed a 180-degree turn. He suspected it had been him.

He'd done a parachute drop once, overseen by the military. Low opening, they called it: pulling the cord at the last possible moment. River still remembered his feet hitting the ground; it was a memory stored in most of his bones, including those in his ears and thumbs. This was similar. There was also an old joke here somewhere. *The good news is, your airbag works.*

River buried his face for a moment in the soft mass, then tore it from its casing. It deflated with a Lamb-like noise.

'You bloody maniac!'

The other driver was standing next to his door.

'Sorry,' River mouthed.

'I'm calling the police. I'm calling the police. You bloody — '

'Sorry.'

' — bloody stupid *maniac.*'

River nodded, because it was the least he could do. He was a bloody bloody stupid maniac: pointless to argue the toss. Or to waste more time. He tried to recreate his sudden turnaround, which proved a lot more complicated when done consciously, with an angry man providing the chorus. But it got done and then he was away again, still driving too fast down a narrow dark lane, but conscious of something having shifted inside him shortly before he didn't crash; some realisation he'd arrived at, the way you might put your hand inside a crowded wardrobe, and pull out exactly the thing you hadn't known you were looking for.

★ ★ ★

The end turned out to be a clearing by the side of the road; a small parking space among trees, from which, Sid guessed, a footpath would lead somewhere picturesque, or interesting, or historical. She was not in the mood for any of these things. But it didn't seem likely that her preferences would count for much.

'Nearly there,' said Jim, as Jane parked in the far corner.

What now? Sid asked, then realised she'd done so without making any noise. She cleared her throat. 'What now?'

'Nothing to be alarmed about.'

'No. But what?'

Jane spoke for the first time in a while. 'There's a lake through the trees. Well, a large pond. Looks nice on the map.'

'Area of natural beauty,' said Jim. 'One of those phrases you hear.'

'We'll take a look, shall we?'

There's a word for questions that don't require an answer.

Sid provided one anyway. 'I'm not going anywhere with you.'

Jim laughed. 'You've come this far. What's a hundred yards more?'

'It's dark.'

'We have a torch. And it'll be lighter by the lake. Water reflects.'

'You know what?' said Jane. 'I think a dip would sharpen us all up. What do you say to that?'

She'd directed this at Jim, who said, 'Nightswimming — why not? It'll only be cold for a few moments. After that, it'll feel quite normal.'

'I don't have a costume,' said Sid. She seemed to be having trouble with her volume control: the words came ballooning out of her mouth, as if she'd taken helium. This was what happened when you got near the end: everyday things slipped away. The last time she'd died, it had happened suddenly, so she hadn't been nervous. This time, there was too much warning. These people were going to kill her. She didn't know why, but didn't feel she'd find any reason acceptable, even if it were carefully explained.

'Skinnydipping,' said Jim. 'Why not? We're all adults.'

He reached over and released Sid's seat belt. The strap brushed her breasts as it spooled back into its cavity. 'Or,' he said, and for the first time his voice became his own: no longer the jolly vicar but the ice-toned intruder. 'We could finish it here in the car. Which will be messier, but we can do that if you prefer.'

His head was right up against Sid's, their eyes inches apart. Sid stared into them, and nothing stared back.

'All right,' she said.

Jim tilted his head slightly: a question.

'Let's finish it here in the car,' Sid said, adjusting her sleeve.

Lamb said, 'You realise, if this goes on much longer, I won't have two spooks to rub together.' He in-then exhaled, a thin cloud that drifted away across the canal. 'Not that they won't enjoy that,' he added. 'Last time Ho experienced friction, someone was giving him a Chinese burn. Well, just a burn in his case.'

'You've gone dark,' Diana said, a refrain she'd played earlier. 'Stay that way. All of you. Another few days, a week at most, and you can safely graze again. We'll find this hit-team, send them home in a padded envelope.'

'I love it when you talk stationery.' Lamb turned to look at her. His face was the moon's: craters and hummocks and random patches of grey. 'White and Loy, I can live with. But Sid Baker was in that file too. And that's a different story.'

Diana said, 'She's dead,' but didn't put a whole lot of effort into it.

'She was dead,' he agreed. 'That's the official line. But you needed it on record that she actually wasn't, in case it came back to bite you. I mean, it was your fuck-up that nearly got her killed. So you buried the truth in Molly's archive, where no one was likely to look. Because everything goes straight to digital now, right?'

'Except you.'

'Pretty much a last resort where I'm concerned, yeah.'

She said, 'I wouldn't be the first First Desk, and I won't be the last, to hide things among the paper-work. So okay, yes, I wanted Baker out of the picture. I've kept her safe all this time. New name, new footprint. Nice little cottage near the Lakes.'

'I'm hearing the world's biggest but coming in to land.'

'She's gone absent. Her milkman reported it a couple of days back.'

'And you did what?'

'I didn't get the report until earlier today.'

'That's what I like about the Park,' said Lamb. 'Always on the ball. Any chance you included her hideaway details among that paperwork? Don't even bother answering that. Found out where she went yet? And why?'

'We're looking into it.'

'Let me save you the bother. She's at David Cartwright's place. Remember him? Used to be the Service's pied piper. He played, everybody danced.'

'And why would she go there?'

'Because joes on the run look to other joes for help, and Sid was close to River Cartwright. Whose grandfather's address would be on record as his main contact on account of River living in a six-month rental. She'll know that from having seen his file back in the day, and our bad actors'll know it courtesy of your friend Cantor. So now they're on a two-for-one. They turn up looking for Cartwright, they'll find Baker too.' He paused. 'I hope you're keeping up. I'm fucked if I'm repeating any of that.'

'Her address wasn't in the file,' said Diana. 'But the facility she'd been treated at was.'

'Stone me. How could they ever have found her?'

She studied her cigarette, which was all ash and filter. 'I'll send a team out.'

'Don't bother. Cartwright knows we've gone dark. He may be an idiot, but of all the idiots I'm proud to call my own, he's the idiot who's memorised the protocols. He'll have vanished and taken her with him.'

'Unless the GRU team got there first.'

'Yeah, well, in that case we'll need the cleaners in.'

'The past never stops coming back to bite us, does it?'

'It never stops coming back full stop,' said Lamb.

She ground out what was left of her smoke. 'I appreciate that you're pissed off. But it's under control now, or will be soon. So don't make waves, Jackson. Barricade yourself somewhere with a case of Talisker. By the time you've drunk yourself to death, it'll be safe to come out.'

'Nice to hear words of comfort. It's like being offered a glass of water by the arsehole who's just burned your house down.'

'Oh, and one other thing,' she said. 'Two of your lot beat up a civilian tonight. Stole his wallet and phone.'

'We've all got ways of making ends meet,' said Lamb. 'But how do you know they were mine? It's not like I've got a monopoly.'

'Because Wicinski was being tailed when it happened. My agent reported him lurking in the gents at Old Street station. Actually spoke to him there. Ten minutes later Wicinski left in a hurry, along with — quote — a squat-looking she/he. I'm assuming that was Dander. And they'd left their victim in a toilet cubicle.'

Lamb considered this. 'I'll give you squat-looking. But Dander's more of a he/she, I reckon. Your agent's very rude.'

'And last time I checked, mugging was a criminal offence. So once Slough House's lights are back on, expect that pair to be clearing their desks. Aside from

240

whatever the Met do with them.'

'Clear their desks? Dander'll probably do a crap on hers.'

'More work for the cleaners then.'

He said, 'This Judd business. The angels. You've stepped into a bear trap, you know that.'

'I can handle it.'

'You think?'

'I know.'

'Your funeral.' He offered her an outstretched palm. 'Meanwhile, I'll need your keys.'

'You'll need my keys. What does that mean?'

'It means I'm going dark, as requested, which means I'll need a safe house. And for obvious reasons, I don't currently have faith in the Park's ability to boil a kettle, let alone keep me or mine out of harm's way. So if you'll let me have the keys to your place, it'll save you having to sweep up broken glass in the morning.'

'You're not using my house!'

'Like I said. Broken glass.'

'Jesus's blood,' she said, the words coming out of nowhere. Then found her key ring, and detached a pair. She recited an address, not her own.

'Been dipping a toe in the property market?'

'Just leave it as you found it, all right?'

'My philosophy of life,' said Lamb, taking the keys.

* * *

It was clear that damage had been done. There was a noise from the engine suggesting distress, what had started as a polite knock fast becoming an irritated rattle. River had passed several cottages but encountered no further vehicles; couldn't see anything suggesting tail lights when he reached the occasional straight. He had no idea where he was. Probably he'd cycled this way as a boy, but the curves and twists were lost to memory. These might be ditches he'd already ended up in once. Nice to have had a practice run.

In his stomach now, a tightening knot. He was breathing hard and his teeth were clenched. What had been excitement had drained away, and he was in the grip of dread; dread of not finding Sid; dread of finding her body. He'd been half a second away from piling into that oncoming car: subtract an atom of luck and he'd be dead or badly injured. And whatever was going to happen to Sid would carry on happening, unless it already had. And she'd never know he'd tried to stop it.

A gunshot broke the evening in two, but it was only his engine, the knock that was a rattle reaching new heights.

And then a dull grey something shone through trees on his left, and River remembered a lake, a picnic spot. A small piece of his boyhood fell into place, and he slowed approaching the next long curve, suddenly sure there'd be a parking place here, behind a line of trees. Even as the thought formed, reality arrived to meet it: déjà vu made physical. He turned off the road, drove into the darkness, and came to a halt twenty yards from the space's only other vehicle: silver, its registration ending *XTH*. The doors hung open, but there was someone in the back seat. Someone not moving.

River killed his engine, and for a second or two was aware only of how loud his breathing was.

The airbag was still in the footwell, and tangled his foot as he climbed out. His heart was beating too fast, and his legs trembled as he approached the other car, thinking *No, Christ, not again.* Remembering the blood on the pavement the last time Sid had died.

* * *

'Let's finish it here in the car,' Sid said, and pushed the O.B.'s letter opener up through Jim's jaw, into his head. She was surprised at how easy this was, if not as surprised as Jim. Because his seat belt was still in place he didn't fall forward but sagged back against the car's upholstery, and bubbled some nonsense, and died.

Jane screamed.

Sid opened her door and tumbled out.

She was away already, running along a track to the water's edge. Speed mattered. Maybe Jane would wait to check that Jim was beyond help, but Sid already knew he was. She hadn't even bothered trying to remove the blade, it was in so deep.

He had only been cold a few moments, but Sid guessed it was already starting to feel quite normal.

The trees thinned out, and she reached the lake. The path turned into a narrow wooden jetty, lapped by lake water, and leading to a wooden shack on stilts: a bird hide. It wasn't much bigger than a telephone box, and Jane could probably tear it down with her bare hands. So Sid stuck to the shore, veered left, ran a few paces, then ducked among trees, which immediately attacked her, slashing her face and hands with low branches. She stopped, and they calmed down.

Her clothes were dark. She could blend into shadow. But she'd already used up a lifetime's luck, along with her only weapon.

243

The look in Jim's eyes when he'd known he was dead. There'd been outrage there, rather than fear.

All was quiet.

There were no birds, no traffic; only the fussing of the lake as the wind skated across it. You'd have thought there'd be lovers, or drinkers, or both; you'd have expected at least one small group of idiots looking for romance or similar oblivion. But there was only Sid and Jane, who'd be coming for her now, armed and with urgent intent, because this was no longer a job, it was personal. Whatever toxic bond had fused Jim and Jane, she'd avenge its sundering. So it was likely that Sid would die in this unfamiliar place, and with the thought she pressed against the tree trunk, as if trying to melt inside it, become invisible, become tree.

Tt Tt Tt said the bullet, and a gunshot broke the evening in two.

Sid yelped, but it hadn't been a gun, had been a passing car, and she opened her mouth to scream for help, then snapped it shut. A scream would bring Jane, and it wouldn't take Jane a moment to finish her job. Which was what Sid had become: an unfinished job. Like an unswept floor, or an unwashed dish. Fuck that, she thought. *Tt Tt Tt* said the bullet. Fuck that.

She could slip back onto the track and keep running. She doubted it went anywhere. It would circle the lake and bring her back where she'd started, but didn't most paths do that? Look at her own travels. When she'd fled Cumbria she'd imagined River a place of safety. For some reason he was a fixed point among a mess of scattered detail: a pair of shoes in a wardrobe, beyond use, but never thrown away. Rubbish littering an office floor. Bad coffee drunk in a car at night. *Why did you come here? . . . I couldn't think of anywhere else. And you're safe.*

There was no fathoming what the mind kept hold of.

'Bitch!'

She was grabbed by the arm and pulled onto the track, flung to the ground and kicked hard. She tried to roll with it, a lesson supposedly burned into bone memory on the Park's training mats, but she landed like a bag of wet sand, the air punched out of her.

When she opened her eyes Jane was a fuzzy rim of light, which brightened and dimmed to the beat of Sid's heart. She crouched to be sure of being heard.

'I could put a bullet in you now. Kill you one piece at a time. But you're still going in that water in the end, and you're going to die with your lungs bursting. Because that was the *plan*.'

'That' and 'plan' were where she kept the beat: her tool the handle of her gun, her drum Sid's head.

Tt Tt Tt.

The world was flaring grey and white, like a washed-out flashback in a creepy movie. Sid's head hurt, as did her knees, and everywhere between.

'So small and harmless, so fucking wounded you looked. Holding that lump of metal as if that was your only weapon.'

Another blow. Another moment of nearby lightning. Sid felt her teeth scream.

'And all the time that fucking knife up your sleeve.'

Sid spoke, but the words came out so thickly they might have been made of mud.

Jane shook her. '*What?*'

Sid spat. 'He helped me on with my jacket,' she said. 'He let me have the knife.'

Be Villanelle. Be Lara Croft.

245

She'd been Sid Baker, but the old one, not the new.

'Get on your fucking feet.'

Jane dragged her back to the jetty, her gun hand round Sid's collar, the gun itself pressed to Sid's ear. Sid's feet were next to useless, and seemed to slide off the earth, but progress was made.

The walkway to the bird hide was solid and new. Halfway along Jane sent her sprawling again.

'I should gut you like a fish. Make you eat your own entrails.'

You can borrow my knife. I left it in your lover's head. But the words wouldn't emerge: Sid's throat was locked.

There ought to be birdwatchers. Crews of twitchers, awaiting the dawn chorus. But it wasn't even early yet; was still getting late.

Then Jane was kneeling beside her, one palm flat on her back, the other pulling her hair, forcing her to look up. 'What you'll see when you're dying. My face, laughing at you. And all your dead friends too.'

Sid said, 'His jaw was soft. The knife went right through.'

Jane banged her head on the woodwork, then heaved her across it, one hand still on her collar. She forced Sid's head over the edge. The water was high and stared back at her, an ever-folding blanket laced with sequins, reflections from nowhere. Sid could only see two inches in front of her, but the view reached all the way to life's end. And then it was gone and her head was underwater, held there by Jane's hand.

You're going to die with your lungs bursting.

She tried to kick, but Jane was on top of her, one knee in her back, one hand pressing her right arm to the jetty. These sensations were happening in a differ-

246

ent time zone. Meanwhile, Sid was holding her breath, while Hercule Poirot wheezed inside her. *Tt Tt Tt*, he said. Then *Pp Pp Pp*, and finally *Qq Qq Qq*. The water tightened round her head, and memories broke from the mass of her past: the shape of the bedknob on her first bed. The coat she wore on her first day at school. Something was burning inside her chest, and might swallow everything, if she let it. A piece of coloured paper on which she'd fixed gold stars and drawn a friendly horse . . . It would be simplest to breathe in now, and let the lake's cool water put the burning out. She had forgotten why she was here. But all paths lead back to where they started, don't they? The coloured paper crumpled and vanished, joined all the things she couldn't remember yet, and then Jane's hand released her and she almost slid into the water anyway, because that seemed the obvious move. But with what was left of her free will she pulled back, and breathing air seemed the most extraordinary event: unusual, unprecedented, worth lighting a candle for. It hurt, and her chest still burned, but for a minute she couldn't get enough of it, and lay there gasping, staring at the clouds, while a yard away Jane, taking a break from killing Sid, was killing River instead.

★ ★ ★

When River followed the path through the trees, it led him to the lakeside he remembered from boyhood, or thought he did, though this was new: a wooden jetty, ten yards long, leading to a small hut, probably a bird hide. The jetty was low, or the lake high: either way, its elevation allowed a woman to drown Sid Baker by holding her head under water while kneeling on her back. Sid was alive because her feet were kicking, just barely. Something silver on the planking caught a random sliver of light: a gun. She'd put the gun down the better to drown Sid. This thought took a moment to process itself, and by the time it was done River was halfway there.

The woman turned before he reached her, and her face was pure calculation: work in progress versus approaching deadline. She abandoned her task, leaving Sid flapping like a landed fish, and lunged for the gun, which River's foot reached first: he sent it flying towards the hide. It hit the door and clattered to the woodwork. He tried to kick her in the face as a follow-up, but was unbalanced. She was on her knees, a good height at which to direct a jab at his balls, but his forward motion had propelled him past her, and she hit his thigh instead, which went briefly numb. He turned, dipped and reached for the gun, but she was on her feet now and kicked out, catching him on the shoulder, but only because he averted his head in time. Before she could snatch the weapon he sprang forward and caught her midriff, rugby-tackle-style: now they both went down, River on top. He felt her knee thrust upwards between his legs and jammed his thighs shut, and crashed his forehead onto her nose. Blood spurted. Then her open palms slapped both his ears at once, and the resulting thunderclap split his head open. She pushed him off, and for a moment they shared a look: one of them was going to kill the other. Whoever had the gun was favourite.

She was nearest.

She scrambled onto all fours and scurried for it, but River recovered in time and leaped on her. He tried to grasp her collar, and gain leverage to smack her head on the platform, but she rolled without warning, throwing him off. He nearly went in the water; she nearly reached the gun, but he grabbed her wrist, and when she tried to smack her forearm into his face, bit her. She screamed in outrage, and he hauled himself over her, stretching for the gun, but two swift punches to his side stopped him. He jabbed his elbow into her face in response and she loosened her grasp, and this time his hand did reach the gun, but before that could matter, she punched him in the throat. His whole body convulsed, fingers included, and the gun went off: a sudden firework against a dark background. The bullet could have gone anywhere. The gun did; before she could wrest it from his breathless grip he launched it, hard as he could, into the night: the splash it made when it hit the water met the gunshot's echoes coming back.

Still trying to breathe, feeling like his head was wrapped in plastic, he tried to crawl free, but he was on his back and she was clinging to him tight as a lover: her face soaked in blood, her teeth a grimace. And then she hit him in the face, twice, each blow sending pain rocketing through his head. Before a third blow could connect he arched his back violently and threw her aside. For a second he felt weightless, and had to anchor himself: there was work to be done. He scrambled to his feet, lost balance, and tumbled against the bird hide again, but didn't fall. She was on her feet too, in the crouching dragon position, unless it was flying tiger: she was about to launch herself, and almost did, but something stopped her — Sid Baker, wrapped around her legs like an angry toddler. River stepped forward and punched her in the face and she fell back over Sid and hit the deck. River threw himself onto her while Sid clung to her legs; she was kicking madly, but Sid wouldn't let go. Kneeling on her stomach, River put his hands round her throat and squeezed. It was like wrestling a fish: she arched and flapped and tried to punch him again; then seized his wrists and tried to break their grip. He felt himself winning, but she freed a foot; kicked Sid in the head, and dislodged River. She rolled, began to crawl, but he was on her again, and this time for good: for good? Was this good? River was suddenly aware of the *noise*, all the noise they were making. Yelps and snarls and pained mouthfuls of air. She was flat on the deck and he was on her back, and the water was there in front of them. She'd tried to drown Sid. It seemed like a plan. He hauled her forwards, and she struggled when she realised what he was doing, but it didn't help her, not with the two of them holding her down. And then River had her head in the water, like some God-awful Baptist ceremony, and her arms flailed about, desperate to grab hold of something; she caught his ear and tried to rip it off, digging her nails in, but River wouldn't relax his grip, couldn't, and now Sid was pulling the woman's hand away and holding it in both her own. Her feet were beating a message in Morse code, just a loose collection of vowels expressing who knew what. She had never died before. It was new territory. And then the letters spaced themselves out, and the message fragmented, as whatever it was the woman was seeing outgrew her ability to describe it. One last shimmered attempt at resistance, and she fell silent. It was over. It would never be over. But it was over.

River gave it another full minute before letting go of her head.

There was no sudden reanimation; no last-minute movie shock.

He drew back from the edge, still on his knees, every muscle trembling. Sid, too, had shuffled away. With distance between them they were breathing in unison: hard ragged gulps of air. He was soaking wet, he noticed. Sweat and blood. Lake water. Something to think about if this ever happened again: bring a change of clothing. He wanted to be sick. Even as he had the thought, Sid threw up. He wiped his mouth, as if it were hers.

Somewhere behind them an owl hooted. And then, from the other side of the lake, another replied: *Hu-whit. Hu-whuh.* Life went on.

10

A crowd defaults to its dominant emotion. Recent years had seen children taking to the streets, angry at the damage their elders have done to their planet, but fired by hope nevertheless. For others, rage remained the easier option.

That evening, the Yellow Vests had gathered around Oxford Circus. Though traffic continued to flow, the protestors were confident of their right to occupy the pavements, and their presence had swollen to cover all four corners of the junction, blocking the entrances to the Tube. But rush hour was over, and there was no sign, tonight, of any counter-demonstration by those who were similarly angry but for diametrically opposed reasons, so the usual business carried on at the usual pace; chanting and jeering and outbursts of ragged song. Leaflets, as always, were thrust on anyone passing; these leaflets, as always, now littered the pavements. And all the while the usual targets attracted attention shading into abuse: the too well dressed, the obviously indigent, the clearly foreign, cyclists, drivers who sounded their horns in derision, drivers who failed to sound their horns in support, women in groups, women in pairs, women on their own, and anyone whose skin tone deviated from the yellow-vested norm, which self-identified as white, though would have passed for pasty grey. It was a scene that might have been playing out in any British city, any European town, though if you looked upwards, over the heads of the furious, you could only have been in London, among London's beautiful buildings, framed by London's starless skies.

Not far off — up Regent Street, just this side of Portland Place — a black cab hovered, its passenger having requested it to wait while he made a phone call.

'I watched you on the news,' he was told.

'It's important to remember the camera adds pounds.'

'I suppose you're expecting my thanks.'

'Oh, I never expect thanks. I simply expect repayment, in due course.' Peter Judd shifted in his seat, so he could see himself in the driver's mirror. Put his free hand to his jowls, and gripped. His face tightened in response, and he became several years younger. Hmm. 'They were wondering if you'd be available for an interview.'

'I'd be delighted.'

'I said no.'

'You *what?*'

'You're not ready, Desmond. You don't mind Desmond? I'd use Flinty, but I'd sound like an idiot, or a sportsman. Which yes, I know, same thing.'

' . . . What do you mean, not ready? I've been giving interviews for months.'

'To spotty interns on freesheets, or virgins from websites. Channel Go is hardly *Newsnight,* but its presenters can at least conduct a grilling without falling off their desks. So if, for instance, you should reveal your understanding that *Downton Abbey* was written by Jane Austen, you're unlikely to find them agreeing with you. As happened in that Q&A with, what was it? *The Little Englander?*'

'*A New England.*'

'Thank you.'

On Oxford Circus, with no apparent triggering event, a protestor whose red sweater was visible beneath his high-vis tabard hoisted a newspaper dump bin, earlier stacked with *Evening Standards*, at the curved glass window of a clothing store.

It bounced off, to jeers, and some laughter.

Judd released his chin, and his face resumed its current age.

Flint said, 'So you're saying I need a crash course in general bloody knowledge before I'm allowed to lay out my vision for the future of this country?'

'It wouldn't hurt. But no, what I'm saying is, we need to be sure that the agenda you'll be called upon to address will be focused on those issues you're happy discussing. Rather than on anything which might reveal any, ah, gaps in your hinterland.'

'Bloody cheek!' That this sounded to Judd's ears a token protest was no surprise. Token protests were the bedrock of Flint's campaigning history. 'And I suppose you have an idea as to how to set that agenda?'

'I always have ideas, Desmond. It's why I'm in such huge demand.'

'It sounds like you're in traffic.'

'I am,' said Judd. 'I'm in a cab watching your troops perform their evening manoeuvres. Extraordinary. Like watching the Home Guard morris dancing, with malicious intent.'

'Why do you never say anything I can understand first time?'

'Blame my schooling. But let's try this — you might want to get down here.'

'I was there earlier. And it's a peaceful protest. As usual.'

'Yes, well. It is at the moment,' said Peter Judd, as the red-sweatered mastermind on the corner collected the dump bin and threw it at the window again. 'It is at the moment.'

★ ★ ★

White walls meant a clean conscience, Catherine liked to imagine. Back in her worst days, in that Dorset retreat where the Service sent its damaged people, she'd had fevered nights; dreams of being trapped inside a glass house, whose shifting rooms offered no escape. And during the days spent coming to terms with her new reality — *my name is Catherine, and I'm an alcoholic* — she found herself longing for bare, unvarnished shelter; somewhere with no traces of her previous life, or anyone else's. Somewhere she might be brand new. Vacant possession.

Well, here it was.

The mews cottage Lamb had led them to, on a cobbled lane near Cheyne Walk, had the white walls she'd dreamed of; white walls and little else. The kitchen was functional — a fridge hummed; an oven waited — but there was no furniture, no carpets, no art; only windows, each framing a view that perfectly matched the time of day. It was a blank canvas, with no regrets. A small house, but one that seemed pure and unsullied. Not yet stained.

'Well, fuck a number of ducks,' said Lamb. 'Someone spent a lot of time on all fours for the keys to this pad.'

Louisa, Lech and Shirley checked it out: two rooms upstairs, plus bathroom; kitchen and sitting room down. Approaching two million quid, Louisa thought:

like everyone who'd recently bought property she'd acquired an estate agent's gene, impossible to switch off. Lech and Shirley, both London renters, viewed it as they would a palace or a cathedral; somewhere they might get to visit, but short of revolution, meteor strike or raging zombie virus, nowhere they'd ever live. Lamb, meanwhile, had perched in the sitting-room's window recess, where the incoming light etched a golden thread round his bulk. Henry VIII, Catherine found herself thinking. Minus the finery, obviously. But with the same propensity for getting his own way, and not much caring who faced the blade.

Roddy Ho had found an outlet in the corner, and was charging his laptop. This was possibly at odds with the going-dark scenario, but he'd roll his eyes at any suggestion that his online presence might be detected. That was the thing about Roddy, thought Catherine. He couldn't open a door without hurting himself or offending a woman, but give him a keyboard and he could skip a fandango with his eyes shut.

The others reappeared. The house was clean, as advertised: no bugs, no tripwires.

'What about the neighbours?' asked Louisa.

'We'll tell 'em we're rat-catchers, and might be here a while,' Lamb said. He turned to the others. 'So — Dildo Baggins and Captain Coke. Been sandbagging tourists, I gather.'

'It was an accident.'

'We thought he was Park.'

'Well, according to Taverner he wasn't, which means you two shat in your porridge. So you might as well start planning your leaving party. I can't come, by the way. I'm drinking in my office that night.'

'We were going to return his stuff,' Shirley sulked.

'Is that the highest priority right now?' said Lech. 'I mean okay, we screwed up. But people are dying.'

'River's still not called in,' said Louisa. 'Nor has Sid.'

'Cartwright's gone dark,' said Lamb. 'So either he's remembered his training, or someone's pulled his blinds down. We'll find out which when he turns up or his corpse starts to smell. Meanwhile, I've got my own problems. Anyone got a light?'

Catherine said, 'Just for once, could we try not polluting the air?'

He stared at her as if she'd just invoked an impossible creature, like a unicorn, or a secret vegan. 'And how would that help?'

'We'd all breathe more easily.'

'Help me, I meant.'

'You don't seem surprised Sid's alive,' Louisa said.

Lamb had conjured a cigarette from nowhere, but tucked it behind his ear. 'I'm more surprised some of you are. She was the only one of you smart enough to look both ways crossing the road.'

'Thanks.'

'Mention it. Of course, she's also stupid enough to turn to Cartwright for assistance. Bit like seeking Prince Andrew's advice on choosing your friends.'

'Editorialising aside,' Catherine said, 'do you have a next move planned? Because if all we're going to do is lie low, we might as well sort out sleeping arrangements.'

'Happy to share with anyone,' said Lamb, raising a buttock and farting long and loud.

Ho said, 'Three rooms, six of us. We should probably pair off.'

'In your dreams,' Louisa told him.

257

Lech said, 'There's a team of GRU killers out there knocking off slow horses past and present. Maybe that's what we should be focusing on.'

'Hashtag-face has a point,' Lamb conceded. 'Anyone care to contribute? And remember, there's no such thing as a bad idea.' He retrieved the cigarette from his ear. 'Just the time-wasting fuckwit who offers one.'

Shirley said, 'How many of them are there?'

'How many clowns fit in a car?'

'GRU crews operate in pairs, don't they?' Catherine said. 'And these attacks have been spaced out. First Kay. Then Struan, a couple of weeks later.'

'If there was more than one pair, they could have done them at the same time,' said Louisa. 'And given us less warning.'

'I didn't know these people,' said Lech.

'Yeah,' said Louisa. 'But let's pretend we care.'

'No, I'm making a point. They were before my time. And there's no record of me being in Slough House anyway. Because Taverner had us wiped at the same time I joined.'

'Before my time too,' said Shirley.

'So you want to know who's gone dark?' Lech said. 'Me and Shirley. Because if they're using out-of-date records, they've no idea we exist.'

'And that's what comes of supportive leadership,' said Lamb. 'Anyone would think you were strategic thinkers, instead of a bunch of useless no-hopers.' He levered himself off his perch. 'Our Moscow murderers are operating from Molly's file, which doesn't include Butch and Sunglasses here. So yeah, we have the advantage that they care even less about you than the rest of us do. Of course, that only stays an advantage until you both go to prison for mugging a tourist.'

'Seriously, he was not a tourist!'

'He was hanging around in a public toilet,' Shirley said. 'Probably cottaging.'

'Which would make it a hate crime,' Lamb said sorrowfully. 'And time's up on that sort of thing.'

'So how do you propose playing this advantage?' Catherine asked. 'And please don't say you're sending Lech and Shirley out against a pair of trained hitmen.'

'Be a good way of using them up, wouldn't it?' said Lamb. 'But no, that wasn't my first thought. My first thought was — '

'River and Sid,' said Louisa.

'My first thought was, there must be a takeaway round here somewhere. But I suppose, once they've snuck out and got me some food, they can go round up the missing.'

Louisa said, 'You can borrow my car. So long as Shirley doesn't drive it.'

'What's wrong with my driving?'

'Your lack of basic motoring skills.'

'I'll need drink, too,' Lamb said. 'And a lighter.'

Louisa scribbled the O.B.'s address down, and explained to Lech where her car was, while Shirley fidgeted. Roddy had returned to his laptop. Catherine watched all this with the sudden sense that it was beyond familiar. Even Lech, the relative newcomer, slotted in: his obvious damage plain to see; the other stuff bubbling inside him, looking for an outlet.

She remembered J. K. Coe, and the direction his long-buried trauma had sent him, and thought *It doesn't help* — putting them all together in one place, fastening them up in Slough House, didn't help. It just provided them with the opportunity to nurture old bad habits, or foster new ones. But it was a little late to make that observation. Lech was taking the keys from Louisa, Shirley all but tugging at his coat hem. 'Don't mug any strangers,' Lamb advised as they left, an unlit cigarette dangling from his lips.

'Sneaked, by the way,' she said.

'...What now?'

'It's 'sneaked'. Snuck's not proper English.'

'Do I look like I give a feaked?' said Lamb.

They settled down to wait.

★ ★ ★

Don't leave your kill in the open. He couldn't remember whether that was Bond, Bourne or *The Lion King*, but it seemed a rule, so they'd half-carried, half-dragged Jane's body back to her car. The track seemed twice as long as it had been, and the night twice as noisy, and when a vehicle slowed on the road beyond the trees both their hearts moved up a gear, pounding in unison. Halfway there Sid fell: she was fine, she was okay. She clearly wasn't. So River hoisted the body onto his back, and staggered the rest of the way solo. Getting a corpse into a boot looked easy in a movie, but Jane's sodden clothing got twisted on the locking mechanism. She'd gone waxy to the touch, and looked foreign in a way she hadn't while alive, as if the role she'd been playing had drifted away in the water. This was the kind of thought it would be best not to share. He got the clothing untangled at last, and the body slumped like a bag of vegetables. Death was a savage bastard, robbing both giver and given of grace.

Jim — that was what Sid called him — was just a

260

shell. The letter opener embedded in his jaw took a while to lever free.

'We should put him in the boot too.'

Except Jane was occupying most of it, and the effort required to fold her more compactly was beyond them. So he just freed Jim from his seat belt, and let the body collapse to the floor.

'It's a bit obvious.'

Sid's voice was a faraway niggle.

'Can't be helped. And nobody will see it while the car's moving. I'll take this one, you take mine. You okay to drive?'

But she wasn't.

'We need to get back to the house. I'll call Lamb, he'll talk to the Park. They'll deal with it. But we can't leave them here. Anyone might come.'

And probably would, given time, but it made no difference. Sid's hands were trembling madly. They couldn't have handled cutlery, let alone a steering wheel.

'Okay,' River said. Plan B: he'd let the Park know where the bodies were. But even before he could look for his phone he remembered Catherine's text, the one events had erased from his mind.

Blake's grave. Now.

'Shit.'

Sid said, 'Oh. Is something the matter?'

'Very funny . . . We've gone dark.'

'We?'

'Slough House. Probably something to do with this pair.'

Another car was approaching, its headlights grazing the trees. Sid flinched but the car didn't slow. The darkness it left behind it seemed heavier for its passage.

'Okay,' said River again. 'We leave them here. Get home. I'll contact Lamb from there.'

Once they weren't standing next to a vehicle whose passengers were dead.

It was far from ideal, but the whole evening had been like that. When he got behind the wheel he realised his own hands were trembling too, the hands he'd used to hold a woman's head underwater. *Until she died.* He started to say something, but stopped. Wasn't sure what it would have been.

'River?'

'That knife belonged to Beria,' he said.

'. . . Knife?'

'The one you took from the study.'

'Oh.'

'My grandfather paid a lot of money for it.'

'. . . Who's Beria?'

'Doesn't matter. Tell you later.'

His headlights picked out the killers' car when he turned them on. But you'd have to be standing close, peering through the window, to make out the body within; you'd have to open the boot to find the second. He started up and left the scene, heading for the O.B.'s.

★ ★ ★

In a different car with the same destination, Shirley had opened the glove compartment. 'Hey, Sunglasses! Lamb called us Butch and Sunglasses.'

'Yeah, I think you were meant to be — forget it.'

She put them on. They covered half her face. 'Do I look like J-Lo?'

More like Jeff Goldblum, Lech thought. *In The Fly.*

262

They'd eaten on the move, after having delivered a metric ton of Indian takeaway to the mews house. In keeping with Louisa's restriction, Lech had refused to countenance Shirley's offer of driving 'just until we're clear of the city', because, her opinion, 'it'll be quicker that way'. For one thing, he pointed out, she was way over the limit. And for another thing, there didn't need to be another thing. Because she was way over the limit. He still wasn't sure his argument had hit home, but the fact that he held the keys, not her, was the clincher.

The O.B.'s house was outside Tonbridge, Kent. The rain had moved west, and rush hour was over; all in all, there were worse ways of spending an evening, were it not for the company, and his awareness of impending doom.

Still with the shades on, Shirley said, 'How much trouble do you think we're in?'

'Well, we mugged someone in a toilet and the whole world seems to know about it. So quite a lot.'

'At least we didn't kill him.'

'The fact that you see that as an upside worries me.'

'It'll be all right.'

She sounded confident.

Lech said, 'Gut feeling? Or do you know something I don't?'

'We're Slough House, not Park. Lamb'd sack us if he felt like it, wouldn't need a reason. But he won't let Taverner.'

'Yeah, one small thing? Taverner's his boss.'

Shirley just laughed.

She toyed with the sunglasses, letting them dangle from her ears, cupping her chin. 'What's it like?'

'What's what like?'

Shirley waggled her fingers in front of her eyes, like a celebrity signposting fake tears. 'Having your face mashed up.'

'Empowering. You should try it.'

'Do you wish you hadn't?'

He'd hit rock bottom the day Lamb had handed him the razor. *In case a third way occurs to you. Other than stitches or surgery.* The latter was out of his salary bracket, and stitches would have left his face looking like a sampler made from a tabloid headline. So what did that leave, wrapping bandages round his head like the invisible man? Actually, that might have worked. But no way was he going into this with Shirley, so he just grunted, and concentrated on overtaking the sixteen-wheeler in front. Spray misted the windscreen. 'You didn't know this Sid woman, then?'

'Nah. She was dead before I started.'

'Or not.'

Shirley shrugged. 'She was shot in the head. She might still be alive, but I doubt she's the person she was.'

Lot of that about, thought Lech. He said, 'You think Lamb'll go to bat for us, then?'

He could hear her alcohol intake in her laughter. 'Lamb with a bat in his hand. I wouldn't want to be anywhere near.'

Lech felt much the same about Shirley and any blunt object. Sharp ones, he'd done as much damage to himself as anyone was likely to.

She said, 'But Taverner was taking the piss, wiping Slough House. So yeah, I think he'll nobble her. Not 'cause he wants to keep us. Just to stop her taking us away.'

He thought: And this is the world I move in now.

264

Where decisions are based, not on the greatest good or the most just cause, but simply on fucking up the opposition, even if the opposition's your own side.

Rifling through the glove compartment again, Shirley had found some chewing gum. 'Do you ever get déjà vu?'

'I feel like I'm about to.'

'We should check the boot,' she said. 'See if Louisa bought a new monkey wrench.' And when Lech raised his eyebrows, said, 'You never know.'

★　★　★

At the third time of trying, the dump bin went through the window, and the resulting scatter of glass was accompanied by a roar of approval from the Yellow Vests, as if the windowpane had been all that was hemming them in. En masse they swept onto the road, causing traffic, which had been grumpily processing past, to come to a halt; a line of buses and taxis, taxis and buses, soon blocked both Oxford and Regent streets, while cycle-drawn hansoms took to the pavements. From a distance it might have seemed like a celebration in progress — Victory Over Europe Day, perhaps — but in the immediate area, a violent undercurrent was palpable. One broken window wasn't such a mess, in the scheme of things. But it seemed like a start.

Oddly, a TV crew had been in place throughout, though Yellow Vest gatherings were barely newsworthy these days; were just another street hazard, like wobbly paving slabs or charity muggers. But Channel Go had sent a van earlier in the evening, and its crew were on the street, filming the commotion. From the

265

cab window Judd watched them weaving through the crowd with interest, not least because one of them had just the kind of legs he admired: long, and attached to a woman.

Noise rose and fell, like a wave breaking over silt.

'Meter's still ticking, guv,' the driver said.

'I'm immensely glad that you reminded me of that. But it's of no importance, I assure you.'

'Your money.'

'And soon to be yours.'

This promise gladdened the driver's heart, or at least loosened his tongue. 'Interested in these jokers, are you? The Yellow Vests?'

'Mmm.'

'Yeah, no, I say jokers, but they've got a point. It's the voice of the people, you get down to it. I mean, it's been a joke, hannit? These last few years? A flippin' circus. It gets you wondering, who are the government to tell us what to do?'

'A strikingly acute question. And now, I have a favour to ask.'

'Anything you say, guv.'

'Stop talking. And step outside for five minutes. I'm about to take a meeting.'

Which commenced twenty seconds later, when Desmond Flint joined him.

'What the hell's going on?' he asked, climbing into the cab.

'I know,' Judd beamed. 'Almost as if your people had a mind of their own.'

'I mean — this wasn't . . . A peaceful gathering. That was my instruction.' He closed the door. 'But this, this . . . The police are lining up on Oxford Street. This'll make us look like criminals.'

266

'As so often happens when laws are broken,' said Judd. 'But do stop worrying. Here.'

He handed Flint a silver flask. Flint took it, uncomprehending.

Judd said, 'The Home Secretary is unlikely to order the police to move in without the PM's say-so. And since he has a way of being hard to find when decisions are called for, we have a little time.'

'This was deliberate. A troublemaker. None of my doing. This is the work of one of those, what did you call them? An Asian something?'

'Victoria's Secret Agents,' said Judd.

' . . . What?'

'Just my little joke. *Agents provocateurs.*'

'And you said they'd been dealt with. That you'd persuaded MI5 to withdraw them. But now this happens. And there are TV crews, for God's sake!'

Judd said, 'Take a drink. Calm your nerves.'

Flint looked at the flask, then raised it to his mouth. Swallowed and said, 'And you're making jokes. I thought you were going to be my political saviour. Just earlier today you said that. And here we are now, and my movement, the movement I started, looks minutes away from building a bonfire in the middle of fucking London! And what have you done in the meantime?'

'Well,' Judd said, 'I arranged for someone to throw a bin through a window.' He held a hand up to forestall interruption. 'And I know what you're going to say. That can't have taken more than a phone call. But you have to know who to call. That's where the expertise comes in.'

' . . . You are out of your bloody tree, mate! You are mad as a box of Frenchmen!'

'And the same person I called to borrow a bin chucker from arranged for the first of those TV crews to be here. Channel Go. I think I mentioned them earlier. Now, be a good chap, take another belt of that rather special brandy, and run a comb or something through your hair. Because it would be best if you made your play before they do light actual bonfires. The optics would be a little, what shall I say? Reminiscent of darker times?'

'. . .What you on about?'

'Channel Go isn't here to film a riot, Desmond. It's here to film you.'

'. . . Me?'

Judd nodded in the direction of the increasingly restless mob. 'Oh yes. You wanted an opportunity to shine, didn't you? Well, that's what I'm giving you.' He leaned across to open the door of the cab. 'Your destiny awaits. You can thank me later. Here, take this. Oh, and leave the brandy. There's a good chap.'

He made no attempt to hide the thoroughness with which he wiped his hip flask before drinking from it. But Desmond Flint had left the cab by then, and had far too much on his mind to take offence.

* * *

River pulled into a lay-by half a mile short of home, and Sid handed him his dismantled mobile. He inserted the battery and powered up.

'If you've all gone dark, won't Lamb have disabled his phone too?'

He remembered the last time Lamb had switched Slough House's lights out: he'd gathered their mobiles and posted them down a drain. On the other hand,

268

Lamb was freer with other folks' possessions than he was with his own. But 'Soon find out' was all he said.

Lamb answered on the seventh ring. 'What fresh bollocks is this?'

'Me.'

'Not dead yet, then.'

'It would seem not.'

'And Baker?'

'I'd probably have mentioned it first thing.'

'So you're breaking protocol why, to tell me you finally got her knickers off?'

'Someone came for her. Two someones.'

'And . . . ?'

River said, 'They're no longer a problem.'

'Well, treat my billy goats rough.' Lamb paused. 'Okay, good. Unless they were just pollsters or window cleaners or something. You wouldn't be the first pair to go to town on a passer-by tonight.'

River didn't know and didn't care. 'There's a car. It'll need tidying away.'

'So now I'm your valeting service.'

'Jackson, I'm not in the fucking mood.'

'That's clear. I assume you're calling from nowhere?'

The middle of. River said, 'I thought it best to put some distance between us and the . . . '

'Recyclables,' suggested Lamb.

'Yeah. So, are we still dark? Or can I get the Park to do their thing?'

'No. Just get back where you started from. Wicinski and Dander are heading there now.'

'And then?'

'And by then I'll have a plan. Are the, ah, empties likely to be noticed any time soon?'

'Let's hope not.'

'Yeah. When did hope ever let us down?'

Lamb disconnected.

Sid said, 'Well, anyone eavesdropping on that'll assume it's just another Wednesday evening.'

Her voice was stronger.

River said, 'He knows you're alive. Probably always has done.'

'He sounds like he hasn't changed.'

'No. If anything, he's more so.'

'What were those names he said?'

'Wicinski and Dander. Lech and Shirley.'

'And he'd already dispatched them to the O.B.'s. So he was worried about you. Us.'

'Not sure worry comes into it.' He removed the battery from his phone once more. 'It's all a game. He's just shifting pieces round the board.'

'Isn't that what your grandfather used to do?'

'There's no comparison.'

'If you say so.'

'Barely common ground, even.' He scowled quickly, for no reason. Then asked, 'You all right?'

Sid looked at her hands. They'd almost stopped shaking. She said, 'There was this voice I kept hearing. In my head.'

'That's okay. We all get them.'

'Shut up. It was . . . I thought of it as my bullet. The one I was shot with? It was like it talked to me.'

River pulled away, his eyes on the dark road ahead. 'Okay,' he said again.

'Only it kind of drowned. When she was holding my head in the lake.'

Tt Tt Tt. Pp Pp Pp.

'Not a peep since.'

Qq Qq Qq.

270

River drove on. The road had grown familiar again: the usual bends, the usual straights. The patch of trees ahead were squared off where they overhung the road, remodelled by the regular passing of a bus. 'I'm not an expert. But maybe that's what happens, maybe traumas . . . cancel each other out.'

'Seriously? You're not an expert?'

'Yeah, shut up.'

'Because that sounds like seven years of medical school talking.'

River said, 'You sound fine. Maybe you should walk from here.'

She smiled, and looked down at her hands again. 'Thanks. By the way.'

'No need.'

'She'd have killed me.'

'I know. But you did pretty good yourself.'

Sid said, 'I'm not sure good's the word I'd use.'

'You or him.'

'Yes. I know.'

'And I don't ever want it to be you again.'

He pulled aside to allow an oncoming car to pass, and they rounded another corner, and then were home.

★ ★ ★

Catherine said, 'They're alive, then.'

'The night is young.'

Louisa said, "Recyclables'? 'Empties'?'

'It seems our hit squad caught up with Romeo and Juliet, and wonder of wonders, came off second.' Lamb shook his head. 'Good job I'm not a gambling man. I'd have lost the house.'

271

'And they're both okay?'

''Spect so. What am I, NHS Direct?'

'It's over then,' said Catherine.

'Yeah, sure it is,' said Lamb. 'Someone sics a hunter-killer crew on me, I'm basically just happy to call it bygones.'

Roddy said, 'I was hoping to see some of that action myself.'

They all stared, and Louisa said, 'You do realise you said that out loud?'

Because there were no tables, the floor was a mess of foil trays and cardboard covers, plastic knives and forks. In place of the new-paint smell that had lingered like a not-yet-broken promise, the mingled aromas of baltis and bhajis, dhansaks and dhal had taken over, along with — because Shirley had fetched Lamb a plastic lighter — cigarette smoke. Catherine had retaliated by opening the window. Lamb had glared at her as if this were the first skirmish in what might turn out a prolonged war.

Louisa said, 'And you know who this someone is?'

'His proxy was a Dog called Tommo Doyle. But the man himself's some kind of media playboy. Like a Bond villain, without the cool name.'

'Which is . . . ?'

'Damien Cantor.' He looked at Ho. 'Box of tricks all powered up, is it?'

'Always,' said Roddy.

'Except when it isn't, you mean. Okay, go fetch me Damien Cantor.'

Roddy looked momentarily confused.

'Information relating to him,' Catherine explained.

'And tell him to be quick about it,' Lamb said.

But Roddy didn't need that translated, and

shuffled off to his laptop.

'I've read about Cantor,' Catherine said. 'He's the Channel Go man. Pegged as the new Branson.'

'Haven't we suffered enough?'

'He wields a lot of influence.'

'And tried to buy more by selling Slough House.' Lamb found another cigarette. 'So pardon me if I don't rush to take out a subscription, or whatever you have to do to watch the fucking telly these days.'

'Does Taverner know he sold us out?' Louisa asked.

'Yeah, but he's currently got her bollocks in a mangle. And she hasn't worked out what to do about that yet.'

Catherine said, 'If Diana Taverner's been compromised, she's not fit for office.'

'And if being compromised got you the sack, we'd have vacant desks from here to Number Ten,' said Lamb. 'Not that that's a bad idea. But I barely have time for a quiet smoke, never mind cleaning the orgiastic stables.' He adopted a martyred expression, lit his cigarette, and — presumably out of habit — threw the lighter over his shoulder. It disappeared through the open window. 'So let's deal with one bastard at a time, shall we?'

'Oliver Nash is chair of Limitations,' Catherine persisted. 'We should talk to him.'

'Nash is a bureaucrat. If I want my bins emptied, he's who I'd trust to put the bin-emptying contract out to tender. But Taverner goes to the mats, which is what you want First Desk to do. And besides, we've had our moments.'

'Didn't she once try to have you killed?'

'I didn't say they were good moments.'

Looking up, Roddy Ho said, importantly, 'Cantor

lives in the Needle.'

Louisa, who had memories of the Needle, said 'Lives there?'

'It's where his offices are. But he's got an apartment too.'

'It's like having my own personal Yellow Pages,' said Lamb. 'Or, you know. Just Pages in his case.'

'So what exactly do you have in mind?' Catherine asked. 'Bearding him in his den?'

'Isn't bearding when you marry the Earl of Wessex? He'd probably sooner I killed him.'

'If you're planning a murder, the rest of us are leaving. I mean it.'

'And there's that moral high ground you love.' Lamb reached for the whisky Lech had furnished, which he had received with the grace of a minor royal being offered a turd. 'Must be cold up there. Explains the late-onset frigidity. Does he have family?'

Ho said, 'Married, two boys. But they live in Hove. He lives here, mostly.'

'Sensible man. Well, I say sensible. But cutting deals with Russian intelligence? What's he doing, running for office?' He uncapped the bottle. 'No, I plan to reach out to our Mr Cantor. Let him know he's playing with the big boys.' For a moment he studied the whisky's label, frowning, as if troubled by the ordeal ahead. Then he tipped the bottle and poured a glassful into his waiting mouth.

That done, he said: 'And as it happens, I've just the man for the job.'

11

Careful editing made it seem heroic: Desmond Flint, approaching the mob swarming Oxford Circus.

Police were massing on the approach roads, but focusing their attention on calming traffic, rather than crowd dispersal. Nor had there been violence, broken window aside. But there was noise and heat and movement; that mixture of anger and unwarranted triumph that can turn a pub quiz into a war zone. From a distance, it wasn't clear where the lines had been drawn. A bus driver had opened his door to engage in what might have been debate, might have been an exchange of threats: it was hard to tell. But what was certain was that this was an interim stage, a balancing act; as in any other circus, a tightrope was being walked. And one slippery moment might bring the tent down.

So into the spotlight walked Desmond Flint. His first steps seemed hesitant, but something changed the nearer he drew, as if he appreciated that the next few moments would define him ever after. He'd never be mistaken for Gary Cooper — he was a man for whom 'match ready' meant a fridge full of beer and a new battery in the remote — but he walked taller the last twenty yards, his strides longer. He developed purpose.

There was speculation afterwards as to where he'd laid his hands on a megaphone — did he take one everywhere, just in case? — but he brushed the question aside, saying only 'Someone put it in my

275

hand,' never adding who or when; never mentioning Peter Judd. And when the camera caught him raising it mouthwards, the resulting image became a photoshopped meme: Desmond Flint facing a tank in Tiananmen Square, planting his foot on the Moon, standing on a balcony in papal white. *You all know me — it's Flinty.*

As Judd remarked later, 'History has an open-door policy. Any fool can walk right in.'

Flint's appeal to the crowd appeared in several British newspapers the following day, though the punctuation differed in each.

'You all know me — it's Flinty. And I'm proud to be standing here wearing the same vest as the rest of you. The vest of the British worker, us who dug these very roads, built these very buildings all around you. The heart of London, this is — the heart of what used to be a great and proud empire. And I know why you're angry, why you feel like kicking off. I do too. I do too. Because that birthright, that word 'Great' that comes before Britain, we've seen it trampled in the dirt, haven't we? We've been lied to and talked down to for years. And I'm as angry about that as you are, trust me. Because I'm one of you, and you all know that. We've stood shoulder to shoulder, we've drunk from the same flasks of tea. Nights like this, and worse nights too — nights when it was cold and wet, and it was only our knowledge, only the knowledge that we were doing the right thing, kept us out here, making sure our voices would be heard. Heard all the way down the road there, at the BBC — which ought to be ashamed of itself, pretending to speak for Britain — and all the way in the other direction too, in Westminster, where the fat cats spend their days with their noses in the cream. And we're going to keep doing that, brothers. Yes, and sisters too. We're going to keep doing that, and the day is coming when they'll stop pretending to listen and actually open their bloody ears. And when that happens, I'll be the one letting them know what we're demanding. And you trust me to do that, don't you? You trust me to see you right!'

In the pause he allowed here, a heartbeat's silence filled the streets before the response arrived: a muttering that grew to a roar, accompanied by the stamping of feet, and the slapping of hands on the sides of cars and buses. Up the road, leaning against his taxi, Peter Judd nodded, appreciating the timing. You couldn't call it oratory. But it was getting the job done.

'Thank you. Thank you. I can't tell you what it means to me, to know I've got your support in the battles that lie ahead. Because that's what's important. But right now, right this moment, what I want you to do is call it a night. I want you to call it off now, this legal gathering of like-minded citizens, and go back to your homes. I've been assured you'll be allowed to leave peacefully, just as I've been assured that the police will be looking very carefully for those saboteurs, those victorious agents of provocation, who came here tonight to deliberately cause misrule. Not our people. Not our message. These people are the enemy, and they came here to make it seem as if we were the violent ones, that our protest is violent. Which it isn't. It isn't. We only want to have our voices heard. But for now, for right now, we need to make it clear that it's us who's the victims here, us who's seeking justice. And we won't allow our movement to be sullied, tarnished, by the enemy within.'

The unknown 'victorious agents of provocation' were another cause of speculation in the press, and the assurances Flint spoke of were as mysteriously sourced as his megaphone. But by the time the questions were asked, the answers had lost relevance. Once you have them by the headlines, as Judd had been known to observe, their dicks will surely follow.

'That's right. Just pack it away, now. It's been a good evening's work, because we've shown we won't be treated like dirt, and we've shown how calm we can be when we're provoked. So we can hold our heads high now, and we'll be back, won't we? We're all coming back. Thank you. God bless. God bless.'

Channelling a televangelist for some reason, but it didn't matter: the rousing cheer it produced put a seal on events. The crowd began to disperse. A few vests paused to nod to Flinty, or clap him on the back, but nobody tarried long. That would have been to tempt fate; to take what felt like victory and hold it to the light. Some things are best not examined closely.

Though there were several TV crews in place by this time — and dozens of phones had captured Flint's address — only Channel Go had been there for the moment that started the disturbance, the breaking of the window. But although that small piece of action featured prominently in the channel's coverage, at no point did the camera get a clear view of the trouble-maker's face.

And while the red sweater was recovered from a bin once the crowd had dispersed, its wearer was never found.

★ ★ ★

278

The two cars arrived at the O.B.'s at much the same moment, River having just put his complaining vehicle out of its misery as Lech's headlights peeped round the curve in the opposite direction, sculpting a long green shape from the darkness. Sid gripped his elbow. 'It's okay,' he said, recognising Louisa's car, and only mildly perturbed when he saw that it contained Lech and Shirley. 'They're with me.'

The four converged on the lane, and River, conscious that he and Sid were both wet and damaged, made brief introductions.

Shirley said, 'So you're the dead chick.'

'Thanks.'

'No, I meant it in a good way.'

Sid looked at River. 'Slough House hasn't changed, then.'

'Not so you'd notice.'

Lech said, 'Maybe we should take this inside? I'm presuming that's your house?'

Mine, yes, thought River. It had taken a while, but felt true now: this was his house. He led them round the back, shuffling broken glass aside with his foot as he held the door. Lech, he saw, was carrying a mobile. 'I thought we'd gone dark.'

'Situation's fluid. You know there's a GRU team out there?'

'We noticed.'

They went into the study, Sid automatically heading for the O.B.'s chair. She snapped the standard lamp on, and the room adopted a soft yellow sheen, a cosiness that felt unreal after the evening's events. As if they'd reassembled on a stage, having murdered the supporting cast in the wings. River, standing by Sid, noticed she smelled of lake water. He must do too.

279

Lech said, 'You've been swimming? Or mud wrestling?'

Sid said, 'They found us. Found me.'

'Okay . . . '

'And they're no longer a problem,' said River.

'Hey, cool,' said Shirley.

Lech raised an eyebrow.

'You think we're kidding?'

'I'm just getting to grips,' Lech said. 'I'm an analyst, not a field agent.'

Shirley had found the melted gun. 'Did this just happen? Or is it one you prepared earlier?'

River took it from her and put it on its shelf. 'They came after us. And they're both dead. In a car. Back the way we came from.'

'They died in a car?'

'They're dead in a car,' River clarified.

Something in his tone dissuaded even Shirley from seeking details.

'So what happens now?' Lech asked.

River could feel his body complaining: new-born bruises waking up. Stretched muscles, thudding aches. He'd held the woman's head under water until she'd ceased to be. That was something he'd have to live with, and he guessed he was up to the task: she'd come to kill him, Sid too. It was the very definition of self-defence. So yes, give it time, he'd climb over that memory, but here and now he could feel the aches and pains of their struggle, and all he wanted was sleep. On one level, he was grateful to Shirley and Lech for coming; grateful even to Lamb for sending them. On another, he wanted everyone except Sid to fuck off and leave him alone.

But what he said was, 'We'd better collect that car.

Before anyone finds it.'

In the dimly lit room, Lech's facial scarring looked like ten o'clock shadow. 'Collect it and then what?'

For a moment River thought about pushing it into the lake, letting it settle among the weeds. A movie-solution, which in real life would end in a half-submerged fiasco, a crowd of onlookers, and everybody wet. 'Bring it back here,' he said. 'Once we've gone light again, the cleaners can take it away.'

The best kind of problem was one that highly trained specialists would turn up and deal with.

'I'll drive,' Shirley said.

'You're still drunk,' said Lech.

She made a so-what? face, but he wasn't looking, so she turned to River. 'How messy are they?'

Instead of answering, River took Sid's hand. 'I'll be back soon.'

'I'll wait here.'

A glimpse of the old Sid showing through, he thought.

Shirley said, 'And what am I supposed to do?'

'There's a kettle, there are tea bags,' River assured her. 'You'll think of something.' He let go of Sid's hand, and he and Lech went outside. He was cold; could usefully have changed into dry clothing, if he'd had any. Brief, vivid snapshots of the struggle by the lake kept bursting into mind. He flinched involuntarily, and to cover up asked, 'What happened back in town?'

There was a pause long enough that River figured he wasn't the only one who'd had an interesting evening. Then Lech said, 'Lamb had a showdown with Taverner. Now we're safe-housed.'

'Everyone all right?'

281

'We left them eating an Indian takeaway.'

'Did you keep the receipt?'

'Gave it to Lamb,' said Lech. 'Why?'

'No reason,' said River, deciding this wasn't the time to explain that expenses claims filed through Lamb were a lost cause.

The drive felt shorter this time, though Lech wasn't approaching the mad speeds River had reached. Several times, they had to pull into the side to allow an oncoming car to pass. He'd got lucky, River thought, on his earlier journey. Just the one near-collision. And only two assassins. Could have been worse, which it was about to be. Because as Lech turned into the parking space among the trees, his headlights caught movement: there were now three other vehicles there; two in the far corner, and one beside the car containing the bodies. Around it, three shapes had gathered.

'Oh shit,' said River, and remembered the hide. 'Birdwatchers?'

'Uh, not exactly,' Lech said. 'I think they're dogging.'

* * *

I've just the man for the job, Lamb had said, so Louisa was heading into the underground again, alongside drinkers and filmgoers, the theatre crowd, late-shift retailers, and those with cleaning and maintenance jobs, heading from one place of work to the next. You could always tell day from night on the Tube, she thought. Lighting was constant, temperature didn't much vary. But you could always tell day from night.

Roderick Ho was with her, not because she needed back-up, but because Lamb wanted rid of him.

282

Waiting, she scanned ads for banks, for estate agencies, for online services. Credit was available, at rates set by Satan. She thought of Lamb's face on the phone to River; that pause when River told him the hit team was dead. No details, but River had no gun, and improvisation was messy. Meanwhile, people went to and from work, and stopped out late for a drink, and sank deeper into debt. She had a foot in both worlds: owned her own flat, drove her own car, had shot a few people. But she never had money over at the end of the month, her pension forecast wasn't rosy, her team had gone dark, there were bodies somewhere, and Lamb had a plan up his sleeve.

A train was approaching. She glanced at Roderick Ho, engrossed in an ad for bathroom fittings, which featured, inevitably, a barely clad female. He'd answered no when Catherine asked who remembered Kay White, who remembered Struan Loy, but Louisa would bet he remembered Sid Baker. Sid had been smart, and while that wasn't likely to figure among Ho's priorities, she'd been a looker too, and that ticked his box. Roddy was a looker himself, but only in the active sense: when a woman wandered into view, he looked. Sometimes, she'd noticed, his lips moved, as if he were adding a silent voice-over. In some ways she'd like to hear that, but in many more ways wouldn't. What happened inside Roderick Ho's head was best kept secret, like a nuclear launch code, or the PM's browsing history.

The train stopped, and as they boarded Louisa said, 'Probably best if we don't sit together.' With a quick movement of her head, she indicated the other travellers. 'You never know.'

Roddy nodded wisely. He'd been going to suggest

the same thing. They didn't call it the underground for nothing. Well, it was under the ground, but even so: exactly the territory you'd find the opposition lurking. You had to be sharp to spot a pro, mind. Case in point, Roddy himself: black hoodie, black jeans — classic, but blended in. Edgy undercurrent, because you couldn't switch *that* off, but it wasn't like he was making it obvious; not like he was sporting a branded baseball cap . . . There was a poster on a council building near his home, something about fostering children. 'Not all superheroes wear capes,' it read. Well *duh*, thought Roddy. Spider-Man? Captain America? *Sheesh*. Who writes this stuff? But anyway, yeah, there was an underlying truth there: you didn't have to dress the role, you just had to play the part. Always be alert, that was the key. Always bring your A-game. Like earlier, when he'd lured that tail into Lamb's trap — they'd only got this far because he'd done that. The Rodster on all cylinders as usual, ensuring Lamb got the outcome he needed, and now working the underground with the same silent dedication: never a moment's downtime. Dude has no off button, they probably said about him. Dude is like *permanent*. Though now he thought about it, a branded baseball cap might be cool. There was a place near him, they did T-shirts and stuff, he could probably get them to slap a slogan on some headgear. *Spook at work*. Little private joke, because everyone would assume he was wearing it to win cool points, never realising that beneath the outward flair lay constant vigilance.

Someone was kicking his foot. 'Hey!'

' . . . Huh?'

'It's our stop.'

Up the stairs and out of the station. It was full-on dark, and the streets had fallen into alternative ownership, those who were deferential by daylight having less reason to play meek now, given that any civilians still abroad had either spared all the change they were likely to, or long since grown blind to those asking. A few middle-aged men in yellow vests passed, discussing the events of their evening, the name Flinty featuring largely. Soon Louisa and Roddy were off the main drag, most of whose restaurants had perspex canopies sheltering pavement tables, and into the back streets, whose terraces were a mixture of shared-residential and business premises, the latter with posters pasted on their doors: made-to-measure tailoring. Gold bought. Cleaning services. A shop window displayed a collage of property cards: flats and houses to let. The next door along was the one they were after.

'What was his name?' Ho asked.

'Just ring the bell,' she told him.

Late to be a social call, which meant he might be out, might be in bed, but he was neither; was coming down the stairs, she could hear his tread. And remembered how Lamb had described him, so wasn't fazed when he opened the door and looked up at them.

'You're Reece Nesmith?' she asked.

'Who are you?'

'I think you've met our boss,' she said. 'Can we come in?'

* * *

'So. How does it look from here?'

'Here' was a hotel hard by the BBC, one Peter

Judd favoured for its bar, fifteen floors up. Its views of London suited him, especially after dark, when they revealed the city as gleaming clusters of power and influence; a collection of properties arrayed for the delight of those with the altitude to appreciate them. Which he was now doing, large brandy in hand.

Desmond Flint gave the question some thought. 'It looks . . . expensive.'

Judd laughed. 'You've got that right.'

'Out of the reach of the ordina — '

'Oh, please.' With a hand on the other man's shoulder, he encouraged him into an armchair. 'Those who've settled for ordinary have only themselves to blame. And anything expensive can be bought and sold. Like the man said, we've established what you are, we're simply haggling over the price. Which brings us rather neatly to tonight's events.' Judd sat in the facing armchair, London to his left. 'So. How was it for you?'

Flint looked around again before answering. If he didn't feel at home yet, he was starting to relax. Presumably the brandy helped. He said, 'It felt . . . different.'

'In what way?'

'Just different.'

'I see. Let me explain. You've been used to telling those people to do what they already want to do. And you've proved good at that, but it's a bit like pitching in baseball. All you had to do was chuck the ball. Tonight you had to dissuade them from doing something they'd clearly have enjoyed. That's more like bowling in cricket. It requires skill and ability. So yes, it felt different. Because you were wielding actual power, rather than simply pointing which way the wind was blowing.'

'So what you're saying, they might have just ignored me.'

'That was always a possibility.'

'And what would have happened then?'

'To you? To me? Or to all the lovely plate glass on Oxford Street?'

Flint waited.

Judd sipped his brandy, nodded in approval, and said, 'If they'd ignored you, I'd be enjoying a much livelier view right now, that's for sure. As for the rest, I imagine you'd be in the back of a van, a lot of windows would be no more, and whatever credibility you've amassed in the eyes of the public would be similarly in pieces, and impossible to put back together again. That enough detail for you?'

'You bastard.'

Judd looked modest.

'They'd not have got out of hand if you'd not put someone up to it.'

'Oh, come on. Left to themselves, they'd have cooked and eaten each other. It's one thing to play the sentimental card for an audience, Desmond, but don't wave the dignity-of-the-working-man flag with me. There's never been a working man who wouldn't bury his shovel in his neighbour's head for a free pint of beer and a fuck. So yes, I applied a little petrol to the flames, but that was a matter of scheduling rather than outright interference. And as of tonight your stock's in the ascendant, so let's not worry about what might have been. And listen, because this is important, you're not holding your glass correctly. Cup it like this, in your hand. See? Warms the brandy. You want it blood temperature.'

287

Desmond Flint adjusted his hold on his brandy glass, and said, 'How does that mean, my stock's in the ascendance?'

'Ascendant. It means the newspapers will be queuing up. *Question Time* is already in the bag, I imagine. They're awful star fuckers at the Beeb, don't you find? All of which puts us in the right place to take the next step. And look for the right ring to throw your hat into.'

'You're talking about standing for election?'

'That I am.'

Flint was shaking his head. 'I'm not one for elections. Nor are my supporters. The reason we've taken our argument onto the streets is because we've lost faith with politicians. Broken Britain starts at the top, any fool can see that. Parliament's a busted flush.'

'Ah yes, your supporters. They've got you this far, which is nice of them, but you'll soon find you won't need their approval quite so much. Obviously you'll want to stay true to your roots and all that, but the only way to climb the beanstalk's by looking up. And that means appealing to those who until now have seen you as beneath their notice. And that kind of approval comes, in the first instance, at the ballot box.'

'But I've said — '

'And I've listened to your objection, given it due consideration, and filed it under I for ignore. How are you liking the brandy?'

'I'm — It's fine. It's fine.'

'Good answer. It is fine. It's not magnificent.' Judd paused to confirm his judgement, rolling the liquor round his mouth before swallowing. 'Not magnificent. Now, I said election, you immediately jumped to Parliament. I was actually thinking of the mayoralty.'

He paused again. 'That means mayor,' he continued.
'Of London?'

Judd emitted an involuntary snort of laughter. '*Ha!*
Good one! . . . Oh, you were being serious. Well then,
yes, London. London mayor. A big, ah, *ask*, but we
have two years to prepare, which is more than Shaw
gave Higgins, so we shouldn't be too downhearted.'

The blank look this provoked might have disheart-
ened a less confident man, but Judd simply smiled
and raised his glass. 'Two years,' he said again, and
held the pose until Flint joined in the toast.

Later, after Flint had left, Judd ordered a second
brandy and applied himself to the view once more.
He'd suggested that this would be livelier had Flint's
appeal to the mob gone unheeded, but in truth, a few
statue-topplers apart, he doubted a British mob's ability to vent its rage properly. There'd have been smashed
glass and torched cars — a few broken heads, a few
cracked ribs — but it would have soon dissipated in
an orgy of petty theft. Looting was the British mob's
default mode, and what began in principled outrage
would inevitably end with high street showrooms
ransacked. Actually, Judd approved. Depend on the
British character — be generous, and call it human
nature — to back away from revolution in favour of
a flatscreen TV or two: instead of aristocrats lined
up against a wall, you had magistrates working over-
time for a few weeks, some hand-wringing columns
in the broadsheets, and then it was back to counting down the shopping days to Christmas. But still,
times were changing. Not so long ago, the notion of a
Desmond Flint even standing for London mayor, let
alone being in with a shout, would have brought the
average Islington dinner party to climactic levels of

self-congratulatory derision; but now, when the time came to announce his candidacy, you'd hear the foreboding the length and breadth of the liberal left. The status quo had been shattered, whether through greed, idealism, malice, or sheer stupid incompetence hardly mattered any more, and while the formerly complacent were still weeping over their losses, there were opportunities galore awaiting those prepared to rejig the shards.

'Here's to rejigging,' he murmured to himself, raising his glass to his lips. It wasn't magnificent, was merely fine, but it was early days yet.

★ ★ ★

Dogging. River didn't know much about it, except that it happened: people watching strangers having sex in parked cars. There might be more to it, but you'd have to have taken part, or known people who had, to grasp the fine detail, and no one he knew had ever indulged. Or if they had, it had never come up.

'Which one's the car?' Lech asked.

River pointed, and Lech pulled up a few yards parallel, causing those gathered in the parking area to stir, attention snagging on this new arrival the way movement attracts zombies. Most were huddled in the far corner, where a car rocked in response to internal activity. The group round the body car — Jane in the boot, Jim in the back seat — were two men and a woman, each in outdoor gear. *Just popping out for a walk, dear,* River imagined them saying. *Just heading down to the bird hide.*

Unsurprisingly, there was little sign of internal activity in this vehicle, but the trio seemed entranced regardless.

Killing the engine, Lech said, 'You're a mess.'

'Style tips welcome. But maybe later?'

'Don't be an arsehole. I meant, let me do the talking.'

He got out, and River followed.

It was dark, and the ground pitted and rough. One of the men had a torch, but held it down, so it acted as ambient glow, not floodlight. He had his back to Lech and River, but turned as they approached. The other two, a man and a woman, were standing on the other side. They might have been a couple.

Lech said to the lone man, 'Anything good?'

The three exchanged glances, then looked away. There was an etiquette, River supposed. Small talk not encouraged. He felt wary about getting close, his hair dirty, his face banged about — people who looked like they'd walked into trouble looked like they'd walk into more — but they didn't much bother with him. It was Lech they focused on, all three backing away as Lech bent and peered through the car window. After a moment, River did the same.

Jim's body was as he and Sid had left it: prone in the gap between front seats and back. A dark lump showing white at the hands and face; the latter stained perhaps, or just in shadow. River was trying to see this as a stranger might — a passing citizen, your friendly neighbourhood sex aficionado — but Jim seemed pretty dead however you looked at it.

The woman spoke softly. 'We were wondering. Just . . . Should we call someone?'

'Anonymously,' one of the men offered. 'We could just . . . leave. And call it in.'

Lech stepped back. 'He's corpsing,' he said. 'You've

never seen it before?'

' . . . 'Corpsing'?'

'Sometimes called deading. It's what it sounds like.' He'd adopted the patient tone you'd need when talking to an infant. 'You lie still as you can, hardly breathing. Sometimes you fake a wound.'

'I can see blood.'

'There you go.'

'But I mean, he actually looks dead.'

'Yeah, he's a good one.' To River's ear, Lech sounded expert. *Let me do the talking*. Fine by me.

'How long does he stay like that?'

'Long as it takes,' said Lech.

'I'm not sure,' the first man said again. 'I still think we should make a call.'

'Yeah, that'll go down well. Because either he's dead, and you three have been staring at his body for however long it's been. Or he isn't, and all'll happen is you've fucked up everyone's evening.'

'There's no call for language.'

There was shuffling, some shared wordless worry.

Peering through the window again, Lech said, 'Look, if you're too vanilla, that's fine. But we've come a long way, so if you don't mind.'

They fell quiet, and clustered round the car. River was counting his heartbeats: eight nine ten. Faster than they ought to be. He wondered if anyone could hear, then thought: yeah, well. Isn't that what's supposed to happen, your heart beating faster? In the circumstances?

He heard a zipper being undone.

After another twenty seconds, one of the men said, 'This is doing nothing for me.'

Lech, sounding gruff, said, 'There's activity in the

corner over there. Maybe more your thing.'

Glances were shared.

The woman said, 'I'm a bit of a traditionalist.'

Lech shrugged. 'Takes all sorts.'

'So I'll just . . . '

She backed away, then turned and walked towards the group in the far corner.

'Yeah, think I'll join her,' the first man said.

The second man moved away moments later, but stopped and looked back. 'He's pretty convincing. I'll give him that.'

Then River and Lech were alone.

'Nice work,' River said at last.

'I'm going to need to disinfect my head.'

'Was that you, by the way? With the zip?'

'Worked, didn't it?'

'Because I can give you a moment if you — '

'Fuck off. Got the keys?'

River had the keys.

'So get in and drive away.'

River got into the dead man's car while Lech returned to the one they'd arrived in.

Some of those congregated in the far corner watched as they left, but most had other things on their mind.

293

12

There were crimes, there were high crimes, there were treasonous acts, and there was the downright unforgivable.

'When I find out who stole my lighter,' Lamb said, 'there will be consequences.'

The early light of Chelsea had crept along the lane, crawled up the safe house's walls and drainpipes, and was now checking out its uncurtained rooms, filtering through the takeaway smells and overnight odours. The only company it found was in the front room: a muted gathering. Louisa occupied a corner where she sat cross-legged, a half-arsed yoga position, the notion of which — half-arsed yoga — was projecting crazy images onto her tired brain, while Catherine, next to her, might have been kneeling: her long dress made it hard to tell. Whatever, her expression was calm and unruffled. There are times when recovering addicts achieve levels of serenity denied the rest of us, thought Louisa. The bastards. As for Roderick Ho, he'd been dispatched to find another lighter, or matches, or anything capable of producing flame, which would save Lamb the trouble of having to travel all the way into the kitchen to light a cigarette from the hob, and the rest of them the pain of having to hear about it.

In the circumstances, she thought, Reece Nesmith III was handling himself pretty well. Especially given the greeting Lamb had offered, its tone suggesting that Reece were the principal cause of inconvenience rather than its current object.

'Well, if it isn't the incredible shrunken man.'

Reece glared. Back in his own place he'd seemed vulnerable, viewing Louisa and Ho as if they were the vanguard of a hooligan brigade. Dropping Lamb's name had changed his attitude: if he hadn't been keen on renewing that acquaintance, he'd evidently wanted to hear what Lamb had to say. Enough, anyway, to boot up, adding an inch and a half, and wrap himself inside a donkey jacket. On the Tube, whose passengers now included Yellow Vests heading home from Oxford Circus, it was as if he'd acquired an extra layer, one which hostile looks and muttered cruelties bounced off, the same way friendly glances did. You'd need it, Louisa thought. You'd need that invisible shield.

'So I'm here,' he said to Lamb. 'What do you want?'

'Nah, I'll wait till everyone's back. Save me the bother of explaining things to two sets of idiots.'

'So I just hang about until you're ready to talk?'

Lamb beamed. 'There. And they say midgets are slow on the uptake.' He regarded the unlit cigarette in his fist. 'Where the hell has Double-Ho Nothing got to?'

'Please don't let him hear you call him that,' Catherine said.

'You think I'll hurt his feelings?'

'I think he'll think you mean it.'

Reece said, 'It's like I've wandered into a circus.'

'Glad you feel at home,' Lamb said. 'Who's this?'

The others tensed, but it was a full six seconds before they heard a rapping on the door. Catherine made to get up but Louisa beat her to it. It was Lech Wicinski and Shirley Dander, the latter looking rough and sleep-tousled, as if she'd grabbed some kip in the car,

295

and been sandbagged by a hangover on arrival. Lech, though: it was hard to tell about Lech. It occurred to Louisa that having grown himself a hedge, he was learning how to hide behind it.

'How's River?' she asked as she followed them into the sitting room. And then, a beat behind, 'And Sid?'

'Bit bedraggled. All right, though.' Louisa waited for more, but Lech shrugged. 'He was fine. I barely met her. Shirley spent some time.'

Shirley said, 'She didn't remember much about it. Being shot in the head, I mean. But she's got a groove there.' She indicated on her own head where it was. 'Sort of cool, actually.'

'And they're not hurt?'

'Well, they'd obviously been in a fight. But so were we earlier.' She nodded at Lech. 'And we got no sympathy.'

'You beat up a stranger,' Louisa said. 'It's not really the same thing.'

'He wasn't *entirely* a stranger. Lech had already met him.'

Lamb said, 'If there's one thing I can't stand, it's wanton acts of violence. Why aren't that pair with you?'

'They're not ready to come back.'

"Not ready'? If I'd known I was arranging a mini-break, I'd have charged a commission. What did you do with the empties?'

This was for Lech, who said, 'Left them in their car, at Cartwright's house. I assume it's secure.'

'Why not call the Park?' said Shirley, still looking mutinous, and fidgeting with something. 'Isn't cleaning away bodies their job?'

Catherine said, 'You're aware we have a civilian in

the room?'

'I wouldn't worry,' said Lamb. 'This is going way over his head.'

'. . . Does the term 'punching down' mean anything to you?'

'Be reasonable. If I punched up, I'd miss him by a mile.'

Reece said, 'Can we move on to fat jokes now?'

Lamb looked hurt. 'There's no need to get personal.'

Lech said to Reece, 'We haven't been introduced. Lech Wicinski,' at the same time as Shirley asked him, 'Are you a new recruit? Because you'd fit right in.'

'That's not a real challenge,' Lamb said. 'And if you're finished with the small talk, could we get on point?' He paused. 'Small talk? Anyone?'

Catherine shook her head wearily, and tried again. 'Should we really be discussing this in front of Mr Nesmith?'

'Well, he started off knowing more than the rest of us,' went on Lamb, 'on account of his boyfriend being murdered by the Russians. Ah, the return of Macho Mouse.' This because Ho was at the door. Once he'd been let in, Lamb said, 'I sent you to buy a lighter, not invent one.'

Ho blinked. 'The shops weren't open.'

'Why is it I only hear excuses? Give it here. You can keep the change.'

'. . . I used my own money?'

'Let's have the receipt, then.'

Ho handed it over.

'Thanks.' Lamb lit the receipt with the lighter, the cigarette with the receipt, and dropped the flaming scrap of paper on the floor. 'Where was I?'

297

'It might be good if we didn't burn the house down,' Catherine suggested.

Reece trod on the scrap and killed the flame. 'These dead people. The ones in the car. They're not who killed Andrey back in Moscow?'

'Doubt it. It's not like the GRU's short of talent.' Lamb studied his cigarette for a moment. 'But the man who gave the order's the one who pointed a hit squad at Slough House, so we have a common foe. And you know what they say about common foes, Noddy?'

'Do they say you can go fuck yourself?'

'He's funny,' said Shirley. 'Can we keep him?'

'I know who'll end up having to take him for walks,' Lamb said. 'What're you fidgeting with, anyway?'

It was a plastic lighter. 'Found it on the pavement,' she said.

Lamb glared at everyone. 'Don't imagine I'm letting this slide. I start letting you comedians take the piss, you'd lose all respect.'

'And then where would we be?' said Catherine quietly.

Lech said, 'We've talked our way round several houses.

Are we closer to knowing what to do next?'

'What we do is, we go live,' said Lamb. 'Because as we've just established, the GRU have more than one hit team.'

' . . . There's another one out there?'

'Bound to be,' said Lamb. 'And closer than you'd think.'

* * *

298

Out in Tonbridge, still groggy with sleep, River staggered for a piss about 6 a.m., and was jolted awake by his reflection in the mirror. He looked like windfall, and his hands were scabbed and torn. He washed them until they tingled with cold, while deep in the bones, the knuckles, the joints, the memory of what they'd done last night tingled too: holding the woman's head in the lake until she died.

Then he walked through the house. It had grown smaller as he'd reached adulthood; was bigger again now, partly because it was empty; partly because property, anyway, looked huge now he was renting a one-bed in the capital. And partly because his past grew larger every day, and this was where most of it was. Even the absences told stories. Constellations of tiny holes in the walls were all that was left of the art that had hung here. He remembered finding Rose on the landing once, gazing at an etching, a few pencil lines summing up a doorway trailing ivy, and he hadn't asked her what she was looking at — he could see what she was looking at — but wished now he'd thought to ask her what she saw.

As for what the O.B. had seen, and thought, River had his own memories to draw on. Some had faded. It had become popular to record the older generation's words while they were around to deliver them, and it had occurred to River to tape his grandfather's reminiscences, but only for as long as it took the notion to form. David Cartwright would never have allowed it, and to do so surreptitiously would have been tantamount to treason. So all River had was the old man's library. If the O.B. had ever consigned his recollections to paper, the results would be hidden there somewhere. It was a memory palace made solid.

To which River now added his own memories, as if daubing a new picture on a used stretch of canvas. Sid was still asleep, curled in the armchair. It was good to see her peaceful, after last night's alarms. He thought about chasing after her in the car; almost headbutting an oncoming vehicle. *When someone you loved was in danger.* That's what he'd been thinking: someone he loved was in danger. And now she was sleeping in the room he'd grown up in.

His phone was on the table, reassembled, though nobody had taken advantage of this: no texts, no messages. He picked it up, looked at Sid, and wondered about taking her photo, before deciding this would be creepy beyond belief. But while the phone was in his hand he scanned the room anyway: the O.B.'s shelves, his books and mementos, the print of *The Night Watch* above the fire; a six-second video that ended with Sid's sleeping form. Okay, still creepy, but he could always delete it. He checked for messages again, but there weren't any. Then remembered there were two bodies in the car outside, and wondered what he was playing at: mooning about like a lovestruck kid. He pocketed the phone, retreated from the room, and left the house.

The car was round back, where they'd left it. He'd thrown a blanket over the corpse in the seat well, a cunning ploy, and as he peered through the window could only make out a shapeless lump: all that was left of a would-be murderer. Well, seasoned assassin. Just not in River's case. He didn't open the boot. It was clear no one had come looking. He flexed his fingers, felt the tingle again; remembered the texture of the woman's wet head. But he'd be better off right now putting together some breakfast.

Before going back in, he surveyed his surroundings. The garden his grandfather had loved had returned to the wilderness nature prefers; the weeds outnumbering the cultivated shrubs; the lawn peppered with dandelions and daisies. Somewhere underneath lay the canvas David Cartwright had painted, and maybe it would see the light again one day. Unlikely to be River's doing. He walked round to the front. *Is this yours?* Wicinski had asked. And in answering — *Yes, yes, it's mine* — River had felt the truth of it for the first time. It was his house. It had always been the house he'd grown up in — always been home — but until now it had been his grandfather's property, and River had simply lived in it. But now it was his. Was he really going to sell? It was the obvious, sensible thing to do. But standing here, knowing Sid was sleeping inside, obvious and sensible took on different shades. Most of his life was here. Assuming the rest of it lay elsewhere suddenly seemed presumptuous.

The other evening, contemplating his future, he'd pictured himself with a hand on the doorknob, ready to step into whatever the next room held.

So okay. Here he was.

River had his keys in his pocket, so used the front door for a change. Unlocked it and twisted the knob.

Stepped into his future.

* * *

Damien Cantor watched the footage from Oxford Circus sitting at his breakfast island: a marble-topped counter which weighed slightly less than a terraced house. Coffee in front of him, he was jiggling his foot to a mental beat, one matching the scenes on his

301

laptop. The film hadn't been broadcast yet — they'd been trailing snippets since five — but would go out with the 8 a.m. bulletin: catch the news cycle where it hurt. Parts were rough, but that was fine — would show the viewer it was raw, and really happened. He particularly liked the bit where the bin went through the window. The crew had grabbed a blurry outline of the man responsible, the red sweater beneath the yellow vest, without catching his face. It was good to have Tommo Doyle back on the payroll.

Good to have Peter Judd owing him a favour, too. He'd made like they were scratching each other's backs — Cantor catches the story; Judd's man Flint catches some headlines — but they both knew where the truth lay. Judd was looking to be a kingmaker, and the last time there'd been one of those without a TV channel providing back-up, everyone involved had been wearing frock-coats. So Judd owed him. It was the way of the world.

He got up, stretched, poured another cup, then spent a moment gazing at the city: its skyline a tourist magnet, its weather a systems glitch. But Jesus, the money pouring through it, day after day. Even on the domestic level. This apartment, forty floors up — the perfect bachelor pad, though he never let his wife hear him call it that — the maintenance charge alone would cripple a prince. But it was worth it for this view, which wasn't just what you could see, it was knowing how few shared it. Sure, there was a viewing platform, but that was just to show people what they didn't have. There was a sense in which this encouraged them to dream huge dreams, but there was another much bigger sense in which it told them to fuck off. Cantor approved of a system which had

302

allowed him to get rich, but he also believed in pulling the ladder up afterwards. If everyone succeeded, nobody did. Anything else was basically communism.

His phone rang, intruding on philosophy.

It was lobby security, the morning guy — Clyde or Claude or something — and was he expecting a visitor? Claude or Clyde looked like a prop forward for Western Samoa, and hadn't sat an IQ test to get the job, but seriously: it was seven o'fucking clock in the morning. He'd have to be having a Viagra-induced emergency to be expecting a visitor.

'Did they give a name?'

'Sir, he says he's from . . . '

Muffled dialogue took place.

'Sir, he says he's from a Diana Taverner?'

Okay, thought Cantor. That'll add flavour to an already spicy morning. 'Thank you, Clyde. Send him up.'

'It's Clifton, sir.'

'Yeah. Send him up. The flat, not the studio.'

The lifts were fast, but not that fast. Cantor had time to finish his coffee before his visitor arrived.

★ ★ ★

There's a sense in which any leader in a field feels closer to her opposite number than to her immediate colleagues. There's another, more important sense in which she wants to mince that opposite number into bite-sized chunks and strew them in the path of hungry beasts, but still: talking to Vassily Rasnokov, Diana Taverner couldn't help but feel that there was a level on which they understood each other better than anyone else. Rather like her relationship with Jackson

Lamb might be, if she and Lamb were on opposing sides. So, rather like her relationship with Jackson Lamb. Though she and Lamb had yet to reach the point where they were counting each other's dead.

'You've put a team across our borders, Vassily.'

'A "team"?'

'Again.'

'We allow freedom of movement to our citizens, Diana. Surely you remember what that was like? And there are many beautiful things to see in your country. All those church spires. Who could blame anyone for wanting to spend their leisure time visiting your fabled attractions?'

'Please. They've not been admiring our architecture, they've been painting our walls.'

'I'm not familiar with the expression.'

Like hell he wasn't.

Diana was on the roof. The phone wasn't a burner, exactly, but it was one she only used for calling Rasnokov — current First Desk at the GRU — and she never did that in her office. Around her, below her, the city was making those incoherent early morning noises, sometimes ascribed to traffic and the raising of metal shutters, which meant it hadn't yet decided what day-face to wear; the happy, sunny, get-things-done one, or the grubby, sullen, no-eye-contact glower.

She knew how it felt.

Rasnokov said, 'We also are concerned about a regrettable murder within our borders. A young woman, a secretary with the GRU, was killed right here on the streets of her own city.'

'A secretary,' said Diana. 'Is that right?'

'I'm sorry, do I have that idiom correctly? You are

304

asking for clarification?'

'No. I understand.'

'I'm pleased to hear that. She was apparently the victim of street crime, which raised suspicion among the investigators, as this is much rarer here than in your West. Much, much rarer. So they examined the case closely, and came to the conclusion that this murder was carried out by foreigners. Foreign . . . mercenaries? I think there's a more accurate term.'

'Hitmen.'

'Yes, thank you. Foreign hitmen. You can imagine the distress. To have a citizen cut down by foreign criminals, professional assassins. Our president was most concerned that such activities should not go unchecked.'

'And was he reminded that the action was not unprovoked?'

'The president remained focused on the details. A grave insult had been paid to an arm of our national security. Such insults must receive the appropriate response.'

'Which is where we came in. That incident was itself a measured and appropriate response to an outrageous act. You damn well know that.'

Rasnokov did not reply. Diana filled the gap by walking to the edge of the building and looking down. She liked to think she had a head for heights, but there was something about watching people far below, people who imagined themselves unobserved, that provoked dizziness.

She stepped back.

'And to continue along this path, this repeated exchange of appropriate responses . . . Where's that going to lead, do you think? Anywhere good?'

305

The silence continued.

It was going to be a long day. The boys and girls on the hub had been at it all night, combing through CCTV, ANPR, whatever they could squeeze from GCHQ, but the team responsible for dropping Kay White off a ladder, burning up Struan Loy, and frightening Sidonie Baker into the shadows had vanished from sight. The last time a pair of the GRU's worst and wildest had broached UK borders, they'd arrived bearing sequentially numbered passports. That might have looked like a schoolboy error, but felt, in hindsight, like a two-fingered salute. The current model had been less openly abrasive, and, murders apart, hadn't left a footprint. Or not one the hub had yet identified.

Rasnokov spoke at last. 'We have no listening ears?'

'None this side, Vassily.'

He hesitated again. 'It is perhaps fair to say that the decision to . . . How can I put this? The decision to visit your marvellous cathedral was taken over my head. And might better have been left untaken.'

That he was saying this surprised her, but not its import. Rasnokov was as capable of brutal thuggery as the next man, but he'd never struck her as mad. And the original attack had been set in motion by a madman.

She said, 'And you can't have expected us to leave it at that, Vassily. We've already spoken of how such actions amount to insults.'

'There was speculation that your Service lacked the necessary resources to indulge in such an extravagant response.'

'Then your speculations are out of date, aren't they? We're not as strapped for cash as you imagine.'

306

"Strapped for cash'?'

'Short of money.'

'Ah, yes. 'Strapped for cash.' I like that.'

'Happy to help. So what about your current . . . tourists? Were they also wished on you from on high?'

She took his silence for assent.

It was going to be a long day, yes, but there was a glimmer of hope here. If she could tie a ribbon round the GRU hit team, she'd be able to focus on her other problems. Making truce would mean allowing the Russians to walk away, of course, but this wouldn't be a public humiliation: the unnewsworthy deaths of a few former spooks hadn't created the waves that the murder of a citizen had. Nobody missed a slow horse.

Jackson Lamb aside, that was. But she could deal with him later.

Rasnokov said, 'Our current tourists. It might be fair to say that in this day and age, a time of environmental concerns, such holiday-making is uncalled for. The costs to the planet are too high. It might have been better had they too stayed at home.'

She took a breath. 'So call them back.'

'That would be one solution. Though I worry that their passage home might not be a smooth one. So many hold-ups occur these days. Major inconveniences.'

'Things aren't as bad as they were. You might find that their journey is untroubled.'

'That would put everyone's mind at rest. But I have to ask, what sort of premium would be charged for such a guarantee?'

It was good of him to offer, and saved her raising the question herself.

She said, 'Well, Vassily, I always find it interesting

to look at other people's holiday snaps, don't you? I wonder if you have any to share?'

Cantor said, 'No way.'
He waited.
'No way are you a spook.'
Reece Nesmith III said, 'I never said I was.'
Cantor's apartment looked like a movie set: the furniture matched; the bookshelves were colour-coded; artworks occupied shelves, and the kitchen area featured a marble countertop big enough to skate on. But mostly there was the view. London was huge, and from here you could see all of it: its towers and bridges, its ups and downs, its pains and its profits. You could see London's edges from here. You could see where London ended.
And in a movie, Reece thought, this would be the lair of a villain who might be able to arrange just that.
And now Cantor was clicking his fingers, retrieving a memory. 'But I know you. I do know you. You were hassling Bud.'
This was true. Bud Feathernet was the Channel Go news anchor, whom Reece had tracked via Twitter to a restaurant, and badgered in a booth; he'd told him about Andrey, how Andy had been murdered on the orders of Russia's president. If that wasn't a headline, what was? But there was a chasm Reece was unable to throw his story across. Andy had been the kind of journalist who ended up dead. Feathernet was the kind who'd end up hosting a chat show. And on the evening in question, he was the kind who'd had Reece thrown out of a restaurant.
'He mentioned it at morning briefing. Some freak kicking off while he was trying to have dinner. Not the

way to win friends and influence people.'

'He wouldn't listen.'

'Course he wouldn't. Look, if your boyfriend hadn't been Russian, we might have had a story. And if he'd been your girlfriend. But frankly, my viewers wouldn't give a shit. You're an American, you're gay, you're a dwarf. Put it on YouTube.' Cantor was on his feet, playing the height advantage for all it was worth. 'Now, you told Claude you have a message from Diana Taverner.'

'I think his name was Clifton.'

'Yeah, because that's what's important, that we get the names of the staff right. That was a lie to get you in, I see that. And the only reason I haven't kicked you back downstairs is, I want to know how you knew which name to drop. So talk.'

Reece said, 'I'm not from Taverner. But I do have a message.'

He was getting into this. He'd spent weeks hammering on doors that wouldn't open, telling his story to people who wouldn't listen. The most attention he'd had was from Jackson Lamb, and even he hadn't cared. *People die. You should get used to that.* But suddenly something was happening. He'd been handed a lever and told to pull it. It wouldn't bring Andrey back, but would hurt those responsible for his death. That's what Lamb had said, anyway.

'He's not going to be frightened of me,' Reece had said.

'No,' Lamb agreed. 'I mean, he might worry about tripping over you. But you're hardly gunna have him quivering in his socks.'

'So what am I supposed to be doing?'

'Softening him up,' Lamb had said.

'What message?' Cantor asked.

Reece said, 'You had your man steal information from Regent's Park. About a particular department of the Service. And you passed that information to Russian intelligence.'

'Russian intelligence? Get out of here.'

'Well, you probably pretended you didn't know that's who they were. But you certainly knew, when you handed the information over, where it would end up.'

'Just supposing you weren't talking nonsense. How do you know any of this?'

'Oh, I hear stuff other people miss. You might have noticed, I keep my ears close to the ground.'

This with an internal middle-finger salute to Jackson Lamb.

Cantor had picked up an empty coffee mug and seemed to be weighing it in his hands. 'Is this some weird kind of blackmail threat? Because Taverner isn't going to make waves. I'm in the inner circle. You know how that works?'

Reece thought: stick to the script. Tell him what Lamb wants him to hear, and get out. It doesn't matter whether he believes you. You're simply sowing the seed.

He said, 'Taverner ordered the Kazan hit.'

Cantor looked startled, but not so much he dropped the cup. 'I know. I was at the after-party.'

'This made people in Moscow very mad.'

'Good.'

'And now they're using the information you gave them to take their revenge. They've been murdering the people in the file you passed on.' Reece leaned on each word equally: 'British Secret Service agents.'

310

Cantor had gone pale. 'I don't think so. I'd know about it if that was happening.'

'Only if Taverner wanted you to know. And this is not something the Park wants in the headlines. But that doesn't mean they won't act on it.'

'What does that mean — 'act on it'?'

'Join the dots. You're responsible for the murders of several Park employees. You think the inner circle's small enough they'll let you get away with that?'

'This is bullshit.'

'Which bits? The part about you having your man steal that file? Or the bit where you handed it on to your Russian contacts?'

'Okay. Time for you to go now.'

But Reece had one last shot to fire. 'You know what's funny?'

'All of it,' said Cantor. 'It's one long fantasy.'

'No, what's funny is, Taverner wants you toasted both sides. But that Russian crew leaving bodies everywhere? As far as they're concerned, you're their best mate. Better hope they reach you before the Park does.'

'Fuck off.'

Before he reached the door, Reece said, 'I wouldn't stand too close to those windows. Regent's Park hire some pretty sharp shooters.'

He was confident you'd need a tank to break that glass. But it wouldn't hurt to have Cantor think there might be one nearby.

* * *

Diana remained where she was after ending her call, adding a cigarette butt to the cairn on an air vent's flat top. The day was settling on its mood: sunny with grim intervals. Her own outlook was pretty much the inverse. It would give her no pleasure to call off the hunt for Moscow's hit squad. Amnesty was too big a concession, even if their victims were ex-Slough House, too lowly for a Spook's Chapel send-off. There should have been retribution. And if Lamb found out about the deal she'd just agreed there probably would be, even if disproportionate and wrongly directed.

But there was sunshine too. Cantor was hers now. If she'd thought she'd get away with it, she'd have let Vassily Rasnokov think she didn't know who'd stolen the Slough House file, but that wouldn't fly. If Rasnokov thought Diana incapable of discovering that much, he'd have been too busy pissing himself laughing to take her call. So there was no chance she could turn Cantor round and use him to feed Moscow a bullshit buffet. Instead, she had Cantor himself, because Rasnokov had holiday snaps all right — everyone took holiday snaps. Rasnokov had sound and vision of Cantor handing the stolen file to his Russian new-media exec pals, because Moscow Rules and London Rules shared this much in common: once you handed over secrets, you became the product. Cantor would have found out the hard way that you never feed a cat just once. You feed a cat, it owns you ever after.

The same sets of rules said you never burned an asset either, but Rasnokov was old-school Spook Street. No way would he leave his crew out in joe country, even when the crew were a pair of assassins, and the mission one he hadn't believed in. He wanted them brought home, because that was what you did. You brought your joes back, or buried them yourself.

If that cost you an asset, so be it.

And hidden in there was another ray of sunshine: Rasnokov's admission that he'd not have sent his crew into the field if he hadn't been pressured from above.

That was more than sunshine; it almost promised a summer. But while the glimmer of a crack in Moscow's walls was a fine thing to contemplate, there was also the possibility that Rasnokov wanted her to believe that such a crack existed; had given her a glimpse of it simply in order to get his joes back. So yes, she'd think hard on that, but not right now. She had other eggs to boil. Her back to the view, she took out her main phone and rang the first number on her contact list.

'I need to see him,' she said.

And then, moments later, 'Four o'clock. Yes. Thank you.'

She put the phone away.

Next, she'd call off the search for the hit squad. This would cause muttering, but First Desk didn't have to listen, she just had to give orders. And if everyone else fell in line, then, grim intervals or not, she could come out of the far end of today back on top.

Just so long as nobody fucked things up in the meantime.

13

A handwritten notice pasted to the window offered thanks, blessings and farewells to friends and customers, and then said the same thing over again, presumably, in, presumably, Polish. That much Shirley Dander had taken in before getting down on her knees. Roderick Ho stood to one side, pretending to speak into a mobile phone, while she got busy with what Lamb had assured her was a set of global skeleton keys, good for any standard-issue lock; an assurance that, so far, had proved as sound as one of his motivational homilies.

'Bastard thing.'

Into his phone, Ho said, 'I've given my instructions. I expect them to be acted on immediately, *capisce*?'

'Supposed to be blending in,' Shirley muttered. 'Not dicking out.'

Because it was a busy midweek morning Roddy Ho had opted for camouflage, and as well as his phone was holding a clipboard Catherine Standish had found. This made him look, Shirley claimed, like a nervous driving instructor, to which Ho had retorted that he was, in fact, as chilled as . . .

Minutes passed.

None of these damn keys fit.

' . . . Samuel L. Jackson's drinks cabinet.'

'What?'

'That's how chilled.'

'You're supposed to be on the phone. Not talking to me.'

Roddy said into his mobile, 'Nah, no one important. Just some underling whose arse needs kicking.'

'Like that's gunna happen.' Shirley had had haircuts that had done more damage than Ho was capable of.

The next key was also a failure.

'Is it opening again?'

' . . . I'm sorry?'

'The shop.' It was an elderly woman wheeling a shopping basket. 'Old Miles's.'

Shirley looked at Ho, who was supposed to be running interference, but was too wrapped up in his imaginary phone call. Then again, it might be the most meaningful encounter he'd had in a while. He'd probably end up arranging to meet himself for a drink.

'Health and Safety,' she said. 'Just entering to check for . . . subsidence.'

'Ooh, are we about to fall down a big hole?'

'I'd not be surprised,' said Shirley, as the current key clicked sweetly into place, the way a jam jar lid comes loose. 'Probably best to be far away.'

Roddy said, 'Okay, gotta run. Hang cool,' and ended his call.

He followed her inside, closing the door behind them.

The shop had only been shut a day or so, and yet an air of finality had dropped on it like a dust sheet. Emptied of goods, the shelving looked rackety and unstable, as if a heavy finger might bring it down, and the space on the counter where the till had sat for decades was seven shades lighter than the surrounding surface. Shirley shook her head. She rarely entered a shop more than two years old. And that retailer's sweet spot, the gap between opening-day bargains and closing-down sale, she made a point of avoiding.

There was a door behind the counter, leading to the stairs Lamb had mentioned, and Shirley headed straight for it.

Roddy Ho put his clipboard down and followed. She had, he thought, taken long enough to get them in. Lamb would have expected this; when handing her rather than Roddy the skeleton set he'd bestowed upon the latter the ghost of a wink, discernible to no one. *You'd be past that lock like a greased ghost. But let's give someone else the chance to shine.* Nice gesture, but men were just better at the practical stuff — facts and stats, dude. Facts and stats. Three more doors off the landing, two of them open. Time to take charge. Holding one commanding hand up to halt Shirley, Roddy put the other on the knob of the closed door. Twisted and pushed in one swift movement.

'Locked.'

'Yeah, try pulling?'

He pulled, and the door opened on an empty toilet.

'Ho,' she said, 'you're as stylish as a man-bun.'

The other two rooms were also empty, with bare floorboards that moaned underfoot, and a lingering odour of cigarettes. In the back one there was a steel shutter over the window, padlocked in place. That was good.

'Okay, gimme the stuff.'

Ho slipped his rucksack from his shoulders.

Shirley unzipped it and got to work.

★ ★ ★

The studio was buzzing, everyone hyper about the morning broadcast — London had a new hero, the riot-quelling Desmond Flint, and only Channel Go

316

had his number. Already they were trailing an exclusive interview, Peter Judd having promised them an on-air sit-down with his man before the week's end; one that would demonstrate that UK politics' former Mr Angry had emerged from his chrysalis; was a man with wise things to say about the mood of the country, and gumption enough to get stuff done. Already Cantor had received calls from the broadsheets, looking at 'expanding the coverage', meaning riding his coat-tails. Yeah, right. But his heart wasn't in it, unable to shake his early morning visitor.

I wouldn't stand too close to those windows. Regent's Park hire some pretty sharp shooters.

It was stupid, pathetic, an obvious ruse. No way would Taverner be looking to cancel his account. Sure, he'd rubbed her up the wrong way, and yeah, Tommo Doyle had lifted a file from Regent's Park's archive, but that was just gamesmanship: Taverner knew that. And maybe he'd passed that file to some foreign media contacts — okay, *Russian* media contacts — but business knew no borders, and favours were made to be traded. The uses to which shared knowledge might be put couldn't be laid at his door. Besides, these windows were high: you'd need a helicopter. You'd need a *satellite*. Simply put, he was too tall to fall. He was out of reach.

'Damien? Someone trying to reach you.'

' . . . Huh?'

'Caller on line one.'

He punched a button. 'Cantor.'

'Mr Cantor?' The voice had a guttural quality, as if the words were being dragged past an obstruction in the throat. 'How good to speak to you.'

'Who is this?'

'This is your new best friend, Mr Cantor.'

'My new best friend,' he repeated.

'Yes. And I'm calling to let you know how much shit you're in, and how best to avoid it.'

Trying not to think about windows, Cantor sank into his chair and listened.

★ ★ ★

When it was done, Lech slipped his phone into his pocket and looked at Louisa. 'Well?'

'How'd he take it?'

'Like he didn't believe a word I said.'

'Well, that's what he'd want you to think either way.'

'Spoken like a spook,' he muttered.

'Glad to hear it.' She raised her own phone. 'My turn.'

★ ★ ★

At 10.43 — Catherine happened to be looking at her watch — Lamb started coughing, and didn't stop for eight minutes. There wasn't a lot she could do. He presumably accepted these fits as a lifestyle tax, so why shouldn't she? Rinsing a takeaway cup, she filled it with water, placed it by his elbow and let him get on with it.

At 10.51, she said, 'Feeling better?'

'I'm fine.'

'That was your version of an aerobics workout, was it?'

'Just the body's way of expelling bad matter.'

'How does it know when to stop?' She handed him a tissue. 'When did you last see a doctor?'

318

'I think it was William Hartnell,' said Lamb. 'Have I missed much?' He dabbed his face, picked up the cup, drained half of it, realised what it was, scowled, and drained the rest. 'Where's the lawn ornament?'

'If you're referring to Mr Nesmith, he left.'

'Did I tell him he could go?'

'You might be mistaking him for someone who works for you.'

Lamb thought about this, then nodded. 'Yeah, I can see how that might happen. He had that miserable-loser look.'

'And yet he fulfilled his mission. Is what you're doing wise, do you think?'

Lamb, who had found a cigarette to soothe his frame, paused in his hunt for a lighter. 'You'll have to narrow it down.'

'Well, that, obviously. But I meant this game you're playing with Cantor. He's the Park's problem, not ours. And I don't imagine Taverner plans to let him walk away scot-free, do you?'

'Well, it's true I like to win in the long term,' Lamb said. 'But I like to win in the short term too. Besides, Taverner's got more problems than you know. She can't settle Cantor's hash until she's sure she won't get caught in the blowback.' He produced his lighter just as his phone rang, and stared at it for a moment as if unsure where the noise was coming from. Then pulled the phone from his pocket. 'What?'

It was Ho, Catherine surmised. Lamb had a particular expression he wore when forced to listen to Ho; it was the same one he wore when forced to listen to anyone else, only more so. When Ho finished, Lamb said, 'So what you're telling me is, you did what I told you to do. How come you can't just say that?'

319

He listened for another moment.

'Oh, I see. No, perfectly good explanation. Thanks.' He ended the call.

Catherine raised an eyebrow. "Perfectly good explanation'?'

'That was Dander in the background. Apparently Ho's a dick.'

'I'm so glad the team-building's working out.' She paused. 'No word from River yet.'

'Yeah,' said Lamb. 'But I imagine there's been some debriefing going on. If you get my drift.'

'I just wonder if he's coming back at all.'

'Why wouldn't he?'

'Whatever happened last night must have been traumatic. Coming on top of everything else — his grandfather's death, all the havoc round here — he might have had enough.'

'Huh.'

'He nearly packed it in last year. He came this close.'

'He's a spook. It's in his blood.'

'And now Sid's back in the picture.'

'Hence my debriefing comment,' said Lamb. 'You see, what I was getting at was — Ah, what now?'

It was another moment before Catherine heard it: someone at the door. With a key, so it could only be Diana Taverner, who duly appeared a moment later, pausing in the doorway, shaking her head.

'This was in showroom condition yesterday.'

Lamb shook his head sorrowfully. 'I blame the younger generation. It's like they still expect their mums to tidy up.'

'I sometimes wonder how you survived under cover. You'd think the Stasi would just have followed the chaos.' Diana turned to Catherine. 'How do you put up with it?'

'I took a long hard look at the alternative.'

Diana said, 'Fair enough,' then nodded in dismissal. 'Adults in the room.'

'She stays,' said Lamb.

'I don't think —'

'She stays.'

Diana rolled her eyes, but went on as if Catherine weren't there. 'I spoke to Rasnokov. He's calling his dogs off.'

Lamb's expression gave nothing away.

'So you can vacate this place.'

'Just when I was getting comfortable. What does Vassily get in return? Let me guess. Safe passage for the pooches.'

'It's a no-mess outcome.'

'Except for the blood on the walls. And isn't that why things kicked off in the first place?'

'Circumstances change.'

'Meaning you've noticed what a balls-up you created when financing Kazan, so you're dropping everything else to deal with that instead.'

Diana glanced towards Catherine.

'Oh, don't worry,' said Catherine. 'I never pay attention when he's sober.'

Lamb lit his cigarette, waggling the lighter as if it were a match. 'Diana invited some celebrities aboard the good ship Regent's Park. They paid for their passage and everything. And now they want a go at steering.'

'That's not going to happen.'

'Yeah, but here's a thing about pirates. They don't take no for an answer.'

His phone rang again. Without taking his eyes off

Diana, he tossed it to Catherine, who caught it. 'Hello, Lech. Yes. But tell me instead.' A pause. Then: 'Thank you. I'll let him know.'

Rather than throw the phone back, she held on to it.

'So let me know.'

Catherine said, 'Both calls have been made.'

'Calls?' said Diana. 'You're supposed to be dark. In fact . . . ' She made a show of looking round the room. 'Where's the awkward squad?'

Lamb snorted. 'Trust me, awkward would be an improvement.'

'What are you up to, Jackson?'

'You might have declared an amnesty, but I haven't. That file Cantor passed behind the curtain was stamped 'Slough House', remember?'

"Curtain'? Really?'

He blew smoke. 'A good metaphor never goes stale.'

Diana Taverner shook her head wearily. 'I can't stress this enough. The last thing I need is help from you.' She looked at Catherine. 'Haven't you learned to control him yet?'

'I'm taking notes.'

Diana returned to Lamb. 'Cantor's up shit creek. Rasnokov has footage of him handing that file to his contacts. Sound and vision. Good for five years at least. So listen, I'm sorry about the dead, I really am. But there's a greater good at stake here, so whatever you're up to, pack it in. Rasnokov is looking to build bridges.'

'He's got a funny way of showing it.'

'We all have political masters to work around.'

'Speak for yourself.' Ash fell into Lamb's lap. He appeared not to notice. 'But what the hell, you've won me over. You want safe passage for the hit crew, I won't get in your way. In fact' — he paused to stub his cigarette out on the floor — 'I've probably got a box somewhere you could pack them in. That'll save on costs.'

Diana stared. 'What have you done?'

'Exactly what you should have done. Taken them off the board.'

Catherine cleared her throat.

'Well,' said Lamb, 'delegation. It's the art of good management. So it's possible Rasnokov'll call your deal off, but don't worry about Cantor. That's in hand.'

'Are you out of your fucking mind?'

'Again, a good manager would call it initiative.'

'Initiative . . . I'm First Desk, you stupid fat bastard! You answer to me!'

'I'll do that when you do your job. Which means not selling out your joes.'

'Joes? Did you forget what Slough House is? It's a punishment posting. No, screw that. It's not even a punishment, it's what we do when we don't care any more. It's where we send those we can't be bothered to deal with, because that'll just mess up the system. Your job's to keep them from seeing daylight again, and that is all. End of story.'

'Not quite,' said Lamb. 'You missed a bit out.'

'And what's that?'

'It's a department of the Security Service. Whose team, like it or not, work for you. Past or present. And when they die, that's on your watch.'

'Jackson — '

'And mine.'

Catherine was clutching Lamb's phone so tightly,

it hurt her hand.

Diana opened her mouth to continue. Closed it again.

Lamb said, 'You wanted Cantor's wheels removed. Consider it done. And now you don't have to deal with Rasnokov, either. Just tell him the next wet team he sends'll come home the same way. Because you don't build bridges over the corpses of your own crew.'

For a while, nobody spoke. The only sound was Lamb clicking his lighter again. But he didn't have a cigarette to hand; he was simply making flames.

At last Diana said, 'You plan to kill him too? Cantor?'

'No,' said Catherine.

'Buzzkill,' said Lamb.

'We're not going to kill him,' said Catherine.

'But he won't come sniffing round the Park again,' said Lamb. 'You can take that as read.'

'You'd better be right.' Diana's voice was taut as a cheese wire. 'Now give me the keys to this place. And get back where you belong.'

'Sure. And I'll be taking my team with me.'

'Now.'

'Including Wicinski and Dander.'

'Just give me the fucking keys.'

Lamb tossed her the fucking keys.

'And close the fucking door on your way out.'

'Forgive her bad manners,' said Lamb, once they were on the street. 'She still has those pirates to worry about.'

'That little outburst, bad manners? She should take professional advice.'

Lamb had found a cigarette, but his lighter had disappeared again. He patted his pockets and said,

'What does Sid being back in the picture have to do with it?'

'I'd explain, Jackson,' Catherine said, raising her arm for a taxi. 'But I genuinely think I'd be wasting my time.'

★ ★ ★

The second conversation had worried him more than the first.

'I'm calling from Regent's Park, Mr Cantor. I presume you're aware of the significance of that locale?'

'The significance of . . . Yes. Yes, I'm aware.'

'Good. Ms Taverner would like to see you here this morning.'

' . . . This morning?'

'Immediately. And in case you have difficulty finding us, there's a team on its way to escort you.'

'I — '

'Oh, and Mr Cantor? Bring your passport.'

And the woman had disconnected.

('Passport?' Lech had said.

Louisa said, 'That'll freak him, don't you think?'

'It would me,' Lech admitted.)

Cantor was back in his apartment, having left the studio in a hurry. Call Peter Judd was his first thought. Judd was an ally — except he was Taverner's ally too, or rather, he was an ally of whoever seemed most useful at any given moment, and as likely to offer succour to those in need as a poisonous snake. So no, don't call Peter Judd. Pack a bag and think things through.

The marital home was a no-go; the first place they'd come looking.

Staying put was out of the question.

A hotel? But this was London, a city with more cameras than pigeons, and the Service had access to any CCTV system they chose. Showing his face in a hotel lobby would be as discreet as popping up on *The X Factor*. Leaving town was a better bet, but he couldn't use his car . . .

He called upstairs. 'I need a car, nothing fancy. On your own card, not the company's. And I need it downstairs three minutes ago.'

'Damien? Is there something going on I should know about?'

'What you should know is, I need a car three minutes ago.'

He packed a two-day bag. How long could this take to sort out? Taverner was throwing a scare, that was all. The dwarf had been part of it — his story about the dead British agents? Hashtag didn't happen. Taverner was punishing him for having flexed his muscles, that was all. Which meant the Russian voice, *I'm calling to let you know how much shit you're in*, that was fake too, and Cantor was being made to jump at shadows.

What he jumped at next was his phone, again.

'Damien? Your car's on its way.'

'When?'

'It will be there before you're downstairs. Damien, are you sure everything's all right? Because you have a meeting scheduled — '

'Cancel it. And get hold of Tommo. Have him call.'

Was he running? No. This was a strategic withdrawal, no more.

As he took the lift down, he thought of last night's news footage being played right now, on screens all over London. The capital's agenda, set by him. Taverner didn't know what she was getting into.

Ground floor. There were people milling about, queuing for the tourist lift, and he had to push through them to get to Clyde — Claude? — who was holding a set of keys on a BMW fob. It's round back, sir. Thanks. This taking seconds: he was starting to feel like he worked for the Park himself. He'd grabbed his baseball cap on his way out, and twisted it now so the peak faced backward. Street smarts.

The car was waiting as promised, and winked its lights when he clicked the fob. But before he could reach it a man was up close behind him, breathing into his ear.

'You don't want to get in that car.'

It was the voice from the first phone call, guttural, throaty, and its owner had a face to match: like he'd lost a fight with a kitchen blender.

'Trust me. I'm on your side.'

Across the road a woman stepped out of the shadows and started towards them.

★ ★ ★

There was a traffic jam, because there were always traffic jams, because this was London. Perhaps there were cities whose streets flowed freely, but they'd belong to the world's more repressive regimes, where state control extended to the driving seat, and you'd need permission to venture onto the roads. So the price you paid for freedom of movement was sometimes lack of movement; an aphorism she might find a use for one day, but meanwhile: screw this. Diana Taverner abandoned the cab and walked the rest of the way. She could use the thinking space.

She'd been ready to melt glass when she left the

mews house, but there was no sense picking over what should have been. And there was always an upside, if you knew which angle to take. What Lamb did best was sit in his office, drinking himself into a waiting grave, but what he did second best, when he could be bothered, was cut his enemies off at the knees. In this instance that was only incidentally Diana herself, was principally Damien Cantor, so if nothing else Lamb's meddling had saved her the effort. Because one way or the other, Cantor was a blown fuse, and whether that was because she had Rasnokov's evidence of his wrongdoing, or because he'd had the fear of Lamb thrown into him, made no difference in the long run.

Besides, Rasnokov's thugs were apparently dead, and whichever angle you examined that from, it was clear who'd achieved payback. And there was, too, that chink of light Vassily had let show, his hint that this vicious tit for tat had been wished on him from on high. A glimpse of weakness on his side matched by a show of strength on her own. That was the kind of balance she wanted to maintain.

So let that go, and all she had to worry about was her other battle front: the one patrolled by Peter Judd. Who thought he had her under his thumb, and who needed showing that he too would end up squashed like popcorn if he persisted in such a delusion.

The door to the club opened for her before she was up the steps, the members' register waiting for her to sign. And no need to ask if Mr Judd had arrived, for there was his name two lines above, each letter fully formed, in a way that perhaps spoke of self-assurance and ego, but to her seemed schoolboyish. In the bar, ma'am, she was told. The bar was up one flight. She did five minutes' battle prep in the cloakroom, then went to find him. Her plan: to come out fighting.

He was by the window, apparently absorbed in his phone, but looked up as she entered. 'Diana.' He rose, offered an embrace, and seemed amused when she sidestepped. From his phone's screen Desmond Flint stared out, as if he were trapped there. She wondered if he yet appreciated that that was precisely the case.

'And that's why you wanted me to back off the Yellow Vests, isn't it?' she said, sitting. 'It's not that you didn't want trouble, you just wanted it happening on your own terms. Which included having Desmond Flint on hand to calm it all down.' She shook her head. 'I have to confess, I didn't see him as your stalking horse. He's so . . . unprepossessing. Don't you think?'

'Now now. If it was a beauty contest, half the Cabinet would have lost their deposits.'

'I wasn't referring to his looks.'

A waiter hovered. Taverner asked for mineral water. Judd, whose balloon-sized glass just barely contained his gin, looked disappointed.

Taverner said, 'I do hope you haven't made a misstep. One thing that comes across quite strongly is that it's his people, his core support, creating havoc in the streets.'

'Denying that would be a problem. Owning it is not.' This was Peter Judd in magisterial mode, dispensing hard-earned wisdom to his lessers. It needed a toga, really. 'For every Radio 4-listening, liberal-voting vegetarian decrying the behaviour of the mob, there are two people in a public house thinking, that's the way to do it. Desmond understands that.'

'But if there's one thing we should have learned by now, it's that once you've incited the mob, you can't turn it off again. And there's never been a mob that

329

didn't end up eating itself.'

'You have a lively imagination, Diana. You should write a novel. Or pay someone to write one for you.' He took a sip of his G&T. 'That's how it's usually done, I gather.'

The waiter arrived with her water, saving her the trouble of responding. When they were alone, Judd continued:

'Besides, it would be a mistake to underestimate our Flinty. He may not know a fish knife from a soup spoon, but he speaks a language these people understand.'

'You make him sound like Tarzan of the apes.'

'I have no plans to parade him in a loincloth. But the analogy isn't unfair.' He leaned back. 'Of course, had the crowd not heeded his words, I'd have had to resort to plan B.'

'Which was?'

'Throw him to the fucking wolves.'

'But instead you're grooming him for higher things. I've no doubt you'd enjoy being the power behind the throne, Peter, but you'll be a long time waiting. It's not like the last election didn't return a decisive result.'

Judd swirled his glass. 'Politics is a long game. And while it's true the PM enjoys a commanding majority, he's also a walking non-disclosure agreement who wouldn't be the first irresistible force to find himself in close proximity to an immovable object. Best to prepare for that eventuality, wouldn't you say?'

'Sounds like the green-eyed monster speaking. But as long as we're on the subject, you should know I'm seeing him this afternoon. The PM.'

'Which you do at least once a week.'

She nodded.

'So you wouldn't be mentioning it if you didn't have something up your sleeve. Please. I'm not one of those insufferable aesthetes who think women of a certain age shouldn't bare their arms in public. Do share.'

Diana said, 'I plan to tell him everything.'

'I see.'

'Do you? I mean everything, Peter. Full disclosure.'

'I said I see. And loath as I am to borrow a line, I do hope you're not about to make a misstep. You've been known to question my sense of loyalty, but next to the PM, I'm Greyfriars Bobby. If there's any chance you'll make him look bad, he'll dump you overboard without a backward glance.'

'I know. But I also know that he's as keen on hogging glory as he is on avoiding blame. And as you so eloquently pointed out the other evening, there's glory to be had here.' She picked up her glass. 'Kazan is an unspun story. It might be making ripples on the Dark Web, but there's been nothing official from the Kremlin, because the Kremlin doesn't want the world knowing it let its guard down, and nothing official from us, because officially it didn't happen. But unofficially I can make it the PM's triumph.'

''Prime Minister orders state-sanctioned murder',' Judd mused. 'That would probably be his all-time second-favourite headline, Diana. Right after 'Get off my fucking laptop'.'

'I'm not talking about headlines, I'm talking about legends. It's no secret the PM sees himself as Churchill reborn. It's just that he's had difficulty persuading anyone else. But this is his chance to look like a wartime hero, even if only in Whitehall's back corridors. If it's known among COBRA staff that he gave the nod on Kazan, well. Nothing he'd like more than to be thought a warrior leader by a roomful of generals. Who currently, you won't be shocked to hear, regard him as a cross between a game show host and a cartoon yeti.'

Judd nodded, as if appreciating a chess move. 'It's risky, though. Could backfire. You're sure that's how you want to play it?'

'A full admission that I dabbled in alternative sources of backing for an operation which ultimately plays to his credit. Yes, I think it'll work. He's been known to display a certain impatience with tradition himself.'

'If by that you mean he's been known to wipe his arse on the constitution, I'd have to agree.'

'So our arrangement has ended. I know you'd planned it as a long-term thing, and I'm not ungrateful for the assistance. But you won't be using me as a way of steering the Service, Peter. Not now, not ever again.'

Another nod. 'There's nothing I like more than seeing you in control, Diana. Gives me quite the rush of blood.' He raised his glass, but instead of a toast said, 'I have to correct you on one small matter, though. You used the words 'full admission'. That's not quite accurate.'

Taverner said, 'What does that mean?'

'I'm simply pointing out that you can't give the PM all the facts about our arrangement because you're not yet in possession of them. And once you are, well.' He smiled, or at any rate revealed his teeth. 'Once you are, I expect the PM is the last person you'll be making full admissions to.'

He replaced his glass on the table.

'I'll order you a proper drink now, shall I? I think you're about to need it.'

★ ★ ★

Sid woke alone, late morning, and spoke his name. No reply. She was about to call louder, but thought better of it. All was quiet, and as broken memories of yesterday assembled themselves in her mind — driving a knife into the man's chin; drowning the woman in the lake — it seemed better to leave it that way. He was upstairs. Or had gone to the village for food. She was ravenous, she noticed. Food would be good.

But he wasn't in the bathroom, as she ascertained quite swiftly; nor did he reappear in the study during her absence. Next thing she did was draw the curtains, and let the day in. It was like charging a battery — rooms left dark become crabbed and pokey. They need light to remember what they are. This was a simple formula to apply to herself, and hard not to touch a hand to the groove in her head while doing so. Her muttering bullet was gone; no Hercule Poirot voice in her head. It might return, but for now she was on her own.

On her own, back in the world, and with decisions to make.

She'd already made some. She would not be returning to Cumbria, for a start; nor resuming the identity she'd been assigned during her recovery. That had been a non-person; a shell she'd never filled. Nor had she been Sid Baker, or not so anyone would notice. She'd been a character absent from the stage, her dialogue mere gaps in the conversation. Action had been elsewhere. After yesterday, she didn't want to

333

see action again. But she thought she was ready to be Sid Baker once more.

Last night, she'd talked with Shirley Dander while River and Lech Wicinski had returned to the scene of the slaughter.

'You've been living here?'

'Staying here.'

'But it's full of *books*.'

Said as if this precluded anything Shirley might think of as living. Or perhaps even just staying.

'Think of it as being well insulated,' Sid suggested.

'Did you kill them both?'

'No.'

'Did River?'

'We got lucky.'

'Yeah, sure,' said Shirley. 'Except they were professionals, know what I mean? The number of people who got lucky before you is zero.'

Which, as far as Sid was concerned, made her very lucky indeed. Though Shirley had seemed impressed.

Jane and Jim had been dispatched on a vengeance tour, titting the Park's tat, as Shirley had put it with a Lamb-like leer; the Park's crime having been to assassinate one of those responsible for last year's outrage, a ham-fisted episode Sid had followed in the press during her Cumbrian interlude. The target then had been a pair of Russian ex-pats, but two British civilians had wandered into the line of fire, one of whom had died. The murder method had created headlines worldwide: the smearing of a toxic substance — Novichok — on a doorknob.

Well, if she was back in the world, this was the world she was in.

Shirley Dander had been jittery, and possibly

high. Lech Wicinski's scars were plain to see, but he was hiding behind them all the same. Min Harper was dead, as were others who'd come along after, but Louisa Guy was still a slow horse; Roderick Ho remained Roddy Ho, and Catherine Standish still carried the keys. As for Lamb, Sid could only assume he was unchanged, self-damage notwithstanding, because without Jackson Lamb there'd be no Slough House. Slough House was the stage and those were the actors, and all the time she'd been emerging from her head wound River had been living among them, mostly bound to the same old beat — the paperwork, the pointless chores, the soul-killing drudgery — but occasionally, just occasionally, finding himself on the sharp end too.

Which was an end Sid knew about. She'd found her own on a rainy pavement in London, years ago; had nearly found it again last night, hiding in this very room while the couple she and River later killed had rattled the doorknob at the front, tapped the glass round back, like evil figures in an adult fairy tale. Then spirited Sid away. *We could finish it here in the car. Which will be messier, but we can do that if you prefer.* Making an invitation of a death sentence . . .

She uncurled from the O.B.'s chair and stretched. A gust of wind shook the windowpane, and she startled at the interruption, an echo of last night's haunting. The bell had rung, and then once more. And the flap on the letterbox had jangled, and Sid had imagined the pair taking it in turns to drop to one knee and peer into the hallway.

Life went quiet again quiet again, the only disturbance the faint rattling of a doorknob.

The thought broke the morning in two.

Rattling the doorknob . . .

Where was River?

★ ★ ★

There was a traffic jam, because there were always traffic jams, because this was London; a thought so familiar that someone might already have had it this morning. Cantor was lying flat on the back seat, being driven by the nameless man whose cheeks were ribboned with scars, a walking indication that bad choices produce bad outcomes.

A hooting horn provoked more hooting horns. This too was London: everyone wanting to be heard, even when they had nothing to say.

'Are we being followed?' he asked. The man made a foreign noise in reply, so he said it again. 'Are we being followed?'

'. . . Nyet.'

'Who was she?'

He knew the answer, but needed to hear it anyway.

'From Regent's Park.'

So Taverner had sent someone to collect him.

Taverner wants you toasted both sides . . .

It was possible he'd made a tactical error.

The woman at the Needle couldn't cross the road for traffic, and the scarred man had used the delay to hustle Cantor round the corner and push him into this car. Things could happen so quickly, they felt like a good idea. And now they were on the move again, albeit in a jerky, arrhythmical manner, Cantor's head banging against the seat while he tried to reconstruct his earlier frame of mind: Taverner was throwing a scare, hoping he'd jump at shadows. But the shadows

336

seemed solider now, and here he was, jumping at them.

A sharp corner, and a guttural apology from the front: 'Excuse.'

Cantor said, 'Where are you taking me?'

An audible shrug from the front seat. 'Somewhere safe.'

'Why?'

'You help us. We help you.'

But I didn't mean to help you, thought Cantor. I was just trading favours. I didn't mean to end up hiding in a car, evading capture by the British Secret Service.

Bad choices produce bad outcomes . . .

The man spoke again. 'There are no worries. My people and your people, they'll iron out their difficulties. And then you'll go back to making your news programmes, and helping my people too, yes? No harm done.'

'I'm not . . . I don't work for your people. I was doing a favour for a contact, that's all.'

'So you do more favours.'

'No, that's not . . . This has all been a misunderstanding. I'm not going to be doing any favours.'

There was silence. Then: 'It's not a good time to be telling me this. Not when I'm helping you.'

The car jerked to a halt. When Cantor peeped through the window a young Chinese man was hopping onto the pavement, as if he'd been safeguarding a parking space. 'We're here,' the driver said. Here was Soho, a familiar street whose name evaded Cantor right that moment, his mind still reeling. He clambered out. There were people everywhere — London, London — but nobody was paying attention, or if they were, were doing so in a successfully covert way. There was an open door, leading into an apparently abandoned shop. 'Quickly.' So quickly it was: through the door, into an empty retail space. The young Chinese man had disappeared, but in front of Cantor stood a short, wide woman. 'Upstairs,' she said, in what sounded to Cantor like a bad-movie German accent.

In a similarly bad-movie way, he was getting a bad feeling about this.

'What's upstairs?'

'No time for questions. They're looking for you.'

The driver had closed the shop door and was leaning against it.

'I just —'

'Now.'

The stairs creaked. There was a small landing at the top: a toilet, two other rooms. The woman nudged him towards the back one.

'A safe house,' she said.

The scarred man had come up with them. 'Yes. You'll be safe here.'

Cantor said, 'I need to make some calls. Just ten minutes to make some calls, and I'll be on my way.'

He had his phone out before he'd finished speaking, but it was snatched by the square-shaped woman.

'No.'

'But I —'

'No.'

He looked around. The floor was uncarpeted, and the window covered by a steel shutter. The only light was a bare bulb, swinging on a cord. No heating, no furniture.

And at his feet, newly screwed to the floorboards, a metal ring with handcuffs attached.

'You're safe here, provided you don't wander,' the man told him.

'Which you won't,' said the woman. She dropped to her knees, and before Cantor could react had fastened the loose cuff around his left ankle.

'What the hell—?'

'Water,' said the man, producing a two-litre bottle from behind the door.

'And an empty,' said a new voice. The woman who'd been at the Needle had appeared, holding another two-litre bottle, uncapped. 'But I'm sure you'll fill it.'

'What are you doing?' Cantor said. His mouth was dry.

'We're leaving you to ponder your actions,' said the scarred man. His accent had gone, his voice softer.

'People tell me I ought to do that,' said the squat woman, getting to her feet. Her voice had also altered. 'But I've never really found the time.'

'Which isn't going to be a problem for you,' the other woman said. 'Bags of that coming up.'

The young Chinese man who'd been holding the parking space had arrived too. He alone was hanging on to the B-movie vibe. 'You picked the wrong guys to mess with, friend.'

The second woman tossed Cantor the empty bottle. 'You can shout as loud as you want,' she said. 'But if anyone hears you, they won't care.'

'Who are you people?'

It was the Chinese man who answered. 'We're Slough House,' he said. Then added, '*Hasta la vista, baby*,' before following the others down the stairs.

Cantor pulled against the cuff, but it didn't budge.

And the woman had been right about this much: Cantor shouted as loud as he could. But no one came.

He said, 'I enjoy being a member here, don't you?'

'Don't change the subject.'

'I rather think I'm about to provide an illustration. Do pay attention.'

The waiter arrived with a fresh G&T for Judd; a large Chablis for Taverner. She resisted the temptation to dive straight in.

I'm simply pointing out that you can't give the PM all the facts about our arrangement because you're not yet in possession of them . . .

'I'm fond of that plaque in the lobby. The one that says this club was founded fifty-odd years ago by a chap whose name escapes me but has a VC attached. Lovely detail. If you're going to tell a lie, tell a big one. Stick it on the side of a bus.'

'Get on with it.'

'Because we both know the club's not twenty years old. And that its founder was one Margaret Lessiter, who, unless I'm mistaken, you were at college with. One of the brighter lights, no? Alongside that chap who crashed a bank and the conman's daughter who pimps for royalty. Sterling year. I bet the gaudies are fun.'

'I'm not sure either attend. What's your point?'

'That the badge doesn't tell the whole story.' He picked up his glass. 'Take my own little enterprise. Bullingdon Fopp.'

The PR firm Judd had been running since he left the Cabinet.

'The thing is, Diana, I needed start-up money. A life dedicated to public service doesn't leave one over-burdened with ready cash.'

'Really. But your property portfolio weighs more than the average bungalow. Let's not pretend your public service prevented you amassing a fortune.'

'There'll always be those who resent the enterprising. But we've moved past the moment at which your antennae should have twitched.'

Oh, they'd twitched.

Once you're in possession of the facts, I expect the PM is the last person you'll be making full admissions to.

She reached for her Chablis. You could drown in two inches of water, she knew. Two inches of wine was starting to look like an option. 'You have backers,' she said. Her voice sounded flat and unnatural, as if she were still in rehearsal. With luck, the director would soon shout Cut.

'Whose names don't appear on the paperwork,' Judd agreed. 'Discretion being the better part of investment. How many commuters know who owns the tracks their trains run on? Whose fuel keeps their lights on?' He waved his free hand lightly: the walls, the floor, the ceiling. 'Who owns half of central London, come to that? New builds and old? Doesn't matter whose names are on the deeds.' He leaned forward. 'You know why national sovereignty's so treasured by the great and good? Because they get a damn fine price for it when market conditions are right.'

'Just tell me.'

'Forty per cent of my company's initial funding came from overseas sources.'

'Overseas.'

'Quite a long way overseas.'

'You used Chinese money to launch Bullingdon Fopp.'

'Well, it was good enough for the steel industry.'

341

'The company that organised backing for the Kazan operation.'

'Among the various other uses you found for the money.'

'Oh, you mad bastard.'

'So a clean breast to the PM might be self-defeating, don't you think? I mean, he's made a career out of gaslighting the electorate, but there's clear blue water between fooling others and being fooled. And discovering that his intelligence service carried out an unsanctioned hit on foreign coin, well. He hates to be shown up for the dick he pretends to be. You might not get the absolution you're after.'

Diana was experiencing something like an out-of-body moment, as if she'd just detached from herself, and was floating in the ether, bombarded by raw emotions. Chief among these was shock. She was thinking about those visitors' tours, designed to show strangers around the Park's outer corridors. Had she really thrown the doors wider without knowing it? Burned down her own firewalls and allowed a foreign power in?

Judd said, 'You're tense. Take deep breaths, then finish your wine. It'll help.'

'You fucking maniac.' Her voice was low, but she might have been shooting off sparks.

'Careful. This is not a conversation you want overheard.'

'You've put me, the Park, the whole fucking country in an impossible situation. This could start a war, you realise that? An actual full-scale war.'

'And now you're being melodramatic.'

What she was was homicidal. 'Melodramatic? You're telling me you put Chinese money into a

Service op — '

'No, Diana, I put *money* into a Service op, and money doesn't recognise borders. So calm down.'

'It's beyond treason. It's a fucking *coup*!'

'Again, melodramatic. But finish your drink. We're going in for lunch soon, and they've a rather nice Zinfandel breathing.' He downed a healthy percentage of his gin. 'My backers know nothing of our current, ah, *angelic* arrangement, still less of any involvement I might have had in your recent Russian adventure. So don't worry. I have no plans to endanger national security.' He smiled the way alligators do. 'I am, if you like, my own Chinese wall. A perfect model of discretion.'

'Which you'll drive a bulldozer through when it suits you.'

'The point being, it doesn't suit me. Not as long as we're on happy terms. An injunction you're free to interpret as widely as you like.'

Her glass was shaking in her hand, not a huge amount, but enough that he'd notice. She took a swallow, wishing it were brandy, whisky, or something being served at a beach bar many decades away. 'You wanted Number Ten,' she said. 'Always have done. Now your mirror image has got there instead and fouled your nest. And this is your revenge, isn't it?'

'Revenge? No, Diana, this is simply me being me. Nothing's changed. I have plans, and you'll help me achieve those plans, and nobody need know anything about it. I appreciate that you're not entirely happy with some of those I recruited — '

'Cantor's been dealt with.'

'Really? I was going to make the offer but, as always, you're ahead of me. So, yes, we'll be discreet,

343

and we'll be careful, and your angelic choir will sing in harmony when called upon to do so. My backers, who are purely businessmen, I assure you — nothing to do with the state apparatus — they'll remain ignorant of any dealings we have outside the public sphere, and no breath of their financial association with the Service need ever trouble the air. Provided, as I say, that we continue on happy terms.' He reached across the table, his palm open. 'So. A moment of truth. The alliance continues?'

Diana finished her drink, not taking her eyes off him. There was a rather nice Zinfandel breathing in the dining room; there were no doubt other delights in store, and every step they took would be dictated by him from now on, until such moment as she could reclaim the initiative. It didn't seem likely that this would occur within the next few minutes.

She had served for years under Ingrid Tearney, who had occasionally dispensed wisdom. *If you can't choose your enemy, choose your moment.* In that spirit, and still not taking her eyes off Judd's, she put her hand in his.

'Excellent girl. Shall we go in?'

Like a gentleman, he allowed her to precede him into the dining room.

★ ★ ★

Sid found River in the kitchen. He had been to the village while she slept, and had returned with the usual provisions — bread, cheese, milk, coffee — all of which were neatly arranged on the kitchen counter, while River himself was on the floor. She found his phone in his jeans pocket, the battery in another. He was still dark, a thought she pushed away. This is how you insert the battery, she told her hands, which fumbled and dropped and had to try again. This is how you press the buttons. She'd called 999 before remembering there were protocols; numbers you called when a Park operative hit the ground. Not that River was Park, exactly, but once you'd hit the ground, the meaner distinctions dissolved. So she called the Park too, its number still high on River's contact list, as if there'd never been a rift. Nerve agent, she said, toxic attack, and said it again when asked to clarify.

Then sank to the floor next to him. There were things you did, were supposed to do; recovery position, cardiac massage, oral resuscitation, any one of which might sign her own death warrant if she attempted them. *Nerve agent. Toxic attack.* Best advice: put on a rubber suit and stand somewhere in the next county. But instead she sank to the floor and held him, words circling her mind like wagons: *don't die don't die don't die*; the useless instruction, prompted by love, that shatters on impact with reality. Everyone dies.

Sid Baker never knew how long it took the ambulance to arrive. But well before it did she could hear its ululation, as if an unleashed spirit were hurtling towards her, screaming through trees and howling through hedges, before finally coming to rest here, in the house that would do for its haunting: a house like many another, and only incidentally the one in which River had grown up — a house with ordinary windows, an intact roof, a garden that had once been loved, and ivy still growing around its poisoned door.

★ ★ ★

Afterwards the sound disappears, howling along the lanes, the roads, the motorway, all the way back to where it started, because endings swallow their beginnings eventually, so you can't tell one from the other. Later the same day, or early the next — at any rate, long after dark has fallen — Louisa Guy is ruining a new pair of trainers, running in the rain that has descended on London like a punishment, and every slap of her feet on the unmetalled towpath finds an echoing thud in her heart. *Don't die.* Meanwhile, in the grim kitchen of his current lodgings Lech Wicinski is making bread again, or at least thumping dough with his fists. In this light, which is harsh — an overhead tube which fizzes steadily, as if there were insects hatching within — his scars present as individual razor marks rather than the undifferentiated battleground they usually appear to be; here, now, he has a face like a first draft, all crossings out and scribblings over, which is nevertheless the finished text: as good as it's going to get. What he thinks about this is impossible to determine, but what's certain is that he continues to pound the dough long after it has reached the point where it should be allowed to rest; is as blindly intent on this activity as, some distance away, Roderick Ho is on his computer screen, the Rodster currently being ankle deep in blood on a blasted landscape, doing combat with recognisably humanoid forms wielding recognisably inhumane weapons, a gallimaufry of swords and pikes and axes, between whose swings and roundhouses Roddy weaves, or Roddy's avatar does, this being a slightly tweaked version of Roddy 1.0 — taller, more chiselled of feature, more lustrous of hair, and significantly ripped: an Alpha male in an Omega world — he's confident he's

346

got that the right way round. *Don't die*, he instructs this other Roddy, knowing the instruction to be otiose, for the RodMan is an indestructible force, with moves as slick as Skywalker's and dialogue to match, and a smile tickles his lips as he recalls his parting shot to Damien Cantor — *We're Slough House.* Hasta la vista, *baby* — though it vanishes as he also remembers that Cartwright didn't come home, and before he has quite finished processing that thought his avatar's head is pirouetting across the cratered battlefield, skipping across mud and debris as slickly as if it were the dance floor Shirley Dander occupies, for Shirley is dancing again, or dancing still, because there is a sense in which Shirley never stops dancing; the dance of being Shirley continuing even while she sleeps, which she has been known to do, when she runs out of alternatives. Nobody is watching as she achieves lift-off, her unaerodynamic shape unhampered by gravity for a moment, and for that short space of time she is at ease with herself, as if it is contact with the earth that causes her dissatisfaction, leaving her in constant need of a series of minor highs. This one ends, as all highs do, but the dance continues, and as always when she dances Shirley's lips move to the lyrics, as if she were mumbling in prayer, the way Catherine Standish is doing — words addressed to no one in particular, because all that matters, Catherine feels, is that they be spoken, for words released into the air acquire power, and the possibility is that when she says *don't die* the world will bend itself to fit, though it is equally likely that the world will refuse to listen. Certainly, words spoken aloud have had no noticeable effect on Damien Cantor's situation, since he remains where the slow horses left him, shackled to an iron ring in an empty room. He is dozing now, his head resting between two half-full plastic bottles, and his dreams are not unlike the images summoned up by Roddy Ho's war game, full of noise and nuisance; disordered scraps of intelligence whose meaning remains as elusive as that of the tadpole scribblings left behind by Andrey, on scraps of paper marking pages in his books, a jumble of which Reece Nesmith III is now attempting to assemble into some sort of order. But some of Andy's scribblings are in Russian, and others so illegible that they might as well be, and before long Reece hurls the scraps into the air again, making another brief paper snowstorm. *You shouldn't have died*, he thinks; an admonition hurled into the past, so less likely to be heeded than one levelled at the present, but it needed thinking. Other thoughts are best tamped down before they've sparked, and this might describe Diana Taverner's preoccupations as she slips out of bed and pads downstairs, where she finds the outside security lights lit — a fox is vacating the lawn, and she hears the scrabble of its claws on the fence. Diana is in an insomniac limbo, unsure if it is the end of one day or the beginning of the next, but whichever it is, she knows that bad things lie both behind and ahead of her. These bad things coalesce around Peter Judd, who has managed to compromise her so absolutely that she is in no position to refuse him anything, but no problem is insuperable, even if some solutions seem unpalatable at first glance. What's important is that she maintain her composure, a resolution which forms in her mind at precisely the moment the security lights switch off, which is also, by curious coincidence, precisely the moment at which Tommo Doyle regains consciousness. His evening had started in an East End pub, and has ended in a skip, an itinerary from which a number of details are absent, though some are starting to emerge through a fog of pain. He recalls a fat man with swept-back greasy hair and bristling jowls, who struck up conversation with Tommo in the evening's first pub and was still matching him drink for drink in the last, after which — it's coming back now — the fat man led him up a blind alley and broke his legs. 'Who's the crip now?' he'd asked, before dumping Tommo like unwanted furniture, the way debris from the O.B.'s house will be thrown into a skip, shortly after its facade has been dismantled brick by brick, frame by strut, to eradicate any trace of the toxic substance smeared there. The building will be shrouded in canvas like an artwork, the artists in question favouring hazmat costumes rather than smocks, and the contents of its one furnished room — armchairs and tables, curtains and carpet — will be junked, and the O.B.'s carefully collated books hurled into random bags and boxes. If any messages were encoded in their shelving, which seems possible given the mind responsible, then those secrets are gone forever, while the house itself is left to be badgered by the elements. If houses die, this one probably will. Others persist, despite encouragement to the contrary. Back in the present, on Aldersgate Street, in the London borough of Finsbury, Slough House has weathered another day despite having been wiped from the map. It remains an estate agent's nightmare, all leaky drainpipes and flaking woodwork, but even at this late hour exerts a pull upon its occupants, one of whom approaches now, from an unexpected direction, and vanishes into the alley that leads round back. If it were possible to see through walls, a shadow might be viewed soon afterwards, a bulky shape attached to the glowing tip of a cigarette, and rising floor by floor, its heat and light leaving tiny scars in the air behind it. When this shadow reaches the top floor the cigarette expires, but another is lit from its dying breath. And while the smoker speaks no words aloud, the dark and empty rooms below take up an echo regardless, and for a while it whispers round Slough House, *don't die*, until all that is left is its tail, *die*, and this persists for a while, *die, die*, and then it stops.

Acknowledgements

Readers may notice in *Slough House* echoes of events in Wiltshire between March and July 2018, when four people were poisoned, one fatally, by the nerve agent Novichok. They should be aware, however, that this novel is pure fiction. Various details have been radically altered; none are intended to be accurate.

It might be worth adding that the novel was completed in March 2020, a week or so before the UK went into lockdown. Hence the absence from its pages of social distancing, face masks, workouts with Joe Wicks, and other aspects of actual life in the summer that followed.

My heartfelt gratitude, as ever, to all at John Murray and Soho Press for their unstinting efforts on my behalf; to Juliet Burton and Micheline Steinberg for their constant vigilance; to friends and fellow authors for companionship and support; to booksellers and librarians for lighting candles in the dark; and to readers, for making it all worthwhile. Special thanks to Mark Richards, for the huge difference he made to my career, and for leaving me in such good hands.

MH
Oxford
August 2020

Other titles published by Ulverscroft:

JOE COUNTRY

Mick Herron

'*We're spies, Standish. All kinds of outlandish shit goes on.*' Like the ringing of a dead man's phone or an unwelcome guest at a funeral . . . In Slough House memories are stirring, all of them bad. Catherine Standish is buying booze again, Louisa Guy is raking over the ashes of lost love, and new recruit Lech Wicinski, whose sins make him an outcast even among the slow horses, is determined to discover who destroyed his career. And with winter taking its grip, Jackson Lamb would sooner be left brooding in peace, but even he can't ignore the dried blood on his carpets. So when the man responsible breaks cover at last, Lamb sends the slow horses out to even the score. This time they're heading into joe country. And they're not all coming home.

THIS IS WHAT HAPPENED

Mick Herron

Twenty-six-year-old Maggie Barnes is someone you would never look at twice. Living alone in a month-to-month sublet in London, she has no family but an estranged sister, no boyfriend or partner, and not much in the way of friends. Working in the postal department of a large corporate office, she struggles to make ends meet. Maggie is just the kind of person who could vanish from the face of the earth without anyone taking notice. Or just the kind of person MI5 needs to thwart an international plot that puts all of Britain at risk. They need someone inconspicuous to infiltrate her office and interface with the security system, a simple-seeming task. Maggie has the chance to be a hero — but the stakes are about to escalate beyond anything she ever dreamed of ...

LONDON RULES

Mick Herron

Tasked with protecting a beleaguered prime minister, Regent's Park's First Desk, Claude Whelan, is facing attack from all directions: from the showboating MP who orchestrated the Brexit vote and now has his sights set on Number Ten; from the MP's wife, a tabloid columnist who's crucifying Whelan in print; and especially from his own deputy, Lady Di Taverner, who's alert for Claude's every stumble. Meanwhile, someone's trying to kill Roddy Ho. And over at Slough House, the crew are struggling with personal problems: repressed grief, various addictions, retail paralysis, and the nagging suspicion that their newest colleague is a psychopath. But collectively, they're about to rediscover their greatest strength — that of making a bad situation much, much worse. It's a good job Jackson Lamb knows the rules, because they aren't going to break themselves.